# DARK ESCAPE

## TALES OF ARABELLA

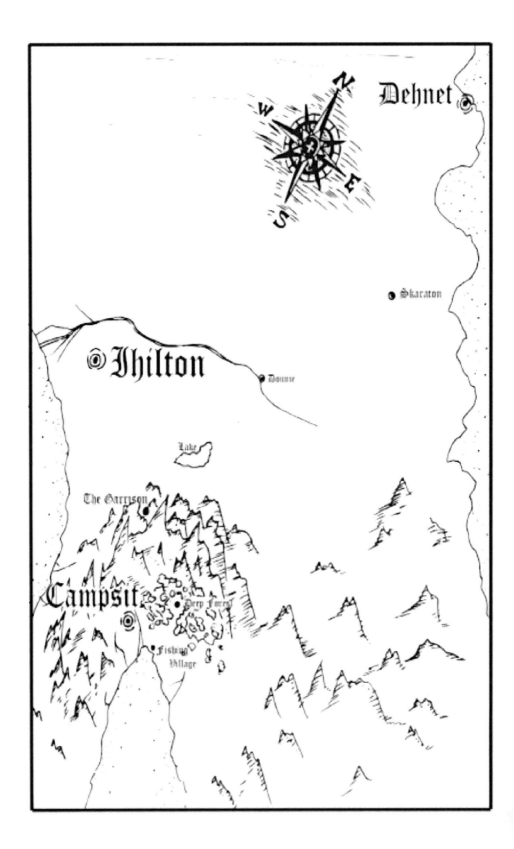

# DARK ESCAPE

## TALES OF ARABELLA

### AARON GEE

ARABELLA PRESS LLC.

Dark Escape
Tales of Arabella

Published by Arabella Press LLC
West Jordan, UT


Publishing History
First paperback edition published July 2013

Cover art and design by Dane Low
Map by Chandelle Gee


For information and inquiries:
inquiry@aarongee.net


Library of Congress Control Number:  2013911446


ISBN-10: 0989436101
ISBN-13: 978-0-9894361-0-6
010101713


Story typeset in 12 point Adobe Garmond Pro, and Charlamagne standard.

Dedicated to my loving wife Sandy.
Without her, Arabella would not exist.

# Chapter 1

# THE ABSENT PRINCE

Arabella drifts through the blackness of space as it slowly orbits the star Sakphata in its own blissfully unique way. Turned on its side by a cataclysm eons ago, it forever spins with its north pole continually facing the sun. It is a planet of extremes. One hemisphere basking in the light while the other freezes in the darkness of unending night.

On the northern side of Arabella, it is always day, only the circular motion of the sun denotes the passage of time. Despite these conditions, life flourishes in a habitable zone where the hot air and water from the North Firelands mixes with the icy temperatures emanating from the dark recesses of the Southern Black.

In a nearly impenetrable valley, surrounded by the high Wall Mountains, sits the tiny enclave of Campsit. There, a few brave souls have sought refuge from the persecutions of the neighboring kingdom of Ithilton. Those that have committed to the harsh lifestyle find comfort in its borders.

The only path to the reclusive kingdom is a rugged narrow pass that is protected by the Campsit Guard. For almost two centuries, they have kept the kingdom safe by strictly enforcing the law that forbids all foreigners. The penalty for trespassing is summary execution. Man, woman, or child, anyone entering Campsit territory is killed. There is no exception. There is no mercy. It is a harsh law, but necessary to maintain the ideology of the utopian kingdom.

Campsit is ruled by Tremmon and his wife, Aurora, who reign as servants of the people, sworn to protect and administer the laws. Their only heir, Tam, will eventually rule the kingdom, but his destiny is in limbo.

Like all children in Campsit, Tam was schooled from an early age. At the Campsit Academy, under the tutelage of Master Thales, he honed his mental abilities, and like all male children, his physical prowess was sculpted by rigorous combat training with Athon, Captain of the Campsit Guard. Unlike his peers,

Tam did not enter his apprenticeship when he turned sixteen. Now, two passes later, he struggles to reconcile the monotony of his life and the entitlement of his birthright, with the ideology that founded his kingdom.

Athon was up early, as usual, walking the battlements before beginning the turn. An imposing man, he was taller than most, a fact that had always served him well. His well–proportioned physique had given him the advantage in combat, and quickly caught the eye of his superiors. Early in his career as a guard, they groomed him for leadership. Not only was he blessed with the strength and agility, but also a keen mind that absorbed everything he could learn. His charisma and physique accentuated his handsome appearance, making him a natural leader.

For all his comeliness, he had no companion. He had attracted the attention of many of Campsit's women, but he couldn't bring himself to reciprocate their affections. He had been in love once; but was forced to leave the only woman he had ever cared for, and it had broken his heart. Fortunately, his duties left no time for love. It was his responsibility to ensure the safety and security for the entire kingdom, as well as train Prince Tam.

As the sun began its steady rise over the mountains, Athon made his way to the dining hall for breakfast. The aroma of sweet roasted meats drifted through the air and greeted him. As he sat in his place of honor, a cook's assistant brought his food, and he heartily dug into the plate. Midway through his meal, his First Sergeant, Parth, joined him to discuss the routine matters of the watch. Parth was in command during the sleep–watch. He still had several hours left of his shift, but now Athon would take command. After the briefing, they left the hall and headed up the cobblestone street for the courtyard where the guards trained.

The central street of Campsit was beginning to spring to life. Villagers were opening shops, setting out fresh fruits and vegetables, making the sunrise deliveries, and the general activity that signified the start of a new turn. It was a guard's job to protect this idyllic existence, and it gave Athon a sense of achievement to know that it was his responsibility to make this life possible.

The sun had now risen above the high mountain peaks, erasing dark shadows and replacing them with the warmth of wake–time. In the courtyard of the inner keep of the city, guards were gathering in anticipation of the challenge that soon would commence.

Athon and Parth strode to the growing crowd of warriors, taking mental notes of those in attendance. Something caught Athon's attention, causing his brow to furrow. His eyes made a second sweep of the anxious faces, searching for the absent prince; but he didn't see him. An irksome feeling began welling at the base of his neck, slowly traveling up to where it began burning at his ears and cheeks. Could it be that he had simply fallen behind, and was running late? Athon glanced up at the sky to get a reckoning of the time. No, the sun was too high. It was the appointed time, and tardy participants were punished severely. Tam was no exception.

"By the shadows," Athon muttered under his breath. "Parth!" he barked. "Get the men warmed up, and start some hand–to–hand drills. I have to see if the prince will grace us with his presence." With that, Athon turned and stormed off toward the royal quarters. He breathed heavily, and wished he could drag the youth by his ankles back to the training grounds. Prince or not, Tam would have to answer to him.

From the beginning of his combat training Tam had demonstrated a certain disregard for the rules. He would be tardy to his training and lessons from time to time. At first, it was not apparently intentional, but slowly Athon had become aware that there was a certain level of smugness behind Tam's excuses. It was as if he felt the whole concept of work and stewardship was beneath his station as prince.

The more Athon thought about the egoism of Tam's behavior, the more it made his patience dissipate. How inconsiderate of his time, and the time of his men. How was the prince going to be a good a ruler, if he didn't place the needs of others above his own? Sacrifice was required of all men who serve others. It should be no great sacrifice to be on time and willing to learn the fundamentals of combat.

Athon hoped to rectify this continued disobedience. He had been, he felt, more than tolerant. He needed to impress upon Tam that expectations must be met.

The royal house was nestled at the northeast corner of the inner keep. The tallest building in Campsit, it was half–carved into the cliff. The palace stood as a man-made monolith juxtaposing the waterfall on the other side of the keep. The highest tower jutted out from the cliff face to overlook the valley below. It was a full fifteen levels high, giving it a commanding view of the surrounding area. The large sopha wood door was the last obstacle as Athon ascended the stone steps at its base. The massive portal moved surprisingly easily inward as he entered with a mighty shove on its heavy iron handle.

"Where is the prince?" hissed Athon, to the guard standing watch.

"I'm not sure. I haven't seen him. He might be in the dining hall."

"You check there, and I'll check his room," Athon ordered, his brows furrowing. "If you find him first, hold him until I get there." The guard gave a smart salute and charged down the hallway on his errand. Athon headed in the direction of the royal apartments several levels up.

As he moved through the large Grand Hall and past the raised dais holding the thrones of the King and Queen, he began fortifying the grand tirade that would soon be unleashed on the torpid prince. With each step, his fury built, welling from the depths of his soul, waiting like a trague to pounce on its unsuspecting prey. He climbed the long spiral staircase toward the living quarters on the uppermost levels. At last, he found himself on the landing that led to the royal bedrooms. He opened the door. Tam was in his bed, and by the sound of his deep breathing, in heavy slumber.

The Prince was an attractive young man, tall, lean, and above average strength for his age. His long, curly brown hair sprawled out over his pillow as he slept. Lying there, he seemed almost innocent. In a way, Athon almost felt guilty about interrupting the respite, but it wasn't enough for him to stop. With all the wrath he could muster, Athon focused all his vocal ability to make this the most jarring moment of the young man's life.

"Tam!" Athon's sharp tone echoed through the palace.

The youth was so startled that he nearly jumped out of bed. He frantically searched the room in a disoriented haze for the source of the reprimand, his mind foggy with the soundness of his sleep. Slowly, his brain began to make sense of the familiar surroundings, and the tall figure standing in the threshold of the room. He blinked bleary eyed at the captain.

"Athon?" Tam asked, in a haze that quickly faded. Suddenly it dawned on him what had happened. "I'm late!"

"Yes, you are," Athon said in an icy tone. "You didn't show up, so I came to see what was keeping you. Here I find you're asleep. Has Master Thales been working you too hard?" He stared at the youth as if he could see through to the soul.

"I'm sorry, Captain. I must have overslept."

"That much is obvious. Is this a test, or are you insulting me?"

Tam's face flushed with the embarrassment of having been caught doing something he knew to be very wrong. "No," he stammered. "I must have stayed up too late. I'm sorry."

"Your highness must understand that your obligations and duties can't be simply ignored. It is important that you be prepared for combat. How can you possibly gain any respect if you fail to show it? What's worse is that you seem to think that your duties can be ignored."

"Captain," Tremmon's voice came from behind, and startled them both. "The prince will join your training as soon as he is dressed." The king approached from the stairwell.

"Your Highness," Athon said with a deep bow. He flushed as he realized that he had broken protocol.

The king halted just short of the door and eyed both the prince and the now blushing captain. "Tam, get dressed and report to the training grounds at once." He turned to the captain. "Athon, I wonder if I might speak with you in my study."

The now sheepish captain abashedly nodded his head and followed the king down the corridor, closing the door to Tam's room behind him. The two men said nothing on the way to the king's private office on the level below. Athon was certain that there would be some measure of reprimand for the lack of decorum. The righteous indignation he felt on his way to Tam's quarters was replaced by contrition. How stupid could he be? Raising his voice at the prince inside the confines of the royal apartment left a sharp sting when he thought about it. Why did he allow his quick temper to overtake his common sense?

The king's study was not used for official visits, but reserved for his normal working duties. The more mundane aspects of administering the kingdom's affairs could hardly be managed in the great hall effectively. He did most of his work here. Its utilitarian nature was readily apparent to anyone who entered the door through the antechamber that connected it to the hall. The study was large, with a good–sized desk at the far end of the room. The walls were lined with shelves littered with books and parchments. A single large window interrupted the shelves on the south wall, and filled the room with sunlight.

"If you would please close the door we can begin." Tremmon settled into the large high–backed leather chair behind the desk. He motioned for the captain to sit in one of the chairs. "Athon, you seem to have forgotten your place. I love my son, and you are not to raise your voice to him in this house. Have I made myself abundantly clear?" He spoke as if he were reprimanding an errant child.

"Very clear, Your Majesty. It will never happen again." Athon, now flushed with embarrassment, squirmed slightly in his chair in anticipation of the verbal lashing he was about to receive. "I'm sorry, I lost my temper."

"I'm sure it won't happen again," the king replied. "A reprimand was in order, but it could have been said differently, and we can do without the shouting."

Athon couldn't believe his ears. The expected harsh punishment had failed to materialize, and that unnerved him.

After letting the statement sink in, the monarch continued. "I have noticed that Tam has become a bit temperamental lately. He has been tardy to your exercises several times in the last ceanor, and you probably aren't aware of this, but he has given Master Thales quite the headache recently. It took me some time to divine a reason for this apparent lack of responsibility. Do you know what I discovered?" Athon could only shake his head in stunned disbelief, so Tremmon continued. "He is bored, and has no real direction. I'm not old, sick, or feeble. That means that I will reign as king for some time. Tam has finally come to the realization that it will be a long while before he ascends to the throne. It's very difficult to continue down a road with no foreseeable end. Another path must be presented to make the journey interesting and worthwhile. That is where you come in. I need Tam to learn leadership, discipline, and have something to occupy his time. He has to serve the citizens of Campsit, and he has yet to learn what service is in a practical fashion. He can't do that if he sits around being drilled by Master Thales. You need to teach him how to serve this kingdom."

A blow to the head could not have stunned Athon more. He sat dazed and confused by what he was hearing. It sounded like there was a major change in Tam's life that he would be expected to oversee. "Majesty, I'm not quite sure that I fully understand what you're asking me to do. Are you expecting me to take over for Master Thales?"

"Yes and no." Tremmon paused for a moment. "Tam will no longer be requiring the headmaster's services. I want Tam to experience what life really is, not the sheltered existence he has here."

"What did you have in mind?" Athon's mind had caught up with Tremmon's. He surmised it would be better if the king were the one to say it aloud, because the mere thought of it was almost too terrifying to think of. How could the king even entertain such an idea? Certainly, there must be some other way to deal with the unpredictable nature of a boy who has too much time on his hands.

"Come now, Athon," The king said in an almost patronizing tone. "You know where I'm going with this. I want Tam to join the guard, and I want you to train him."

The force of the command hit like a heavy blow to the gut. Athon was being relieved of his command to play babysitter to a spoiled brat in the mountains. No Captain of the Guard had ever been summarily dismissed like this. Surely, this couldn't be happening.

"Majesty, I take it that you are displeased with my services. If there is anything I could do to repent —"

The king gave a sudden look of shock. "Athon, don't be so hard on yourself. I don't wish you to leave my service as Captain. I want you to take someone I love dearly, and mold him into the kind of man that you are."

"But, Xacthos has a very good mentoring program. He can execute this duty far better than I ever could."

"You and I both know he has his hands full with the latest batch of recruits, but that isn't the only reason why he's not suited for this assignment." Tremmon cleared his throat and continued. "Xacthos is too impulsive and short tempered. Oh, he's a fine leader, and an excellent teacher, but he won't be able to divide his attention between the rest of the recruits and Tam without retaliating. No, the prince needs the undivided, diplomatic attention of a senior officer, and you're my first choice."

"I don't understand how you expect me to fulfill my duties as Captain when I am so far away." Athon was grasping at straws. He knew that the king had already made up his mind about the move, but he still tried to force him to see reason.

"You will appoint a second to lead the guards here, but you will still maintain your status as head of the defenses and security. I don't see why you can't perform all your duties at the garrison instead of here." Tremmon gave a warm smile. "Can you think of anyone that would be able to take command here?"

"Parth." Athon didn't even have to think twice about who would be best suited for the job. He was second in command here anyway.

"You and I are of the same mind." Tremmon rose to his feet and moved toward the window. "Do you think you can be ready to leave in the next turn or two?"

"Yes," Athon said. He stood and joined Tremmon at the window. "I need time to get my affairs in order. How long do you plan on having me mentor Tam at the garrison?" He asked the question with some hesitation, knowing that he might not like the answer he would receive.

"I don't think it will take you more than a pass or two, but that will greatly depend on Tam," Tremmon said, gazing out over the kingdom. "Will he learn quickly, and be satisfied with his station? Perhaps he might excel enough to be given a command. I don't know. It all depends on his ability to adapt to change." Tremmon paused for a moment, and then looked keenly at Athon. "You are concerned that if you stay there long you will no longer be captain?"

"I fear that the longer I stay away from my duties, with someone else in my position, the more difficult it will be to resume them when I return," Athon answered bluntly.

Tremmon nodded his head slowly. "It is possible that might be a problem, but right now, the problem of a temperamental prince is more pressing. Parth will obey my commands just as you do. I will make sure that he understands his place in this affair. Now, I've kept you from your duties long enough. When the training is over, please return to my study with Tam and Parth, so we can explain the plan to them."

Athon nodded his head and gave the king a smart salute. "Yes, Your Majesty," he said. He left, his mind still reeling from the sudden turn his life had just taken. He was not thrilled about becoming a babysitter to the prince, but there was nothing he could do about it.

# Chapter 2

# FALLOUT

T am cursed himself silently as he pulled on his tunic and hopped into his boots. How could he have been such an idiot? Staying out too late with Anker and Proteus was no excuse for sleeping in. He had never seen Athon this mad before. He could still see the look of seething anger on the captain's face, and that shout could have scared the dead. Tam quickly raced down the spiral staircase to the Great Hall. A stunned sentry met him halfway down. He didn't even stop as the guard hailed him.

"Your highness, Captain Athon is looking for you." The guard's voice echoed down the steps, and Tam refused to break stride

"He found me!" Tam cried over his shoulder, as he yanked the heavy door open to gain the freedom outdoors. He didn't even bother to close it as he ran down the cobblestone steps toward the courtyard near the entrance to the keep. Mentally he cursed his lack of responsibility. There would be repercussions later, but there were more immediate concerns.

As Tam approached the training area, he could see the men practicing the single weapon hand–to–hand combat techniques he loved so much. A combination of grappling and weapon use was lethally effective in close quarters. It was a change of pace from the dual weapon drills they normally practiced.

Tam prided himself on his ability to force his opponent to lose his balance long enough for the blunt wooden dagger to find its mark. Tam slowed his approach to the ring of guards awaiting their turn, not wishing to draw undue attention, but Parth saw him right away.

Guards, waiting their turn, ringed the two entwined in mock combat. Mythos was attempting to back Belen over his leg, and cause him to lose his balance. Belen went backward, but clung to the arms of his attacker. As his back touched the soft grass field of the courtyard, he kicked his legs into Mythos' chest, and pulled the larger guard over with all his strength. The surprised Mythos was jerked off his feet and flung head over heels onto his own back. Still clinging to the stunned guard, Belen kicked himself over to a kneeling position. He released his grip on his dagger arm and made a slashing motion over the now supine foe's chest and neck. The surrounding ring of guards gave an approving shout. The two opponents clasped hands as Belen helped Mythos to his feet.

"I thought you would have countered that last move, Mythos," Belen said, slapping his opponent on the shoulder.

"I was too surprised," the larger man said, shaking his head in disbelief. "I really thought I had you. I should have continued the roll, and thrown you clear to begin a new attack, but it just didn't occur to me at the time."

"Your Highness, how nice you could join us this fine turn, I hope it isn't too early for you?" Parth's voice rang over the crowd and his gaze connected with the sheepish eyes of the tardy prince. Tam shook his head at the sergeant in dismay. "I think it's time to see if you have learned anything from your prior lessons." Parth signaled Belen to give Tam his weapon. He then proceeded to take the wooden dagger from Mythos' hand. "These are close combat dagger drills, so nothing too fancy. I want you to try to disarm me. Are you ready for that?"

"Something I could do in my sleep," retorted Tam, trying to regain his composure. He entered the ring of men, and accepted the wooden dagger from Belen. Tam had faced off with Parth before, but had never been able to overpower the older and larger man despite his bravado to the contrary. The size of the opponent was never the issue, but his skill with a blade, agility, and sense of balance were the deciding factors. Parth was adept at knowing where his center of balance was, and had skillfully manipulated Tam in the past. He knew why he had been selected to fight Parth this time. This was punishment for his lack of punctuality.

Parth was shorter than most of his contemporaries and very agile despite his stocky build. He wasn't the strongest man in the guard, but could hold his own in a fight. What Tam feared most was Parth's graceful ability to grapple. It was like watching a trague in the act of stalking its prey. He would analyze every move his opponent would make. The swift, fluid attack was calculated to surprise his opponent before they could react.

The sergeant took up a ready stance and moved the wooden dagger so it ran along the inside edge of his forearm. Tam gripped the weapon in a similar fashion in his right hand, ready to parry, strike, or grapple if the circumstance called for it. The two men locked eyes and began a slow circling spiral toward each other.

Tam began scanning his surroundings with his peripheral vision watching for the slightest hint that an attack was pending. Parth sensed the youth's posture, and began to probe his defenses. A quick slash to the right brought back with a stabbing motion in the opposite direction. Tam parried both intrusions. He knew that Parth was testing him, searching for weaknesses. Tam countered with a series of thrusts and slashes that were expertly blocked.

The two were quite close now, and their free hands began their own assaults. Punches were thrown as well as searching for a grip that would catch the opponent unaware. Parth switched his dagger to his other hand, and began a flurry of assaults, pushing Tam back in order to evade the offensive. Tam had to force his mind to keep his vision from narrowing to the point where he would miss the sweep of Parth's leg as it tested his footing. Tam brought his weapon down in a slash, changed to a sword grip and thrust up in an effort to catch Parth off guard. Before Tam could react, Parth's free hand swept in underneath to catch his arm, parrying the attack. With a sudden jerk, Tam was pulled forward, throwing him off-balance. The next thing Tam knew, he was falling over backward after meeting Parth's leg. He felt the dagger spin out of his grasp as he tried to catch himself, but fell with a thud on his side. Tam looked up to see Parth looming over him, extending an assisting hand.

"You over–reached, and that left you vulnerable. Remember, keep your center of balance, and let your opponent come to you." Parth slapped the young man on his back. "Tam needs more practice. Who is next?"

Tam turned with wide eyes toward the surrounding guards. He knew that the beating was punishment, but did he deserve more? Tam's pleading eyes met with Parth's, and then he knew that he was in for it.

"You get to practice, until you've learned," Parth said with a malevolent smile.

The next half hour was a lesson in humiliation for Tam. He faced off with most of the guards in the circle, attempting to disarm his opponent, one by one. Each time he tried various techniques to turn the conflict to his advantage. Each time he tumbled on his back. Sweat was dripping down his face. He could feel the bruises where punches had connected, or he had hit the ground. The sheer effort of almost constant fighting was draining his youthful reserve, but Tam refused to give in to the desire to admit defeat and throw down his weapon in submission.

Tam was breathing heavily, fighting yet another guard, when Athon approached. "That is enough for now," Athon said. He raised his voice so that all assembled could hear. "I need the prince. Parth, Tam, you're with me, the rest of you can carry on."

Tam, bent over with exhaustion, threw the dagger down and slowly began to shuffle toward Athon, who helped the prince to a standing position. "Parth, did you give this young man a proper training?"

"I certainly hope so." Parth chuckled. "With the beating he took, you would think that he hasn't learned a thing, apart from how to lose."

"I could win if I wasn't so tired," Tam protested. "I just started the turn off–balance."

"Battle doesn't wait. You need to be ready. That's why we train. Now, don't be a wimp. Move through the pain or you'll make things worse," Parth chided.

Tam began moving more under his own power as they neared the palace. By the time they had reached the threshold, Tam had shrugged off the assistance from the two older men and moved stiffly along the route to his father's office. Athon knocked on the door. There was a muffled sound granting permission to enter, and the three walked in. The prince took the lone seat in front of the desk while Athon and Parth stood.

"I suppose you're curious why you're here," Tremmon said, wringing his hands. "Captain Athon and I had an interesting discussion, and we made some decisions which will affect you both. Tam, it is high time that you actively serve the kingdom." The king looked directly at his son. "Athon will take you to the garrison, and teach you how to be a guard."

Tam's eyes flashed with incredulous anger. "What? I'm not going to be a guard!" Tam bellowed, as he sprang to his feet. "I'm a prince, born to rule this kingdom!"

"Sit down, and don't talk while I am speaking!" Tremmon said sharply. "You have a lot to learn about your place in this kingdom. You think that just because you're the prince you're fit to rule?"

The reprimand startled the Tam, but he continued to stare defiantly at his father. "I am the prince of Campsit, and heir to the throne. I was born to rule, and have no other purpose."

"My dear boy," said Tremmon coolly, as he raised himself to lock eyes with the prince. "What do you think a king is? If you think Campsit exists to serve one family you are very much mistaken." Tremmon circled to a position in front of the desk, mere inches from the defiant prince. "You don't even begin to comprehend how I serve this people." Tremmon's words were measured now, as if each were a heavy brick being laid in a wall with intense purpose. "I *am* a servant of this kingdom. The rulers are the citizens, and we're *not* above them. As of this moment you are under the direct command of Captain Athon."

"But, father please—what I have done to deserve this?" Tam pleaded, his eyes welling with tears. His mind was racing with desperate thoughts of escape. It was a harsh punishment for being tardy. "I overslept. I won't do it again. Please don't do this!"

"Tam," said Tremmon, his tone softening with loving sympathy. "I know you think I am punishing you for what happened earlier, but I'm not."

"You must be," said Tam, tears began falling down his cheeks.

"No, I'm not." Tremmon caressed his son's face, wiping away the tears with his thumb. "I know it may appear as if I am angry with you, but I assure you that isn't true. I have been contemplating this for a long time. I have noticed that you have become restless lately, and have been somewhat irresponsible. I wasn't sure what to do about it until now."

"What changed your mind?" Tam asked.

"Athon said that you couldn't command respect if you didn't *learn* it." Tremmon said bluntly. "You've learned that you hold an exalted place in the kingdom, but you haven't learned your duty to those who gave you that position. Respect and honor come from serving others. It isn't given because you are born into it. You have to earn your place in this kingdom by virtue of your deeds, not just because you think it's your birthright."

"Father," Tam pleaded. "I'm sorry, but don't ruin my life."

"I think you'll be better for this experience." Tremmon looked lovingly at his son. "Don't think of this as a punishment. Think of it as an opportunity to learn more about the kingdom, and what it takes to keep it free."

"I don't want to." Tam knew Tremmon couldn't be persuaded to change his mind. "I don't want to leave my friends, or my home."

Tremmon held his hand as if to silence the objection. "I know you don't want to go, but that's my decision. You'll leave with Athon in two turns. I assume that you'll depart with the sunrise supply cart?"

"That was my thought," Athon replied, nodding in agreement.

"Parth, you'll take over the Athon's duties here while he tends to Tam's training," Tremmon said, turning to the sergeant. "Athon will retain his authority as Captain of the Guard, but you will command in his absence." The faintest hint of a smile crossed Parth's lips.

Tam was sullen now. He knew his father had spoken, and that altering the edict would be impossible. Once the king had issued a command, it was not questioned. His defiance gone, Tam slumped into the waiting chair. The temporary burst of energy just moments ago had evaporated faster than water on a hot stove. He was feeling as if someone had siphoned the very life force from his body. The physical effort of combat training coupled with the emotional drain of his father's news left him feeling limp. Slowly he lifted his eyes to meet with his father's warm gaze. He knew his father loved him; but he still could not penetrate this reasoning.

"Athon, I expect that you will have Parth fully briefed before you leave." Tremmon continued. "Parth, I fully expect that you will continue to follow Athon's fine example while he is preoccupied."

"You won't notice a difference, Your Majesty," Parth said with a bow.

"Then it is settled," Tremmon said, returning to his chair. "You two may leave us," he said, waving his hand to dismiss the guards. They gave a quick salute and left the room. "Tam, I know you're hurt, and I don't blame you. I need you to trust me."

Words seemed to form in Tam's mouth, but no sound emanated for a few seconds. "I can't believe that you would do this to me. I am the prince, and your son. I shouldn't have to leave the comforts of my own home to go off guarding the mountains like a commoner. What will mother say?"

"I'm sure that she has reservations, but we're in agreement. Sometimes, we have to make difficult decisions, and this is one. We don't want to send you into danger, but it can't be helped. We're sending you with the best warrior I have. Athon is an excellent guard, and a good teacher. I can't have you continue with this irresponsible behavior." Tremmon looked at the sagging prince. "You look as if you have done battle with all of Arabella. Go upstairs and rest. We'll talk later." The king helped the prince to his feet and hugged him. "I love you far more than you realize."

Tam trudged out of the room and headed for his bedroom. Like a death march, his feet seemed to plod down the corridor as if they were made of stone. Each step was more arduous than the last. With his strength completely gone, his movement was controlled like a puppet on a string. Somehow, he managed to make it to his room, shut the door, and collapse onto his bed. Although his body and spirit were completely drained, his mind kept his body from the sleep it so desperately demanded.

He thought about the wilderness of the mountain garrison. The ignominy of being reduced to a guard, and having to sleep in barracks with the rest of the pitiful men assigned to the outpost. He thought about the unending training, and the countless defeats he would suffer at the hands of Athon. He thought about how his friends would laugh at him. If they continued to be friends, once they learned of his subjugation. This was the worst thing that ever happened to him. Somewhere in the intense speculation of his thoughts, his conscious mind faded into the most restless sleep he had ever experienced.

# Chapter 3

# WANDERLUST

S unlight streamed into the royal chambers as Tova opened the thick drapes. It was nearly an hour past second–quarter sun, and it was well past normal wake–time hours. Even for royalty, it was time to wake up. Indura stirred with a groan.

"You have slept long enough," Tova said. "It is time to wake, and be productive. There are many things to do with the life we have been blessed with, and loafing about does not qualify."

"I don't have to be anywhere. Just let me sleep," Indura groaned, as she tried to seek shelter from the light under the covers of her bed.

"You think that just because you have nothing scheduled, it is reason to sleep the entire turn away?" Tova asked rhetorically. "I give you far too much latitude. Do not think I am willing to let you get away with whatever you want. I would be remiss in my duty to allow behavior so unlike a princess."

"A fact that you seem to delight in reminding me *repeatedly*," Indura said, the sound muffled by the heavy covers. With one swift yank, the protective linens Indura had been cocooning herself in were pulled from around her. "Tova!"

"I will tolerate no more," Tova said, gathering the heavy covers in her arms. "Now get up. I have drawn a bath. Get in before the water gets cold."

Indura beat her fist into the soft mattress in a perturbed manner as she brought her head up. Her tousled auburn hair spilled about her face and shoulders, only partially obscuring her vexed expression. She gave an angry grunt, and hoisted herself to her feet. Tova had interrupted a pleasant dream. One she had hoped to finish. She shot Tova an icy glare through a gap in the long flowing locks, and stormed into the bathing chamber.

It seemed that most turns began similar to this. It wasn't that Indura had any problems with Tova, quite the contrary. Tova was practically her mother.

She was Indura's mistress. It was her duty to supervise, protect, and teach the young princess, a duty she had performed since Indura was young. Lately, she had become more of an annoyance. It was as if the mistress had run out of anything new to teach, and was just nagging her, and it was tiresome being treated like a child.

The warm bath was refreshing. It was usually the only time alone the princess had when she was awake. She was never without the company of her handmaiden, Mai, or Tova, except now. From the time she awoke until she was tucked into bed at late–sun, she was constantly attended.

Indura enjoyed the heat of the lightly perfumed water. Her thoughts were her own for a short span of time, which always passed too quickly. It wouldn't be long before Mai would shatter her solitude. While there was still time, she tried to recall her dream.

Closing her eyes, she could still see a handsome young man who had come to the castle. He was tall and strong, with penetrating blue eyes. He boldly entered the castle, and walked past the guards. She stood atop the throne next to her parents. His eyes seemed to pierce to her very soul, but she couldn't look away. He silently ascended the stairs. It was obvious he wanted her.

Time slowed as he drew near. Her heart fluttered. Although she had never seen him before, she wanted to be in his arms, and feel the warmth of his lips. She couldn't explain why, but she loved him with every part of her soul. As he neared, she extended her arms in longing anticipation of an embrace. She knew as soon as they touched their love would overflow, cascade out, and fill the world.

A knock startled her from the trance. "Indura? It's time to get dressed." The handmaid's voice pierced the silence, breaking the serenity of the vision.

Not again! Indura thought angrily, cursing the inability to fulfill the vision. "Can't I get a moment's peace?" It was a rhetorical question, blurted in frustration.

"Highness, have I offended you?" Mai entered with a worried look on her face.

The realization that her curt reply was uncalled–for caused the princess to apologize. "No, sorry, I was just preoccupied. I didn't mean to take anything out on you."

"Something pleasant, I trust," Mai said as she entered the room, holding a thick towel. "I didn't mean to interrupt. I can come back later."

"No, Mai, it's all right. I was trying to finish a dream." Indura stepped out of the bath into the large, soft towel Mai was extending.

"He must have been handsome," Mai teased.

Indura couldn't help blushing. Mai knew her too well. They had spent so much time together that they had become like sisters. She was easy to talk to, and understood her better than Tova did.

"Yes, he was." Indura flushed.

"Anyone I know?" Mai said tauntingly.

"No! I've never seen him before." Indura was giggling with the guilty pleasure of knowing something Mai didn't.

"A mystery dream man? Or, are you trying make me guess?" Mai asked, pouting her lips playfully.

"I don't know, or I would tell you," Indura said coyly. "He didn't remind me of anyone I know, but can't forget his eyes."

"His eyes?"

"Yes, the deepest blue I have ever seen. I can't describe it in words. It was as if I was looking into love, and it was looking back at me," Indura hesitated, briefly recalling the recent vision.

"Did you kiss him?"

"No, I wanted to," Indura said with longing, "but then you interrupted."

"No wonder you were cross," Mai chuckled as she selected a gown from the wardrobe. "I'm sorry I disturbed you. I wish I hadn't, so I could hear how it ended." She paused for a moment. "I wonder if he actually exists."

Indura looked wishfully at Mai as she slipped into the dress. "I sure hope so. There has to be a man like that, somewhere."

"It sounds romantic," Mai said with a sigh. "When you see him, ask if he has a brother. I haven't met anyone like that, yet. Knowing my luck, he would only pay attention to you anyway."

Mai began the ritual that transformed Indura into the stunning beauty that made her the envy of every other woman in Ithilton. Exquisite clothes, makeup, and hairstyle complemented the princess' natural allure.

As Mai was putting the final touches to Indura's hair, she stopped and gazed admiringly at the princess' reflection in the dressing mirror. She was the epitome of glamour. Her long auburn hair flowed down her back and shoulders with graceful curls that seemed locked in a mesmerizing dance about her face. The red of her hair only accentuated the brilliant green of her eyes, and light copper hue of her skin. She was perfect.

"If the perfect man exists, he better not be blind," Mai chuckled. "It would be a shame to waste this on a man who can't appreciate it."

The two girls giggled at the idea of a blind suitor, and left the dressing room and headed to the Grand Hall. They passed by a large picture window. The sky was a wonderful shade of blue with small puffy white clouds. It was such a nice change from the constant rain of the past ceanor. Such a wonderful turn couldn't be spent locked up in the palace.

Indura needed to be outside, feeling the warm sun on her skin, and the wind in her hair. She loved riding her hestur, Urdin, and now she had the perfect excuse. She only needed a friend to in the adventure. "If I really have nothing scheduled," Indura asked mischievously. "What should we do?"

"You could parade yourself about court, and catch the eye of every man there." Mai said playfully.

Indura didn't really like spending much time in that formal gossip fest. "Perish the thought. It's nice outside. Let's take our hesturs out for a ride."

"Tova won't approve."

"We won't ask." Indura gave a sly grin. "Tova can—"

"I can what, Your Highness?" Tova asked, startling the two young women. She had an incredible knack for approaching undetected. It was like she had materialized out of thin air.

Indura hoped Tova hadn't overheard their conversation. Unfortunately, her mistress had exceptional hearing, and she knew it. There weren't many times Indura could whisper something to Mai that Tova didn't overhear.

"I would ask that you at least tell me where you are going, and take a full escort with you on your ride." Tova said frankly.

"Thank you, mistress," Indura said. "I'm glad you approve. It's such a nice turn. It would be a shame to waste it."

"I do not approve," Tova interjected. "It leaves you vulnerable, and I cannot protect you adequately outside the palace. However, I have found there is not much I can do to stop you. I only ask that you be careful and take adequate soldiers with you."

"Nothing will happen," Indura said. "No one would dare harm me, and I have Mai."

"Do not underestimate the animosity of your subjects." Tova said tersely.

"You worry too much," Indura said.

"It is my duty to worry," Tova said, turning to Mai. "I would go with you, but I have other matters to attend. You, and the soldiers, will never let her out of your sight."

Mai nodded. "Yes, mistress."

"Would you please go to the stables, and make sure the hesturs are readied?"

Tova said, looking at the young handmaiden. "I would like to talk to her highness alone."

With a quick curtsy, Mai left the room, giving Indura an encouraging glance as she exited. Tova motioned for Indura to join her as she went to the small sitting area near the fireplace. The older woman sighed as she sat down. "I have tried to be fair to you, Highness. I have tried to make sure that you are given an amount of freedom." Tova had a reflective expression on her face, as if she were remembering times long since passed. "It has not been easy to keep you protected, and allow you the opportunity to experience life beyond the palace. Do you understand what I am telling you?"

"Not completely."

"You like your little adventures." Tova said diplomatically. "But, it is dangerous outside the palace. There are people who would harm you. You could be kidnapped, killed, or worse. Inside the walls of the palace, you are heavily guarded, and safe from those who would do you harm. Outside this sanctuary, it is very different. You are vulnerable to those who would use you as a means to destroy your father. Your father loves you so much that I suspect he would do anything to keep you safe. It is my duty to protect you, and I must set limits. You are *never* to venture out of the palace without a full escort, *and* my permission."

Indura had never felt more like a prisoner. She hated the idea that she had to ask permission to venture anywhere outside the palace walls. Riding with an escort was always tedious. She could never steer Urdin where she wanted. Soldiers always surrounded her, and they decided everything. For once, she wanted to have the right to command her own destiny. It was clear that Tova had overheard her talking to Mai. All she wanted was the freedom to choose her own destiny.

Indura was flush with anger at having to submit to Tova's will, and embarrassed at having been discovered in a plot to thwart that authority. She could feel the heat rise in her cheeks. Tova must be aggravating her on purpose. It took great effort to quell the desire to lash out at her oppressor, but she kept her expression placid. She didn't want Tova to know she had succeeded in making her angry. Unfortunately, she was less successful keeping her tongue in check. "I understand you perfectly," she said in an icy tone. "I thank you for the privilege of being allowed outside my beautiful prison." She stood haughtily and left, not waiting for Tova to dismiss her.

Each footfall Indura made as she stormed down the hall reinforced the futility of the situation. The palace was beautiful, full of people, and safe. She knew it as well as the people who had built it, but it was still a prison.

Prisoners, by definition, are unable to leave. Indura lived in luxury, but still wasn't free to come and go as she pleased. Soldiers, nobles, and even servants could, but she was better than they were. She was the princess. She should be able to do whatever her heart desired. It was patently unfair, an injustice against her royal person. She was angry with a world that enjoyed a right that she had never known: the right to come and go as she pleased.

How she longed to ride Urdin past the soldiers at a full gallop, the wind whipping past her face as her hestur rhythmically pounded the ground. Rider and mount free from the invisible chains that had held her back for so long.

How Indura envied the sycophantic people that infested the palace. Each one oblivious to the contempt she held for them. She entered the crowded court looking for the one person she knew would sooth her bitterness.

The Grand Hall was a massive edifice. There was nothing to rival the space in all of Arabella. On one end was the raised dais, which contained the thrones of the king and queen. Towering pillars lined the sides of the hall on either side interspersed with numerous galleries ascending a full ten levels above stone floor. Crowds of nobles gathered to discuss the political gossip and intrigue which always seemed to permeate the air. The scintillating prattle would normally merely annoy, but now it seemed to close around her, reducing the capacious room to a claustrophobic closet.

Indura searched the sea of faces, continuing her desperate attempt to find her handmaiden. After a few moments, the feeling of captivity began to grip her to the point of panic. Her steps quickened, and she nearly lost her indifferent facade. As she made her way toward the main entrance to the chamber, she spied her quarry.

"Mai!" Indura quickly raced to her friend, struggling to maintain her composure. "Quickly! The walls have ears." She grabbed Mai's hand and nearly yanked her through the main entrance toward the stables. There was a room, used to keep riding tack, and it would be relatively private. When they arrived, she urgently ushered Mai inside, giving a cautious glance around the hallway to make sure the coast was clear.

The room was filled with leather saddles, bridles, reigns, and other accouterments needed for hestur riding. The effect was much like a saddle–filled library. They moved to the far end, and concealed themselves behind a rack.

"Did you make arrangements for our ride?" Indura asked, with the realization that a stable boy might soon interrupt their conversation.

"Yes, of course," Mai said. "What's going on? What did Tova say to you?"

"Can I trust you?" Indura's eyes seemed to plead with her handmaiden.

"Yes, of course," Mai said. "Indura, I would *never* betray you."

Indura eyed her handmaiden while her soul was pounded by swirling emotions she struggled to control. It was as if she stood in a stormy sea caught between the surging waves and the rocky shore. The envy she had for the apparent freedom Mai enjoyed and her love for her dearest friend battered her psyche. She wanted to scream, and cry for her lamentable situation. The internal turmoil was completely masked by her well–disciplined countenance. Finally, she spoke. "What is it like to be able to leave the palace whenever you want?"

"What?"

"I can have anything I want, but I can't ride off to visit the ocean, mountains, or even your mother. I have to ask Tova. She tells me how to act, and what to do. I feel like I have no control over my own life. But you can leave whenever you want."

"That isn't true," Mai said defensively. "I just can't leave you. I live to serve you."

"But, you're my best friend," Indura pleaded. "You don't stay because you have to."

"Yes, I do." Mai was firm, but her face spoke of understanding. "We are friends, but I can't just leave when I feel like it. I'm bound to you."

Indura was stunned. It was as if someone had splashed her in the face with cold water. "You're right. I'm sorry I'm being selfish. Please forgive me. I know you're my servant, but it's easy to forget. If it makes you feel any better, I don't think of you that way. You're more like the sister I never had." The feelings she had been repressing finally broke the surface in a well of tears. It had never occurred to her that her handmaiden was by her side out of duty and not pure friendship.

"I don't mind our relationship," Mai said, wiping a tear from the princess' eye. "When I first started, it was different, but as time passed my duties became less of a chore."

"I'm still sorry," Indura said, weeping softly. "Here I pity myself, and you have to spend every turn catering to my spoiled nature."

"It isn't so bad," Mai said. "I enjoy my time with you." A stable boy entered the room, grabbed a saddle and bridle, and left without noticing the two young women in the back of the room. "I don't like seeing you sad, so let's leave. It will make you happy to get out."

Indura nodded, wiping her tear-stained cheeks. The two quietly left the room and entered the stable. The boy was placing an ornate saddle on Urdin as the women approached.

"How soon will the hesturs be ready?" Indura asked as politely as possible. She was suddenly feeling sick of having others serve her every need, but outfitting a hestur was something she hadn't learned to do.

"Not long," he replied.

"Mai, would you please tell Captain Glafindr that we will be departing as soon as our mounts are ready." It was another task, and she felt guilty for requesting it. How could she be so selfish? Mai touched her shoulder briefly, smiled warmly, and left.

Indura patted Urdin's long neck with affection while the stable boy cinched the saddle tight. She looked at the stable boy. He was like Mai. They both worked at the palace since they were young, and probably couldn't leave if they wanted to. Did he envy her for all the privileges she enjoyed? Her thoughts couldn't reconcile a nagging question: was anyone truly free?

# Chapter 4

# BROODING

Tam's body ached so badly it woke him from his nap. He couldn't remember a time when he felt this awful after sparring with the guards. Combat training always resulted in bruises, but he had never fought so many before, or been beaten as badly. Usually the guards restrained themselves during the training sessions, but not this time. It seemed like most of them unleashed their full might.

Tam knew he had to move or he would stiffen up. Groaning with pain, he rolled out of bed and shuffled over to the window. It was high–sun.

He was supposed to be in class at the academy, but didn't think it mattered much anymore. Surely, his father must have spoken to Master Thales about the change by now. Knowing Campsit's resident genius, he already understood what was happening. Tam didn't know how that was possible, but the man seemed to know everything about everything.

When Tam had been tardy to class in the past, Master Thales already knew exactly why, and would chastise him for whatever bad habit had interfered with his punctuality in his usual polite manner.

"Never let vain desires distract you from noble purpose," Tam muttered, mocking the tone of his mentor. He shook his head and sighed. There really wasn't any way of avoiding that conversation, but if anyone could explain his father's logic, it would be Master Thales. He ran a brush through his tousled hair, and made his way to the building at the far end of the inner keep.

The academy was one of the larger buildings in Campsit. It housed the school where every child was taught the skills necessary to help the kingdom grow. Everyone learned to read, write, apply a trade, and the ideals that made Campsit different from the rest of Arabella.

Since Tam's situation was unique, he took most of his lessons from the academy's headmaster, Master Thales. The elderly man taught the more advanced classes in math, science, engineering, philosophy, and medicine. Most students would take at least one or two classes in these subjects, but only a few took them all.

It was after high–sun, and he would be in the middle of his engineering lecture. Engineering was one of the larger classes due to its popularity with the various guilds and craft halls. Because of the size, it was held in the main auditorium. Tam thought he might be able to enter relatively unnoticed and find a seat in the back.

Just before he entered the hall, he stopped to listen at the door. He could hear Master Thales, and quietly opened the door a crack. He could see the back of the master's head as he was drawing a diagram on the chalkboard along with some equations detailing how much rope it would take to lift a given weight using a pulley. Tam figured that now would be the perfect time to slip in.

"It's rude to skulk around in hallways eavesdropping, Tam," Master Thales said, without turning around.

"How does he do that?" Tam mumbled, as he swung the door open to the stifled laughter of the other students.

"Come in and have a seat in the front row," Master Thales continued, still intently scribbling on the board. "I saved one especially for you."

"How did you—"

"Know you would be late?" Master Thales said, finishing Tam's sentence. He turned and gave a sly wink. "I saw the guards using you as a throwing dummy, and thought you deserved a rest." The class openly laughed at the reference to Tam's beating, but Master Thales raised his hands to quiet the raucous moment. "Children, it isn't wise to laugh at another person's pain. After all, I seriously doubt any of you would be standing so soon, if the roles were reversed."

Tam quickly found the only empty chair in the center of the front row. It had a small sign neatly inscribed with his name placed in the exact center of the seat. He picked it up and took its place.

With a warm smile, Master Thales turned, and resumed his discourse. Tam was certain he picked up exactly where he had left off. The rest of the lecture went by without further interruptions. Unfortunately, Tam really couldn't concentrate on what was being said. He hadn't brought anything to take notes, like the other students. Somehow, it seemed pointless to continue his studies. He would be leaving in a couple of turns anyway.

Master Thales ended his lesson at the exact moment the timing bell heralded the change in classes. Unlike the rest of the students, Tam remained in his seat as the room cleared.

"I don't know why you think I will be able to explain things more clearly than they already are, Tam," Master Thales said, in his usual warm tone. "I can't make your father change his mind either."

"I guess I don't understand why he thinks demoting me will help."

"For a young man who has learned Campsit ideology, you demonstrate an acute failure to understand its most basic principles."

Tam scowled. The insinuation that he was stupid didn't sit well with him. "I learned them," he said defensively.

Master Thales raised an eyebrow. "Then care to explain how you are above doing any job you're asked to do?"

"I'm not above it," Tam countered. "I'm just meant to lead, not follow."

"You feel you should replace Athon now?"

"What? I didn't mean to imply that."

"You're afraid that once people see you in uniform, they will somehow forget you're the prince?" Master Thales chided. "You forget that every person in Campsit is vital to its continued existence, and because of that, no *one* person is *more*, or *less*, important than another."

Tam scoffed. "I know all that."

"You say that, but I feel you don't fully understand it yet, and that is why you are being given this opportunity."

"It's punishment, not opportunity," Tam said sourly, folding his arms in a huff.

"You believe that, but that doesn't make it true," Master Thales said gently. "You think you misbehaved, and your father is punishing you for it."

"Isn't he?"

"Not remotely. I proposed the idea when you were very young, but it took your father longer than I planned to adopt it."

Tam has always thought of Master Thales as a friend and mentor. For him to be behind this was an unspeakable betrayal. "Why would you do that?"

"To help you reach your full potential," Master Thales said. Tam was speechless. "How much longer do you think you can stay here and continue to progress? You've learned practically everything I can teach you." The first students began to enter the lecture hall. "You have to move forward, and for that you have to take what you've learned and apply it." Master Thales leaned over and whispered in Tam's ear. "Some people are born into greatness. Others have it thrust upon them, but even the mightiest must be tempered by experience. The trick is to be humble enough to accept the destiny the gods have planned for us, and I can tell the gods have something extraordinary for you."

Tam glowered at his teacher. "That isn't very convincing."

Master Thales sighed. "Tam, you can either do things the easy way or the hard way. I cannot give you wisdom. You have to do that yourself, but I can tell you that if you persist in fighting the change it will only cause more pain. Now, unfortunately I have class, so go home and think about what we discussed."

Tam was furious. He grit his teeth and silently began making his way through the incoming crowd of students.

"Never let vain desires distract you from noble purpose, Tam," Master Thales called out, just as the prince exited the room.

Tam silently walked back to the palace, unwilling to acknowledge anyone. He was angry at the world. He thought Master Thales could help him understand, or maybe talk some sense into his father, but instead he had discovered that everyone was conspiring against him. As far as he was concerned, he wouldn't learn anything by being a guard.

Despite his anger, or perhaps because of it, he began to feel a tinge of guilt. Maybe he was putting himself above others, and that was troubling.

People in Campsit understood that everyone was equal. There wasn't a single person that wasn't wanted, needed, or appreciated, and everyone was expected to contribute to the advancement of the kingdom. Each person's talents and desires helped them select a job, and then they gave their best effort. Even people who were disabled or suffering from illness did what they could.

The net result put everyone on the same level. No one felt as if they didn't contribute, or that some people worked harder than others did. Everyone had work, and was happy doing what they could to help their fellow citizens. No one was left behind.

In theory, Tam wasn't any different, but in practice, he was special. Campsit law forbade the royal couple from having more than one male child. This practice served to ensure that no argument for succession would ever occur. The downside was that once a male heir was born that child had to be protected until he could ascend to the throne, and sire a male child to continue the royal line. His fore-ordination as king governed every aspect of his life. Everyone treated him differently, so didn't that make him unique? Why should he feel guilty when it was obvious he was meant to be superior?

Tam brooded in his room for the next two turns, emerging only when necessary. He continued to fathom his place in the kingdom, and the sudden change in his father's attitude toward him. Wasn't being a guard more dangerous than a game of tvinga, a sport he had been barred from playing due to its brutality?

When the gong sounded, announcing supper, on the second turn Tam sulked downstairs to the dining hall. His father and mother sat at the table waiting for him. Usually the cooks, butlers, maids, and others who worked at the palace were there to enjoy the meal with them, but not this time. The room was empty except for the royal family.

"Where is everyone?" Tam asked.

"They just finished," Tremmon replied. "I wanted to talk to you over supper, and didn't feel our conversation needed to include them."

Tam plopped into his chair. "What's there to talk about? You've made up your mind," he said, sullenly.

"We're worried about you." Aurora gave Tam a concerned look. She was a beautiful woman. Despite being in her fifties, she looked younger. The only sign of her age were the streaks of gray in her otherwise dark brown hair. It made her look regal.

"What for?" Tam muttered. "It's not like my opinion really matters."

Tremmon sighed. "Son, you entirely miss the point."

"Well, what is the point then?" Tam asked bitterly.

"We've made some mistakes in your upbringing," Tremmon said.

"It's all my fault," Aurora blurted.

"Now, now, we made these decisions together, so you can't take the blame here, darling," Tremmon said, patting Aurora's hand gently. "We've been a little overprotective with you, Tam. We should have let you live a more normal life—"

Aurora interrupted. "We just didn't want anything to happen to you. I—we had to protect you from all the danger. Well, you know the law. We couldn't put you in a situation where you could get hurt."

"The problem is that by doing that we deprived you of the opportunity to learn the important lessons in life," Tremmon said with a pained smile. "Lessons only experience can teach you."

"I'm not deprived," Tam protested. "I've learned plenty."

Tremmon shook his head. "No son. What you've learned is entitlement, and superiority. By sheltering you from the harsher aspects of life, we have taught you that you're somehow above things. That has to stop."

Tam was shocked. He hadn't really thought of himself as entitled or superior. "When have I ever acted like I'm better than anyone?" He said defensively.

Tremmon held up his hand. "I said that we've taught you that. I never said you act that way, but based on your actions you're headed that direction. Campsit needs leaders that follow the path your ancestor, Themis, blazed."

"Even though you're special," Aurora said. "You have to be humble enough to recognize that, if anything, the citizens of Campsit are our superiors. We serve them. We owe them for everything we have, and for the privilege of living a perfect dream. No other kingdom in Arabella can say they have what we have. Your father sees to that. He makes certain that everyone is treated fairly, and that everyone's needs are met."

Tam groaned. "I know all that mother. I just don't know why I have to up and move to the garrison."

"To teach you service," Aurora said bluntly.

"Experience is the best teacher," Tremmon said. "I talked it over with Master Thales, and he thinks the best place for you to learn that is working as a guard."

"For how long?"

Tremmon shrugged. "As long as it takes."

"What about the danger? You won't even let me play tvinga because it's too dangerous" Tam was incredulous. "You know as well as I do that several guards die every pass up there."

"Athon and Master Thales assure me that you'll be in no danger. Athon promised he wouldn't allow you to do anything that would put you in harm's way." Tam sat, arms folded, still somewhat unconvinced.

"Tammerand," Aurora cooed gently. It was her pet name for Tam that she used whenever he was scared or injured. "If we didn't know this wouldn't benefit you, we wouldn't do it. Please, trust us."

"We love you very much, and want you to be the best king Campsit has ever seen," Tremmon said. "The only way that's going to happen is if we teach you correctly."

Tam was confused. "But, you're a great king. Shouldn't I want to be like you?"

Tremmon smiled. "The goal is to have a lineage that improves with each generation. Too often, you have a great king whose offspring degenerates over time, and they become tyrants. Themis wanted to put a stop to that. He wanted his descendants to carry on his dream of a perfect kingdom, so each successive generation had to try to improve; to ensure freedom, equity, and justice for each and every citizen."

"I could learn that from Master Thales."

"He said that he had taught you as much as he could," Aurora said, "and that it was time you learned by doing."

Tremmon clapped his hands together. "We've beaten this hestur to death." He began piling food onto his plate. "I'm starving."

The meal passed with no more discussion on the topic that weighed so heavily on Tam's mind. He still had reservations, but at least he had some idea of why he was being shipped off. Unfortunately, it didn't make him feel any better about the arrangement.

When Tam was full, he retired to his room, and tried to sleep. He knew Athon would come around sunrise, and that made him too anxious. The unknown bothered him, but at least he had accepted the change thrust upon him. Eventually he drifted off into restless slumber.

# Chapter 5

# A Frozen Journey

T am woke up just before sunrise, and couldn't get back to sleep. After a half–hour, he decided that he would get dressed and wait for Athon to come get him. When the knock finally came, it gave Tam a sense of relief. He entered the hall, prepared to meet his fate.

"I'm ready," Tam said, closing the door behind him. He was sullen–faced, and refused to look Athon in the eye. He was dressed in some warm wool clothes with a light cloak.

The mantels worn by Campsit civilians were good for most situations, but not extended periods out in inclement weather like the ones the guards used.

Athon handed him a thick olive colored cloak. "Put this on. It's raining and this one will do a better job at keeping you warm and dry."

Tam gladly completed the exchange. "What about my armor?"

"It's still a few turns from being finished. I'm glad to see I don't have to carry you all the way to the stables, your Highness." Athon said sincerely. "We have one thing that needs to be done before we leave, and I would rather not have to lug you around to do it." Athon brought Tam under his arm and led him out to the waiting hesturs.

They rode to the stables used by the guards in silence. After they secured both hesturs, they made their way to the dining hall. It was deserted except for Parth, who was seated at the Captain's table.

"About time you showed up," Parth said, as they entered the room. "I was beginning to think I would have to send reinforcements."

"We aren't that late," Athon said with a smile as he led Tam to the table.

A warm fire was burning in the hearth, filling the room with its heat. The cook had set three places, and the table was laden with fresh breads, fruits, sweet meats, and a large bowl of eggs. He directed Tam to sit.

"It is important for us to start this journey with full stomachs. There will be no time to stop once we get on the road, and it is not the best weather." He poured Tam a large cup of steaming atole, and began to load his plate with the various foods from around the table.

"You only hurt yourself if you don't eat heartily, Tam," Parth said, tearing into a warm loaf of bread.

"I don't want to go," Tam said, staring blankly at the food in front of him.

"Tam," Athon said sympathetically. "You must understand this doesn't depend on your wants or wishes. You're going even if I have to tie you to Pyta. Either you can accept it, or you can fight it and be miserable. The choice is yours, but it doesn't affect the outcome." Tam gave a heavy sigh, waited for a moment, and then began to fill his plate.

"That's good, Tam," Parth said. "Trust me when I tell you that you need lots of food in your belly. You won't eat again until you reach the mountain garrison, and it is a very long time when you're riding."

The trio feasted while anticipating the arrival of the wagon master. At last, the burly man entered the hall complaining about having to delay for their sake. They took their cue, and left the remnants of supper for the cooks to clean.

As they entered the stable, they were met by Tremmon and Aurora. "I trust you weren't expecting to leave without letting us say farewell to our son," Tremmon said, walking towards Tam. "I wanted you to know that I am proud of you. You are taking your first real step towards becoming a true leader. Pay attention to Athon. There is no room for error in the wilderness."

"I will, father," Tam said, "although, I still don't want to go."

"I would rather not have you leave either," Aurora said sweetly. "But, it is better that you have this experience in your youth." Tears stained the cheeks of the fair queen as she embraced Tam. "Take care of him, Captain."

Athon looked at both monarchs. "I will defend him with my life. Majesties, we must be leaving if we want to reach the garrison before the end of the turn."

Tam embraced both parents, and though he wasn't accustomed to losing composure in front of the stalwart guards, he broke down and cried. The farewell lasted only a few moments, but it was much longer than the wagon master apparently could tolerate. At last, he announced that he would be leaving with or without his escort.

After a final hug from his parents, Tam mounted Pyta, spun his cloak about his shoulders, and urged his mount into the cold damp of the drizzling rain. There was a crack from the wagon master's whip and the party began moving.

Tam urged Pyta forward and swiveled in his saddle to watch as his parents disappeared behind a corner. He slowly turned around and followed the wagon closely toward the main gate. A shiver ran down his spine as the cold air enveloped him; a cold that was only amplified by the misery of the rain and isolation he felt.

The pace was increased to make up for lost time. It didn't take long for the convoy to reach the edge of the forest and disappear from sight in the dense vegetation. Happy that they were finally underway, the wagon master began to sing. Tam supposed that it was his way of keeping company on the long and lonely road from Campsit to the high mountain garrison.

The road was cut through the trees and dense ground cover like a tunnel through rock. On a normal turn, the light barely penetrated the thick canopy of trees. It created a surreal feeling, as if just beyond the brink of the thoroughfare, something unimagined was lurking, waiting for the right moment to pounce. However, the rich baritone voice of the wagon master eased Tam's fears.

Athon and Parth had been accurate when they said it would take the entire turn to travel to the garrison. The first part of the journey eased through rolling hills that eventually gave way to steep switchback turns, which steadily climbed the side of the mountain. Tam felt as if the steep, winding road would never end. "You weren't exaggerating the length of this trip," Tam said.

"It *is* a long way," Athon replied as he turned to face Tam. "I make this trip several times each pass. This is your first time going to the garrison?" Tam nodded. "That actually comes as a bit of a surprise to me. I would have thought you made the trip before."

"I don't know why. I suppose it is something that I should have done, but other things have always been a higher priority."

"I suspect that your mother has never been too keen on your exploring. It can be dangerous if you leave the main road."

"I figured that my studies with Master Thales took priority over my adventuring out into the kingdom."

"You'll have a lot to learn if you're going to survive," Athon said. "The mountains are not for the uninitiated. I won't fulfill my promise to keep you safe if I can't teach you."

"Well, when do you plan on starting?" Tam asked the question with enthusiastic apprehension. He didn't really wish to start the training per se, but he didn't know how he could stall it any longer.

"I suppose I should start giving you the rules. It isn't going to be the same as living in Campsit. The most important rule is that you must never leave without the watch commander knowing where you are. It is vital for your safety and those around you. The mountains pose a significant threat with the weather and steep terrain. Throw in wild beasts and the constant threat of invasion, and the work becomes very hazardous. We only have the other guards and scouts to keep each other safe."

Tam wasn't convinced that the dichotomy of being dangerous and safe at the same time was possible. He would do his best to follow Athon's instructions on how to live and work at the garrison. He continued to question Athon about the rigors of life as a guard. Much of Tam's time would revolve around the watch cycle and combat training. Eventually, he would learn to track and move through the forest. "How long does the training take?" Tam asked, somewhat anxiously.

"Well," Athon mused, "it depends on how quickly you learn. It will be different from what you have experienced so far. You will have to learn how to follow orders, track, hunt, survive the wild; all while keeping a careful watch around you."

"I don't want to do this," Tam said, surprised he said it aloud. "I don't want to try, but seeing as I don't have a choice. I'll do my best."

"At least you're being honest with yourself," Athon said. "I have several additional rules for you."

"What are they?" Tam quickly asked, moving his mount slightly away from the captain, as if distance would soften the blow.

"First," Athon said ticking off his fingers for emphasis. "Never lie to yourself, or me. Second, do everything that you are asked to do without complaint or question. Third, make sure you memorize everything you're taught. You have to be able to do it in your sleep, or you'll be vulnerable in a crisis. Lastly, I want you to trust me. I want you to know that you can come to me with any problem, and we'll solve it together. Do you think you can do that?"

Tam nodded. "I'll do my best."

Thick mist began to blanket the road as they ascended the mountain. Soon, it became difficult to see the path ahead in the dense fog. The air was significantly cooler than it had been just a short while before. It was as if the rain wasn't falling anymore, but was surrounding them, suspended in midair. The freezing temperature penetrated the thick uht wool cloaks and chilled them to the bone. They pulled their cloaks tighter, in an almost vain attempt to ward off the icy air.

"H—hoow mmmuch f—farther?" Tam tried to ask the question, through chattering teeth and spasmodic shivers. He could not remember being so cold before. Campsit had its fair share of cold weather, but not often. Snow occasionally stayed for turns during winter, but the cold was always tempered by the warm fires of the keep. His only protection from the elements was his heavy rain cloak, and it wasn't enough.

His cloak was a rather ingenious article of clothing, made of laminated layers of heavy uht wool bound together with tar to make it waterproof. The finished garment kept the wearer warm and dry in inclement weather. However, the front was still open to the elements, so the cloak offered only partial protection against the high humidity and the colder temperatures of the mountains. Tam knew armor would have helped keep him warm, and silently cursed Master Orpheus for not having it finished in time.

"I figure we'll be at the garrison in a couple hours," the wagon master called over his shoulder. "Should hit some snow an' ice here'n not too long. That'll slow us down a piece. 'Fraid it's goin' to be worse before'n it gets better."

I'm going to freeze to death, Tam thought to himself. He hunched over and tucked both hands under his arms as he pulled the cloak around him as tight as he could.

Time seemed to stand still for Tam. Each agonizing second was a battle to stay warm in the increasingly cold weather. Soon, the water droplets that surrounded them turned into ice crystals that gently floated to the ground around them. The water that soaked his clothes, saddle, and boots formed a thin sheet of ice around his body. He was quite certain that his cloak had formed into a rigid shape about him. His feet and legs were like two blocks of ice. He was tired now, and it was becoming difficult for him to keep his eyes open.

The snow was now quite deep. It was with some difficulty that the wagon was moving forward. Tam could barely make out the edges of the road. The forest had given way to rocks and cliffs. He couldn't make out much of the surrounding area due to the driving snow. Ahead, he made out the outline of a rock wall with a large cave opening. As they neared the opening, it became quite apparent that it was the outer wall of the garrison. It was a welcome sight. As they neared, a horn sounded, and the heavy portcullis lifted. The giant main door opened, and the three were ushered quickly into the stable area.

The warmth of the stable was a huge relief for Tam. A guard helped him off his mount, and he shuffled after their escort to the dining hall. He could barely feel his legs, and his feet were numb. The hall was full of guards enjoying a delicious smelling supper. Several sculphounds made their way around the tables, eagerly accepting scraps from the men. At the far end was a large hearth with a warm fire.

A man stood at the commander's table and shouted. "Captain Athon, Prince Tam! I'm so glad you made it safely. I was beginning to worry with the storm and all."

"Xacthos, my dear friend," Athon said, placing his hand on his lieutenant's shoulder. "It's good to see you. We have a lot to discuss, but I'm afraid the young prince wasn't dressed for this weather." He glanced at Tam who was glass–faced, moving stiffly, and shaking. "I think he could do with a hot bath."

"Naturally," Xacthos said, motioning to an attendant at the far side of the room. "Draw a hot bath for the prince and the captain immediately!" The attendant left the room, and Xacthos beckoned them to follow him. "I'll send someone for your bags, and we'll warm your clothes up so they will be ready when you are done." He stared at the clumsy manner in which Tam was shuffling after them. "We'll get you warmed up, your highness. Hope you don't have any frostbite."

"Thhhank y—you," Tam stuttered.

"Wasn't expecting it to be as bad as it was," Athon said bluntly. "Don't think I've traveled up here through a storm like that."

"It can fool you," Xacthos said. "It can be raining in the valley, but once you get up here it's snow. I thought you would have remembered that."

The three entered a very warm and steamy room with partitions separating the entry area from the bathing stalls. Each stall contained a changing area and a tub that was filled by water through a series of pipes carrying hot and cold water. The attendant was busy checking the temperature of the water flowing into two of the tubs. The heat felt inviting on Tam's cheeks, and he could smell fresh herbs that had been added to the water.

"I'll let you both bathe," Xacthos said, turning for the door. "We'll talk more over supper."

Tam attempted to remove his cloak, but found his fingers incapable of clasping the fastener. The attendant saw his predicament and began assisting him with his clothes. "Thank you," he said. "I don't know why, but my hands don't seem to want to work." She took his cloak and then began to help him with his outerwear. Tam was somewhat uncomfortable by this help. She seemed to be about fifty or so, easily old enough for her to be his mother.

"I'll tell you what," she said. "I'll get your boots and such off, and let you take care of the rest so as not to make you all mortified. Put your hands in that water while I'm fussn' with your boots and it'll unfreeze 'em in no time."

"Thanks," Tam responded. He was glad he wouldn't have to suffer the embarrassment of being undressed by a total stranger, and a woman at that. She did as promised, and then promptly left him alone to undress. The warm water had helped get his hands working again so taking off the frozen clothing wasn't too much of a chore.

As he slid into the water, his feet and legs could barely tell that the water was warm at all. After a short time, the attendant came back in to gather his clothes and hustle them off for cleaning. By the time she left, the feeling began to return to his feet. Icy cold was replaced by sweet warmth that penetrated his body to the core.

Tam sat basking in the sheer luxury of the bath. The sweet smell of the herbs and warmth of the water not only refreshed him, but also seemed to cause his mind to drift into a cloud of oblivion. The attendant entered again, and set out clean clothes and a towel on the changing bench.

"You ought to get out before you fall asleep there, Highness," she said as she left.

Tam sat with his thoughts for a few moments, and then got out and dressed. He made his way back to the dining hall. It was deserted except for Athon and Xacthos. A place was set for him near the fire. The hot meal was just as welcome and delicious as the hot bath. It seemed like an eternity since breakfast. He was famished, and ate helping after helping of the nourishing soups, breads, and roast meats. Athon and Xacthos were involved in a long conversation revolving around him.

Tam didn't pay attention to them. He was physically exhausted, and mentally weary of discussing the subject. All he wanted was to fill his stomach and find a place to collapse in a heap. He wasn't used to travel, and this voyage had taken a lot out of him. When he first arrived, the aches and pains of riding a hestur a long distance didn't register compared to the cold he had to endure, but now his body was crying out in pain. With his belly filled, and the warmth of the fire, a glazed expression came over his face.

"It looks like this conversation will have to wait until after we have had a chance to sleep." Athon said. He helped the dazed prince to his feet. "If you will excuse us, Xacthos, the prince will use the table as a bed if we don't do something quickly."

"We have prepared quarters for you, so you don't have to use the inn this time." Xacthos said, as he led them toward the garrison sleeping quarters. "It won't be like the one you had at the palace, but oh well."

"They'll be just fine. Will you make sure to have the watch commander wake us at the customary time?"

"It's up to you, but I had left orders for you to sleep as long as you wanted." Xacthos had sounded slightly surprised.

"I think we need to begin training as soon as possible. No sense in delaying what we came here for," Athon said earnestly.

Tam followed the two men in a zombie–like fashion. His brain hadn't registered the implications of what time he would be awakened. He stumbled along the corridor in a mind–numbing haze. The only thing that kept him from falling asleep was the constant effort of putting one foot in front of the other without tripping. They seemed to go through a maze of corridors until they stopped in front of two opened doors. The rooms were lit with a single lantern revealing the rather sparse furnishings. Each room was equipped with a simple bed, desk, chair, and trunk. The room was just big enough to contain all of the furnishings and accommodate standing with the door closed. Someone had already been here, as their belongings were waiting for them.

Athon thanked Xacthos, and bid him farewell. He led Tam into his room, helped him into bed, and then blew out the lantern. It seemed the instant Tam had curled up under the warm covers; he slipped into unconsciousness.

# Chapter 6

# Tragues

Time at the garrison was long and arduous for Tam. As the pass progressed from the spring storms and into the warmth of summer, the homesickness that plagued his initial arrival evaporated along with his rebellious attitude. For six ceanors, he learned everything there was to know about life as a guard, and it was more exhausting that he ever imagined. There was a lot of manual labor: cutting wood, cleaning stables, and clearing the roads and trails of fallen trees. Every strenuous task was assigned to the junior guards.

At least Tam had some friends stationed at the garrison, but he didn't see them very often. Most junior guards worked the sleep–watch after they completed the first three ceanors of orientation, but Athon had other things in mind. Tam worked the wake–watch, which put him on an opposite shift from his friends. It would have been lonely except for Brixos, another junior guard who had befriended Tam on his first turn, and they had become nearly inseparable during that time.

Brixos had grown up at the garrison, and had joined the guard only a few turns before Tam arrived. Since they were both new, they were in the same orientation group. They were often partners during training exercises, and had time to get to know each other. They soon found they had many common interests, and before they knew it, they were best friends. Their rapport made the more arduous tasks easier to bear.

It wasn't all work. Athon regularly took Tam out, and taught him how to track and hunt. The prince found he had a natural talent for it. What he lacked in innate ability he made up for as a quick learner, catching on much faster than Athon had anticipated.

The forest was intimidating at first, but quickly lost its mystique. There was a natural order to life in the wild, which he understood very well. Much of

Athon's teachings were reiterations of topics Master Thales had already made Tam commit to memory. He knew many of the plants and animals by name. Tam loved being in the forest, and seemed to relish every moment he was outside the high walls of the protective fortress. Every turn was filled with adventure.

One, seemingly unremarkable turn, Tam roused himself and began his early ritual like every other in the past few ceanors. He tidied his room and headed for the dining hall where he sat next to Brixos. As Tam entered the hall, he noticed the usual jovial faces were grim. The air was thick with tension. "What's going on?"

"One of the scouts hasn't reported in," he said with a frown.

"Really?" Tam asked in disbelief.

"No one has seen him."

"Who was it?" Tam was still getting to know everyone. He knew many of the guards, but wasn't familiar with the scouts.

"Drastos," Brixos replied. "He's a legend around here."

Tam had heard the name before. It was said that he once infiltrated an Ithilton raiding party while most of them slept and single–handedly killed them all. For such an experienced man to go missing was very odd indeed.

"Could he have been captured?" Tam's mind reeled with the thought of a potential attack.

"Not likely," Brixos replied. "He wasn't the only one on patrol in that area, and everyone else has checked in."

Tam's food arrived, and he began to eat somberly. He wasn't anxious to have to face real combat. The thought was both terrifying and exciting at the same time. Still, it didn't leave a pleasant feeling in his gut. "When did we find out?"

"Word came in just before the watch change. A runner was sent back when he didn't show up for the relief rendezvous." If Brixos had anything further to say, he never got the chance.

A runner burst into the room gasping for breath. "Captain Athon, Xacthos!" He ran to the two leaders seated at the head table. The pair had been grim faced and softly talking amongst themselves. Their attention was instantly diverted to the messenger, and they both leapt up to meet him midway into the room.

"Report!" Athon demanded.

"They found him," the messenger gasped, "out in the Great Meadow, he's been attacked."

"Attacked! By what?" Xacthos said angrily.

"A trague," the messenger said still gasping for air.

"What? How can you be certain?" Athon said in disbelief.

"Impossible!" Xacthos exclaimed. "He's fended off countless attacks."

"I know," said the messenger, "but it's a trague. The prints are there, and he's been—eaten. We found where it happened, and then followed the trail to what's left of him."

Athon looked around. There was a rather sizable audience. Trague attacks weren't anything new, but it was very rare that one turned fatal. There was only one standing rule regarding tragues. Once they had a taste for human blood, they would be back for more. "Where is the rendezvous?"

"They're waiting at The Crossing."

"Tam, Brixos, front and center. Xacthos get thirty guards and form a hunting party."

"Men," Xacthos said, "you heard the captain. I want that beast's skin for this floor! Who are my volunteers?" Every man in the room stood, and every man gave a deafening cry.

Xacthos went through the room and selected his thirty, leaving the rest dejected. It wasn't prudent to have the entire garrison empty, leaving it unprotected, while they went hunting. The disappointment in the men's faces was evident.

Tam wondered why Athon had included him and Brixos. They were junior guards, and should have been left behind. He hoped it was because Athon held his ability to hunt, but it he was probably just keeping an eye him.

In no time the entire hunting party was saddled and ready to ride. Athon led the charge through the main gate and down the road toward the Ithilton valley. The hesturs thundered down the mountain, through the narrow pass, and then out into the forest beyond. Tam wasn't sure how far it was to the rendezvous, but he soon began to realize that he was in an area he had never been before.

Onward they pressed until they came to a river. Athon reined his hestur, Zuri, to a stop. He raised his hand high in the air and gave a whistling call. An answering call was given from across the river, and a camouflaged scout raised his hand as he stood from his crouching position on the opposite bank.

"Cyrix, is that you?" Athon asked.

"What, you don't recognize me?"

"You all look the same when you're suited up."

"Yes, It's me. You're late Athon." Cyrix chided. "I was beginning to think you weren't coming."

"You should know better!" Athon spurred Zuri on, and led the rest of the men across the ford. "Dismount, and hobble your hesturs," he commanded when the last man had crossed. "We walk from here. Xacthos have one group stay here and stand watch."

With all the efficiency of a well–planned military exercise, the hesturs were moved off the road, and the front legs hobbled to prevent them from moving far. Cyrix grabbed Athon's arm. "I'm not kidding about the time. The longer you ladies sit here and doddle, the harder it's going to be for me to find these mongrels."

Athon roared for every man to hear. "We will be hunting until we find our prey. It could make for a long turn, but we lost a brother. We do not suffer without retribution. The beast could be anywhere on our path, so keep a sharp eye."

Tam and Brixos were close behind Athon and Xacthos as they followed the scout into the brush. This was not the stealthy movement of hunters tracking game in the forest, but it was still quiet. For a group as large as they were they passed surprisingly fast through the dense undergrowth. Just over an hour after they left the rendezvous, they arrived at the Great Meadow. At one end was a fern covered rocky outcropping that overlooked a lake in a large, open meadow. On the opposite end, Tam thought he could make out a wide path just beyond the tree line.

"Is that the road?" Tam asked Athon incredulously.

"Yes, but much further down from the crossing. We took a bit of a shortcut."

"Why didn't we just ride to that meadow?"

"We're hunting," Athon glowered. "We don't want to spook our prey. It's bad enough with all these men, but add the hesturs and we don't stand a chance. With tragues, you never know what their up to until you start tracking them, and you don't want a bunch of hobbled hesturs milling around a known kill area. You want Pyta as bait? Hesturs are far too valuable for that."

Tam flushed at the reprimand. Athon was right, of course, there weren't enough hesturs to go around, and they were essential. He looked around at the meadow. It was now obvious why they were standing here. This was the first large open space he had seen near the road. It had a good water supply and was a natural staging area for an invading army. This outcropping was a perfect place to spy on any force large enough to mount an assault on the garrison.

"Here is where the attack happened," Cyrix said. "His body's over there the far end of the field." He pointed to the tree overhead. "Stenos has kept watch. Seen anything yet?"

Tam looked around for another scout in the brush, but couldn't see any signs. A slight rustling from the tree preceded the camouflaged figure lighting to the ground.

"Haven't seen 'um," Stenos said through the mop like face of the suit.

"How did the attack happen?" Xacthos asked. No doubt, the two seasoned scouts had already dissected the scene.

"Most likely there were two of them," Stenos said.

"Two?" Tam blurted out without thinking. He couldn't see the look from either scout as their heads turned simultaneously toward the interloper.

"It isn't common, but tragues can hunt in pairs," Athon said. "It means that they most likely have a litter of cubs somewhere nearby. They must have smelled Drastos, and figured he was a threat."

"We found tracks there in the center of the meadow," Stenos said pointing into the field. "We figure the male drew his attention while the female came up over here from behind. He put up a fight, until the male finished the job. Then they drug the body over to the cubs at the far end of the meadow."

"Has anyone touched the remains since the attack?" Athon asked the question, already knowing the answer.

"No," the other scout said.

"You four," Xacthos pointed to the guards behind Tam. "When we get to the body, wrap it in your cloaks and take it back to the garrison."

"Show us," Athon said to the two scouts. The group then walked in silence to the grizzly scene where the half–eaten carcass of Drastos lay. The four guards solemnly removed their cloaks, reverently wrapped the body, and somberly walked toward the crossing.

"Break into teams of three and fan out to the east and west," Athon said to the remaining Guards. "Everyone head north at sight line intervals from my party, Xacthos, Tam, Brixos, Stenos, and Cyrix are with me. Who's the best tracker?" he asked, turning his attention to the two scouts.

"I am," Stenos said.

"I assume you have already established the direction the tragues went after they were done here," Athon asked.

"Naturally."

"We'll follow you, then," Xacthos said.

"Tam, Brixos, stay close." It was the first time Athon sounded worried about the safety of the prince.

"No talking from here on out," hissed Cyrix. "Hand signals only. You're already loud enough to wake the dead."

Silently, the group of six hunters took up the trail, following the family of tragues. The remaining guards grouped up and fanned out. The whole army, bent on vengeance, moved like a whisper into the forest. Almost immediately, the two scouts produced bows in readiness for the kill to come. The guards all followed suit, ready with anticipation.

Tam looked up. Just before high–sun, he thought, a long time before they would be expected to return to the crossing. Good thing he had gotten in the habit of stuffing extra food and water into his pack.

The group tracked the predators in an erratic trail across the road several times, through thickets, over streams, around bogs, all leading further down the mountain. At the base of a small hill, Stenos stopped and examined the ground closely. "*The den is close,*" he signed in the guard's hand language, and then gave the signal for the others to wait. He moved cautiously forward.

The silence was palpable. The air was thick with the stench of rotten flesh and the rank odor of trague urine. Tam could feel the mephitis choking his every breath. The air began to taste bitter and foul. He held the hem of his cloak to his nose and mouth in a vain effort to sieve the air. Without warning, a great scream erupted ahead in the distance. Instantly, the air was filled with the squeals of hesturs, and the cries of men. Every head of the party shot to attention, and without hesitating, Tam began sprinting in the direction of the commotion. The others were close behind.

It was a foot race. Tam knew that hesturs from the hunting party were still at the crossing, but the screams were definitely those of frightened men. He didn't see the stream of guards pouring in from all sides, or his companions near him. He was focused on the noise in front of him. Tam knew that he was a swift runner, and would easily beat most men to the fracas. His heart pounded in his chest as he moved closer to the yelling. He ran faster toward certain danger, faster than he had ever run before. It was as if something unseen was accelerating him toward an unimaginable calamity.

He came to the top of a short hill, and saw the source of the scream. The scene below was horrifically chaotic. Six hesturs lay dead, and two others bolted rider–less in terror. Armed men lay strewn about, bloodied from the onslaught of the two tragues that were beginning to focus their attention on the two remaining hesturs. They were occupied by obviously terrified women. The pair of tragues deftly circling their frightened prey, their deep black hides glistened in the patchy sunlight. Tam could tell that the tragues next attack would prove fatal to the maidens. He would not let that happen.

He was a good shot with his bow, and could easily hit his target from this range. Constant training made his next actions seemed as if his body had a mind of its own. The world around him froze as if suspended in the moment. His movements were steady and calculated as he drew his bow and marked his target. In a moment, the entire world seemed to be clear and focused. He could feel his heart beat as if a single pulse lasted an eternity. He breathed deep, and with deadly accuracy released his first arrow.

The first trague was caught mid–air in the head as it began to pounce on its hapless victim. It keeled to the side and fell dead instantly. The poison soaked arrow would have proved lethal without the added toxin, but he wouldn't get so lucky next time. The second, larger monster, startled by the fall of its mate, shifted its gaze and spied Tam. The snarling beast acrobatically leaped past the two hesturs, and sprang for the new threat. Tam fumbled for his next missile, but his fingers found only air. He couldn't be out of arrows. He knew he had a full quiver. Frantically his hand searched his back in vain.

He could hear the terrifyingly deep breath of the trague as it raced gracefully toward him. The pounding paws seemed to shake the ground now as it neared. Athon and the rest of the party drew close enough to see the entire scene.

"Tam!" Athon cried out in horror, as he saw the trague spring for its next victim.

What happened next was instantaneous but seemed to last forever. Tam dropped his bow and drew both his swords. The others drew their bows, and fired. The trague pounced, claws unfurled to tear at limbs, fangs bared wide ready to crush its foe. The long sword met the fierce gaping mouth with a tip of sharp steel that penetrated deep into its skull. The short sword slashed at the mighty paws, and found the vulnerable soft neck. Four arrows found their marks with deadly precision. One arrow skittered off into the brush and was lost. The trague fell on Tam, forming a motionless bloody heap.

# Chapter 7

# PRINCESS INDURA

Athon raced single–mindedly to the crumpled body of the dead trague. He didn't know if he could live with himself knowing that he had placed the prince in such great harm. His mind tried unsuccessfully to shut out the mental image of a lifeless Tam, and the anguish of explaining the death to the king. "Gods, don't let him be dead," he muttered.

Blood flowed in great spurts from the trague's near severed head. The crimson liquid was everywhere. With a mighty shove, Athon tried to move the trague, but it was no use. The female trague was too big. The others reached his side, and with their help, he was able to roll the heavy beast off the motionless body of the prince.

"Tam! Tam!" Athon cried. It was impossible to tell if any of the copious amounts of blood were his, but presently the eyes blinked, and he began to move. "You're alive!"

"What happened?" Tam was obviously shaken.

"You killed a trague. Are you hurt?" Athon began wiping the blood away with his cloak.

"I don't think so," Tam said with a shaky voice.

"Water!" Athon demanded, and Brixos quickly produced his flask. Athon began washing the blood off in a desperate search for any serious wounds. He couldn't find anything.

Tam sat up, dazed from his near death encounter with the largest trague he had ever seen. He had never been this close to one before, and was certain he didn't want to repeat the experience. He quickly collected his wits and sat up.

"Steady now," Athon cautioned. "Don't *ever* scare me like that again."

"I didn't want to in the first place," Tam said standing against Athon's protests. He quickly got his bearings, and his attention was then focused on the road. Some of the guards surrounded the two female trespassers, while others were checking the fallen men for signs of life. The two women seemed on the verge of near panic, as if they were still in great peril.

"Who are they?" Tam asked

"I don't know," Athon said. "But it's time we found out. Stenos, Cyrix find that den, and kill the cubs. We can't afford to have tragues around." The two scouts turned and swiftly moved back in the direction of the den. The four guards joined the others at the scene of carnage below.

One of the females was now protesting. "I demand you release us at once! I am Indura, princess of Ithilton. I command you to release us."

She was the most beautiful woman Tam had ever seen. Even with her face red, with an odd mix of rage and embarrassment, she was stunning. Her auburn hair draped its soft curls around her face. Her eyes shone like perfect emeralds. Her skin color he had never seen before. Tam couldn't seem to take his eyes off her.

"You won't be going anywhere, Your Highness," Athon said as he pushed his way through the press of guards. "You are under the protection of the Campsit Guard. You'll need someone to look after you, now that your escort has been slaughtered."

"Are you in command here?" Indura nervously began.

"I am Athon, Captain of the Guard, and I believe some gratitude is in order."

Indura swallowed hard. "I beg your forgiveness. My handmaiden and I are grateful for your rescue. Particularly of the young man who came to our aid. Is he injured?"

"I'm all right," Tam chirped. "At least, I think I am."

"As you can see," Athon said, "he's just fine. Please, let us escort you back to our garrison. Stay until you're rested and then we will return you to your father unharmed."

"I really must be going back," Indura pleaded.

"Princess," Athon said, with an understanding voice. "I cannot in good conscience allow you to leave without a proper escort. I'm sure Preanth would expect nothing less. Unfortunately, we don't have our hesturs. Now, come down and we will escort you to our garrison."

"Come down?" Indura said, confused.

"We will need your hesturs to carry the dead," Athon said. "We can't carry them that far, so you will have to walk until we get you back to where we left ours."

After a moment, she dismounted Urdin and handed the reins to the nearest guard. Mai mirrored the princess' actions.

"Get the bodies on the hesturs, and clear this road," bellowed Xacthos. "Someone skin those tragues. I believe our dining hall could use some decoration."

The guards moved quickly to clear the road of the carnage that littered the ground. Before long, Stenos and Cyrix returned, the skins of three trague cubs proudly hung from their shoulders.

Indura and Mai spent the time alone on the edge of the road. It wasn't long before the grizzly site of her deceased entourage made her cry.

Tam couldn't help but watch the young princess as she sat there, weeping in misery. He felt like comforting her, but he was afraid there wasn't anything he could say that would help. It was all he could do to stop from staring at her. Her elegance was unmatched by any woman he had ever seen, and he couldn't shake the uncontrollable desire to drink in her vision of beauty. He would have to make sure that he was the one that escorted her back to the garrison. Unfortunately, he was certain that a blood–covered man was not very attractive. He dismissed himself and sought out a nearby stream to wash the sticky blood from his clothes and body. He wasn't able to remove it all, but it would have to do.

As Tam sat by the stream's edge, he couldn't shake the thought that he had nearly been killed by a giant trague saving the most beautiful woman he could ever imagine. It hadn't quite dawned on him that what he had done was incredibly heroic. He just kept thinking that he had to be the luckiest man ever. He could have easily been savagely shredded by the razor sharp claws, or crushed by the massive jaws. He vividly recalled the terrifying moment when the enormous snarling beast lunged at him. He closed his eyes to erase the terror from his mind. When it was clear that he would be only marginally successful, he returned to the group.

As he approached, Athon met him, and pulled him aside. "You look a lot better without all that blood on you."

"It didn't all come off, but I feel better," Tam said. "It really stinks though."

"I'm proud of you, Tam, and that I'm sorry." Athon's eyes started welling with tears.

"Sorry?" Tam was confused. "For what?"

"For putting your life in danger," Athon said. "When your father learns about what happened I'll be lucky to stay as captain. I was reckless with you, and I shouldn't have been. You could have died, and I've grown rather fond of you. Like the son, I never had. I hope you can forgive my thoughtlessness."

"Don't apologize, Athon," Tam said reassuringly. "There is nothing to forgive. I shouldn't have run so far ahead. I don't know why I did."

"I've learned," Athon said, placing his hand on Tam's shoulder, "that you should never regret an experience that makes you stronger. I think I have seen a boy become a man with a single act, and you managed to do it without killing yourself. I am proud of you." Athon gave Tam a hug, and walked back to the group. "Let's move!" he ordered, and the company began the long march back to their hesturs.

Indura and Mai walked next to Athon, so Tam didn't need an excuse to be near the princess. She walked somberly, still wiping away the tears that wouldn't stop flowing. An hour into the march, Tam noticed that Indura and Mai were starting to have difficulty keeping up. They both looked exhausted. Tam poked Athon, and gestured his head in the direction of the women.

Athon nodded. "We'll rest here for a moment," he said, guiding Indura to a nearby rock. "Xacthos, send several of your best runners ahead to ready the hesturs, and maybe meet us part way."

"I wondered why we didn't think of it sooner," Xacthos replied. He summoned five guards out of the dispersing crowd, explained the plan, and they ran off down the road.

Tam decided it was time to introduce himself to this remarkable princess. He went for his backpack when he noticed that his quiver was firmly entrenched under his cloak. Suddenly, it dawned on him that the reason he couldn't draw any arrows earlier was that they were safely tucked away under his cloak. Silently cursing his own clumsiness, he took off the pack and found the food stowed inside.

"You look a little hungry," Tam said, stooping to eye level with Indura. "I have some food, and water. It isn't much, but it will help you keep your strength." He scanned her eyes for the faint glimmer of recognition that she had heard his offer. He took out a salted meat roll and waved it in front of her.

Indura blinked after a moment. There was a faint glimmer of recognition, and she smiled. "Thank you, I am hungry, and it's been a while since we last ate." She took the roll from Tam, broke it in half, and then gave the rest to a silent Mai. "You're the guard who saved us, aren't you?"

Tam chuckled softly. "I guess you could say that."

"What's so funny?" Indura asked perplexed.

"Oh, nothing," Tam said with a smile. He handed her his canteen, and pulled out a piece of fruit. He contemplated the irony of finally meeting a princess, only to have her think of him as a lowly guard. It had occurred to him to blurt out that he was the prince, but he was curious how she would treat him. For now, he thought, he should improvise.

Tam's gesture had not gone unnoticed. Xacthos looked at Athon and mused. "So, do you think he is over there telling them how the prince just saved them from certain death, and they should just fall in love?"

"I would not presume to make such assumptions," Athon said. "Tam may be many things, but he isn't a show off. I think being a guard has humbled him somewhat. He may just be interested in finding out who she is."

"What?" Xacthos was incredulous. "I don't believe it. You don't see he's enamored?"

"He maybe," Athon said bluntly. "But I'm not convinced that he would be so uncouth as to approach a woman romantically after such a traumatic experience. Give it time."

"If he doesn't, I will think less of him as a man." Xacthos said.

"It was an incredibly brave thing you did," Indura said. "Taking on two fully grown tragues by yourself."

Tam snorted. "I'm not so sure it was bravery as much as it was sheer stupidity. I didn't think the others were as far behind me as they were."

"Were you frightened?" Mai asked.

"You speak?" Tam had come to think that the handmaiden was somehow mute. "I suppose you might even have a name?"

"Of course," Mai said indignantly. "I just prefer to let my princess talk in matters of state. As for my name, it's Mai."

"Matters of state?" Tam jokingly inquired. "I'm not sure how this qualifies."

"It is," Indura said insistently. "Ithilton and Campsit aren't on friendly terms. In case you didn't notice. I have to make sure that nothing is said that could bring the two kingdoms to war."

"Ah, I see."

"Time to move out, men!" Athon said, rising from his seat.

"You feel up to more travel?" Tam asked.

"Not really," Indura said, wincing as she stood, "but, it doesn't seem to matter if I do or don't. We need to get out of here."

They walked for more than an hour before the sound of hoof beats echoed down the road. Soon, the guards arrived with the other hesturs in tow.

Tam insisted that Athon let the princess ride with him. After a sly glance from Xacthos, Athon agreed. Xacthos had Mai ride with him, and they were off. Tam noted that it was not quite low–sun yet. He was starting to feel the strain of the turn, but he knew that there was a long ride to come.

It was well past low–sun when the convoy entered the gates of the garrison. Guards and mounts were hungry, thirsty, and near exhaustion. Athon went to the inn on the north side of the garrison, to secure accommodations for the guests. He roused Iason, the innkeeper, apologized for the unexpected late arrival, saw the women to their room, and let them know he would be back when a meal was ready. The fallen soldiers were placed in a vacant corner of the ice cellar next to Drastos.

Xacthos gave orders that those involved in the hunt would be excused from the next turn's duties to recuperate from the ordeal. He also found a stable boy to tend to the women's hesturs and bloodied tack. The exhausted guards filed into the dining hall where the cooks were franticly trying to ready breakfast several hours earlier than usual.

As the first meals were being brought out, Athon entered with the two women and escorted them to the head table. The room was more crowded than usual, with sleep–watch guards lining the walls, eager for some word from their captain. As the two women entered the room, every man stood until the women had been seated next to Athon, Xacthos, and Tam.

Athon stood and raised his hands for silence. "As you know this turn has brought us great sorrow, and great victory. First, to our sorrows, all of you have heard of Drastos' bravery, and his tragic death. He was our best and most experienced scout. He taught most of you at one point or another, and died doing what he loved. We will miss him dearly." Athon raised his fist high. "Let us toast to his memory, and honor the man. I owe him my life, as do we all."

A thunderous roar erupted in the confines of the large room as men stomped feet and pounded fists on tables. "Hail Ceanor's rest!" the men chanted for several long moments.

Athon raised his hands for silence. "At third–quarter sun the funeral pyre will be lit. We shall sing of his deeds, and greatness. We shall see that he makes it to paradise, and honor him one last time. While most of you will sing his praise, we will return the princess to Ithilton." Leaning down to Xacthos, he whispered in his ear.

Xacthos stood. "We have great reason to celebrate. It took two large tragues to slay Drastos. They are dead! We have one warrior who was mighty enough to slay them both. When he first arrived, he was a boy, but now he's a man! He has conquered the enemies of all boys: fear and doubt. Now we raise our mugs and toast our beloved Prince Tam, slayer of tragues!"

A great roar emanated from the throats of nearly two thousand men, as mugs of celis were raised high. The women were stunned. Their jaws dropped open, and they immediately turned to stare wide–eyed at Tam.

"What wrong?" Tam asked, placing his mug on the table.

"Who are you?" Indura asked, incredulously.

"Didn't you just hear," Tam said glibly. "I'm the slayer of tragues."

"No, not that," Indura said, slightly irritated. "You're a prince?"

"Oh, that. What does it matter?" Tam said indignantly. "It isn't like it made a difference when I saved you." Tam was right, and he knew it. At least he knew that she had an interest in him. He wasn't sure how he was going to proceed with this budding infatuation, but he was sure he would think of something.

Midway through the meal, Indura's head snapped up as she caught herself beginning to nod off. Her eyes glazed with exhaustion she gently touched Athon's arm. "Captain, you have been most kind, but I'm so exhausted I can't stand."

Athon briefly examined the fatigued expression of Indura's face. "We'll escort you to your room. Tam, would you please accompany us?"

"Absolutely," Tam replied.

As the women stood, the entire room rose to their feet. Indura addressed the crowd. "To all you brave men, thank you for your kindness, hospitality, and for saving our lives." She then turned, grasped Tam's arm for support, and left the hall for the comfort of a warm bed.

Indura and Mai took their leave of Athon and Tam at the door to the inn. Their rooms were modestly furnished, but the soft feather beds were a welcome sight, and the windows had drapes that darkened the room enough to invite deep sleep.

Indura dismissed an exhausted Mai, overruling her objections to help her get ready for bed. She closed the door and shut her eyes. Her emotions swirled about her like a powerful cyclone, battering her soul in its wild fury. Men were dead because of her wanderlust, and now she was at the mercy of her enemy. She threw off her riding clothes, and sank into a tearful heap on the bed. Her weeping lasted only a few moments as she lost her battle to exhaustion.

Sleep provided no escape from her circumstance. She dreamed of the black coat, sharp fangs, and yellow eyes of the trague, and the cool blue eyes of the mysterious prince who had saved her.

# Chapter 8

# To Ithilton

Athon's gentle shaking seemed to come all too early. Tam felt like he had just fallen asleep. He blinked, bleary–eyed, sore, and feeling like he only wanted to roll over and drift back to sleep. His body felt like he had fallen off a cliff. "What time is it?" he groaned.

"About an hour after high–sun," Athon said, as he seated himself in the chair.

"Go away. I'll be up in a little while," Tam countered, as he rolled back into the shadows cast by the lantern.

"Come on," Athon cajoled. "You need to clean up, and we have to talk over a few things."

"Can't it wait?" Tam asked with a wince. "Preferably until after I'm dead?"

Athon snorted at the sarcastic tone emanating from the obstinate lump on the bed. "No, Tam, it can't wait. Now get yourself out of bed before I drag you out. You still smell like a certain dead trague. Did you even bathe?"

Tam grew annoyed. "Yes! Of course I did!"

"Well get up and do it again. I'm sure the princess wouldn't want to smell your stink."

At the mention of the Indura, Tam whirled to face Athon. "Why bring her up?"

"Come on, Tam," groaned Athon. "Do you think I'm blind? The entire garrison can see you're attracted to her."

"I've been that obvious?"

"Do birds fly?" Athon said sarcastically. "I think if she hadn't been traumatized she would have noticed, but I can't fault your taste. She is beautiful."

"She is *really* pretty." Tam was fully awake now.

"Yes, she is," Athon said. He winced and held his nose. "Whew! I'm not kidding it's ripe in here. Honestly, I think the maid will have to burn incense for a full turn. Now get out of bed and scrub that stench off. My eyes are watering it's so bad." He turned, and then stopped to add one more thought. "Before we leave to fetch the princess, I want to talk to you, but it can wait until *after* your bath." He helped Tam out of bed, and turned down the hallway. "Meet me in the dining hall when you're finished, and make sure you use lots of soap!"

The two men separated, and headed in opposite directions. Tam went to the bath, wondering what Athon was so eager to speak to him about. His body ached from the strain of the previous turn's activities. Getting into the warm, fragrant water eased the tension in his muscles.

Tam scrubbed the clotted and dried blood still clinging to every strand of hair. He thought about Indura. He wondered if she could be interested in him. Will she like me? Would she ever want to see me again? How am I going to court her if she does? It was apparent he would need to give the matter some serious thought.

The maid entered, left some clean clothes, and departed leaving Tam absorbed in thought. He spent nearly a full hour soaping and scrubbing his skin until it was nearly raw. When he was satisfied that he had completely rid himself of the remaining stench, he got out and dried himself off. He examined the clothing closer and found that it wasn't the uniform he had been wearing. The tunic was emblazoned with the royal crest, and there was a corporal's insignia under it. Even his armor and weapons had been scrubbed clean and freshly oiled. He gave a satisfactory smile and donned the new uniform, and went straight to the dining hall.

Athon was seated alone at the barren head table. The captain examined the prince in the new attire with a proud air of satisfaction. "I see you found the new uniform to your liking," he said. "When we arrived, I thought you might do well enough eventually to earn it. I had the master weaver make it after the first ceanor here. I'm not giving you command of a squad just yet, but you've earned the rank."

"I like it," Tam replied with some pride. "It is rather nice, even if it's only ceremonial. Now what did you want to discuss?"

Athon looked Tam in the eye. "I hope that you don't take the situation with princess lightly. This is a serious diplomatic problem. Six Ithilton soldiers are dead, and we are have the princess. Preanth might see it as an act of war."

"But, we didn't kill those men," Tam said defensively. "Or kidnap his daughter. We are protecting her. We couldn't just leave her to die like that."

"Everyone on this mountain knows that," Athon said evenly. "Unfortunately, Preanth isn't on this mountain."

"We have to tell him," Tam argued. "Make him see the truth."

"It won't be that easy, Tam," Athon interrupted. "He won't listen, and probably think we're lying. Remember the law. No outsiders are allowed to live once they step foot on our soil. Preanth knows this."

Tam flushed. He knew the law also applied to Indura, but wanted to make an exception for the princess. "You aren't going to kill her, are you?"

Athon shook his head. "No, and if we followed the law we'd be in a war we might not win. Right now we need an ally. Someone Preanth *will* listen to, and more importantly, believe implicitly."

"You mean Indura."

"You need to get to know her. It will take at least two turns to get to Ithilton. I want you to be with her as possible during that time. Use your charm, and let her know that we don't pose any kind of threat. We only want peace between our two kingdoms. Campsit has neither the desire nor resources to mount any kind of war. We can defend ourselves against a large army from this position, but we can't hold them off forever. Under no circumstances can we provoke King Preanth to attack. Our primary goal *must* be to safeguard the freedoms and peace of the people of Campsit. I need your assurances that you will do everything in your power to gain her trust."

Tam had never stopped to consider the more sinister ramifications of rescuing and safeguarding the princess. It was sobering to think of his people in chains, or worse. He now had a purpose, and more importantly, a blessing to be with the princess. "I was hoping to get to know her, and I will do my very best to win her confidence."

"Be careful, Tam," Athon said sternly. "This is not a game. This is very serious. Don't push yourself on her. Make it natural, and draw her in. Let her come to you. If you come off overbearing, you'll ruin everything. If you fail, it means war and certain death. However, I don't want you to get too attached. You're fulfilling your duty as a servant of the people, not cultivating a romance."

"Why me?" Tam realized that Athon had given this matter a great deal of thought.

"I have done my part," Athon said. "By treating her as an honored guest I've shown that we mean her no harm. You're the perfect person for this job. You're her age, and she has already developed a rapport with you. Moreover, you're the prince, and you have a fascination with her. But, now it's time to meet our guests and have a meal before Drastos' funeral." Athon stood up and motioned the prince to follow.

"I have one question," Tam said. "Indura was out for a ride in the country. Won't we encounter an army of searchers when we get to Ithilton?"

"There were tents and sleeping rolls on her hesturs," Athon said. "I'm hoping she was planning out being out for a while, so there is a possibility that they may not know she's missing."

"What happens if there are searchers, and they find us?"

"Then, let's hope you have the gift of a silver tongue, and gain her confidence before then."

"And, if I can't?"

"Then the war will begin with us." Athon opened the door to the courtyard, and stepped into the late turn air. The walk to the inn was short. They found Indura and Mai waiting for them in the sitting room that overlooked the Ithilton valley. They were wearing new dresses provided by the tailor's guild. It was not as fine as what she was wearing before, but Tam thought she looked stunning. A simple, leaf green dress accentuated her eyes, and her flowing auburn hair. Even in a humble Campsit dress, she was the epitome of elegance, grace, and charm.

"Your Highness," Athon began. "I hope the clothes I sent meet your approval."

"Yes," Indura said gratefully. "Our riding outfits were quite filthy."

"I'm told they're still drying and will be ready after our meal. I know the dresses are not quite as nice as you're used to, but I thought something clean would be welcome."

"It was very considerate of you, Captain." Indura said genially.

"May we escort you to the dining room?" Athon bowed, and offered his arm to Mai. Tam followed suit, and offered his to Indura.

"I would like that," Indura said politely as she took Tam's outstretched arm.

They went downstairs to the inn's dining room where Xacthos was waiting. The innkeeper's wife, Daphne, had outdone herself in preparing the meal. The table was festooned with the trappings of a royal meal. A fine violet linen tablecloth, elaborately decorated gold goblets, and fine china were a far cry from what Tam was used to. The finest cuts of meats had been slowly roasted to perfection. Fresh vegetables and fruits adorned the table, and there was plenty of celis.

Athon explained to the gathered party that they would leave for Ithilton after the funeral pyre was lit. As soon as they arrived in Ithilton, they would take Indura to the palace.

"Who will be escorting us?" Indura asked.

"Myself, Xacthos, Prince Tam, twenty of my best men, and the wagon master of course," Athon replied.

"Is Brixos coming?" Tam winced as he heard himself speak out of turn.

Athon looked at Tam with a slight hint of disapproval. "No, sorry, he's too junior for this mission." Athon continued with his briefing. "I have assigned the prince to be your escort during the voyage. He'll see to your needs. Is that acceptable?"

"Yes," Indura said, dreamily. "I would appreciate his company. I do have one question. Why will we not be staying for the entire funeral service? Don't you want to stay, and honor your comrade?"

"We have a long journey ahead of us," Athon said, evasively. "You need to get back as soon as possible. Waiting for hours while all the songs are sung and memories rehearsed is not an efficient use of our time."

"I have a question, princess," interjected Xacthos. "What were you doing so far from Ithilton?"

All Campsit Guards learn a form of sign language when they first join. It is discrete, silent, and very effective in delicate situations. "*What are you doing?*" Athon signed furiously. He shot his lieutenant a disapproving scowl.

"*Asking a question*," replied Xacthos.

"*Stop it!*" Athon commanded.

"We were riding through my kingdom," Indura replied. "I like to see life outside the palace walls."

"What were you doing in Campsit?" Tam asked the question, not seeing the clandestine exchange between the two officers.

"I beg your pardon?" Indura indignantly shot Tam a cold look. "I was still in Ithilton."

"That claim is disputed," Athon said, nonchalantly.

"Disputed by whom?" Indura asked, her anger beginning to simmer.

"You claim the land, and we dispute that." Athon said curtly. "Your highness, this is not an argument worth having. The exact boarders of our two kingdoms have been the source of contention for generations. We were hunting the tragues that killed my friend, slaughtered your soldiers, and nearly killed you. Animals know nothing of borders, and certainly don't care if you're of royal blood or not. If it were not for our intervention, we wouldn't be having this conversation, so let's not bicker over a quandary best left to others." Indura's face grew red with anger, but she didn't respond.


The rest of the meal proceeded in relative calm. The conversation shifted to more general and less controversial topics. After everyone had eaten their fill of the delicacies, Indura and Mai dismissed themselves and went upstairs to their rooms. As promised, their riding clothes had been cleaned, and were laid out for them, still warm from the sun.

When the door was finally closed, Indura began removing her dress so forcefully she nearly ripped it off. "Arrogant captain," She fumed. "How dare he speak to me that way?"

"Please calm yourself, Highness," Mai said, soothingly.

"I can't believe I'm held captive by our enemies." Indura succeeded in pulling off the dress, and threw it spitefully to the floor.

"What makes you say that?"

"We're being held against our will," Indura said defiantly.

"We aren't prisoners." Mai said reassuringly.

"Yes, we are. They captured us," Indura began to rant. "They forced us to come to this place. They should have just let us go home."

"Indura," Mai said softly. "They haven't treated us like prisoners at all. We are free to move about. We have been treated as royalty. They have given us food and shelter. They have catered to our every need. There are no bars on the windows, and the doors are unlocked. They have even offered to escort us safely to our home. I don't see that we are being treated as an enemy of this people."

"You don't need bars to tell you that you are not free to go," Indura countered.

"True," Mai conceded. "However, have you considered that maybe the captain is telling us the truth? Maybe he is trying to protect us because the men sworn to do that are now dead."

"I know!" Indura yelled, tears welling in her eyes. "I killed them! It's all my fault! I pressured the commander to let me stay out longer, and ride into the mountains! Now, they're dead, and when Tova hears what happened she'll never let me leave again!"

"You didn't kill those men," Mai said reassuringly. "You cannot blame yourself for their fate. Those tragues would have attacked anyone that came into their territory. You cannot take responsibility for something you had no way of foreseeing. You also can't mistake kind actions for something more sinister. I believe the soldiers of Campsit mean us no harm, and they only want to see us safely home."

"I don't know, Mai," sobbed Indura. "It's like a terror I can't wake up from, and I don't know what to do."

"You have to believe that things will be all right." Mai wiped away the stream of tears that flowed down Indura's cheeks. "Now, let's get changed. Once we get back to the palace, everything will be fine. You'll see."

"I don't know that I can ever see it that way," Indura said. Tears continued to flow, but the torrent had passed its crest. "But, you've never been wrong before."

"It will take time," Mai said reassuringly. "Right now, try not to dwell on dark thoughts."

The proceeded to change into their riding gear, but Indura couldn't help, but focus on her situation. For her, the attack was horrific on several levels. The beasts came within a hair's width of gruesomely killing her as well as her best friend and confidant. The soldiers had sworn to lay down their lives for the kingdom in battle, but Mai hadn't.

The journey had been Indura's idea. It was her plan to visit the high mountains. She had instigated the whole affair. The selfishness behind the escapade made the deaths unnecessary, which made them more tragic.

Tam knocked on the door to Indura's room, and the handmaiden opened it. "It's time, Princess," he said. "Are you ready?"

"Yes," Indura whispered. She looked rattled. Her red eyes and tear–stained cheeks belied the smile that graced her face.

"You've been crying," Tam said. "Are you all right?"

"I'm fine," Indura lied very unconvincingly.

"Is there anything I can do?"

"No, I said I was fine!" she insisted.

"All right." Tam didn't want to press the matter, but it was obvious that something deeply troubled her. He knew that he would have to try to discover the source of her anguish. If she reached Ithilton with this temperament, he was sure that all of Athon's fears would be realized. As she stood, she composed herself. "Indura, I know it's been hard on you. I wanted to let you know I'm very sorry. If there is anything I can do to help, please let me know." He instinctively gently patted her shoulder in a show of empathy.

"You're very kind," she said softly, "but I'm all right." She pushed past just into the hallway, and Mai followed.

The conversation would have to wait for now. They left the humble comforts of the inn and proceeded to the central courtyard where a large, solemn congregation of guards had gathered around a great pile of firewood. Athon and the contingent of escort guards sat atop their hesturs at the head of the unlit pyre, waiting for the trio to join them. When they mounted, Athon spoke.

"We are all brothers on Arabella," he began. "We received the gift of life, and our mortal bodies to journey in the company of our brothers and sisters. We are born into this world with nothing. In death, we leave our bodies behind to the womb of Arabella from whence we came. We leave our memories entrusted to those with whom we shared this life. We take our knowledge and experience with us to the paradise that awaits us. Drastos has left us, and given the most precious gift, life. Bring forth the honored dead."

A procession of six guards reverently emerged from the door to the great hall. The body of Drastos was still lovingly wrapped in the cloaks of his brothers in arms. They carried their sacred package to the neat pile of wood, and respectfully laid him in the center. Athon dismounted and walked up to the bundle. He leaned over and whispered something that Tam couldn't hear, looked up at Ceanor.

The words were barely audible over the crowd. "Gods be with you till we meet again." Athon mounted again, and spoke for all to hear. "We send him to the waiting arms of his ancestors in paradise," Athon said. He signaled a torchbearer, who began to ignite the dry kindling of the funeral pyre. "May he live in Ceanor's peace." He gave a sharp whistle, and the escort group turned and departed.

The funeral pyre, fueled by the oil soaked kindling burst into an inferno. The heavy black column of smoke ascended into the sky; a beacon of the sepulchral sentiment of the grieving guards.

The caravan rode down the mountain in silence. The pace was a slow, steady descent to accommodate the wagon team. The road was not as well maintained on the Ithilton side of the pass for good reason. Armies can use good roads just as effectively as traders can. The leaders of Campsit had intentionally used the road as a strategic weapon against invasion. They had created the path through the dense forest to control the route any invading army might take. If there were an existing road, the enemy would most likely use it. This allowed the ancient founders to force potential invaders through a series of natural choke points, where ambushes could be conducted. They also minimally improved and maintained the roads to make supplying any army more difficult. Large rocks were left in places where wagon wheels would hit them. Hit enough rocks, and you can break a wheel. Break enough wheels, and the supplies aren't going anywhere. One thing that the ancient strategists knew was that armies are only as effective as their supply chains, and it would take a large army to overcome the disadvantages of the natural terrain. The caravan had to move slowly so that the wagon master could deal with the subtle defensive hazards.

"Captain," Indura finally spoke. "Why are we moving so slowly?"

"I'm sorry?" Athon was roused from his reverie.

"At this rate we won't make it back to Ithilton for turns," Indura said impatiently. "Why are we going so slowly?"

"This road is good for hesturs, but not so good for wagons," Athon said. "It will be like this until we reach Ithilton territory, when the road gets better."

"Faster would be better," Indura grumbled.

"We'll get there in due time, Princess," Athon said. "No one wants you back home more than me."

They traveled for nearly five hours before they came to the crossing. Once everyone had forded the river, Athon called a halt for a break. Mai and Indura walked away from the main group and found a log to sit on. Tam soon joined them with a small meal of meat rolls, bread, and fruit.

Tam looked up to the beautiful opal blue of the sky. White puffy clouds gracefully moved through the heavens along the ridgeline of the majestic mountain peaks. Dortic was the only moon visible now, its bright red surface in stark contrast to the sky.

"Nice weather," Tam commented to the pair.

"I hadn't really noticed," Indura said, glancing up to see the spectacle.

"This season is usually quite rainy. I'm just glad we don't have to travel in the wet. It can get pretty miserable." Tam remembered his experience arriving in the cold, driving snow, and wasn't anxious to repeat it knowing there would be no warm bath at the end.

"Aren't you normally asleep at this time?" Mai asked, trying to lighten the princess' mood.

"Just about," Tam said between bites of a meat roll. "It just depends on what I'm doing at the time. Sometimes, it takes a while to finish a job. You have to work until it's done. That doesn't always mean that we get off duty when you think you should."

"There's something that I don't understand," Indura said. "Why are you a guard in the first place, and why do you take orders from Athon?"

"That is a question I'm not completely able to answer," he said, giving a slight shrug. "I suppose I became a little too rambunctious for my father's taste when I lived in town. He sent me out here with Athon to train. It has something to do with learning to serve the people."

"He just sent you away like that?" Indura said incredulously.

"Well, I wasn't doing anything productive, really," Tam admitted. "In a way it's been good for me. I've been able to learn things about Campsit that I hadn't seen from my sheltered life in town."

"You don't resent being sent away?" Indura asked in disbelief.

"At first, I did," he said. "But as time went on, I stopped trying to fight it, and now I actually like the work. It's challenging, and I'm gaining new skills all the time."

"Like what?"

"Hunting," Tam sighed. "I never did any when I was living in town, and now I get to do it almost every turn. I'm pretty good at it, too." He felt a brief swelling of pride in his recently discovered ability.

Indura smiled at Tam. "I don't think I would take being banished to a remote mountain fortress very well."

"I wasn't banished," Tam said defensively. "In a big way it's liberating. I get to be outside the garrison walls doing something I enjoy."

"You really think it's freedom?"

"I think so," Tam said definitively. "Haven't you ever wanted to feel free?"

Indura looked suddenly shocked. "Yes, I have," she whispered.

Tam could tell he had just struck a nerve. He decided to shift the topic to something more comfortable. "Tell me what it's like to live in Ithilton."

"Why would you want to know something like that?"

"You know about me, but I know almost nothing about you."

Indura didn't get to answer as Athon strode up to the group and interrupted. "After giving it some thought, I've decided that we will make camp here, and rest. We are all still a little tired, and could do with some more sleep. Tam will make sure you have a place to bed down."

Tam crammed the rest of his meat roll into his mouth as he stood, and left to retrieve the tents from their hesturs. He returned a few minutes later and set up the small shelters.

As Tam busied himself with the tents, Indura and Mai whispered quietly to each other. "What do you make of him?"

"I like him," Mai whispered. "He's strong, and nice, and handsome."

"There's something about him," Indura replied, trying to keep her words just audible enough for Mai to hear. "It's like I've seen him before, almost like something out of a dream. I can't really explain it."

"Is it good or bad?"

"It's good, I think," Indura said softly. "It's really strange. I've never felt anything like it in my life. I need to get to know him better. Maybe if I found out more, it would come to me. I don't want to encourage him until I know why I'm getting this impression. It could be just some figment of my imagination, but I'll have to see where it leads."

Tam was an enigma to her. He disguised his royal nature, accepted his confinement, saved her life, and was so humble. It was foreign to her way of thinking. She wanted to know more about him. To be closer to him, as if she were guided by some instinct she couldn't control.

Tam rejoined the women. "The others will be taking watch for now, so we can all get some rest. I've set up your tents. We'll leave all too soon, so don't waste any time trying to sleep. If I know Athon we won't be stopping to rest until low–sun.

"Thank you," Indura said. She and Mai both moved toward their respective tents.

Tam helped Indura into her tent. "I'll be right here if you need anything," he said. "Pleasant dreams, Princess."

"Please call me Indura,"

"And, you can call me Mai," she said, not wanting to be left out of the conversation.

"Fair enough, Indura and Mai," said Tam, as he closed the tent flap.

# Chapter 9

# REVERIE

The rattle to Indura's tent seemed to come almost immediately after she felt herself slip away into the peaceful sanctuary of sleep. It was difficult to feel rested when you are normally used to the comfort of a nice soft bed. She was sure there was a rock the size of a small fist that had wedged itself into the small of her back. She moved and her stiff muscles howled in pain. Her head was still in a fog as it tried to make sense of where she was. She winced as her body revolted against the commands to roll to a more comfortable position. The tent flap opened and light flooded her small, dark tent with a blinding brilliance. Her mind made out a dark shape kneeling over her head. It was Tam.

"Indura," he said. "It's time to wake up. We'll be moving out soon, and I need to get things packed away."

"What time is it?"

"It's just after first–quarter sun. You've been asleep for nearly five hours." Tam said soothingly.

"Where's Mai," Indura said, still trying to free her mind from the sleepy haze that continued to maintain its grip.

"I was going to wake her next," Tam said. "Do you need help?"

"I'm so stiff," Indura moaned. She accepted his outstretched hand, and began to emerge. "It feels like I've been sleeping on a bed of rocks."

Tam gently tugged on her arms until she slid out of her tent, and stood beside him. She rubbed her eyes and staggered, still trying to gain her bearings. He caught her by the waist and steadied her. It was the first time she had ever been held like that. The warm feel of his arm on the small of her back sent a ripple through her body. Instantly, the fog left her mind, and things clarified. She suddenly relished the thought of being in his arms. The foreign sensation swept through her body, and demanded more. She gazed into his eyes and wondered what fortune fate had bestowed on her.

It lasted only a brief moment, and then Indura's reasoning mind overwhelmed the sentimental desires of her heart. She steadily planted her feet on the ground, and instinctively pulled away. "I'm all right; I can stand on my own now."

Tam nodded and left her to rouse Mai. After they ate, they broke camp and continued down the road toward Ithilton.

Tam took up a riding position next to Indura. "Did you get any rest?"

"Not really," Indura said. "I had a boulder jabbing me right in the center of my back."

"I'm sorry about that," he said sheepishly. "I'll do a better job of picking out a boulder free sleeping spot next time."

"I don't blame you," she said. "I'm just not used to camping."

"Beds are a lot nicer than the ground; fewer bugs, too." Tam smiled at her warmly. "Before you know it, you'll be home, and soon it will be a distant memory."

"I don't know that I'll ever forget," she said. "Some memories can't fade fast enough, other's I never want to escape."

"I like that," he said cheerfully. "Forget the bad. Remember the good. Hopefully there's more good than bad."

"It's tough to tell at this stage."

"Why's that?" He asked, puzzled by her cryptic answer.

"It isn't over yet," she said.

"That's a rather pragmatic way of thinking," he scoffed.

"Tell me I'm wrong," she said, it was her version of verbal swordplay.

"You're not wrong," he conceded. "But, I think there are better ways of viewing things. You could assume that the whole trip is an utter disaster, or you could see it as a golden opportunity for our two kingdoms to ease tensions."

"I didn't come here to act as an emissary."

"No, I'm sure that wasn't your intent," he said. "But, why waste the opportunity? It isn't like we have anything better to do with our time."

"Very well," she said coyly. She would play his game. "Since I have nothing better to do, I'll go along with this impromptu diplomatic dialogue. Where would you like to start?"

"Tell me about life in Ithilton. I don't know much about your people, or your kingdom."

"If you are interrogating me wouldn't you rather hear about our army? I hate to disappoint you, but I don't know anything." She wasn't quite sure what his motives were, and didn't have the patience to try to ferret out his intentions.

"I'm not interrogating you," Tam said, defensively. "You don't have to tell me, but it would help me understand you better."

Indura was satisfied with his argument, and couldn't see the harm in telling him what a wonderful place Ithilton was. She spent the next several hours describing the great city of Ithilton, and the surrounding villages and kingdoms. He listened intently as she told him of palace life and the daily drama that unfolded in the court of her father. She was particularly eager to tell him about her loving father, King Preanth, ruling justly over his subjects. She painted a vivid picture of the paradise of Ithilton, and the beauty she encountered on her excursions. Her eyes lit up as she described the endless white sand beaches she loved to visit, and the majestic forests on the north slopes of the Wall Mountains.

Tam rode along, listening silently to Indura expound on her life as princess of Ithilton. Fortunately, he had been taught the truth about Ithilton by Master Thales. He found her perspective on palace life was interesting. He took particular note that she mentioned that her father routinely sat in judgment over peasants who had broken some law or another. He didn't interrupt her as she expounded on the virtues of her kingdom.

It interested Tam that Indura had to have guards accompany her when she left the safety of the palace. To him, it seemed a foreign concept to need constant protection from the citizens of Campsit. He never felt uncomfortable going anywhere. He knew many of the people by name, and often had long conversations with his subjects. His father held court, but usually to discuss the mundane affairs of the kingdom. There was the occasional petty dispute, but Tremmon never had to preside over a criminal trial.

Tam realized there were very few guards for its population compared to Ithilton, and their primary duty was the defense of the land, not policing the people. He knew Indura's kingdom wasn't the paradise she purported it to be, not for everyone, at least.

Athon stopped the column and turned to the two women. "I'm afraid I must blindfold you for the next portion of our trip."

"Why?" Indura asked, in a demanding tone.

"Trust me, it's for your own good," Athon said.

"No, I will not be bound," she said defiantly.

"No one is talking about binding you," Tam said reassuringly.

"Highness, we will be approaching the site where you were ambushed by the tragues," Athon said. "There really isn't another way to get around this portion of the road, and I don't want you to have to relive that event. Please, let us blindfold you for this part. I promise you that as soon as it's over, the blindfolds will come off."

Indura had mixed emotions about the proposal. She didn't like the idea, but she didn't want to be reminded of what happened either. "Thank you for your concern, Captain, but the answer is, no."

"Don't be afraid, Indura," Tam pleaded. "I'll be right next to you the entire time. If you need to, all you have to do is reach out your hand."

Indura started to fume. "I said, No!"

"As you wish," Athon said. "But, if you feel like changing your mind the option is open to you."

They proceeded down the road at the same slow steady pace, drawing steadily closer to the narrow section where the tragues ambushed them. Anxiety began to envelop the princess with each step Urdin took. Everything looked so foreign and yet oddly familiar. The realization that she was near the place she had come so close to death filled her with dread. Her mind was burning with the vivid memories that would forever char her soul. She gripped the reins tighter, turning her fists white with the strain. The thought suddenly occurred to her that there might be more tragues lurking in the recesses of the forest's dense undergrowth. Her breathing quickened and she feared that she would soon lose all self–restraint and urge Urdin into a gallop to escape her peril.

"Tell me more about your homeland."

Tam's question startled Indura. "What? Right now?" He can't be serious, she thought. "I hardly think this is an appropriate time."

"It's the perfect time," he reassured her. "Come on, it'll help you get your mind off things. Tell me about Mai. Is she your friend or sister?"

"My sister?" Indura laughed. "Why don't you ask her?"

"She doesn't seem to do much talking when you're around," Tam said.

"I can speak if I wish," said Mai nervously. She was also gripping her hestur with both hands flushed. "I choose to let my lady speak in polite company."

"She serves me," Indura interjected. "She is also my dearest friend."

"Is there any other kind?" he asked.

"You're making light of something I hold dear to my heart." Indura could feel the anger beginning to build in her stomach.

"Not at all," he said apologetically. "Everyone serves each other, but I've never seen anyone act like her."

"Mai accompanies me on all of my excursions," Indura said. "In truth, she is the only one whose company I really want."

"You have other servants like her?" Tam said.

"I have many who serve me, but Mai and Tova are the only servants who are assigned specifically to me."

"Who's Tova?" He asked.

"My mistress."

"And what does a mistress do?"

"She's practically her mother," Xacthos interjected, "without having to be bothered by the whole birth thing."

"She does many things," Indura said, scowling at the lieutenant, but glossing over his jibe. "She is my teacher, oversees the other servants, and is just generally in charge of my life."

"I see," said Tam. "What does she think of these outings?"

"She says they're too dangerous, but I've convinced her that isn't the case." Indura shuddered at the thought of Tova's reaction when she arrived at the palace. "Although, I'm not sure she will allow them to continue now."

"It could have been worse," he said reassuringly. "You are still alive, unharmed, and safe with us."

"What else do you want to know?" Indura seemed to feel more at ease talking to Tam. He had been right; their conversation took her mind off things.

"Tell me about how you met Mai."

It seemed to Indura that this would be a waste of breath. She recalled the first time she had been introduced to her new servant when she was eight, and Mai was twelve. It was a learning experience for both of them, and they soon found themselves thick as thieves. It took some time to relay how they had both learned to appreciate each other's little idiosyncrasies, and they had found themselves treating each other more like sisters. She let her mind drift as she wistfully recalled some of their more mischievous exploits. She was so lost in her own narrative that she completely failed to notice her surroundings.

When it dawned on her that they were near the site of the attack, she became suddenly anxious again. "I've been here before. Are we there yet?"

Athon chuckled lightly. "We passed in nearly a half hour ago."

"Really, are you sure?" Indura said, with a mixture of embarrassment and relief. She was thankful that she hadn't relived the memory of the terrible event.

"Everyone's been too enthralled by your tale, Princess," Xacthos chirped.

"I guess that includes me," Indura blushed at the thought of her own self–centered behavior.

"Good thing too," Xacthos said under his breath.

Athon shot him a disapproving scowl and shook his head. "This is as good a place as any to stop," Athon said. "We'll rest here long enough to eat and stretch our legs."

The break consisted of bread that was quickly becoming stale, meat rolls, and fruit. As had become their own routine, Tam, Indura, and Mai ate separate from the main group. Indura had developed a desire for greater personal space.

Tam enjoyed drinking in Indura's magnetic aura. She exuded beauty and charm, and he reveled being near her. The back of his mind drifted to the fact that his time with her would be limited. Occasionally, the thought would float into his consciousness like a piece of drift wood in a pond, make its presence known, and recede back into the realm of matters of the less important.

"How are you fairing?" Tam handed Indura a flask of water to wash down her bread.

"I'm better now," she said. "It feels good to get that place behind us."

"I can't imagine," he said. "Hopefully, you won't have to travel that way again."

"Didn't it bother you," she asked. "Being in such a terrible place?"

"Not really," he said frankly. "Somehow, I don't think that my experience was nearly as terrifying as yours."

"But, that monster nearly tore you apart," she said, incredulously.

"I think you're giving it more credit than it deserves," he said with a snort.

"You're bragging now," Indura said.

"Not really, I was ready for him."

"How could you possibly be ready for something like that?"

Tam thought about that question for a moment. "I've trained nearly every turn for as long as I can remember. I didn't need to think, I just did it."

"Well, however you managed it, I'm glad you were there."

Tam thought about that fateful moment that brought the two of them together. He wondered if he would have changed anything. He looked at Indura. Her matchless beauty attracted his attention like no woman he had ever known. Could he ever look at another woman the same way? Even though he still knew very little about her, he would have to say no. It is true that he was very attracted to her, but there was something deeper that drew him in.

Tam's thoughts were interrupted as Athon called for the caravan to get under-way. They had rested only long enough to eat and stretch their legs. Soon, the entire cadre of guards was moving down the road again. The slow, steady pace established from the very start of the journey would continue unabated for the next several hours.

Indura was just as fascinated by the young prince as he was with her. For her, his physical appearance was not the major impetus for getting to know him. There were handsome young men aplenty from the nobles at court. All of them had tried to win her affections one way or another, but she found them all to be wanting. Tam was different. While others paraded around like great birds with beautiful plumage, Tam was humble and rugged. He had come to her rescue without any expectations, or demands. He had been there for her when she needed him most. The fact that he was a prince simply put him in the category of eligible men.

It was late in the turn before they reached the smooth roads that denoted that they had entered the domain that was clearly in Ithilton's territory. They stopped and set up camp. Indura knew this would be the last time she would sleep outside the palace.

# Chapter 10

# Preanth's Bane

The screaming woke everyone in camp, ripping them from deep slumber. In a flash every man armed himself, and raced to the source of the terrifying cry. Tam felt as if he was still half–dreaming as he flung open the tent flap and vaulted to his feet. It was Indura. She was screaming as if someone had plunged a knife into her stomach.

Franticly, she flailed at an invisible assailant. She thrashed at her tent walls, collapsing it into a tangled mess about her, all the while screaming at the top of her lungs. It took only a few moments for Tam to realize that she was fighting thin air, and must be dreaming. He placed his sword back in its scabbard, and pulled the hysterical woman, tent and all, into his arms. "It's all right, Princess," he assured her. "Calm down. It was just a dream. It was just a dream. You're all right. I'm here. You're safe." The fitful screaming subsided, replaced by the frightened tears of a mortified girl. "Indura, I'm here. It's all right." He held her tightly in his arms, and patted her back gently.

"A terror dream," Athon mused, kneeling beside the two. "Princess, are you awake? Can you hear me?"

"Yes," Indura sobbed.

"Highness, I'm here with you," Mai said, taking her hand.

"What happened?" Tam asked.

"Big eyes," Indura replied in a disjointed jumble, racked by waves of tears. "Big teeth—coming to get me—couldn't move—tried to run—couldn't move."

"There's no trague here, Princess," soothed Athon. "It was only a dream."

"It wasn't real," Mai added.

A glimmer of recognition that she was not in the nightmare broke on Indura's face. She scanned the sea of mostly unfamiliar faces. Tears streaming down her checks, her eyes met Mai's. "I'm not dreaming?"

"No, highness," Mai said, clasping her hand. "You're not dreaming."

Indura wiped her tear-stained face. "I'm sorry," she said. The barrage of sobs began to fade, replaced by the erratic sucking breath of post hysterics. "It seemed so real to me." She struggled to stand, and extricate herself from the prince's arms.

Tam realized that she had become uncomfortable in his embrace. He helped her to her feet, and reluctantly released his grip around her waist. It took a few moments to untangle her from the folds of the tent, but she was soon free of its confines. "Are you all right now?"

"I'm fine," she said, unconvincingly. "Thank you."

"You gave us all quite the start," Athon said. "Do you think you can go back to sleep, or should we get moving again?"

"No," Indura said softly. "I'm awake now. How late is it?"

"Just before even–sun," Athon said. "We would have woken everyone up in about an hour anyway."

"Then, I would prefer to go now," Indura said. "I think I will be able to rest once we get to the palace."

"Very well," Athon said, turning to the men that surrounded the commotion. "We'll break camp after we eat."

"You sure you feel up to the journey?" Tam asked Indura.

"I'm tired, but I'll be fine," she replied.

After a quick meal, they broke camp. With the better roads, the pace was much faster. Soon the steep switchbacks gave way to the gradual rolling foothills. Indura and Tam continued to exchange pleasant conversation through the changing scenery.

The caravan had traveled for several hours before they exited the forest in the high foothills. On the road in the distance, they saw a cloud of dust from approaching hesturs. It wasn't long before they could make out the ten Ithilton soldiers that galloped toward them. Instinctively, hands reached for weapons in preparation for battle.

Athon raised his hand high. "Put them away men!" he commanded. "No one makes a move unless I give the order." He prodded Zuri forward. "Tam, bring the princess."

Obediently, Tam motioned Indura to follow Athon. The three rode out about fifty feet and stopped. The approaching soldiers surged forward as they closed on the trio.

"Tam," said Athon. "Stay behind me, and follow my lead. Don't let your guard down. If this goes badly, I want you to take the princess, and get as far away as you can. Princess, I may need your help with these soldiers. Neither of us wants a war."

"I can assure you, Captain, I will do everything in my power to prevent a conflict," Indura said, rising in her saddle in a regal manner.

The soldiers thundered up the hill and skidded to a stop in front of Athon, a little too close for Tam's liking. Each Ithilton soldier grasped a lance that was lowered to strike. The tips of the blades came just shy of Zuri's unflinching head. A lesser steed would have turned and run at the site of the ten fully armored men bearing down on them, but master and mount were too disciplined. The captain sat with his hand above his head as a sign of parley.

"Why do men from Campsit dare to invade this land?" Obviously, this man was the leader.

"We are here to escort Princess Indura, and what is left of her retinue, to the palace at Ithilton," Athon said calmly. "There is no other purpose."

"Highness," the commander said, looking past Athon and finally recognizing the princess. "Do these brigands speak the truth?"

"They do, Commander," Indura said haughtily. "Lower your weapons. They are no threat to you." The soldiers remained motionless, their lances maintaining their threatening posture. "I said stand down, Commander. You will do as I command."

"Highness," the commander said, sternly. "How do I know that you are not being coerced? You could be a prisoner, and they may have threatened to harm you unless you do their bidding."

Indura pressed past Athon toward the small band of soldiers. "Do you recognize me, Commander?"

"Yes, Your Highness," the commander said, shifting his lance away from her direct vicinity, but keeping it ready for a charge. "I didn't notice you at first, but every soldier of Ithilton knows their beloved princess."

"Then you must obey my commands," her voice was thick with irritation.

"There are many questions that must be answered, Highness," the commander protested.

Indura interrupted him. "Questions that will be answered quicker if you cease threatening our guests; now stand down!" Slowly, reluctantly, the lances moved to a raised position.

"I'm Athon, Captain of the Campsit Guard, and this is Prince Tam of the royal house of Campsit. We have rescued your fair princess from a pair of tragues. We are escorting her, and what is left of her entourage, back to her father."

"I am Eyvindir, commander of the Fifth Legion. Ithilton accepts the safe return of our princess. We will escort her safely back to the palace."

"You may escort us to the palace, but I have promised to see that the princess and her slain guards make it to the palace safely." Athon was polite but firm in his demand.

"Slain?" Eyvindir looked accusingly at Athon. "Her guard was slain? By you, or was it the mysterious tragues?"

"Mind your accusations, Commander," Indura hissed. "My guard fell prey to tragues, as the captain said. They follow us in a wagon, so that we may mourn them properly. You will allow them to escort us to the palace."

"I cannot allow these men any farther," Eyvindir said through his teeth. "I do not see the wisdom of allowing our enemies into our territory."

"It is your duty to follow my orders, Commander," Indura said. "Do not question my judgment, or you will answer to my father when we arrive."

"I beg your forgiveness, Highness," Eyvindir said. "I mean only to protect and serve you."

"There is no need for hostile words, Commander," Athon said, spurring his hestur forward. "I give you my word as captain that there is no treachery here, and my men will not threaten you in any way. If you desire, you may ask any question you wish."

"Your word," Eyvindir said in a condescending tone. "The words of a traitor's offspring are worthless."

"Commander," warned Indura. "I will not tell you again. Keep a civil tongue, or I will have it removed. Since you won't take his word, you shall have mine. I assume that will be good enough for you?"

"As you command, so shall it be," Eyvindir said with a bow. "We will escort you to Ithilton, and I will hear your story of how this came to be directly from you, Your Highness. Erad, ride ahead, and tell them we are coming." With that, one of the soldiers at the back wheeled on his hestur and charged back down the road toward Ithilton.

Athon signaled for the rest of the convoy to move forward, and the two rival groups of soldiers formed a precession behind the remaining Ithilton soldiers. Eyvindir took up a position next to Indura, and for the first time since this journey had started, Tam felt a sense of loss. He had grown fond of their conversations and had the slightest twinge of jealousy that he would not have Indura all to himself. Mai took up her place on the other side of Indura, and Tam was relegated to the position next to Athon and Xacthos. Tam wanted to be closer so he could overhear the conversation between Indura and her soldiers, but Athon held him back.

"It's better to give them a little room, Tam," Athon said in a hushed voice. "I don't want to give them the impression that we are manipulating the situation. If the commander is convinced we pose a threat, it will make matters worse."

Tam had learned to trust Athon in these matters. Master Thales had gone to great lengths to teach Tam the finer points of diplomacy, but he had never seen them put into action. He didn't want to aggravate things by inserting himself into a situation he was unfamiliar with.

The caravan traveled for a short time when it crested another high hill unencumbered by trees. They were met with the view of the valley below. Tam had never seen it this close before. It was breathtaking.

From the vantage point of the garrison, the city seemed small and insignificant compared to the surrounding valley. From here the magnificence of the metropolis could be easily seen. Lofty spires rose from the central hill where the castle seemed to float above the buildings below. The city was enormous compared to Campsit. Tall structures jutted from the valley floor in a vain attempt to rival the palace. There seemed to be countless edifices crammed together inside the giant ring of the outer wall. It easily dwarfed Campsit in size. The city was situated on the edge of a great river that emptied into the sea. Farmland surrounded the city in every direction. Dotted amongst the fertile fields were numerous villages and towns, spreading across the land in every direction. Tam noticed there was a lack of forest on the valley floor. Ithilton seemed to rest easily on a plain that stretched for miles. Only small groves of trees could be discerned throughout the valley. For someone who came from the sheltered existence of Campsit, the sight was awe–inspiring.

"Not quite what you were expecting, is it Tam?" Xacthos chuckled. "Don't be fooled by the grandeur. It isn't the paradise the princess made it out to be."

"Really?" Tam said, still dumbfounded. "How are you so sure?"

"Athon and I have both lived here." Xacthos replied in a whisper that stunned the prince more.

"What?" Tam stammered. "When?"

"Keep your voice down, Tam," Athon cautioned. "Xacthos, you know better than to open your big gob about that — idiot!"

Tam's head was swimming. How was it that he had never heard of this? Somehow, his father and others were aware of the happenings in Ithilton, but he had never been told how. He thought he knew every story about Athon, but this was something new. "Why was I never told?"

"Tam, there are some things that are best not shared." Athon whispered just loud enough for Tam to hear. "We always have several spies in Ithilton to keep us abreast of what is happening, but we don't speak of it openly, and certainly not now!"

The stern reprimand removed the wistful smile from Xacthos' face. "Sorry," he said. "I was just waxing nostalgic. It won't happen again."

It was several long hours before the company approached the gates of the city. Tam had been enthralled by the sites as they passed through the villages and fields en route to Ithilton. He wanted to be with Indura, and have her regale him with the stories about her travels among her people. Unfortunately, the commander seemed determined to segregate her from her Campsit escort. As they crossed the threshold of the gates, the loud blare of trumpets could be heard from the battlements far above them.

They moved slowly through the crowded streets and ascended the hill to the palace above. It was well past even–sun now, late by Campsit standards, for a crowd of this sort. The castle was truly an amazing building. Tall spires towered above the thick walls of the outer keep. Hundreds of guards lined the road as they entered the massive edifice. They came to a stop at the base of a wide flight of stairs that led to the main door of the castle. Athon left half the contingent of guards to tend to the hesturs, and they walked up the steps.

Eyvindir halted them before they entered. "Captain Athon, I wish to apologize to you. The princess has told me of your kindness, and hospitality. I am grateful that you would show such uncharacteristic and extraordinary mercy. As much as I am able, I will see to it that you are treated similarly."

"Your offer is received with thanks," Athon said cordially, "and I hope King Preanth shares that sentiment."

Eyvindir escorted them through a corridor toward the Grand Hall. As they neared the entrance, a lavishly uniformed officer approached them. "General Naestir I present Prince Tam of Campsit, Athon, the Captain of the Guard, and his men. They seek audience with His Majesty King Preanth on the return of Princess Indura."

"Eyvindir," said Naestir. "The king will see the emissaries of Campsit, but I cannot let them enter with guard or arms."

"Athon you will need to choose your representatives, and leave your weapons here," Eyvindir said.

"Prince Tam, my lieutenant Xacthos, and I will act as plenipotentiary," Athon replied. They then began the arduous task of disarming themselves.

As they handed their weapons to the other guards, Indura took a mental inventory. Each was equipped with a bow, a quiver full of arrows, a long sword, a short sword, four daggers, a handful of throwing knifes, a hurlbat, and a large knife. "Aren't you overdoing it with the weapons?" she asked.

"We feel like being prepared," Athon responded flippantly. He turned to the guards, and quickly signed his order. "*Do nothing unless you hear the eryr's cry.*"

The three officers turned and followed their escort into the Grand Hall. Tam had never seen such a gargantuan space in his life. He thought the great hall of his father was the biggest place he had ever seen. The ceiling seemed to touch the sky as it hovered high above the floor. Those standing seemed to be dwarfed by the lofty columns that supported the walls. At the far end, a raised platform holding the thrones of the king and queen towered above the heads of the subjects that surrounded it. A long red carpet flowed down the center of the room like a great river of blood. Tam realized he shouldn't show his astonishment, but it was difficult.

As the group reached the base of the pedestal, the soldiers, Mai, and Indura knelt and bowed. The three guards likewise fell to their knees and bowed.

"Your Majesty, Lord High King of Ithilton, Ruler of the five Realms, Lord Protector of the Land, Guardian of the Sacred Chalice, and Steward of the House of Fadir. I present your daughter, Indura, Princess of all Ithilton, and Daughter of Elina. She has returned from a voyage to the Wall Mountains in the company of the Guards of Campsit." Naestir said, with a booming voice. Tam felt the elaborate way the general addressed the king was completely unnecessary.

Indura stood and ascended to the top of the platform. She turned, and in a loud voice addressed the room. In the same flowery, overdramatic language Naestir used, she recounted the tale of the trague attack, and subsequent rescue by the prince. He thought there was far too much emphasis placed on his role, but the narrative seemed to enthrall the courtiers. Tam surmised the purpose of this peculiar form of storytelling was to entertain the assembled masses, not relay vital information in any useful way. As far as he was concerned, court was not a form of entertainment.

It took longer than Tam thought was necessary for Indura to tell her story. When she finished, the king stood and walked majestically to his daughter's side. He embraced her tenderly, and turned to the three guards at the bottom of the dais.

"Have you anything to add to my daughter's account, brave Guards of Campsit?" Preanth asked the trio kneeling beneath him.

"Your daughter speaks the truth," Athon said, looking up. "I ask only that we be allowed to rest, and return to our lands in peace, oh great king."

"You are the prince?" Preanth asked Athon.

"I am the prince, Your Highness," Tam said. "This is Athon, captain of my father's guard, and Xacthos, one of his lieutenants."

"Approach me," Preanth said. "I wish to meet the man who saved my beloved daughter."

Tam stood and began ascending the dais. Indura gazed admiringly down at him. He looked so steady and handsome in his uniform. Their eyes met, and she had the distinct feeling she had done this before. His brilliant blue eyes penetrated her to the core. His walk was steady and confident as he made his way up the steps. Suddenly, everything coalesced in her mind. She knew why she had the feeling of déjà vu. She recognized him in a flash. It was the man from her dream.

A flood of emotions broke upon Indura as if someone had released the dam that held them at bay. She didn't love him, did she? What a preposterous notion that she could have fallen in love with someone like him, and in such a short time. The force of the conflicting emotions battered her ferociously. He was almost near her. A great swelling of undeniable love filled her heart to near bursting. She fought to control her composure, but it was useless. The torrent of feelings swirled about her, tugging at her exhausted body. The room began swirl, as if the palace were melting with the intense heat she was now feeling. Her vision began to narrow and fade. Tam's face seemed to distort and contort like melting wax. His eyes never wavered but seemed to separate and float toward her in mid–air. She heard him call her name. The cry floated to her from the distance like a lazily drifting cloud. Her knees buckled, and all went black.

# Chapter 11

# RECKONING

Tam reached Indura in time to catch her as she fell toward the dais. He had seen her start to swoon as he reached the top of the steps. His swift reaction had saved her precious head from crashing to the hard stone floor. The room gave a collective gasp as they realized what was happening. Soldiers raced to the side of the king drawing weapons in a misguided attempt to save the princess from her erstwhile savior.

Athon and Xacthos impulsively tried to react, only to be confronted by stunned soldiers with bared steel. Athon abruptly halted and grabbed Xacthos by the arm, restraining him from escalating the situation.

King Preanth was the first person to come to the realization of what had just happened. "Stay your weapons," he ordered. "What have you done?" He demanded.

"She must have fainted," replied Tam. "I didn't want her to crack her head."

"Your Majesty, if I may be so bold as to suggest that the princess has simply been overcome by her journey?" Athon shouted, in a desperate attempt to defuse the situation.

"You are bold," Preanth growled as he wheeled on Athon. "You forget your place, Captain."

"Majesty, I believe my captain is right," Tam said. "Indura has barely slept since the attack, and she has traveled far with little rest. She must have collapsed out of sheer exhaustion. Let me take her to a place where she can rest."

"You?" Preanth said in disbelief. He seemed to mull the idea in his mind for a moment. He leaned over and whispered in Tam's ear. "Pick her up and we will escort you to her chambers." He turned to the masses, and addressed the crowd of onlookers. "The princess has merely fainted. Her exhaustive journey has gotten the best of her, and it seems the prince has saved her from injury once more. Now if you will excuse us, we need to see to her needs."

Preanth turned and led Tam down the steps toward the royal chambers and motioned for Athon, Xacthos, and Mai to join them. Once they had passed through the crowd of gawking onlookers, they moved swiftly through the palace towards the royal quarters.

They burst through the doors of Indura's room to find Tova anxiously waving them to the large bed in the center of the room. Tam gently placed her on the soft pillows, and turned to find a scowling monarch glaring at him.

"All of you leave," Tova ordered. "I have sent for the doctor, Majesty, but I must insist that she be left in my care for the moment."

"Do not forget your place, Mistress, or I will have you educated! You will inform me directly on her condition," Preanth said sternly.

"I apologize, Majesty," Tova pleaded. "I did not mean to offend. If it pleases you, I wish to care for your daughter in private right now. She needs her rest." Her eyes fell on Mai. "You need your rest, as well. I will care for her for now."

"But, Mistress," Mai protested.

"I will have none of that," Tova said sternly. "You are relieved of your duties until you have recovered." She then shooed the concerned group out of the room, and closed the door firmly.

"Mai," Preanth said. "Thank you for being there for my daughter. You are exhausted. Do as Tova commands. Go to your quarters and rest."

"Yes, Majesty," Mai said quietly, and left them in the hall as she nearly sleep-walked to her room.

"Now sirs, you will tell me all I want to know about what happened," Preanth said, turning to the three guards.

The trio answered the barrage of questions from the king as they walked to his private office near the Grand Hall. He seemed to be very interested in the particulars of how the hunting party had come to be in the area they were, and why they had come to the aid of his daughter. Every detail was scrutinized of how she had been fed, sheltered, and treated.

The flowery language was gone, replaced by the shrewd, direct questions of a man who ruled by sheer force of will. Tam felt the need to answer his questions honestly. He answered partly because he felt empathy for Preanth's position as Indura's father, but also because the soldiers, which that had accompanied them since the Grand Hall, had never lowered their swords.

After what seemed an eternity of constant questioning, Preanth was satisfied. "I am sorry if I seem ungrateful, but I can never be too careful. One does not become king by trusting everything he is told. I have to be sure you are not lying to me."

"Our kingdoms may have differences," Athon said. "But we have no reason to lie about this."

"We simply wanted to make sure your daughter was returned to you safely, and her guards given proper respect," Tam said.

"And what, exactly, do you want as your reward for this great deed?" Preanth eyed the three with the suspicion born of an ancient paranoia.

"Reward?" Tam said.

"Nothing is required, Majesty," Athon interjected. "We simply wish to have a place to rest, and return to our lands in peace."

"Surely that can't be all?" Preanth said skeptically.

"No, Majesty," Tam said firmly. "Our hospitality is not for sale. We simply wish to be allowed go our own way in peace."

"Well then," Preanth said. "We shall afford you with the same conviviality as you have shown my daughter — Page!" The door to the study opened and a young man entered. "Find accommodations for these men in the city. See that they are fed and their hesturs stabled. Send men to fetch our dead soldiers, and have them burned immediately. They are probably stinking by now, so burn the wagon they came in. We wouldn't want our guests to take that diseased filth back to their homeland." The page gave a quick salute and promptly exited.

"You don't wish to honor them?" Tam asked, shocked by the king's cavalier attitude.

"Those men failed my daughter completely," Preanth said, coldly. "The tragues saved me the trouble of having them executed. No, they are a disgrace to my army, and don't deserve to be honored."

Tam was dumbfounded by the lack of compassion for the fallen soldiers. He looked at Athon who seemed unconcerned at Preanth's callousness.

Preanth smirked. "I take it you disapprove?"

"Your men were slain in the service of your daughter," Tam said. "It seems to me that they deserve a better fate, in death, than their memories cast aside so casually, Majesty."

"I see," Preanth said with a menacing frown. "You would have me reward the failure of cowardly men who must have frozen in fear when the attack occurred? Those men deserved their fate. I could forgive them if they died in the act of killing the tragues, but they died with their weapons still in their scabbards." Preanth spit the words out as if they left a bitter taste on his tongue. "That kind of cowardice is inexcusable. You survived because you acted. It is because of your actions that I will not throw you in the dungeon as I ought to."

The hairs on the back of Tam's head rose, and a chill trickled down his spine. He hadn't thought that Preanth would react with brutal malice toward them. It had never occurred to him that he would be welcomed as anything other than a hero by the father of the woman he rescued. He looked into Preanth's eyes and saw the cold malevolence of a man who held absolute power. The king's true vicious, cruel nature belied the warm façade he showed is daughter. Tam was beginning to understand how delicate the thread was that kept the sword of doom from falling on them.

"However," Preanth continued. "I love my daughter very much, and am grateful that you came to her aid. I promised you that I would treat you as you treated her. You held a feast in her honor, sheltered her, clothed her, and escorted her to safety. I will do no less. You will be fed, housed, celebrated, and when it is over, escorted from my lands."

"Your Majesty is most generous," Athon said, trying to relieve the tension.

"You have left me with quite a lot of preparation to do. If you will wait in the antechamber, the page will be back and escort you to your quarters. Tomorrow, at late–sun, a celebration will be held to commemorate your heroism. I'm sure you lack formal wear, so I will have some sent to your apartments. Then you may rest until even–sun when you shall leave—Naestir!" Preanth bellowed. The general quickly entered from the antechamber. "I expect you all to behave as good, honored guests. Just in case you have other intentions, soldiers will accompany you wherever you go, and I must request that you leave your weapons with them, for safekeeping. Naestir, see to our guests."

The general motioned for them to follow, and they were led out of the study, then out of the palace. They met the other guards who were waiting in the courtyard. The page approached the general, whispered in his ear, and then headed back into the palace.

"Men of Campsit," Naestir said loudly. "You are honored guests of the kingdom of Ithilton. There is no need for your weapons. Surrender them and follow me. They will be returned to you when you leave."

Athon signaled the guards that it was all right to comply with the order. Reluctantly, they removed their armament and placed them on the ground at the general's feet. No one liked the idea of being unarmed in enemy territory, but they were trained to use their entire body as a weapon. If they were attacked, they wouldn't be that way for long.

"You will need your hesturs, as the inn is outside the palace," Naestir continued. "There is a stable there, and rooms procured for all of you. You may feel free to move about the hotel and stable area, but you are forbidden from venturing off the property. Any violation will result in immediate death to your entire party. Am I understood?"

"Threats are not necessary, general," Athon said calmly. "My men will comply without question."

After depositing the last of their weapons they got on their hesturs and headed into the city. A contingent of more than a hundred soldiers escorted them through the streets. The ride to the inn didn't take long. It was midway between third–quarter and late–sun, and men and beasts were exhausted from the long voyage. Tam was glad to give Pyta some feed and water and after he was satisfied his mount was ready to bed down, he left to collapse in his room.

Tam's quarters were sandwiched between Athon's and Xacthos'. His apartment wasn't much larger than the one he had at the garrison, but the furnishings were quite a bit better. He had his own washbasin, and he decided to put that to immediate use. It wasn't as soothing as a warm bath, but the dirt and grime from two turns of hard, dusty travel came off just as nicely with the water from the basin. Sufficiently cleansed from his travels, he pulled the drapes closed over the window, crawled under the inviting warm covers of the bed, and fell asleep, dreaming of holding Indura tightly in his arms.

# Chapter 12

# TRIUMPH OF LOSS

Tam's sweet, warm breath rippled across Indura's neck, causing the tingling sensation to reverberate through her spine, and focus all its resonance on the small of her back. The sensation ignited her skin with a pleasant response that made every part of her ache to be caressed. His velvet lips glided over the nape of her neck, kissing her softly. He held her firmly about her waist with his strong hands. Slowly, she turned to meet his mouth with hers. Every part of her body seemed to pulsate with the rapid beat of her heart. Nothing seemed to separate the warm and supple touch of their lips pressing together in the sweet embrace of a passionate kiss.

Indura leaned in with anticipation, but met air. Her eyes were closed, but her mind's eye could see the mouth she longed to taste. She pushed further, but was still frustrated in her efforts. Perplexed, she opened her eyes and found herself alone. She searched for the love of her life, but couldn't find him anywhere in the palace. After she scoured the upper levels, she found herself standing at the door of the dungeon. Had her father imprisoned the man she loved? She dreaded the thought of him languishing in the depths of the palace, so she frantically raced down the steps calling his name. At last, she heard him returning her call. She continued down the interminable staircase following the sound of his voice. Finally, she came to the very depths of the dungeon.

At length, Indura came upon a small door with a small barred window. Tam's face was pressed against the bars. She tried furiously to pry the door open, but it wouldn't budge. She looked around to see that prison cell was actually a small coffin like box. She looked up and noticed that it was suspended by a thin chain. She glanced down and saw that beneath it was a large hole in the floor with no apparent bottom. All around was darkness.

Tam pleaded with her to open the door before the chain snapped under his weight. Indura scrambled around, looking for a key that would open the cursed door. She couldn't find one.

Suddenly, the chain broke, and the cell plummeted down the hole. She screamed, and tried to snag anything that would arrest his fall, but it was too late. She called after him, peering over the edge into the abyss. There was only silence.

Indura was alone. Darkness enfolded the princess. A profound sadness overcame her, and she felt as if her heart would break. Fate had only taunted her. Now, all was lost. In the gloom behind her, she heard Tova calling her name.

"Indura," Tova said, her voice cold and ethereal. "Indura, wake up. You are dreaming."

"Help!" she cried. "Tam's gone! He fell! I lost Tam!"

"Wake up, Indura," Tova said, starting to shake her. "It is not real, it is a dream. Wake up!"

Indura eyes flung open. She was in bed. She looked around the room in stunned disbelief. "What happened?"

"You fainted in the Grand Hall," Tova said, calmly. "It is a good thing the prince was there to catch you."

"How long have I been asleep?" Indura rubbed her eyes as if it would rid her of the weariness she still felt. She glanced down at her dress. Her riding clothes had been replaced by a sleeping gown. She must have been completely exhausted to be dressed without waking.

"Since they brought you here," Tova said, pulling the drapes open. "That was sometime after late–sun, but it is well past high–sun now. I felt it best to let you sleep as long as you needed. It is a good thing that you chose now. The feast will be at late–sun. I imagine that Your Highness would be expected to be there to greet our guests of honor properly."

Indura was stunned with how late it was. Normally, Tova would have never let her sleep so long. What was the feast she was talking about? Honored guests? Clearly, things had happened while she was comatose. "I assume that this is for the Prince?"

Tova gave a sly smile. "Naturally, your father would celebrate your safe return. The prince made that possible. This feast is in his honor, as well as yours." She paused for a moment. "It seems you are attached to this young man. Was that who you were calling for in your dream?"

Indura sighed with the relief that Tam hadn't left without saying goodbye. "What?" she said dreamily.

"You were calling out his name just before I woke you. You seemed in distress, and you were crying out for someone named Tam. I can only assume that you meant the prince." Tova asked. "Was he attacking you in your dream?"

"No!" Indura hadn't fully come to grips with the emotions she felt just prior to blacking out, or what she felt in the dream. It was possible that she loved him, but determining that would have to wait. The thought that Tova had been there when she cried his name out in her sleep was somewhat unsettling. She may not have decided her feelings, but she was certain she didn't want Tova knowing about them. "It was only a dream Tova, nothing more."

"If you say so," Tova said, with a wry smile. "You should get ready for the festivities. I will draw a bath, and fetch Mai. Now, finish waking up while I ready things for you."

Indura was happy to be alone. It was no good to try talking to Tova. She knew that Tam was the man from her dream, and in that dream, she loved him. If the feelings were real or some fantasy imagined by her subconscious, she didn't know yet. For now, she would make the most of the limited time she had with him, but there was a problem. How was she going to communicate with him once he returned home? If these feelings were real, separation would be difficult. She mulled the problem over while she had time.

It wasn't long before Tova was back, and Indura slowly pried herself from the comfort of her bed. Her bath was a refreshing cleanse, as she stayed lost in the deep recesses of her thoughts. She didn't even notice when Mai came into the room.

"Highness?" Mai said softly.

Indura was startled from her trance. "I didn't hear you come in."

"You were lost in your own world, I think," Mai said, pulling a dress from the wardrobe.

"I was, wasn't I?" Indura gave a laugh at her own predicament. "I guess I just have a lot to think about."

"You want to share?" Mai teased. "Or, do I just get to sit and wonder?"

"Oh Mai, I don't know. I'm not even sure I understand my own mind right now."

"About what?"

Indura paused, knowing that Mai was the one person she could trust. "Tam."

"Oh," Mai said, knowingly. "I thought I sensed a connection between you two."

"I've been having dreams about him." Indura emerged from the bath into the warmth of a soft towel.

"What kind of dreams?"

"I'm not sure. I don't even know if they can be called dreams."

"What do you mean by that?" Mai was perplexed by the princess' evasive answers.

"You know how you can tell when you're dreaming?" The handmaid nodded. "When I dream about him, I can't tell if I'm asleep or awake. Even stranger, some of the things I have dreamt about have come true." Indura started dressing.

The hair on the back of Mai's neck stood on end. "Are you saying that you had a vision of some kind?"

"I don't know that I wouldn't say that."

"What do you dream about?"

Indura stopped for a moment. She wasn't sure that she wanted to verbalize her feelings, but she knew that if anyone would understand, it would be Mai. "Promise not to laugh?"

"I would never laugh at you."

"In my dreams, I love him, more than I've ever loved anyone before. I know it seems stupid, but I don't know how else I can say it." Indura felt a little ashamed, but she knew that she couldn't phrase it any other way.

Mai looked at the princess thoughtfully. "Do you feel the same way when you are awake?"

"I don't know," Indura said. "I'm not really sure to be honest. I just know that when I'm with him, everything just seems right."

# Chapter 13

# THE BALL

It was high–sun when Tam had been roused by Athon knocking at the door. A maid was standing there with him. She had come in to give him a smock to wear while she laundered his clothes. An hour later, a messenger arrived with formal attire made especially for the feast.

The ensemble was comprised of a heavy lapis blue jacket, spotless white shirt, and matching gray slacks. Everything was of the finest craftsmanship. It was amazing how exquisite the cloth was compared to his uniform. The fabric was of a material that was smooth and light to the touch. It was unlike anything he had ever felt. When he put it on, it fit him perfectly. It was amazing considering no one had measured him for the garment.

Tam was alone in his attire. It seemed that the king only furnished clothes for the young prince, and it made him stand out from the others. He felt self–conscious riding with the other guards toward the palace. He felt out of place, but Athon had assured him that refusing to gift would be seen as an insult.

The servants had been busy in their absence. The palace was festooned with brightly colored banners and flags. A thick red carpet covered the stairs that led to the main doors. Hallways were similarly adorned with bright decorations. Tam was both impressed and amused that the king seemed to have gone overboard in creating a festive atmosphere.

The palace dining hall was cavernous, but bustled with hundreds of people. The head table was on a short, raised platform at the far end of the room. Instead of several long tables running the length of the room, there were dozens of round tables filled with elaborately dressed nobles. A large fire pit in the center contained the several beasts that were slowly being roasted on rotisseries. The smell of the delicately seasoned flesh wafted through the hall, providing a pleasing aroma that made Tam's mouth begin to water.

Naestir heralded their entrance with the flowery language that irked Tam. It seemed that the only reason why someone would put such effort into using extravagant speech would be to demean those of lesser stature. It was a verbal segregation that he found unsettling.

They were led to a set of reserved tables, and seated according to rank. He, Athon, and Xacthos were escorted to the platform where they were seated on the left side of three large chairs, presumably for the royal family.

"There are two goblets at your place setting. Don't drink from the large one," Athon whispered.

"What?" Tam said, confused by the order. "Why?"

"It shouldn't matter, but trust me on this one. It isn't celis juice," Athon said firmly. "Don't drink it."

"The toast," Xacthos hissed. "He can't toast with water."

Athon sighed. "Ugh, I hadn't thought about that."

"If he doesn't do it, the king will look like a fool," Xacthos whispered.

"I know, I know," Athon groaned. He paused for a moment to formulate a plan. "Fine, here's what we'll do. If the king offers a toast, pretend to drink, but don't let it past your lips."

"I still don't understand. Is there something wrong with the drink?"

"It's forbidden by Campsit law," Athon said curtly. "Just leave it at that. As delicate as things are right now, it will only make matters worse if we offend Preanth, and we can't afford any more complications. Just follow my lead, and don't actually drink it." Athon made eye contact with one of the guards in the audience and gave a silent command regarding the drink.

Horns shattered the din in the room, and Naestir announced the royal family. Through a small entrance near the head table, the three royals emerged, and all in the hall stood. As the royal family approached the table, Tam found that he couldn't take his eyes off Indura. The deep green dress accentuated her perfectly, and seemed to set her sparkling eyes aflame. Her face lit up when she saw him. He was thankful when everyone was allowed to sit, because his knees seemed to have lost their strength at the sight of her.

Preanth welcomed his guest, clapped, and the feast began. There seemed to be no end of food as the revelers were served with bounteous portions of freshly roasted meats, breads, and fruits. Minstrels, jugglers, jesters and other entertainers wove their way through the hall to the delight of the crowd. Despite the chaos, Tam took every opportunity to glance over at Indura. He tried not to seem overeager, but he couldn't stop looking at her.

After over an hour of feasting on the most succulent dishes Tam had ever eaten, Preanth stood and called for silence. "Nobles, fair ladies, and honored guests; I am happy you could join us for this celebration. On this occasion, we are pleased to have with us the brave men of Campsit, and their heroic Prince. If it were not for his bravery, my daughter would not be sitting next to me. For that, I will be forever thankful." He raised his large goblet and turned to address Tam personally. "You do your kingdom great credit by your actions. May your countrymen follow your fine example and ever be valiant."

Everyone raised goblets high and then drank. Tam was careful not to consume any of the liquid. It smelled oddly familiar, like a mixture of celis and old bread. Whatever it was didn't smell very appetizing. After the king returned to his seat, the servants hurriedly filled the goblets in preparation for a reciprocal toast. Tam eyed Athon nervously.

"You have to toast him back," Athon whispered, his lips barely moving.

Tam had been schooled by Master Thales in formal etiquette, but he had never had to honor anyone with a toast. He was nervous, and unsure of what exactly he would say. His mind raced, trying to formulate a proper response, well aware of the time slipping away. He glanced in the direction of Preanth, who was eyeing him with a sly, malevolent smirk.

Tam slowly rose to his feet, still unsure of himself. He mustered all of his faculties to keep a confident façade, despite his knees feeling like jelly, and the almost uncontrollable urge to vomit. He took in a deep breath to calm himself. His thoughts coalesced into a coherent notion. The extemporaneous words began to flow through his mind. "I wish to thank our gracious host for this magnificent gala. It is an honor to serve the princess and your kingdom. Our two nations have been at odds for far too long. May these events serve as a preamble to a more peaceful co–existence between us." He raised the large goblet high toward the king. "May you live long, forever wise."

Tam pretended to drink to the king, and sat down slowly. In truth, he wanted nothing more than to hide from the uncomfortable attention. He didn't like being put on the spot. A wave of nausea accompanied by a euphoric feeling of relief swept over him. He glanced over at the king who looked quite amused, then turned to Athon.

"You look as if you are going to pass out," Athon whispered.

"Either that or lose my stomach," Tam whispered back. "For some reason I wasn't expecting that."

"You did fine," Athon reassured him. "I couldn't have done better myself."

"Let's hope I don't have to do that ever again."

"Really?" Athon quipped. "I wanted to see you go until one of you couldn't stand." Athon's gentle teasing had the desired relaxing effect.

The feast continued for another hour as people slowly overindulged in the gastronomical delights. Everyone seemed to have their bellies filled and their thirst slaked. Most of the guests had quite a bit of the liquid that was liberally poured into the large goblet, and appeared to be befuddled. The laughter was more boisterous, and people seemed uninhibited and out of control.

The royal family rose, and beckoned the party to follow them into the Grand Hall. Music filled the air as the coterie entered. Tam came to the sudden realization that the celebration would include dancing.

Preanth turned politely to the Campsit guards. "I noticed that you did not come with appropriate companionship for a ball. I have taken the liberty of arranging some companions for you."

A group of elegantly dressed young women emerged from the shadows of the galleries. Each woman approached one of the stunned guards, curtsied, and one by one, lightly took them by the arm.

Indura looked on helplessly as one of the women gracefully approached Tam and ensnared his arm. She felt a swell of jealous anger. She looked at her father, veiling her disappointment so as not to break regal decorum. She knew he had arranged precisely enough young maidens for the men of Campsit, including Tam. Preanth saw the look on her face, and turned unapologetically to whisper in her ear.

"I assume you had other plans for the prince," Preanth said. "You may dance with him, if he has the backbone to ask you, but I'm not offering my daughter to him."

"Do you not care, at all, for my happiness?" Indura said coldly.

Preanth smiled warmly at his daughter. "You know I would do anything for you, my dear, but this is politics. I cannot simply bestow your hand upon any man that comes along. It takes more to make a man than a simple act of bravery. It takes even more to make a man worthy of my daughter. Let us see if he is a man yet, or if he is still a boy." The music picked up in tempo, and the king grabbed his daughter's hand. "As for the first dance, it belongs to me."

Preanth led Indura to the center of the Grand Hall. The others formed a large circle and watched as the king and his daughter gracefully danced together. As the waltz concluded its final sweet notes, the royal pair bowed to the applause of the audience.

"We have come to make merry," Preanth said, "and, I did not invite you here so you could stand and watch me. Please enjoy yourselves!" With a wave of his hand, the musicians began a lively tune, and the king, queen, and Indura walked to their thrones.

Mai was waiting for Indura at the top of the dais, dressed in her finest gown. She looked stunning. They quickly sought a corner of the platform away from the king to talk.

"It's sad," said Mai. "We're here at a ball celebrating our safe return, and you have no one to dance with."

"I'm painfully aware of that," Indura said dejectedly. "Father made sure the only eligible man was accompanied by someone else."

"You didn't expect him to make it easy, did you?"

"I hoped he would," Indura said glumly. "He's testing him."

"Does your father know how you feel about him?" Mai whispered.

"Shush," Indura whispered sternly. She glanced at her father, but he was intently watching the scene below. "No, and I don't want him to. Let's keep it between us."

Mai and Indura followed the king's gazed out onto the floor and began to giggle at the somewhat comical scene that was taking place. It was obvious that formal dance was not something that the men of Campsit were used to. Even Athon was having difficulties with some of the dance steps, but managed to look like he had learned to dance at some point in his life. Most fumbled clumsily, and were red with embarrassment, but they refused to give up. Some of the maidens were flustered, tired of having toes stepped on. The more patient of them were trying to lead their partners with less than ideal results. The king seemed delighted by their plight, and grinned broadly.

Tam seemed to have less difficulty weaving his way around the stumbling couples. He moved around the floor as if he were gliding on ice. He paraded himself through the mire, working steadily toward the base of the dais. His timing was impeccable. He arrived at the steps just as the melody ended. He kindly kissed the hand of the fair maiden, and thanked her for the dance. He then confidently ascended the steps to the throne platform, and bowed deeply.

"Oh gracious, King Preanth," Tam pleaded, using as flowery a language as he could stomach. "You are wise, and generous beyond measure. You have provided beautiful companions, and I thank you for your generosity."

"It has been a true joy and pleasure," Preanth replied.

"I ask that I have an additional honor and be allowed to dance with your daughter, the most beautiful maiden in your kingdom."

"Are you not satisfied with the one you were presented with?" Preanth asked, mildly irritated. "Does she not please you?"

"She is very lovely, and a fine dance companion," Tam said, to the dejected woman. "However, I believe that it is customary for someone of my stature to accompany someone of equal esteem."

Preanth stared at Tam sternly for a moment. "You have a point. A prince deserves the company of a princess. You may dance with her for the duration of the gala, if that is her wish."

"You are most kind and giving, Your Majesty." He turned and bowed to Indura. "May I have the honor of this dance, Highness?" He presented his arm to Indura, which she joyfully took. They then proceeded to the floor, and took their place among the dancers.

"That was as unexpected as it was generous, my husband." Elina, the Queen, didn't speak often, a plus as far as Preanth was concerned, but when she did, she was quite perceptive. "I thought you would have done a better job of keeping them separate."

"I did my best to discourage him, but there are rules even I must follow," Preanth said. "What would you have me do?"

"It is not my place to question your decisions, husband," Elina said. "I am simply trying to comprehend your reasoning."

"You, of all people, should understand me," Preanth retorted. "Whom you should be trying to conjure a motive for, is your daughter."

"She does seem to be quite infatuated with the prince, doesn't she?"

Brief horror passed the king's face. "Can you imagine such a thing? We have to discourage such impulsive behavior, but if I were to forbid it, I would only encourage her defiance. If I allow her to make a few decisions, but don't encourage them, she will eventually see the folly of her ways and forget all about this infatuation."

"For now, it seems, we have to watch," Elina said.

Athon knew most of the guards weren't much for formal dancing. Campsit dances were nothing like the ones in Ithilton. This kind of dancing was taught at the academy, but rarely seen at the celebrations where dancing occurred. Athon envied Tam. He had tried, along with the other guards, to remember childhood lessons long since forgotten, but the results were tragically embarrassing. Instead of continuing to embarrass themselves, the guards had thanked their companions, and retreated to the safety of the gallery to watch.

In stark contrast to the rest of the guards, Tam was debonair. He danced with the beautiful princess in the midst of the sea of colorfully dressed nobles. Without the clumsy guards in the way, the dancing became a spectacle of well–choreographed art. Athon could only look on in humiliated awe at the kaleidoscope before him. It was better this way, he thought. It was much more relaxing to enjoy the entertainment of watching than to stumble about trying to imitate the moves of others as they glided in synchronized rhythm.

Eyvindir approached from the shadows of a neighboring alcove, and greeted Athon. He was wearing a dress uniform. There was no heavy armor, just the bright red tunic of an Ithilton officer, and a very ornate dress sword. "I think you were brave to even try to compete with the charlatans who learn that sort of thing. We are fighters, not dancers."

"You are most kind to soften the blow to our obvious defeat on the field of cultural relations," Athon said, acknowledging the officer. "I train my men to be graceful on the battlefield, not here."

"Yet, you attempted it despite your deficit," Eyvindir said. "It shows spirit, even if it is foolhardy."

"You've come to gloat?" Athon felt a little defensive, but didn't wish to provoke a fight.

"On the contrary," Eyvindir said. "I have come to offer my apologies. You should have never been placed in such a situation. I think my king meant to embarrass you."

"He succeeded," Athon, admitted with a chuckle.

"Such petty humiliation does not befit men like us."

"Men like us?" Athon wasn't sure of Eyvindir's motivation for this conversation, but was determined to ferret it out.

"Men who choose fighting as our profession," Eyvindir said. "You and I are alike. We both prepare for a fight that we hope never comes. It all depends on the decisions of those that command us."

"Command you," Athon corrected. "You and I both know Campsit has no desire to mount an offensive against Ithilton. Our guards are strictly for defense. That is why they are called guards, not soldiers."

"I stand corrected," Eyvindir acknowledged with a nod. "You think of me strictly as an enemy?"

"Not specifically," Athon said cautiously. "It depends on your intent. If you intend to harm those I protect, or bring them into subjugation, I would have to say, yes. If your motives are friendlier, I would not be so harsh. So, are you friendly, or must I consider you my enemy?"

"I assure you, I mean you no harm." Eyvindir looked steadily at Athon as he spoke. "I am merely attempting to know my counterpart. I have no use for politics. I admire bravery and fighting skill and value actions more than empty words. Your actions are far nobler than the sycophants who consistently parade in this court with their verbose speech, and hollow deeds. In my esteem, your integrity is unimpeachable."

"That is very high praise for a simple an act."

"Is it simple?" Eyvindir asked skeptically. "You could have killed Indura, or allowed the tragues to do it. It was within your power, and your people aren't known for letting trespassers live. If you hadn't killed her, you could have ransomed her for any number of concessions from the king, and yet you only asked for safe passage. You acted honorably, and returned the princess unspoiled and unharmed. Such a man deserves my admiration and respect."

Athon was speechless. This type of response was unexpected, and meant more coming from this line officer than it would Preanth. The respect of an adversary was common ground that could be built upon. "I think we understand one another," he said at last. "I believe that there might be hope for our two kingdoms. Unfortunately, it depends on the ambitions of one man."

"I'm not so sure that it is entirely up to him," Eyvindir said. "I think there are two people who have an even greater say than he does." He gestured simply to the two young royals who seemed enthralled with each other in their own personal ballet.

Tam relished every moment that he spent with Indura. He was grateful for the opportunity to be with her, but as the hours slipped by, he knew that eventually it would end. It would not be long before he had to return to the inn and get some semblance of sleep.

Once he left, he didn't know if he would ever get the chance to see her again, and he wasn't thrilled with that. For now, he savored the precious time he spent in her presence. Her skin was warm, soft, and creamy smooth to the touch. He longed to feel his fingers intertwined with hers in a gentle embrace.

Dancing, even at the measured pace of the courtly promenade, takes a physical toll. After nearly two hours, Tam was ready for a break. Turns of sporadic rest and meals had left him feeling less than one hundred percent. He bowed politely to his graceful companion. "I need to take a break."

Indura was relieved. Even with her extended respite, she hadn't fully recovered. She heartedly accepted, and the two retreated to an unoccupied portico off one of the galleries.

Soon her time with Tam would end, but she refused to accept that these would be the last moments together. She suspected he held similar feelings, but she wasn't sure. Unfortunately, time was a commodity that was swiftly running out, and she had to be certain before she could proceed.

Tam stood by Indura in the shade. It was past fourth–quarter sun and the vista of the Wall Mountains to the south was magnificent. Almost without thinking, he brushed his fingers against her dangling hand. Instinctively her fingers reciprocated the subtle advance and entwined with his. A shock surged through them both, and they realized the symbolism of the simple gesture. They simultaneously looked at each other and smiled. It was the first time either of them had been openly affectionate.

Tam hadn't expected this to happen. It was one thing to have incidental contact, but quite another for it to be intentional. All he could do, was state the obvious. "You're holding my hand."

Indura giggled. "Really? I didn't notice," she said sarcastically. "It isn't a problem for you, is it?"

"I'm not complaining," he said.

"Good, for a moment I thought I was clasping another man's hand, and I would have to scream if that were the case."

"And, ruin that beautiful voice? Perish the thought."

"So, what do we do now?"

"That's a good question, and one that's been much on my mind. What to do with you in the time I have left?"

"What time is that?"

"Even–sun is only a few hours away. We don't have long together."

"Nothing escapes you."

Tam flushed with embarrassment. She was teasing him, and he knew it. "I'm not subtle. It's a talent I've hidden as long as I've known you."

Indura giggled again. "It's a talent now?"

"It is, and I've mastered it." Tam paused to reflect for a moment. "I still don't know what to do with you."

"You could hold my hand."

"I am holding your hand." Tam winced at the thought of yet another conspicuous fact. "I'm a little tired of dancing, so perhaps we could just sit and talk for now." He led her to a nearby stone bench. He looked back toward the mountain peaks. Somewhere at the top, too distant to be seen, was the garrison. "I've never seen them from this far away."

"What?"

"The mountains," he said. "Campsit is at the base of the high cliffs on the other side, and the garrison is somewhere on those peaks. I've never seen this view of them before. It's quite spectacular."

Indura looked at the distant vista, a sight she had grown up seeing. "I had never thought of it that way. I've always seen this side. I hadn't considered that there could be another perspective."

"Indura," Tam said nervously. "I like being with you, and I don't want to leave. I may never see you again."

"Stay a turn or two more."

"No," he shook his head, remembering Preanth's demeanor. "Your father was very specific. After even–sun, we are no longer welcome."

One thing she knew about her father was that once he gave a command, it was obeyed. "I could come to Campsit. Now the tragues are dead, the road is safer."

Tam shook his head. He couldn't tell her that she had been spared, in violation of the law. "It isn't that simple. Our kingdoms are adversaries. You honestly think your father would let you go back?"

"I see your point. We could meet somewhere in the middle."

"I wish, but I have duties. It isn't like I can just go wandering off by myself." Tam knew he was throwing up excuses, but he would be hard pressed to find a legitimate reason to leave the garrison alone. "I wouldn't even know when or where to meet you."

Indura knew he was right, and that any further discussion needed to be covert. She lowered her voice to a whisper. "I might have a way we could do it, but I'll have to make some preparations. We could secretly write each other, if you want?"

"Indura!" Preanth snapped. He stood at the threshold of the portico with Elina and several soldiers. He was livid.

The princess whirled to face her father. Fear gripped Indura as she realized that their conversation might have been overheard. She felt Tam withdraw his hand. By Ceanor! she thought, he faced two full–grown tragues, why is he intimidated by her father? The look on Preanth's face answered that question.

It was stern and disapproving.

Tam knew his time with Indura just ended. The tension was instantly palpable. Holding her hand must have caught Preanth's attention, even from the dais. In retrospect, it was a mistake, but one that he wasn't ashamed of.

"The hour is late, and our guests have a long way to travel." Preanth said maliciously. "They need rest before they leave."

"I'm sorry father. I didn't realize how late it was." Indura was trying to be diplomatic, but knew there was an invisible line they had crossed.

Tam gave Indura a longing look and then faced Preanth. "We thank you for your hospitality. Surely, in all Arabella there is no finer merriment. I do not wish to wear out our welcome, so if we may have your blessing, we will retire." He tried to sound as obsequious as he could. It wasn't eloquent, but it would have to do.

Preanth stepped forward, motioning for Tam to join him by the edge of the balcony. "Young man, you have been here for less than a turn. You are an enemy of my kingdom, and the only reason I allow you to live is the service you rendered my daughter. Do not think that you are welcome here. I've been hospitable as a courtesy, but *do not* insult me by trying to woo my daughter."

Tam's eyes had widened, and his face began to flush with a mixture of humiliation and anger. He bit down hard, nearly grinding his teeth in an effort not to lash back at the monarch. It was like getting caught daydreaming in class by Master Thales, and then being called out. He wanted to defend himself, but he knew that he couldn't win. He quietly took the verbal abuse, but he couldn't hide his emotions. For now, he would stay silent and accept the withering assault.

Preanth continued his tirade unabated. "She may be mesmerized by your charm, but I am not. Make no mistake, young prince. I disapprove of you and your ilk."

"Father, stop!" Indura yelled.

"You have until even–sun," Preanth said not stopping to acknowledge his daughter. He whirled on his heels, and strode toward the Grand Hall. "Come! it is time to close the festivities."

Indura looked at Tam, her eyes full of horror and regret. She turned and ran across the floor of the Grand Hall past the stunned faces of the nobles. Mai was not far behind her as she charged down the halls to her quarters. She couldn't help the tears that began streaming down her face. How could her father be so cruel to the man she loved? Why did Tam have to be from Campsit? Why couldn't he be a noble from one of the smaller kingdoms? Why did she love him? Why couldn't things be simple and work the way she wanted?

Tam turned, red faced, back to the Grand Hall. Athon and Xacthos were standing calmly by the threshold. "Sorry I made such a mess," he said softly.

"We should return to the inn while we still can," Athon said.

They walked silently, but proudly out of the palace to their waiting hesturs. "Well, that's a relief," Xacthos said acerbically. "I was getting dizzy watching that nonsense. So glad you know how to impress the ladies, Highness."

Tam was in no mood for Xacthos' jibes. "That isn't funny, and I'll thank you to keep your big mouth shut."

"With all due respect, Highness, if you weren't so enamored—"

"Enough!" Athon roared. "Both of you, shut up! We'll discuss it later!"

The mute ride back to the inn seemed to take longer than it should. Once they arrived, guards stabled their hesturs and sought the warm comfort of their assigned rooms, but Athon, Xacthos, and Tam found their way to a deserted lounge.

"Tam, what you were thinking?" Athon asked tersely.

"What are you referring to?" Tam replied defensively. Being cornered by the two officers was something that happened all too frequently. The interrogation wasn't unexpected, but he didn't want to hear it.

"Don't play dumb!" Xacthos snapped. "You know exactly what we're talking about."

"Xacthos, please," Athon said in a calm but firm voice. "I'm sure the prince has a very good explanation for his behavior."

Behavior? Tam thought. He had done nothing wrong, had he? He danced with the princess. They had talked and held hands. Surely, he hadn't been dishonorable. He leveled his gaze at the captain. "I'm not sure. Perhaps you can enlighten me?"

Athon sighed. "Tam, as far as I'm concerned, you acted honorably and appropriately, for a man that has affection for a woman. It's obvious that you have some feelings toward the princess, and usually that wouldn't be a problem, but Indura is far from your typical woman. Any relationship with her is fraught with political considerations beyond your comprehension."

"I see," Tam said, feeling quite defensive. He had been debased by Preanth, and now felt under attack by his mentor. "You think I shouldn't have been with her tonight?"

"Oh, for the love of—you're not listening!" Xacthos said with exasperation.

"Calm down, Xacthos. Yelling won't help." Athon paused for a moment, and gave a heavy sigh. "Openly showing affection for the princess has complicated things."

Tam was confused at this revelation that simply holding hands had anything to do with politics. "What do politics have to do with my feelings for Indura?" he asked.

"When we came to Ithilton, the only reason we weren't attacked immediately was because we were escorting the princess in good faith. Our purpose was not to ask for permission for you to court her. By the simple act of holding her hand, you communicated your intent to seek Indura. You may not have considered this because it seemed like the natural progression of your shared feelings. I'm sure Preanth saw it as you trying to take advantage of the situation with his daughter."

"I didn't try to take advantage of her," Tam said defensively.

"I know, and I didn't say that you did. I said that it is likely how Preanth saw it. Why do you think he interrupted you? She is his *only* daughter, and I'm sure he has other plans for her. For Indura, marriage is all about money and power. The king will use her politically, not because she loves someone."

Tam looked at Athon dumbfounded. "She can't love who she wants?" In Campsit, he could have a relationship with anyone he chose. There wasn't the stratification of nobility in their society. The concept was completely foreign to their way of life.

"No, she can't. Nobility doesn't marry for love in this part of Arabella. If there is no power or money to be gained, there isn't a reason to marry."

"That's stupid!" Tam scoffed. "I wouldn't think about marrying someone I didn't love."

"That is one of the reasons our ancestors left," Xacthos said. "It's a system put in place for one reason, to perpetuate the cycle of power." He sighed heavily, and left in disgust. "This is giving me a headache. I'm going to bed."

"I blame myself. I shouldn't have put you in a position to become so emotionally attached. I should have seen this coming. You're both young and attractive. Xacthos is right; I'm getting a headache from all this nonsense. Get some rest while you can."

Tam followed Athon to his room, and shut the door behind him. It was good to be alone again. Tam washed his face, and changed out of the brightly colored clothes. He didn't know if he would offend anyone if he kept them, but he was certain any decision he made would be wrong. Exhausted, he fell onto the bed.

Sleep didn't come readily. His brain refused to surrender to the fatigue that racked his body. Instead, his mind focused on the conundrum of his affection for Indura. She was more desirable than anyone he had ever known, but she was trapped by a society that centered on the accumulation of wealth. He wondered if Indura could ever be free to love him.

Indura burst into her room, tears streaming down her face. She was furious with her father. He meddled in her affairs so rarely that caught her by surprise this time. Mai entered the room and closed the door. Indura rounded in a disjointed angry haze. "Why is it that when I like someone who equals my stature, my father intervenes?"

"Are you seriously asking me that question?"

"Of course, I'm asking you that question!" Indura yelled indignantly. "I should be allowed to pursue anyone of noble birth."

"As far as your father is concerned, he isn't noble."

"I don't care," Indura said defiantly. "I love him, Mai."

"Highness? Have you considered that these feelings aren't real?"

"Of course, I have." Indura's eyes misted with emotion. "I've never felt this way. I wasn't sure before, but I am now. You have to believe me."

"I'm trying, but you're getting this from a dream. You have to think this through." Mai said unconvincingly. "He leaves in a few hours, and you'll never see him again."

The thought boiled Indura's blood. Her eyes narrowed, and her resolve solidified in an instant. She would not let Tam slip away. She thought for a moment, and knew what needed to be done. She couldn't involve Mai. It was too risky. She wiped the tears from her cheeks. "I'm tired, Mai. Get me out of this dress."

Mai extricated Indura from the formal gown, and Indura assured Mai that she could handle the rest. Once Mai left, she could proceed with her plan, but she would have to be careful not to be seen by anyone.

# Chapter 14

# SPECKLE TIP

The voice floated like a leaf, gently twisting in a summer breeze. "Tam, wake up." It was beautiful, melodic, and beckoned him to consciousness. "Tam? Please wake up."

"Just let me sleep, mother," He said, pleading for more time.

"I need you to wake up. I don't have much time."

"Mother, please just a little while longer," he insisted. She was shaking him now. This was annoying. Why didn't she get the hint that he just needed more sleep? He was leaving in a few hours.

His eyes flew open. It was dark. The drapes were still occluding most of the light from the window. The minuscule amount that bled around the edges provided enough to make out some of his surroundings. A hooded figure leaned over him.

"Who's there?" He was still bleary.

"It's me, Indura."

"Indura?" Tam was bewildered. He had to be dreaming still. She drew the drapes a small bit. The light temporarily blinded him. This was no dream; it hurt his eyes too much. With one hand, she drew back her hood and sat down on the edge of the bed.

"I'm sorry to wake you, but this couldn't wait. I think it's best that I give you this now. I don't think I'll have a chance later." She had a small bundle that she cradled in her arm. She took it out and began carefully unwrapping it.

"What time is it?" Tam was still coming to grips that she was in his room.

"It's past first–quarter," she said quietly.

"What are you doing here?"

"Keep your voice down," she whispered. "I have something to give you, and you can't let anyone know you have it, understand?"

"What are you talking about?"

"I'm going to give you a parting gift, but it can't be seen by anyone. Do you understand me?"

"Yeah, I got it. Secret, no one can know."

Indura was almost finished unwrapping the carefully packed bundle. Suddenly the roll of fabric moved slightly. It made Tam jump a bit.

"Shush," she cooed. "It's all right. It won't hurt you." At last, the final wrap came off to reveal a small blue–gray creature that fluttered its wings slightly as it sat nestled in her palm, cooing softly. "It's a kyhdue. This one is called Speckle Tip, because of his wings."

"What's he for?"

"This is how you and I will write each other," She said. "You tie a small strip of paper to its leg, and then let it go in the direction of Ithilton. Speckle Tip will fly here, and I'll get the message. Put this cloth where it can see it from the air, but no one can see it from the ground and it will perch there when I send it back. That way, you and I can communicate without anyone knowing about it."

"How does it know how to find you?"

"I don't know. It just does. Kyhdues can find their way home from anywhere, and the palace is its home. Once you release it, it will know how to find its way back. The flag lets it know where to land when I send it to you."

"Will it really work that easily?" He looked at her with some incredulity.

"I've raised kyhdues as pets since I was young, but I've never tried anything like this. I don't honestly know if it will work, but there isn't a reason it shouldn't." She smiled at him. "Just be very careful with him. When you pick him up, just pull his feet back and hold them under his belly like this," she hoisted the bird up showing clearly how she was cradling him. "Keep his legs nestled next to his body. When you carry him, make sure to keep his eyes covered so he will stay nice and quiet and still. Be careful not to wrap him too tightly. He needs to breathe. Keep him in a cage or somewhere safe until you need to send a note. When you're ready, tie a message to his leg and let him go."

"It's that easy?"

"It should be. I've thought about it, and this is the only way to communicate." She began gently swaddling the kyhdue back in its cloth. "I have to get back before someone notices that I'm missing. I was able to sneak out, but if I stay much longer I'm sure to be caught." She finished getting the bird into the cloth and handed Speckle Tip to Tam. "Be gentle. He has to survive your trip without anyone knowing about him."

Tam looked at the bundle. It was not a small package. He wasn't sure how he was going to hide the kyhdue without anyone noticing. "I don't know if this is going to work," he said dubiously. "How did you get this thing out of the palace with without anyone seeing you?"

"The palace has been my home since I was born. I know how to move through the corridors without being seen by the soldiers."

"You don't think that someone will intercept any message I send you?"

"It's a risk, but I don't see another way of writing you." She looked around nervously. "I have to be going. Please be careful. This has to work."

She leaned over and kissed his cheek. For a moment, her warm, sweet breath was on his neck, and her velvet lips were against his skin. He was in paradise.

"It means a lot to me, Tam," she whispered. "I'll see you in a few hours." With that, she swiftly threw on her hood and quietly left his room.

Tam was stunned. The kiss had come as a pleasant surprise, but the kyhdue floored him. He could only sit there, holding the bundle in his hand. It took him a while to come out of the trance. He could scarcely believe what had just happened. It had to be a dream, he thought to himself. He felt the slightest movement of the bird in his hand. He stared down at it in disbelief. How could he possibly transport this delicate creature without anyone knowing?

He had heard about kyhdues from Master Thales, but he had never actually seen one before. He carefully uncovered it. Up close, the creature was quite remarkable. It was mostly an iridescent blue–gray with black speckles on its wings. Its head was a shimmering sea green color that accentuated its red–orange eyes. It bobbed its head up and down in a stuttering rhythmic fashion, and cooed softly. Tam nervously stroked the back of its head as if he expected it to suddenly turn and peck at him. The feathers were soft and very smooth to the touch.

Tam stared at Speckle Tip for a while, contemplating this delicate creature that needed to survive a long journey unseen. He decided that his saddlebag would probably kill the poor thing, and he couldn't wrap it in his bedroll without smothering it. He had to ensconce it somewhere without raising suspicion. At last, he settled on his backpack. It wouldn't draw too much attention, and he would be able to feel its movement. He would have to take special care not to wrap it too tightly, but he would have to work on that later. He was still very tired, and needed to rest a few more hours.

Tam wrapped the kyhdue, being careful it was tight enough to keep it still, but loose enough to allow it to breathe. He covered the eyes, and left the beak uncovered. He gently placed the bundle in his backpack, closed the curtain, and went back to bed. Within moments, he was asleep.

Athon knocked on the door just before even–sun. As far at Tam was concerned, it was too early. Indura's interruption had really thrown him, and his head was foggier than it should have been.

Athon opened the door after Tam had failed to answer. "Oh, good," he said. "You're not dead. Having a problem getting out of bed?"

"Good–turn to you, too," Tam quipped. "Sorry, I didn't sleep well. I'm just a little tired right now. Don't worry though, I'll get over it."

"We need to get moving. There's barely enough time to get something to eat before we have to leave. Are you ready to move yet, or do you need a moment more?"

Tam shook his head in an effort to clear it. "I'm fine," he said, getting to his feet. "Just give me some privacy and I'll get dressed." Athon left the room, closing the door behind him. Tam opened the drapes flooding the room with the early turn light.

Tam quickly dressed in his uniform, and joined Athon and Xacthos in the hall. Breakfast was a light affair. Everyone was still full from the feast. Tam finished quickly and returned to his room. He checked on the kyhdue. It was resting comfortably in its wrap, seemingly oblivious to its place as a stowaway. He stuffed the pack, gently placed Speckle Tip on the top of the contents, and cinched the bag closed. Smuggling the kyhdue only left room for the shirt he received. He doubted he would wear it again, but he thought he would keep a memento. He gingerly shouldered the load, and joined the rest of the guards as they saddled their hesturs.

Eyvindir and his soldiers trotted up to the mustering guards, confiscated weapons in tow. "I am here to escort you to the outer plateau. Preanth wants to guarantee your safe journey."

"How thoughtful," Xacthos said with mild sarcasm.

Athon glared disapprovingly at his lieutenant, but didn't say anything. In short order, everyone was armed and mounted, and they started heading toward the city gates. Tam noticed that the wagon master was riding one of his hesturs bareback; the other was in tow behind. It was an untenable position for a man who was used to riding on the buckboard of a wagon.

As the convoy left the inn, Tam kept looking around for Indura. She was nowhere to be seen. He thought she would have at least shown up to wish him goodbye. He hoped to see her rounding the corner. It didn't happen. Tam gave one last forlorn glance toward the palace, and then turned to follow the others. After they left the constricting city streets, he galloped to join Athon.

Tam rode in silence for the remainder of the turn. It was early fourth–quarter sun before they stopped to rest. They had already reached foothills above Ithilton, and the dense sheltering canopy of the forest. He sat alone, eating the paltry amount of stale bread that remained in his pack. He kept some of the crust to feed the kyhdue when he could remove it from the pack without anyone taking much notice. He was finishing the last morsel, Athon approached.

"You've been pretty quiet since we left."

"Not much to say, really," Tam responded.

"Something on your mind?"

"I guess I've been preoccupied."

"With what?" Athon said compassionately.

Tam hesitated for a moment. "Indura," he sighed. "It comes as a shock I know, but that's it."

"You're really taken by her? She's very beautiful, but it isn't meant to be, Tam. You should be grateful that you weren't around her long."

"Why's that?" Tam looked at him quizzically.

"You didn't have enough time to become attached. Separating isn't easy, but it could've been a lot worse."

"That's the problem," Tam said glumly. "I wish I had more time."

"Trust me," Athon said. "It's better that you didn't. The pain is sometimes worse than wounds from a sword."

"How would you know?"

Athon paused, a pained expression on his face. "What you don't know about me could fill—I don't know—the largest building you can think of. I loved once, a long time ago, but I had to leave her, and that was the most painful thing I have ever done."

"Why did you do it?"

"I had to," Athon said, showing a rare struggle with his emotions. "It's a long story, and I'll tell you later, but not now. You're in a tough spot. Political issues are preventing you from following your heart."

Athon being in love was inconceivable. For as long as Tam could remember, Athon had always been a guard, and he couldn't think of him as anything else. Tam shook his head in disbelief. "How could that be?"

"Preanth doesn't want you near Indura."

"No, not that," Tam said, annoyed that his question was misunderstood.

"Oh, Contrary to popular belief, I wasn't always perpetually single. I wanted a family."

"What was her name?"

"Dissa."

"That's an odd name," Tam said, and then suddenly he understood. "You met her when you were here?"

Athon nodded. "I told you, it was a long time ago."

The captain and his adventures had been a source of mystery since the revelation that he had been a spy. Tam's curiosity couldn't be contained any longer. "Tell me about it."

Athon looked around. Eyvindir and his soldiers were still nearby. "I this isn't a topic we can safely discuss right now. It isn't that I'm keeping secrets; there are too many prying ears. I just wanted to let you know that I understand, and you aren't alone. Try and forget Indura, and be thankful you didn't get to know her that well." He slapped the young prince on the shoulder reassuringly. "Get some rest. It'll be a long ride, but we'll be home before you know it."

Athon got up and left Tam there to think. The prince was exhausted, and really could use the sleep. It didn't take him long to set up his tent and crawl inside. He brought his pack in the entrance of the small enclosure. The inside of the tent was barely big enough to admit him and his sleeping–roll. He placed the pack so he could access the contents, and carefully opened the cinched closure. He found the kyhdue bundle on the top, and was relieved to find the bird had survived the first leg of the journey. He carefully uncovered Speckle Tip enough for it to feed on the sparse crust of stale bread, and drink from his water flask.

After the bird had eaten, he wrapped it, gently placed it back in the pack, and cinched it closed again. Sleep found him as soon as he laid his head on his arm.

Tam awoke to the light tapping on his tent's exterior. He was stiff and every muscle seemed to scream in the agony reserved for heavy travel, followed by sleeping on hard ground. He crawled out of the shelter into the bright even–sun light. As he left the tent, he was careful to move his pack gently, so as not to injure Speckle Tip. Athon greeted him with a small crust of bread, and some dried meat.

"I couldn't help but notice that you shared a lot of your food with the women," Athon said cheerfully. "I managed to procure some food while we were at the inn, but there wasn't enough for everyone to have a proper meal. This isn't much, but it will have to do until we reach the garrison."

Tam was grateful for the morsel, and ate it hungrily. Breaking camp didn't take long, and soon they had resumed a quick pace to the garrison. After they had ridden for several hours, the Ithilton guards came to a halt.

Eyvindir turned to Athon. "We have gone far enough, and I don't feel the need to escort you further. I know that the king didn't seem like he was terribly grateful for your help, but he really was. Continue to your lands in peace with our eternal thanks."

"Thank you for your assistance, Commander," Athon said, extending his hand. "It was an honor to meet you. I hope the next time we see each other it will be in friendship."

"Let us hope," Eyvindir said, giving him a firm shake. He turned to Tam. "Prince, I was asked to deliver a message from Preanth himself. He commands that you stay away from Ithilton, and find a young maid in your own kingdom."

Tam bit down hard trying not to say anything snide in rebuttal. "I will do my best," he said finally. Eyvindir gave Tam a knowing smile, and led his soldiers galloping toward Ithilton.

"Well," said Xacthos. "I'm glad they're leaving. I don't know about you, but I was getting tired of being babysat."

"Me, too," Tam echoed. "One thing I won't miss is their arrogance."

"I'm sure they're saying the same thing about us," Athon said.

"I can hear Preanth now," Xacthos said, mimicking the king. "Thank the gods *that prince* is gone. I nearly had him as a son–in–law."

"That's going a bit far, don't you think?" Tam spurred Pyta forward.

"Not really," Xacthos said. "You were pretty love–struck. You don't have to be Master Thales to see that."

"Everyone makes such a fuss. I didn't realize that showing interest in a woman was such a crime."

"Only *you* could find the only woman who could start a war by falling in love." Xacthos said, giving Tam a sly wink. "We're all just jealous."

"You're joking, right?" Tam asked skeptically. It wouldn't be the first time that the lieutenant's sense of humor had caught him off guard.

"Xacthos is right, Tam. Not all of us can be the handsome prince that rescues the fair maiden. We just wish we could be you."

They rode at a brisk trot, passing through the rugged narrow terrain that led to their home high in the mountains. Returning to familiar territory brought a welcome feeling to everyone. They spent the time singing familiar songs as they passed over the high mountain road.

It was well after late–sun when the troupe finally spied the garrison. Tam never thought he would be so glad to see the high walls of the fortress. It was good to be home, he thought to himself.

It took nearly an hour to water and put away the exhausted hesturs. Pyta was obviously relieved to be free of the riding tack, and back in his stall. As a treat, Tam gave him some fruit along with his grain. After putting some fresh hay into the stall, Tam went to his room.

His quarters were small, but they were his, and he was happy to be back. He was starving, so he left his bags on the bed, and headed to the dining hall. He ate supper, absconding with some bread to feed Speckle Tip. After picking up a change of clothes, he went to wash off the dust of his long journey.

When Tam finished scrubbing the smell of Pyta from his sore body, he went to his room. He stealthily closed the door, eagerly opened his backpack, and withdrew the bundle containing the kyhdue. Immediately he sensed something wasn't right. The cloth wasn't moving. He removed the wrapping as sweat started to ooze from his forehead. He couldn't have this creature die.

Speckle Tip lay in his hands, and fluttered slightly. It was obvious it barely clung to life. Tam stroked the once brightly colored feathers that appeared duller now. He couldn't believe this was happening. His only link to Indura lay in his hands listless and dying. A knock at the door startled him back into reality. He glanced around, but didn't know what to do with the dying animal. A second knock sent him into a near panic, but there wasn't much sense in hiding anything now.

"Come in," Tam said shakily.

Athon entered the room and instantly froze. "What are you doing with that?"

Tam struggled to find any words that might explain his situation. "It's sick. I think I killed it."

Athon entered and examined the bird. "Where did you get a kyhdue? Did she give you it?" Tam nodded.

Speckle Tip's agonal breathing showed the animal's distress. "Give it to me. There's no sense in allowing it to die." Athon gently took the kyhdue out of Tam's hands. "Follow me!"

They quickly moved through the complex to the watchtower at the southern end of the garrison. Tam had never been in this part of the fortress. They ascended a stairway to small room at the top of the tower. Bursting into the main chamber, they startled a number of kyhdues that fluttered their wings in protest. Athon walked to a door at the far side of the room and knocked loudly.

"Cicero? Cicero, I need your help."

A few moments later, a white, scraggly haired man blearily peered out of the doorway. "Master Athon? What do you want at this hour?" Cicero spoke with a singsong tone that was instantly soothing. He noticed the limp bird in Athon's hands. "What have you done to my bird? Wait, this one isn't mine." He took the creature gently from Athon, and walked toward a table in the far corner. He seemed to be oblivious to Tam's presence.

Cicero was a frail, elderly man with stringy, snow–white hair that looked as if it hadn't been combed in some time. His clothes were obviously slept in, and hung about him in tatters. Wrinkles lined his geriatric face and accentuated the skin that hung from his skeletal frame. Despite his neglected appearance, he had a certain kindly air that permeated the room. Several of the kyhdues left their perches and alighted on his shoulder, peering down at the almost motionless bird in sympathy.

"Did I kill it?" Tam asked, not really wanting to raise his voice above the sounds of the kyhdue's gentle cooing.

"What did you do to him?"

"It was smuggled in a backpack from Ithilton," Athon said.

"They were meant to fly, not travel as baggage." Cicero's soft scolding didn't seem to be directed toward anyone in particular, but pricked Tam's conscience.

"Can you do anything to save it?" Tam asked, certain the bird would die.

"I'm not sure," Cicero replied. "Kyhdues are resilient creatures, but this one's very sick. I'll do my best. Leave it with me, and I'll let you know if it survives."

"It's in your capable hands," Athon said. He turned and roughly grabbed Tam as they left the room. "Come, Tam. You and I have some matters to discuss." They rounded the corner, and he couldn't contain his anger. He threw Tam against the side of the wall, seething with rage. "How dare you! Of all the thoughtless stupid things you have ever done, this tops them all! What were you thinking?" He held up his hand to prevent Tam from answering. "No! You weren't thinking about anyone but yourself! Have you any idea of what you've done?"

Tam had thought he had seen Athon angry before, but even the turn he was late for training wasn't close to the rage he saw now. He doubted that anything he said would pacify the furious captain. Of all the people Tam wished to please, Athon was the most important. He knew he had let him down. It was a crushing blow to Tam's ego. "I'm sorry, Athon," he said, finally.

"Sorry doesn't cover it," Athon snapped. "Not even close! You got this from Indura?"

"Yes," Tam said, swallowing hard trying to hold back the tears beginning to well in his eyes.

"Did it ever occur to you that this was some trick by Preanth to obtain intelligence?"

"Indura—" Tam stopped, rethinking his answer. "I didn't get the impression she wanted her father to know."

"She told you she was going to keep it a secret?"

"Yes."

"You're sure? What did she tell you, exactly?" Athon was calming down remarkably fast.

"She told me that no one could know about it," Tam said. "It was the only way we could correspond without anyone knowing. I'm sorry. I just didn't want to lose her."

"How did she get the kyhdue?"

"She said she raises them as pets."

Athon paused for a moment, and relaxed his grip. "Sorry Tam. I didn't mean to lose my temper, but you've put me in a bad spot, and I don't know what I'm going to do with you." Athon growled. "It's my own fault. If I hadn't made you get close, this never would've happened."

"You didn't say I had to *like* her," Tam said.

"True, but I should have seen that you became too attached." Athon sighed heavily. "Sending secret messages to Ithilton is treason."

Tam felt like he had been punched in the gut. He hadn't considered that writing to Indura could be considered anything other than benign. "I would never betray my kingdom," he protested.

"I'm sure you wouldn't," Athon said, "not knowingly anyway. If Preanth discovered your letters, he would certainly scour them for any intelligence he could. You might give away secrets and not even realize you were doing it."

"So, I never get to hear from her again?" Tam said, disheartened.

"I didn't say that." Athon paused for a moment to consider the possibilities. "We're both tired, and I shouldn't rush to judgment. We need sleep right now. We'll talk about this later." He took Tam by the shoulder, and began walking down the stairs leading back to the dormitories. "I'm sorry I lost my temper, but you got off easy. If it were anyone else, they would be dead."

Tam rubbed his sore shoulder where he had struck the wall. He was bewildered by the rapid change in Athon's demeanor from sheer fury to calm and supportive. It was if someone had snuffed out a candle, but somewhere, an ember still smoldered.

"It's all right," Tam said. "It isn't like I haven't had worse in combat training. I'm sorry for disappointing you."

"We'll talk about this later. I'm really too tired to think right now."

"What about Speckle Tip?" Tam asked.

"What?"

"The kyhdue."

"Let Cicero handle it. If it survives, it will be a while before it's well enough to fly. In the meantime, stay away from the aviary."

Tam nodded, and they walked back to the barracks in silence. Tam felt like a major failure. He had managed to kill his one tie to Indura, and alienate his mentor. His attraction to the princess and his duty to his kingdom had collided. How had he not seen this coming? Had he forgotten all of Master Thales' teachings? Were his actions so unconscionable as to be treasonous?

"Get some sleep," Athon said, when they arrived at their rooms. "I'm going to bed. I'll wake up when I've recovered. I expect you to do the same. Sleep as long as you need, and we'll discuss things later."

Tam entered his room, cleared his bed by carelessly throwing everything on the floor, blew out the lamp, and collapsed in a depressed heap under the covers. Despite his exhaustion, sleep didn't come easy to him. He anxiously tossed and turned, but eventually he succumbed to unsettling dreams.

# Chapter 15

# IDLE TIME

I ndura was sore. Her whole body ached, especially her hips. Her arms were so tired she could barely lift them to brush her disheveled hair. Combat training was more physically demanding than she had assumed. It was her own fault she was in so much pain. She had demanded her father allow her to train in self–defense. The perilous adventure in the mountains had irrefutably demonstrated the need for her to be capable of using a weapon. Preanth had reluctantly acquiesced to her wish, and assigned Glafindr, the captain of the palace guard, the task of teaching her.

Training involved familiarizing herself with the vulnerabilities of the body. She learned the best places to strike with her hands and with a dagger. This lesson had been an intensive session of grappling and throws. Even though they had practiced on the thick mat of the domn, it was bruising when he threw her to the ground. She tried to return the favor several times, but he was bigger and stronger. It was an important, albeit painful, skill to learn. She wished it didn't have to hurt so badly.

Glafindr had assured her that the pain would go away once she had grown more accustomed to the rigors of combat. It was something that she hoped would come sooner rather than later. She had questioned the wisdom of such an endeavor, but had the inescapable feeling that it would be useful eventually.

Indura painfully limped up to the aviary that housed the kyhdues raised in the palace. It was a large, open space with hovels built to house the birds. She made the visit twice a turn on the guise of searching for a clutch of eggs to raise as pets. Fortunately, one hen had a small clutch of four eggs. She convinced Rugga, the palace bird master, that she was interested in the beautiful creatures. She knew that he had taken notice of Speckle Tip's absence, but didn't think he had connected the disappearance with her. She would have to be careful when she retrieved messages carried by her secret messenger, but she figured that Rugga's dull wit would hinder his ability to catch her in the act.

Rugga was a simple–minded man with thin, brown hair that draped over his head like a cap. In addition to his mental deficiencies, he was nearsighted. He had infinite patience, but wasn't smart about anything other than his birds. He loved all the kyhdues in the aviary, and knew each one by name, caring for them as if they were his own children.

As Indura entered the room, the birds fluttered their wings in nervous perturbation. Rugga looked up and squinted at the blurry figure. "Who's that?"

"It's me, the princess. I've come to check on my eggs." She looked around the room, scanning the birds for Speckle Tip. She had chosen him because his wings made him easy to spot, but she didn't see him anywhere.

"Ah, pretty princess," Rugga said, kindly stroking a kyhdue. "New fluffies not ready. Not yet."

"I hope it won't be too long," she said pouting her lips. "I'd like to see them now."

"They ain't no rush," he said, cooing at the kyhdue in his hand. "Fluffies need time to grow. When eggs broke, then they ready. You need pay—shunt. Not, now, now, now."

"I can't help it," she said playfully.

"Can't hurry," he said, scratching his head. "They's come when they's ready. Least twenty turns."

"I know, but I like seeing them when they first come out. They are so cute and soft with their fluffy white feathers. They're like a puff seed with little legs, and cute little eyes." Indura wasn't exaggerating her affection for the newborn chicks. She had always enjoyed seeing the new hatchlings. She was even allowed to pet them when she was old enough to know how delicate they were. Still, her primary focus was locating Speckle Tip before anyone noticed that he had returned bearing a message tied to his leg. The prospect of that happening grew ever greater the longer the bird was gone. Why hadn't Tam sent her anything?

It had occurred to her that either Tam had the misfortune of being discovered, or that Speckle Tip had died during the journey. She knew it was a difficult proposition to smuggle a delicate bird back to the garrison without either scenario happening, but she had to hope. She moved toward the nest containing the eggs.

"What you doing?" Rugga demanded.

"I was going to check the nest," she replied.

"No! No!" he said firmly. "Leave fluffies 'lone. Pretty princess not touch. Fluffies still in eggs. Don't see fluffies still in eggs."

"Fine," she huffed. "I'll be back later to check on them." She turned and left the room, troubled by Speckle Tip's absence. As she left, she could hear Rugga muttering something about her not touching his fluffies. She wandered the corridors of the palace, preoccupied by the various scenarios that would prohibit Tam from sending the kyhdue. She tried to reassure herself that there must be a reasonable explanation for the delay, but she kept coming back to the same conclusion. Suddenly, another thought popped into her mind. He doesn't like me.

It had been five turns since they had returned to the garrison, and Athon hadn't spoken to Tam. When asked at the start of every wake–watch, Athon just shook his head. It was possible that the captain had written the king for advice on the matter, and that thought made Tam nervous. Any punishment would be severe, but that wasn't what caused him to lose sleep. It was the unknown possibilities that littered his imagination. He could handle any castigation Athon or his father could mete out, but not knowing his fate was tortuous.

Tam had been occupied with the usual duties. His first turn back, he had to recount his tale to Brixos, and the other junior guards in his squad. They grilled him endlessly on the princess, but it seemed that the entire garrison had heard about what happened with Indura. He told them about everything except Indura coming to his room and Speckle Tip.

As far as the kyhdue was concerned, there had been any word from Cicero. Tam worried that the bird had died, but he doubted Athon would keep that information from him. It just added to his anxiety. He didn't want it to perish.

The wake–watch was eating breakfast as Tam entered the room. He had struggled waking up because his sleep had become so erratic. Dark circles ringed his droopy eyes. He found Brixos and sat down next to him.

"You look awful," Brixos said. "Did you get any sleep?"

"A little," Tam said with a raspy voice. "I kept waking up."

"Some atole will help, but you need rest. Is it because of the princess?"

"Yes, and no," Tam said evasively. "I just have a lot on my mind right now."

Brixos eyed him suspiciously. "If it'd been me, I'd have a tough time too. Try not to dwell on it, and you'll get over her."

"You're a lot of help," Tam said sarcastically. One of the cooks brought out a full plate of food for him as well as a full mug of atole. He drank deeply of the sweet brown liquid, and began to devour the plate of meat and eggs.

As Tam was finishing his meal, Athon came and tapped him on the shoulder. "Highness, I need to speak with you."

Tam swallowed hard. His anxiety spiked. It was the talk he had nervously expected for five turns, and dreaded. His mind began to race with the various scenarios he had been contemplating since Speckle Tip was discovered. None of them was appealing.

"Are you in trouble?" Brixos whispered.

"You could say that."

"Tell me about it later."

"No, he won't," Athon said definitively. "Let's go."

Tam followed Athon to the commander's office. Every step took him closer to his fate. The fact that he walked toward his doom was not in question. What remained to be seen was the extent of his punishment.

The commander's office was located on the upper levels of the tower of the eastern wall. Like most rooms in the garrison, it was small and sparsely furnished. A cluttered desk and two chairs were all that occupied its space, but it had a large window overlooking the fortress and the main road. It was the perfect place for the officer in charge to survey the surrounding countryside.

"Please sit down, Tam," Athon said, gesturing to the chair directly opposite his behind the desk. Tam was silent as he took his seat. "I know you've been expecting this talk, and I apologize for the delay. I wanted to make certain that my decision wasn't a rash one and I wanted to see if your souvenir survived."

"Souvenir?" Tam looked puzzled, and suddenly he realized to what Athon was referring. "Ah, the kyhdue. How is Speckle Tip? Please, tell me I didn't kill it."

"Surprisingly, the bird survived despite your best efforts to the contrary. I think that will be the last time you try and smuggle a living thing in your backpack."

"I'm glad he's all right," Tam said with a nervous sigh. "Tell Master Cicero that I appreciate him saving his life."

"You can do that yourself when you see him," Athon said. "I suspect that you will be seeing quite a bit of them both."

"You mean I'm not in trouble?" Suddenly, it felt as though a large weight had been lifted off Tam's shoulders.

"No, I didn't say that." Athon's denial deflated the prince's spirit as quickly as it raised it. "I'm still rather angry at you, but not for the reasons you might think. I'm disappointed that you didn't come to me with this matter before we left Ithilton. The fact that you concealed it from me tells me that you don't trust me. I told you when you came to the garrison that you could always come to me with any problem. You didn't do that when you should have."

"I'm sorry—" Tam started offering an explanation, but Athon cut him off.

"I'm not done talking yet. You can speak when I'm finished. You need to understand the position you've placed me in. If it were any other man in my command, they would be dead." Tam gulped. "I want you to understand how serious this is. I have sworn Cicero to secrecy, and I'm certain you haven't said anything about it."

"I haven't," Tam said with certainty.

"I know. Keep it that way. You can't mention anything to Brixos understand? You have to make sure no one knows about the letters."

"You're going to let me write to Indura?" Tam was suddenly excited. The thought that he might be able to communicate with the princess swept away all the fear and self–loathing he'd been feeling.

"I asked if you understood." Athon's impatience with the prince was palpable.

"Yes, I promise I won't tell a soul."

"Based on your recent history, you have me wondering if I can trust you." Athon said sternly.

"I'm sorry, I should have told you, but I promised Indura I wouldn't."

"You should be sorry. It's noble of you to keep your word, but your fealty is to Campsit, not the princess. Never forget that fact. This infatuation is never to conflict with your duty to this kingdom again. Is that clear? I'm allowing you to correspond only under the strictest of guidelines."

"What kind of guidelines?"

"Let's start by agreeing that this secret stays between you, Cicero, and me. You can't even tell the princess that I know about the plan. You also need to share the contents of the letters with me."

"What?" Tam was incredulous. Any letters would undoubtedly be very personal, and he wanted to keep that private. He felt embarrassed to share intimate details with the captain.

"I'm giving you some privacy by not insisting that I read every letter sent or received. Discussing the contents of each correspondence will suffice."

"Why bother writing in the first place if I'm sharing my feelings with both of you?"

"I've thought about that myself these past few turns. I, for one, think exploring this relationship is not a bad idea. It's obvious that you're mutually attracted. You are getting to the age where you would start searching for a mate, and she is a logical choice. Normally, she wouldn't present any problems, but she's Preanth's daughter. Some might see that as an insurmountable problem, but I think it could be in our favor. She can influence him and, if you develop a relationship, we might even find and ally."

"How?"

"If you married Indura, Preanth could never invade. He would never attack the only heir to his throne."

Tam had never considered this scenario. Marriage to Indura was something that hadn't even crossed his mind. Betrothal actually frightened him. What shocked him more was that Athon had apparently given the subject a great deal of thought. Tam shook his head in a mixture of disgust and bewilderment. All he wanted to do was explore his attraction. Now this degenerated into a full–blown quagmire. "Why do you have to know what I say?"

"I need to make sure you aren't providing Ithilton with intelligence. I'm assuming that the princess acted alone, and this isn't one of Preanth's tricks. Still, you can never be certain that they won't be intercepted. Never be specific as to what you are doing, or use names of people or places. You might discuss the weather, but I would limit correspondence to your feelings." Athon thought for a moment. "Speaking of emotions, never use the word love in your letters. If you learned anything about Preanth, it's that he has his own ideas about who can court his daughter."

"Fine, I won't use the word love, any other provisos?" Tam was curious to learn if this deal could be any more restrictive.

"Just one," Athon said. "Trust is generally something you earn. I'm not sure I can fully trust you yet, but I want you to know you can trust me. I want you to tell me everything without being embarrassed or worrying about what I will think. I won't judge or belittle you in any way. In this instance, I want you to act like I'm your friend. You'll feel the need to discuss this with someone, but I'm the only one who you can talk to about this, so take advantage of that."

This was a lot for Tam to consider. He knew that he had to disclose the contents of the letters, but it could have been worse. Despite the constraints, it was great to know that he could hear from Indura. He could hardly wait to tie the first letter to Speckle Tip's leg and begin the correspondence. "When can I start?"

"The kyhdue is recovering. I'm not sure when it will be well enough to fly great distances. You can check with Cicero after we're done."

"There's more?" Tam wondered when this lecture would be over.

Athon shook his head. "Not really. When you get finished talking to Cicero, take Pyta and head to the upper pasture. There are some uhts that you need to herd."

"You want me to what?" Tam didn't think it was possible for things to get worse, but they had. Herding the smelly beasts was the last duty he wanted.

"Linus told me he needed someone. One of his wranglers is in the infirmary, and won't be well for a few turns. You aren't above helping a fellow guard, are you?"

"No," Tam said meekly.

"Good," Athon said. "Find out how long it will be before your kyhdue is ready to fly back to Ithilton, and that will be how long you need to spend helping Linus in the upper pasture. I'll check with Cicero myself, so you don't have to report to me. Pack your bags for a trip, because you'll be staying up there."

"You really know how to be a killjoy, Athon," Tam grumbled.

"I try," he quipped. "You're wasting time."

Tam turned dejectedly and shuffled off toward the aviary. The thrill of being allowed to write the princess was tempered by the restrictions. It might not be too bad, he thought to himself. Maybe it will only be a turn or two before Speckle Tip was well enough to fly.

Cicero tended his birds in his perpetual cheery mood, and greeted Tam in his singsong voice. He was informed that it would be at least ten turns before the kyhdue would be well enough to fly, and that his progress had been remarkable.

Speckle Tip was on the ledge cooing softly and looking spry. He looked like he could fly now, but Cicero assured Tam that it was still recovering.

The revelation that he would be spending the next ten turns herding uhts sucked all the remaining joy right out of Tam. It took nearly two hours for him to get ready. He was deliberately delaying as a silent protest of being sent on this prolonged assignment away from the comforts of the garrison. This was the first time he ever dreaded a task. He was always busy doing something, but herding sounded painfully dull and as unglamorous as watching snails crawl.

In his heart, Tam knew this was no different from any other assignment, and it wasn't beneath him. He would accept it eventually, but right now, he felt the same as when he forced into the guard.

It was different this time. The spoiled boy that had been almost forcibly dragged to the garrison was gone. He was leaving of his own freewill this time, even if it was begrudgingly.

It wasn't as if Tam had anything better to do while he waited for Speckle Tip to recuperate. He just didn't want to spend it tending some dumb animals.

Being constantly out in the elements, dealing with the inevitable thunderstorm in the second half of the turn didn't appeal to him. Nevertheless, uhts were an important part of the kingdom.

Uhts were, in Tam's opinion, creatures that smelled bad and spit all the time. They stood roughly twice the height of a man due to their long necks. Their bodies were smaller than a hestur, but looked larger when they had a full season's coat.

Uht wool was a vital commodity, and used throughout the kingdom to make clothing. It was an ideal material because it was soft and breathable, but also water resistant. The biggest advantage was that when fabrics got wet, they still kept the body warm.

Because of the dense forests of the valley floor, the high mountain pastures better suited for raising the animals. The guards tended the herds to safeguard them from tragues, and saw to the animal's every need. They milked the cows, harvested the wool, selected the animals to be used for food, tended to the sick, and helped birth the calves. What they didn't use was sent throughout Campsit. The herds produced enough wool to keep the entire kingdom amply clothed. Like the scouts and miners, there were guards who spent their entire lives as wranglers. Tam didn't know how anyone could choose that as a lifestyle, but men did.

Tam spent the next ten turns in almost constant misery. The weather was terrible. Every waking moment was spent in a cold drizzly rain that marked the high mountain's inhospitable climate.

He found most of the guards to be congenial, but Linus wasn't. He was scraggly, unkempt, and generally short tempered with Tam. He was also nearly impossible to understand. He had a particular way of talking in a kind of drawl that seemed to be of his own making. He would drop any part of a word that seemed too taxing, so his sentences were often a string of nearly incoherent syllables. If you listened close enough, and filled in the gaps, you might understand about half of what was being said. One of the other wranglers commented that Tam would get used to it after a while.

Tam's only respite was when he was alone in his tent. He was thankful he had brought a writing stick and some paper with him. Before bed, he would put his thoughts and feelings on parchment, so he could write a coherent letter.

During his watch, nearly every minute was spent tending the temperamental and skittish uhts. He was instructed in nearly every aspect of herding from cutting, or singling out one animal from the herd, to milking. The latter was more difficult than initially advertised. The first day he tried, he managed to have his foot stepped on, and was grazed by a kick. Linus told him if the ornery beast actually connected, it might have proved fatal, and that he was simply lucky it hadn't.

The whole experience only reinforced Tam's perception that uhts were irascible ugly beasts that were only good for wool and food. What Linus and the other wranglers saw in them the gods only knew. By the ninth turn, he would have gnawed his own limbs off to get back to the garrison. He kept his trepidation in check, and did his best to conceal his true feelings. The sick wrangler he had replaced had been back in action for nearly four turns, but he maintained his determination to remain for his entire commitment.

Tam's last turn at the pasture was interminable. Time seemed to stand still. It rained harder, the uhts were more difficult, and Linus was in a particularly foul mood. The whole scenario brewed the perfect cocktail for misery.

Midway through the turn, Tam brought on a tirade from Linus when he had difficulty cutting a particularly stubborn uht from the herd. He thought it would have been worse if he understood half of what was being said.

Eventually, all things must end, and his work in the high pastures was over. Tam was cold, wet, and hungry, but he didn't want to take his meal there. He bid them farewell, and galloped all the way to the garrison. It was well after the wake–watch had gone to bed when he finally entered the stables, and put Pyta in his warm, dry stall.

Tam was greeted by the deserted halls of the barracks. He took a long, soothing, hot bath, and then wandered into the deserted kitchen to scrounge for leftover scraps of bread before retiring to his own quarters. Although he was exhausted, he wasn't ready to succumb to sleep just yet. He had written pages and pages while in the field, and it would be impossible to attach all of them to Speckle Tip's leg. In the dim lamplight, he began to distill his writing onto a small strip of parchment in anticipation of strapping it to the kyhdue's leg at even–sun.

*Chapter 16*

# GUILT

S unlight began to stream into the room as Tova opened the drapes. Indura winced and buried her face in the pillow. She wasn't interested in waking up. She had been dreaming about Tam, and even though she hadn't heard from him, she still longed to be in his arms. It had been almost a ceanor since she had secretly given him Speckle Tip, and her hope had nearly evaporated. It seemed that the only way she would ever see him was in the velvet recesses of her dreams. She gave a piteous groan in protest of the brilliant even–sun light now filling the room.

"Oh stop complaining, Highness," Tova said, continuing to open the drapes. "It was your impulsive decision for superfluous combat training which obliges me to rouse you so early. I do not understand why you have to punish yourself so brutally."

"Punish myself for what?"

"Why, the deaths of those soldiers, of course," Tova said succinctly.

"You think I blame myself?" Indura was incredulous, but knew the assessment was eerily accurate. Tova knew her far better than she felt comfortable.

Tova sat down next to her. "Oh little one, you might fool everyone else, but you cannot fool me. I know you better than you know yourself, because I have been responsible for you since you were an infant. I saw it on your face the instant you returned to the palace, as easily as I see your infatuation with the prince."

"Why didn't you say anything?" Indura was bewildered by her mistress. She wasn't sure if it was the lethargy, or if her brain refusing to acknowledge the obvious. For some reason, Tova was being more vocal than she had ever been.

"It is not my place to question your motives."

"Why are you bringing it up now?"

"Because, it pains me to see you torture yourself over things you have no control. Every turn since the prince left, you have been spending more and more time training with Captain Glafindr being thrown, kicked, and punched."

"What's the problem with that?"

"Apart from being very unladylike, it is physically leaving its mark on you. You have cuts and bruises that might be fine for a servant, but are not in keeping with a woman of your stature. I know the captain has been good about not leaving marks visible to the casual observer, but if you continue on this destructive course, I fear that you will cause great embarrassment to your father. He may not be able to say no to any of your requests, but I have no such reservation."

"I need that training," Indura protested.

"For what? do you plan to fight in some war? There is no purpose for you taking up arms."

Why was Tova making such a big deal out of this? "I just want to know how to defend myself."

"When would you ever need to do that when you have a palace full of soldiers ready to fight and die for you?"

Frustration and anger boiled deep inside her. She nearly exploded with the fury of a cornered beast, bolting upright to face her accuser. "I nearly died because I counted solely on soldiers for my defense! If it hadn't been for the prince, I would have met their fate! When it was most critical, I could only stand helpless and frightened! I will never be that powerless again!"

Tova has always been the maternal figure for Indura. Her mother, Elina, had delegated the responsibility to the mistress shortly after the princess was born. It was Tova's duty to see to Indura's wellbeing, and teach the difficult lessons inherent with a privileged and sheltered life.

Tova placed an understanding hand on her shoulder. "Shhh, you need to calm down, Highness. I am sorry I upset you, but it is my duty to protect you, even from yourself. I make certain you maintain the decorum of a princess, and this training is spiraling out of control. I know you feel responsible for what happened to soldiers, but you must remember that it was beyond you. No matter how hard you beat yourself, you cannot change what happened."

"I'm not beating myself," Indura pouted, as her eyes began to mist. She knew there was truth in what Tova was saying, but she refused to admit it.

"I wish you would stop deceiving yourself. Accept what happened and learn from it. It is sad those men died." Tova paused for a moment. "They died for you, but they did not die *because* of you."

"How can you say that?" Tears flowed down Indura's face. How could it not be her fault? They were in the forest because of her. It *had* to be her fault, didn't it? She couldn't bring herself to think contrary to that opinion. It only made sense if it was her fault. In the back of her mind, something from her black terror dream stirred. Her breathing quickened. She could not repress the memory invading her waking thoughts. Her mistress continued to speak, but she could only catch a little of what was said, as if her voice carried from afar off. The words swirled about her, but only one sentence coalesced enough to penetrate her trance.

"You did not kill them, the tragues did."

The words were not enough to stop the onslaught of terrifying memories that deluged her. Indura shut her eyes tightly in an effort to evict the horror that viscerally filled her mind. The vivid images of the beasts ripping and tearing through her entourage were as real now as they had ever been.

Even though it had been nearly a ceanor since the attack, she could still feel the breath of the beast on her neck, and see the fearsome yellow eyes sizing her up for the kill. Her heart raced, and she gulped air as if her next breath might never come. Sweat began pouring from her brow as the screams of dying men and hesturs mingled with the deafening roar of the attacking tragues. It was only a memory, but it ripped through the conversation and muted all sound. Her fingernails nearly drew blood as they clawed desperately at her ears in a vain attempt to block the shrill cacophony. Instinctively, she curled up into a ball in an attempt to make herself disappear. If she were small enough, the tragues wouldn't see her and she would be spared. She couldn't tear her mind away. She was drowning in the bloody vision.

Tova was worried. She had never seen this kind of behavior from Indura. It looked as if the princess were under attack from an invisible foe that was tearing at her flesh from every direction. It was a painfully piteous thing to witness. Perhaps she had given too much. This sort of thing was certainly to be expected, but she never thought it would be so intense.

When Indura was very young, and awoke from a bad dream, Tova sang her back to sleep. Instinctively, she enveloped the blubbering mass of princess in her arms and stoked her hair. The demons that plagued the sweet young woman could not be allowed to win. It was her duty to protect Indura and focus her to discipline her mind. It was imperative that she keep the princess grounded, for the sake of all Arabella.

She kissed the princess' tousled auburn mane as she began to sing a soothing old lullaby. It was how she always calmed her.

By the end of the song, Indura had regained her composure. She looked at her mistress with tear–swollen eyes. How many times had that singing comforted her? She threw her arms around her neck and sobbed. "Thank you, Tova. I had forgotten how much I need you."

"Dear child," Tova said tenderly. "I am sorry I put you through that. I was only trying to help. I did not mean to hurt you."

"It's all right," Indura said. "I never told you what happened, or how it haunts me. I don't want to go over details, but it is a terror. I still hear the screams of the men." Her voice began to crack. "I still see the—"

"Stop," Tova said, pressing a finger to Indura's lips. "I think you have had enough for now. I do not wish you to relive the pain, and we shall never speak of it in such terms again. I now fully understand your reasoning. Do what you feel you must, but please stop torturing yourself."

Indura smiled. "You have a deal."

"Hurry and dress, or you will be late for training. Your bath will have to wait until you are finished, but splash some water on your face and brush your hair first. You must be presentable."

Indura gave Tova a grateful hug and retreated to the washroom to get ready for the even–sun training session. After changing into a sparring robe, she ran to the domn. On her way there, she thought about what Tova had said. It was uncanny how her mistress could see through her carefully crafted façade and arrive at the core of the issue. The deaths of the soldiers had weighed heavily on her, and she couldn't help but feel personally responsible. It was her desire for adventure that put them in mortal danger. More than once, she had wished that Tam hadn't saved her. She wished she had died with them. If she had, she wouldn't have to deal with the constant pain of guilt and regret, but Tova said that it wasn't her fault. How she wished she believed that.

The domn stood on the far side of the palace grounds near the barracks. Its purpose was to provide a training facility where the various forms of armed and unarmed combat could be practiced in a controlled environment with a second floor gallery, so people could watch. The sparring floor was a thick woven mat that cushioned the blows that came from being thrown to the ground. Indura always took her lessons in private with Captain Glafindr. This turn was no exception; he stood at the far end of the mat as she entered.

"Good turn to you, Highness," Glafindr said, turning to the princess.

Indura was late, but he didn't mention it. "Good turn to you, Captain," she replied. She noticed he carried two wooden swords in his hands. "I take it we will be learning something new?"

Glafindr had her put on protective leather armor and she began the basic instructions on how to use a sword. After several strikes of the wooden weapon, she was thankful for the protection the armor afforded her. Even with the padded suit she was wearing, several of Glafindr's hits were hard enough to cause pain. She imagined that once she removed the protective armor she would be covered in new bruises.

After the brutal but informative lesson, Indura retreated to her quarters and drew a warm, relaxing bath. She took the sponge and scrubbed hard. It was as though all the guilt and self–loathing had risen to the surface during the sparring session, and left a thick grimy film that coated her skin. It was only after significant scrubbing that she felt clean. Mai came in and helped her dress.

Liberated of the guilt she had felt before, she accepted that no matter what her part might have been in the trague attack, she was not responsible for the deaths of the soldiers. Now a great weight had been lifted off her shoulders, and she was like her old self.

As the two young women left the royal quarters, Indura decided that she would take a detour before heading to the Grand Hall. She usually made her way to the aviary in secret, but this time she took Mai. She had little confidence that Tam would ever return Speckle Tip, and that the kyhdue hadn't survived the journey.

Mai was also in a good mood, and it felt as if nothing terrible had ever happened. They laughed and commiserated all the way to the aviary. "Why are we stopping here?"

"There are some new kyhdue chicks," Indura said. "You know how cute they are. I just wanted to hold them for a little while. I've been so melancholy lately, and I think I've finally found my happiness again."

"You do seem in good spirits and those little puff balls can only make you happier."

The two giggling girls burst into the large room of the nesting aviary, causing several of the birds to take flight to higher perches. Rugga stood near one of the windows with his back to the door. He looked up with his usual kindly smile, and turned to greet the princess. His arms were wrapped around a cooing kyhdue. "Pretty princess has friend this time."

"Yes, Rugga, I do." Indura giggled.

"Have surprise." An exciting chill started at the base of Indura's neck. He motioned to her to join him. "My pretty came back. He disappeared, but now he back. Look at my pretty. Me think he happy to see you."

Indura's attention was drawn to the iridescent bird nestled in Rugga's arms. Mai shot her a look of confusion, but Indura's face spoke louder than any words. Rugga gently took the bird and handed it to Indura, and that is when she saw the telltale speckles on the tips of its wings. She gingerly cradled it in her hand. It was the most beautiful sight she had seen in almost a ceanor. Suddenly, she became aware of a slight irregularity around one of the kyhdue's legs. She looked panic stricken toward the bird master. He must be smarter than she assumed. Did he know her secret? At the very least, she couldn't hide it from Mai now.

Rugga smiled. "You read letter now?"

# Chapter 17

# LETTERS

*My Dearest,*

*I'm sorry I haven't written sooner, but Speckle Tip almost died. I hope you are well. Life hasn't been the same since we parted. I miss your company, and I'm lonely without you. I never got the chance to say goodbye, but hope to hear from you again soon.*

*Yours truly, T*

The note was smaller than Indura had expected, but she didn't see how it could be any larger. The lettering was small, but neat and legible. Written in lead, the prose took up both sides of the tightly curled paper. She read the words repeatedly before she became keenly aware of the two servants looking at her as if expecting some form of answer to questions she knew she could no longer avoid. She sighed and looked into the bird master's anxious eyes. "Rugga, you're my friend right?"

"You're my pretty princess friend." Rugga said, smiling broadly.

"Friends keep each other's secrets," Indura said, caressing his shoulder. "Speckle Tip is our secret. You can't tell anyone. You won't will you?"

The bird master nodded. "I'm good at secrets. Won't tell anyone, ever."

"Not even my father?"

Rugga looked fearful at the mention of the king, but eventually shook his head. "No, won't tell king. Just us secret. I no tell anyone."

The princess smiled at this kind man she had always considered a friend. Inside she felt a slight twinge of guilt for taking advantage of his simple nature, but she had to do it this time. She threw her arms around him in an enthusiastic hug, and gave him a light kiss on the cheek. "Thank you, Rugga. I knew you were my friend."

Rugga blushed. "Never say no to pretty princess friend. I like my friend. Never tell her secret."

Indura blushed and looked over at her handmaiden. Mai looked obviously hurt by the revelation that her princess would keep any secret from her. Indura felt a knot forming in the pit of her stomach. It was a pang of regret. She should have known that this was something that would eventually come out. As awkward as it was, it was better here and now rather than later. "I'm sorry I didn't tell you about it sooner, Mai. I wanted to tell you, but I could never find the right moment. I never know when Tova is about, and she would go straight to my father if she knew. I hope you understand, and that you can find it in your heart to forgive me."

Mai stared back at her with love and understanding in her brown eyes. "I knew something was troubling you. I didn't know it would be so scandalously rash. Your father would go crazy if he found out, and it would be a disaster for everyone, but you. The king wouldn't dare punish you, but he would have no trouble locking us all up and throwing away the key. Come here alone from now on. I would ask you not share the contents of the letters with me, but I'm afraid my own curiosity is far too great. We have to be careful though, or Tova will know."

"Then we'll make sure she doesn't." Indura was glad Mai knew her secret. It would have been more difficult to keep it without her. She rolled the message back into a tight cylinder, and tucked it into the bodice of her dress. She thanked Rugga again for everything, and the girls ducked into the hallway. They made their way through the palace to the west garden. This one had a fountain in the center of a small maze. Indura knew it would be difficult for eavesdroppers to overhear the conversation. Once they were seated at the fountain's edge, she took out the note and handed it discretely to Mai.

Mai read the note twice and rolled it back up, handing it back as if it were a note between friends trying to cheat on a test in school. "He's very sweet," she said in a low voice, so Indura could just barely hear.

"He does have a way with few words," Indura said. She returned the note to its hiding place in her bodice.

Indura and Mai both knew this was breaking protocol. Traditionally, when a nobleman wished to court the princess he entreated the king privately for permission. If a man was of sufficient wealth and social stature, and the king was impressed, he would formally introduce the two in court. It would be up to the suitor to gain the princess' favor. If the man was talented enough to woo the princess, he could then approach the king to ask for her hand in marriage.

Indura had never been formally introduced to any suitor. It wasn't that noblemen hadn't tried to curry Preanth's favor, they had, but he had denied them all. The king had realized long ago that the princess could fetch a high price, and he was saving her for a prince or king of surrounding realms. Campsit was not considered a suitable kingdom. She knew her father disapproved of Tam, but she didn't care. She was in love, and that was all that really mattered.

Mai looked hard at the princess. "Highness, are you sure that you wish to pursue this relationship? Is it really worth the intrigue to have a few paltry sentences from a man you will never see again?"

Indura's became very solemn. "Yes, it's worth it. I know you find it difficult to understand, but I really do love him. As far as never seeing him again, I don't believe it's our destiny to be apart."

"You plan on meeting him?" Mai said, astounded by her boldness.

"Nothing planned, just a feeling. I know I will see him again. I'm just not sure when it will happen."

"Fair enough," Mai said with a sympathetic nod. "So when will you write him?"

"Soon, I don't know what I'm going to say yet, but I'll think of something." Indura saw movement through the corner of her eye. A gardener had started trimming the hedge on the other side of the maze. She looked at Mai. "We should leave." She motioned in the direction of the intruding servant. "There are too many ears here."

It was a long way to fall. The north side of the garrison wall was built on the edge of the cliffs. It was nearly a straight drop from the top of the northern ramparts to the base of the mountain thousands of feet below. Tam was never particularly fond of heights, so he tended to avoid this part of the garrison. It gave him the willies to be on this section of wall. Two things brought him here, the aviary, and the view. From this vantage point, he could see the kingdom of Ithilton far in the distance, and just barely make out the towers of the palace. It was where Indura was, and where he longed to go.

Since he had returned from his stint as an uht herder, he had made coming here part of his after watch routine. He would stop by the aviary to see Speckle Tip. When he received a note he would walk out onto the parapet, look out toward Ithilton, and think of his beautiful Indura as he read her note.

It had been nearly three ceanors, almost an entire season, since Speckle Tip flew toward the distant city with the first note. Each one brought Tam closer to Indura, and each was precious to him. The worst part of the correspondence was reporting the contents of the letters to Athon. It was difficult to relay her affectionate prose to his captain, but it was necessary to continue his relationship. A small price to pay, he mused.

Tam watched several eryrs as they floated on the air currents near the cliffs. It occurred to him that poor Speckle Tip had to navigate through their hunting territory on the journey to the far off palace. He suddenly realized that it was possible that the much smaller kyhdue could easily be seen as lunch for the much larger predator. It was lucky the tiny bird was able to run the deadly gauntlet, and he got any messages at all.

He turned his attention to the strip of paper in his hand. It was much thicker than usual. Indura's writing was incredibly neat and flowing. His own notes seemed crude by comparison. He didn't care. Each note spoke of her love, and how she longed to be in the warm confines of his strong arms. This one was different.

It was Indura's writing, but what it said was unexpected. A chill ran down Tam's spine, and made him shiver unconsciously. He read the note again, but still couldn't believe his eyes.

*Dearest Tam,*

*Each time I see Speckle Tip, I am filled with excitement, but I fear that someone will discover our exchange. It has become difficult to avoid detection.*

*It has been so long since I have seen you, and felt your hand in mine. I need to see you again. I found a lake near our two lands. I drew a map on the back of this note. I will be waiting for you on the north shore at late–sun this coming mid–ceanors turn. Come alone.*

*Love, I.*

Tam shook his head as if to remove a blur in his vision. He stood in stunned disbelief at the paper, turning it over and over. Surely, she must not be proposing to meet in the wilderness—alone. That would involve him finding an excuse to leave his duties for at least a two full turns to make the journey there and back. Was it worth it to see the princess again? Don't be silly, he thought to himself, of course it was worth it. He longed to be near her again. It was one thing to have her notes, but quite another to hold her warm, soft hands. The thought that he might see her face again was exciting.

There were problems Tam had to solve for her plan to work. The immediate dilemma was what he was going to tell Athon. He didn't like the idea of deliberately withholding information from his captain, but he didn't see how he could tell him the real contents of the letter. There was no way that Athon would ever let him go off on his own for some rendezvous, no matter how much he begged. No, this would have to be something he kept secret.

When he was small, Tam told a lie about sneaking a taste of food from the royal kitchen. His father was very harsh, or so he thought at the time, and punished him with a severe spanking. It was the first and last time he ever lied.

His greatest fear was not punishment, but telling a convincing half–truth. The more Tam thought about what he was going to say, the more he convinced himself that he wasn't actually lying if he just omitted the content of the last half of Indura's letter. What Athon didn't know wouldn't hurt him.

He carefully rolled up the letter and tucked it securely into the top of his boot. He looked back toward Ithilton, and cemented his plan into his mind. Mid–ceanor was only three turns away, and he needed to prepare mentally and physically for the journey. He would need to secure provisions, and make sure Athon approved his request to go on a hunting trip alone. He turned and headed to Athon's room.

On the way to see the captain, Tam mentally rehearsed his report. He tried to think of every possible question he might encounter, and be ready for a plausible response.

His mind tried to grasp all the probable outcomes. What if Athon found out? "I'd be in real trouble," Tam muttered aloud as he found himself in front of the door to the captain's quarters. He was nervous as he quietly rapped on the smooth wood planks. He heard the words "come in", and quietly entered the small room.

Athon was in his sleeping gown, a loose fitting shirt that draped past his knees. "You're late, Tam. You have difficulty finding my room?"

"No, sir," Tam said quickly. "I just admired the view from the north wall a little longer than usual."

"It *is* rather spectacular," Athon confessed. "Did you get a note from the princess?"

"Yes," Tam took a deep breath before starting. "She said she was grateful for my letters, but she is finding it increasingly difficult to avoid getting caught. Personally, I'm amazed she hasn't."

"I'm sure that someone knows by now. I would find it difficult to believe that the palace bird master hasn't noticed that kyhdue coming and going. Something tells me that he's either telling the king, or he's in on it with her, but I digress. Continue, what else did she say?"

"She says she misses me, and that she cares for me a great deal. That is really all there is. It was a shorter note than usual."

"I suspect there will be more in the next one."

"She probably kept it small to keep it secret. I wouldn't be surprised if I didn't hear from her in a few turns. It may be more difficult for her to evade detection with the high frequency of our notes."

"You two have been writing enough for almost anyone to take notice of your patterns. I've noticed you have developed a routine that rouses suspicion."

"Has anyone noticed me?" Tam asked.

"One or two concerned guards have approached me. I don't know about Xacthos, but I wouldn't be surprised if someone had come to him. You really must be more careful, Tam. You need to shake up your routine. Don't take the same route, and for the love of Ceanor, pick different times. Don't be so predictable. Haven't I taught you anything?"

Tam blushed. He had forgotten that not everyone at the garrison knew what he was doing. He was lucky that Athon was here to cover his tracks. "Sorry. I wasn't really thinking. I'll try to be more careful in the future."

"See that you are. I can't keep inquisitive minds pacified forever. Someone will be bound to find out if you keep this up, and then we will really have some explaining to do. I'd rather keep this just between the three who know right now. Maybe you should take a rest for a couple of turns to break the cycle."

This was what Tam had been looking for. It was the perfect excuse to make himself scarce. "I have been meaning to go camping. I haven't been for some time, an entire season in fact, and I would love to go out and hunt some game for a change."

"It has been a while, hasn't it? I think that would be a great idea. When do you want to go?"

Tam thought quickly. He couldn't go directly to the meeting site. It would arouse too much suspicion if the scouts watching the road saw him. He would have to go cross–country to avoid detection, and that would add time to the overall trip. If he left in one turn, it would be enough time, but he would have to hurry. "Not next watch but the following one, if that's all right?"

"That would be fine. Who are you planning on taking with you?"

"I thought I might go alone."

Athon raised an eyebrow. "Alone? You aren't serious."

Tam thought quickly. His mind raced to come up with some reason to abandon one of the primary rules of garrison life. Going out alone was strictly forbidden for anyone but senior guards and scouts. It was simply too dangerous to hunt without knowing the mountains extremely well. He knew that the explanation he had to give needed to be phenomenally good in order to satisfy the captain. "I know it doesn't seem like it, but I can handle myself in the forest alone. You've taught me well, and I've even killed two tragues by myself. When I was herding uhts, I learned that being alone has its advantages. It's sometimes nice to be by yourself and not be bothered by others."

Athon eyed the youth closely. "I don't think that is a wise idea to let you go off alone. You're not ready."

This couldn't be happening. The plan was ruined if someone else came with him. Tam knew he wouldn't be able to change Athon's decision with any argument he could immediately conjure, so he spat out the first name that came to mind. "Brixos, what if Brixos came with me?"

Athon groaned. "I can't make a decision about that right now. I need to sleep on it. I'll give you an answer later, but we both need to rest."

Now was not the time to press his agenda. Tam bid the captain good–sleep and retreated to his own quarters. As soon as he entered his room, he removed his noisy accoutrements, and readied for bed. He needed to find a hiding place for Indura's note. Combing his quarters in search of a suitable place, he eventually found a narrow crack in the floorboards under his bed. Once he was satisfied that he could retrieve it, and that it wouldn't be discovered without a significant search, he blew out the lamp and went to sleep.

# Chapter 18

# MISSING

The knock came as usual an hour before even–sun, but Athon was already awake. He only needed a few hours to refresh himself for a full turn's worth of work. He had developed a habit during decades of guard duty. He used the time to write in his journal and review the reports of the previous turn. He had thought that his transfer to the garrison would hinder his responsibilities as the Captain of the Guard, but it had the opposite effect. Most of the intelligence reports came into the garrison, and he had immediate access to them here. The only duty that he couldn't perform was to advise the Council of Elders, but Parth was handling that job.

Athon dressed in his uniform and made his customary wake–up knock at Tam's door. It was time to meet Xacthos in the dining hall to discuss garrison business over a steaming hot cup of atole and breakfast.

The lieutenant was already seated at the head table when Athon entered the large, sparsely populated hall. It wouldn't be long before the room filled to capacity with guards eating before starting the wake–watch. It had been nearly half a pass since he and Tam arrived at the garrison. At first, there was a palpable air of animosity he could feel from Xacthos, but that had quickly evaporated. Athon had made a conscious effort not to alienate his garrison commander. For the most part, he left the command of the mountaintop fortress to Xacthos. He only took command when the occasion called for it. To help ease the load on his lieutenant, he took on the duty of overseeing the wake–watch. He even reported to Xacthos at the end of his own watch. His actions seemed to have the desired effect of mitigating the resentment over his presence. It didn't hurt that the two were already friends, but friendships can be irreparably damaged if there is perceived inequity.

Athon greeted Xacthos with a friendly pat on the shoulder. "I'm sure that you're going to tell me that all is well, and there hasn't been any deviation from the normal."

"No foolin' you is there?" Xacthos said, putting down his atole. "I'll have to work on being less predictable."

The two officers went into a detailed, but routine discussion of intelligence that flowed in from the scouts and spies. There hadn't been much activity on the borderlands, and nothing useful from the spies in the Ithilton army. The supply wagon had come with the usual dispatches, and everything around the kingdom went much the same as it had for countless turns. There were more vegetables coming from the farms because of an unusually good harvest this season. Athon had noticed that the kitchen had taken advantage of this abundance by making dishes laden with the savory tasting delights.

Each man spoke only loud enough for the other to hear. As the room began to fill, there was rise in the cacophony of voices from the gathering men. The noise had its advantages as their conversation became more difficult for others to eavesdrop on, but it also had the caveat of becoming increasingly difficult to make out what the other was saying. Eventually, the conversation shifted to matters outside the realm of garrison business to topics more suited for the gathering mass.

As he sat discussing the weather outlook for the watch, Athon scanned the assembled guards. He marveled how young most of them were. Had it really been such a long time since he was a junior guard seated at one of those tables? There were times that he wished he was young and could sit at each meal surrounded by friends like Parth and Xacthos. Eventually, his gaze rested on a solitary Brixos.

The junior guard sat at the table with a sullen look on his face. All alone, he was playing with his food as if it was a chore to eat. Normally he was quite jovial and talkative. His usual companion for meals, and for almost every other activity, was Tam.

The turn before, Athon had relented and given permission for Tam to go on his requested hunting trip, but only if Brixos accompanied him. They should both be eating together if they were leaving soon. Perhaps Tam had overslept. It wasn't unusual for him to come in late because of his lingering fatigue. He would have to wake up the slumbering prince when he was finished here.

"It's way past time for you to get to bed," Athon said, noticing his lieutenant's fatigue. "We'll talk when you are rested."

Xacthos nodded and the two rose simultaneously from the table. The straggling guards took the cue from their commanders, and all of them quickly left for their various posts.

Athon turned his attention to the young lone guard, now rising from the table. "Brixos!"

"Yes, Captain Athon?"

"Where's Tam?"

"I haven't seen him. I went by his room earlier, but he wasn't there."

"I thought you two were supposed to go hunting," Athon said, quickly becoming anxious that something was terribly wrong.

"Hunting?" Brixos now seemed more confused than Athon, but the picture was now crystal clear for the captain.

"Xacthos, get the sleep–watch guards who manned the gate. Brixos, you come with me, now!" All three men hustled off in the direction of the main exit. Athon and Brixos turned and entered the stables while Xacthos continued toward the front gate.

"Sir, why did you say Tam and I were going hunting? I don't understand."

"I don't know why I'm surprised," Athon muttered. "He wanted to go alone, but I told him that he had to go with you. Obviously, he figured that if you didn't know, he could just sneak out on his own."

"So, what are we doing?"

"Checking if Pyta's still here." They reached the stall and found it empty. They headed out the stable doors and met Xacthos with four guards in tow.

"Tam left about two hours ago, alone," Xacthos said. "What now? Do we go after him?"

"No."

"What? Why not?" Brixos was incredulous.

"He wants to be alone. Let him be alone. For now, we'll wait and hope he doesn't become the hunted."

"He isn't skilled enough to be out on his own." Xacthos said. "It's too dangerous. We must go after him."

Athon was somber. "I don't like the idea much, but I'm not willing to put the rest of the garrison at risk because we have someone who wants to be alone. A man who is lost is one thing, but someone that leaves of his own volition is quite another. Young birds have to eventually fly on their own."

"Tam isn't a bird," Xacthos said sourly. "He's the prince, and it's your duty to watch over him."

"I'm well aware of my duty," Athon said, annoyed his subordinate was questioning his judgment. He knew this could end badly, but he was tired of playing babysitter to this royal brat. "He needs to learn that each man must make his own decisions in life. For good or bad, this is a decision the prince made, and he will have to live with the consequences. When he gets back, I'll kill him."

# Chapter 19

# TOGETHER AGAIN

Escaping the confines of the palace had been trickier than usual. Normally, Indura could slip past the guards by going through the servant's entrance, but she couldn't manage to sneak a hestur through a door meant for people. It had been relatively easy to acquire the sleeping draft she used to drug Mai and Tova, and it worked spectacularly. She did feel particularly guilty about using it on Mai, but she needed to borrow her identity. The risk of being caught as Mai's doppelganger was infinitely greater if there were two handmaidens roaming the halls of the palace.

Indura had dressed in Mai's clothes and donned a black wig to cover her auburn hair, and took Mai's hestur, Azul. She had thought about taking Urdin, but realized the soldiers would think it was odd for Mai to take the hestur of her mistress.

Indura's disguise was so complete she hardly recognized herself in the mirror. Azul seemed to know it wasn't Mai, but he didn't seem to mind when she mounted, or when she spurred him forward.

She was worried the soldiers at the gate would recognize her. Fortunately, they didn't give her a second thought, despite the fact that she had two full saddlebags and the hilt of her sword still visible, but they just waved as she passed. They were focused on people entering, not leaving. For them, it was just another servant on a routine errand.

Indura knew there would be consequences for taking off like this, but the only one she regretted was hurting Mai. It gnawed at her. Mai would be devastated, but she would understand once Indura had the chance to explain. Nothing mattered more than seeing her beloved Tam, and this was the only way it was going to happen.

The journey to the lake had taken a lot longer than she had planned. She had taken a wrong turn, and found herself back on the road toward Campsit. She had no desire to venture that path with an army of men, let alone by herself. It took her hours to retrace her steps and get back to what she thought was the right road. She wasn't sure that this was the right path, but she had to press on. She had never been particularly good at reading maps, and found that she got lost easily. Despite her handicap, she had the overwhelming drive to see Tam.

It was well after high–sun on mid–ceanors turn, and she had been on this road alone for nearly five hours. It had crossed her mind several times that she could be hopelessly lost in this vast wilderness, and that every step of her hestur would lead her further into its dense maze of game trails and heavy vegetation. As she continued on her steady march through the forest, her mind began to play tricks on her. She began to see things that weren't there. Shadows began to move. The forest almost enveloped her like a smothering pillow, closing off her ability to breathe. A rustle came from just off the path. She quickly grabbed the short sword from its hiding place, and tried to quell the terror that rose from her stomach. She began to shake so violently that she nearly dropped the weapon.

Suddenly, a small rodent broke through the edge of the thick vegetation. It stopped, looked inquisitively at the approaching hestur, and scampered back into the brush.

Indura nearly collapsed. "What am I doing?" she asked the hestur. Azul snorted. "You're not scared, are you?" She patted the faithful beast on the neck, her hand still gripping the sword as if her life depended on it. Talking to the animal seemed to calm her a little. "If you're thinking this wasn't a good idea, I'm beginning to agree with you. I hope we aren't lost. That would be just my luck. Tam is probably sitting by the side of the lake waiting for me to show up, but I'm miles away. He'll get tired of waiting, leave, and I'll never hear from him again. All of this will have been in vain, and it will be my own stupid fault!"

Tears began to well in Indura's eyes as she thought of her beloved Tam feeling abandoned. She loved him. She couldn't bear the thought of him thinking that she didn't care. "I'm such a silly girl. Why did I pick somewhere so remote? Why couldn't I have chosen a place easy to find? Why am I continuing down this scrawny little path? I should just turn back and go home. What do you think?" Azul was silent, but kept plodding onward. "I really have gone mad. I'm talking to a hestur like an addlepated twit."

Ahead, the trail seemed to break into the sky. Indura thought she must be seeing things again. Could it be she was walking off a cliff? No, it was blue like the sky, but there was a thin line of green rimming the top. The blue wasn't quite right either. This shimmered in the sun. She dug her heels into Azul's flanks. It wasn't long before they had cleared the tree line and trotted onto the soft high mountain beach.

It was much bigger than Indura had thought, and she wasn't sure which way was north. She pulled out a copy of the map. The Wall Mountains ran along the south side of the lake, and the trail she had just come in on looked like it came in from the northwest. She turned the map around in her hands until it mirrored the vista she held in front of her. If she turned right, she should eventually come to the north point of the lake. According to the map, there was a small 'v' shaped peninsula there. Hopefully, Tam was there, and hadn't given up.

A short time later, the peninsula was in sight. Indura's eyes strained to see even the smallest detail on its shore. A lone figure caught her eye. It had to be Tam.

"He didn't leave me!" She exclaimed, as she urged Azul into a gallop. As she neared, she could clearly make out the green cloak of his uniform. In relief, she began to cry.

As Azul came to a halt in front of a smiling Tam, Indura leaped off, dropping the sword in the process. She fell bawling into his stunned arms. She had never been so happy to see anyone in her life.

"What's wrong?" Tam wasn't quite sure how to handle this weeping woman. He had seen Indura cry before, but he couldn't understand the reason for this uncontrollable display of emotion. She didn't answer him; she just held him tightly and sobbed. "Shh, it's all right, I'm here. Nothing will hurt you. You're safe with me."

"Oh, Tam," Indura managed to say between sobs. "I was so scared. I thought you had gone and left me."

"Nonsense, I would never leave you." He held her soft face in his hands. He looked into her tear-stained eyes, and wiped the streams of water trickling down her cheeks. It was so good to see her, but something wasn't quite right. She looked different from the last time he saw her. Wasn't she a redhead? "What have you done to your hair?"

Indura reached up and touched the hot mat that clung to her head. The mane of normally soft auburn seemed course and thick. She instantly burst into a fit of giggles that erased her fear and her crying. She had forgotten to remove the wig.

She pulled out the pins that held the hot headwear, and gave a swift jerk. The familiar red locks fell about her shoulders in a tousled mess. "I should get a brush," she said. "I'm sure I'm quite hideous right now, but I needed a disguise." She put the borrowed locks and her accoutrements into the saddlebag, and withdrew a stowed brush.

"I'm sure the guards at your palace wouldn't have been fooled if you had tried to leave without doing something to camouflage your looks, although I'm not certain how they didn't know it was you."

"What do you mean? I look completely different, you almost didn't recognize me."

"I'm not quite sure I really count. My only contact with you was for a few turns, and that was three ceanors ago. It had been so long, I wasn't sure I would recognize you in a crowd anyway."

"I left that much of an impression on you?"

Tam blushed, that wasn't quite the message that he had intended to give. He stammered, trying to come up with a plausible excuse to justify what he had just said. "Um, what I meant was that I hadn't been around you as much as your guards, but even I knew it was you, up close." Nice recovery, he thought.

"I see, so my soldiers are stupid?"

This was going downhill fast. "Uh—"

"We Ithiltonians are pretty dumb, aren't we?" Indura teased.

"That is not what I said at all," Tam stammered, trying to recover his verbal footing. What was she doing? He didn't mean to imply that her people were inept. How could he convince her that wasn't what he said? "I would never imply that we have a monopoly on intelligence. I was saying that they must have thought it was just another beautiful woman from the palace—like there are a lot of those around. Um—because, Ithilton is filled with beautiful women—like you—well, not like you, but—"

She looked at him like a captured trague eyeing a piece of raw meat. She had brushed nearly all of the snags out of her hair, returning it to the soft, full curls she was used to. She wanted to play with him some more. Seeing the strong prince in a vulnerable situation was rather a lot of fun. She would let him off the hook in a little bit, but she wasn't quite done teasing him yet. "So, I'm just an average looking woman?"

Argh! he had stuck his foot in his mouth again. What did it take to extract it? "No, not at all, you're the most beautiful woman I've ever seen. You must have a lot of beautiful women at the palace. Maybe your guards are so used to seeing them, they don't pay close attention."

Heh, he's a sweet talker. I'll have to watch that, she thought. He stood there in a sheepish manner that somehow made him look even cuter. Tam was right.

It had been a long time since they had seen each other. She paused briefly from the flirtatious banter to drink in his aura. He seemed much more handsome than she remembered. Uniforms did that to a man.

The noblemen at court frequently tailored their outfits with emblems to make them appear military in nature, but it was never a substitute for the real thing. Indura held the opinion that men who tried to disguise their lack of actual bravery with the trappings of a man that had seen combat were cowards at heart. Tam was not one of those men. Even though Tam's uniform was humble in its utilitarian construction, it had the effect of bringing out his latent masculinity. Each article of clothing was meant to camouflage the wearer in the dense forest, not to make him stand out in a crowd. From the well–worn brown leather boots, gloves, and armor to the green cloak, long sleeved gray–green tunic, and trousers, his uniform was designed for practical use. It still made him look ruggedly handsome.

"I'm so glad to see you," she said, finally. "I've missed you terribly, and I wasn't sure you would come."

"What, and miss shoving my foot so far down my throat I can feel my tonsils? You must be joking," he said, with a nervous laugh. Tam tried to lighten the mood by feigning shock.

In truth, he had wrestled with the whole idea of sneaking out to rendezvous with her. He very nearly didn't make the trip, a fact he was not going to share with her. It was so good to see her again. It had been such a joy to hold her soft body close to his, and smell her sweet fragrance again. She was every bit as beautiful as he remembered. Now that she had finished brushing her hair into the beautiful wavy locks he was accustomed to, she looked even lovelier. Her eyes glimmered in the sunlight. Seeing her in such close proximity filled him with an alien sensation he had only experienced in her presence. As soon as she stowed the brush back in the saddlebag, he approached her, leaning over to pick up the sword that still lay on the ground.

"Are you in the habit of leaving weapons carelessly on the ground? If you don't take care of it, it will rust."

Indura blushed. She had forgotten about the sword. "I was so excited I dropped it. Besides, I didn't want you to think I was going to run you through." She took the blade, wiped it off, and placed it back in the scabbard. As she turned to face him, he encircled her with his arms, his hands resting gently on the small of her back.

She giggled. "What makes you think I need to be held?" She gently pushed against him. She wanted to be held, but she felt liked flirting with him, too.

"I don't think it is a matter of need, but you certainly want it."

Her brow rose over one shimmering emerald eye. "I want to be held? Hmm, I don't think I ever said anything about that."

Two could play at this flirtatious game. "You fell into my arms just a few moments ago."

"I needed it then."

"But, not now?"

She half–heartedly squirmed in his arms. "I have other things I could be doing."

"Like what?" He began slowly drawing her closer.

"My hestur needs to be tended to," she protested. His arms felt so inviting. "I'm hungry. I should fix us something to eat."

"I'm not hearing much of an explanation." The earlier teasing had caught him off balance, but now he was fully recovered. He began reeling her in like a fish on a line. She was so beautiful. Her lips were a deep inviting red. Her cheeks flushed with a crimson tint that accentuated the green of her eyes. Instinctively, his head moved closer to hers.

Her feeble attempts to dodge his forward advance waned along with any resolve she had. She had longed for the passion of her dreams to become a reality. Finally, she would have what she had wanted for so long: a kiss. However, she couldn't give in, just yet. "Do you intend to dispense with all the pleasantries of courtship, or are you just interested in instant gratification?"

The question stopped Tam in his tracks for a moment. She was correct that there would normally be no physical contact more than handholding until a marriage was arranged. Normally, there would be a chaperone to prevent what was surely about to happen. A courtship would last for nearly a full pass before it ever reached this point. However, this was not customary in any way. They weren't even supposed to be writing. "We've ignored protocol so far, what difference does it make if we kiss now?"

Indura pulled back, but this time there was real reservation in her actions. She was still in his grasp, but the distance between their faces had widened so she could look him in the eye. "We can't continue like this. I managed to sneak out this time, but I doubt I can do it again."

"I know," Tam said somberly. "I'm sure Athon will have my hide when I get back."

Indura knew she would have to reckon with Tova when she returned, and it wouldn't be a pleasant discussion. "We could run away."

Tam snorted. "Where would we go?

"Not anywhere in Ithilton. I've been all over the kingdom. There isn't a single villager who wouldn't recognize me. What about one of the smaller villages in Campsit?"

"You really don't know anything about my kingdom, do you?" Tam said, shaking his head in disbelief. "Outsiders are strictly forbidden. I don't know what would happen if I took you back."

"I was there before and nothing happened."

"Athon didn't want to give your father an excuse to start a war, so he spared your life. You're the first person who hasn't been killed on sight."

Indura was shocked. "You mean all outsiders are murdered?"

"Anyone caught near our territory is subject to immediate execution."

Indura was conflicted. She was thankful that she wasn't killed, but she was outraged by the brutality. "That's barbaric!" she said, angrily pushing away. "I suppose I should be grateful, but why do you do that?"

"Do what?"

"Kill people for doing nothing more than being in the wrong place at the wrong time? It seems so — arbitrary."

Tam knew the answer. Everyone in Campsit learned it from an early age, but he had to admit it sounded cruel. "Campsit is different than anywhere else. There's no money to fuel greed, or lust for power. No one is rich or poor. We're all equal, and everyone serves to make the kingdom better — to make themselves better. Outsiders wouldn't understand this way of thinking, so they aren't allowed to contaminate the society. I know it sounds harsh, but it's how we keep our ideals intact."

"So, if anyone disagrees, are they killed too?"

"I don't think so, but I've never heard of a person who took issue with the laws."

Indura couldn't believe what she was hearing. Campsit seemed so harsh, and she couldn't live with people like that, but Tam was different. He had saved her life, and they had fallen in love. There had to be some way they could be together forever. "We could live in the wild," she said half-heartedly.

Tam tried to imagine that, but knew that could never work. "I'm pretty sure running away won't help. We just need to accept the fact that meeting like this won't work in the long run."

"What are we going to do then?"

"I'll just have to march up to your father and demand to court you."

Indura sighed. She knew that was a pipe dream, and that this was probably the last time she would see him, but she didn't care. It was enough to know that they were together again, and even if this moment couldn't last forever, she would make the most of it. She threw her arms around him and held tight. Tears welled in her eyes. She didn't want this to end—ever.

They stood in the bliss of the simple embrace for a long time before Tam's voice broke the silence. "I'm hungry. You want something to eat?"

She looked up at her prince with a serene smile. "That would be lovely. I have some fruit we can share."

"I caught a kanni for us. It may take a while to cook, but I brought some bread and cheese we can have in the meantime."

"That sounds divine."

Tam had counted on eating the kanni for the late–sun meal, and had prepared the animal as well as the fire pit and spit. It wasn't long before a fire roared to life and the meat began cooking. The sweet smell of roasted flesh wafted through the air, causing them to grow hungrier in anticipation of the meal to come. Indura laid out a blanket on the beach and they sat holding each other close. They didn't say much, but basked in the clement warmth of the sun. Waves lapped at the shore, providing a rhythm to counterpoint the steady rush of wind through the canopy of the trees. The melodious songs of the many birds in the surrounding forest completed the symphony that negated the need for conversation. They sat, enjoying the simple pleasure of being with each other. Their reverie was broken occasionally when Tam would get up to turn the spit.

Tam couldn't be happier than right now. It erased the anxiety of his impending punishment. The joy of being with Indura pushed everything else to the back of his mind. She laid her head on his shoulder and all seemed right in the world.

"I think it's done."

"You aren't sure?"

"I'm not a cook. I've only done it a few times when I was hunting or herding."

"Herding? As in animals?"

"Uhts, to be precise."

"You are a herder? I thought you were of royal blood." Indura laughed at the thought of Tam being around the smelly herd.

"I've done it, but that doesn't make me one."

"Yes, it does. Are you sure you're a prince?"

He chuckled to himself at how absurd he must sound to a woman who has never done any work. "Yes, I'm a prince, but I'm one that knows how to hunt, cook, and herd uhts. It's just a hobby right now, but I'm thinking of making it a permanent thing."

"Really?"

"No, not really. Putting up with those stubborn, mangy things is not something I'm really capable of." He felt the meat on the roasting carcass. "It's done. Want a leg?"

"I'd love some."

He took out one of his daggers and quickly sliced off a section of hindquarter and handed it to her. "I'm afraid there isn't much to them, but they're quite delicious. I don't have any plates, but I'm sure we can make due."

"I can manage, but you mustn't think of me as unladylike." She eagerly accepted the hot morsel. The travel had made her very hungry.

Soon, the only thing left of the kanni was the bones. They had satiated their hunger, but not the desire to be together. Warm sun and full bellies began to take their toll; they were exhausted. Tam stoked the fire and lay down on the blanket next to Indura.

"What are you doing?" She was tired, but it would be inappropriate to sleep next to a man.

"I'm going to take a nap. What does it look like?"

"What, now?" She was incredulous. "Isn't someone going to keep watch?"

"You can if you like, but I'm too tired to stay awake. You're welcome to join me."

"I can't do that."

"Aren't you tired?"

"I'm exhausted, but—"

"Then lie down and get some rest."

"Sleep with you?"

He opened one eye halfway. "Sleeping *next* to me is not sleeping *with* me, and I can't stay awake anymore. I need rest. I just need an hour." His last words faded as he slipped into unconsciousness.

She was having a hard time staying awake too, but she was determined to keep watch. The late–sun's rays shone down, warming her skin and making her feel drowsy. A gentle breeze came off the lake and kept her comfortable. It was a beautiful turn. Before long, her eyes became heavy. She tried shaking her head vigorously to stave off the overwhelming desire to sleep, but it didn't help. Her eyes closed, and it felt good. She would just lie down for a moment, and then she would wake back up. If only she had a pillow to rest her weary head. Tam's muscular arm was perfectly positioned. She would just lay her head on it for a moment. He smelled so masculine. It was comfortable here, and she couldn't stay awake any longer.

*Chapter 20*

# FIGHT AND FLIGHT

The sound of a hestur nervously snorting and a throbbing pain in his arm brought Tam out of his deep sleep. He opened his eyes and found his surroundings to be rather disorienting. Where was he? Why did his arm hurt? He blinked several times to clear the haze from his mind. Slowly, it started coming back to him. It was the high mountain lake, the long and filling meal, and seeing his beloved Indura again. He shifted slightly and found Indura cuddled next to him sleeping soundly, her head resting on his aching arm. It was asleep. Trying not to rouse her, he gently pulled his arm away from her head. Unfortunately, he was unable to extricate himself from that position without startling her.

"What is it?" Indura asked, with weary surprise. Evidently, she was just as disoriented as Tam had been waking up. She bolted to a sitting position and looked around wildly, trying to find something familiar with which to make sense of her surroundings. Suddenly, she realized Tam was next to her, feverishly reviving his nearly useless hand.

"We fell asleep," he said. "Judging from the position of the sun, I would say several hours have passed."

The reality of her napping quickly began to filter through her brain, and a flicker of comprehension shown on her face. "I didn't mean to doze off like that. Did I use you as a pillow?"

"That would explain why my hand is asleep." The blood was rushing back into his arm, restoring function as it crept down. With the ability to move came the inevitable tingling sensation that steadily became more painful until it felt as if a thousand tiny needles were being thrust into his skin. He shook it violently to ease the pain. It helped a little.

"Sorry about that," she said, sincerely trying to apologize. Her guilt slowly turned to shame as she realized that she had allowed herself to do that which she swore she wouldn't. "I don't even remember drifting off. I don't know what came over me."

"It really is not a problem. You were tired. I don't mind holding you, even when I'm not awake to enjoy it."

Indura blushed out of sheer embarrassment. How could she be so stupid as to lower her guard like that? If Tova knew — if her father knew, disappointment would be an understatement.

The distant whinny of a hestur caught their attention. On the shore, where she had come from, men mounted on hesturs came into view. They were a good distance away, but she could tell they were uniformly dressed. Suddenly, her mind raced. How did they know where she had gone?

"Who are they?"

"They have to be men sent by my father," she said. "How did they find us? No one knows where I am."

Something wasn't quite right. Tam looked intently at the men with his keen vision. He stood motionless for a breathless moment, watching them proceed slowly down the beach. There must be at least twenty men all in a single file line. Each wore a white hat that encircled their heads, making them look like white mushrooms. Their clothing was all white, and flowed as if it were all cloth. It didn't look like they were wearing any armor. It appeared that all of the men were armed with lances and strange looking swords. "Ithilton soldiers all wear metal armor, right?"

"The ones on hesturs do, and those that guard the palace, but the average soldier wears leather armor like you."

"Those soldiers aren't sent by your father, and they aren't from Campsit."

She turned her attention back to the soldiers. A cry from one of lead men alerted her that they had spied the pair. The column surged down the beach toward them. They were still a long way off, but it wouldn't be much time before they got close. Suddenly, terror gripped her as she recognized the distinctive headdress and uniform of the approaching hoard. "Tam, we have to go now!"

Cold dread filled him. The terror in her voice was palpable and he began to move toward Pyta. "Who are they?"

"We must get out of here, but I can't go back the way I came." She was panicking now. Not knowing where to turn, she stood there almost rooted in place.

"Who are they?" Tam asked, as he grabbed his bow.

"Austicans, they've been at war with Ithilton for years. How did they get so far into my country?" Indura looked around as if she didn't know what to do next. "If they capture me, I don't know what they'll do." She was genuinely terrified.

"See that game trail just across the lake?" Tam gestured toward a small patch of bare ground leading into the forest. She was glancing around, and obviously not seeing where he was pointing. He grabbed her head and directed it to the barely visible path. "Do you see it?" She nodded her head, and he pushed her toward Azul. "Follow it, and you'll get to the main road that leads back to Campsit. We're closer to the garrison than Ithilton. Go to there, and you'll be safe. I'll hold them off while you escape."

"What?" She couldn't believe what he was saying. He hoisted her into the saddle. She couldn't just abandon him. "No!"

"We don't have time to debate this. Get out of here as fast as you can. I'll catch up with you if I can, but you must go. I'll alert the garrison. Don't stop for any reason until you get there. Athon will make sure you're safe." He smacked Azul with his bow and the beast took off. He wheeled around and shouldered his quiver. Tam reached back, retrieved an odd shaped arrow, and aimed skyward. She halted Azul's progress and looked back at her love. Her mind swam with confused questions as he shouted at her again. "Move!"

Almost without thinking, Indura dug her heels into Azul's flanks and he surged down the beach toward the game trail. Tam let his arrow fly straight upwards.

The arrow, called a popper by the guards, was really an ingenious creation of Master Thales. It was essentially a large arrow attached to a fine, tightly wound string at one end. At the end of the string was a small loop that wrapped around Tam's finger. Instead of a blade being attached to the tip of the arrow, there was a hollow tube filled with chemicals and sawdust. In the center was a chemical strip next to an abrasive pad that was attached to the other end of the string. When the string was pulled taunt, it would drag the pad and start a reaction. The chemicals would catch fire, causing the outer walls of the tube to rupture in an explosion. The sawdust would then ignite, but because it burned incompletely, it made a black puffy cloud that would glow orange for a split second and then rise above the point of detonation. It was standard issue for scouts in the mountains and forests of Campsit. It was only to be used when they saw an invasion force. Watchmen would stare into the sky, looking for the telltale explosion, and raise the alarm.

Tam had grabbed two of the devices before he left, just in case. He was far outside the boundaries of Campsit, but he was close enough to the mountains that someone might see. The popper could go unnoticed, but it was a chance he had to take.

Tam fired off the first of the two missiles, and it exploded spectacularly far above his head. The Austicans were much closer now, and were within range of his bow. He quickly pulled an arrow from his quiver and took deadly aim at the first rider. The arrow struck the soldier in the chest, and he fell dead onto the beach.

Tam hoped the others would slow to avoid or help their fallen comrade, but they didn't. A second volley met with similar results. The men were at a full gallop headed straight for him, and spinning some kind of ball weapon above their heads. He fired off another two volleys with equally deadly aim. An approaching rider loosed one of the ball weapons. It spun toward him in an almost mesmerizing way. The weapon made a peculiar low whooping sound as it hurled through the air. He had to duck to avoid it as it splashed harmlessly into the water behind him.

They were getting much closer. Tam calculated that he had perhaps two or three more volleys before they would be on top of him. He quickly glanced over toward Indura, and caught her just as she darted into the forest down the trail. He pulled another popper and aimed skyward. "Please someone see this," he said, as he let the missile go. It had the same effect as the first one. Whatever derogatory comments he had once said about Master Thales in his youth, he took back; he was a genius. It had taken longer than he liked to set the popper off, and he was left with only enough time to take down one more Austican soldier before they would be on top of him. He dodged another ball weapon and fired. His aim was a little off, but instead of hitting the man in the chest, it hit him in the neck. The man grabbed at the arrow and ripped it out. Blood visibly shot from the open wound and the man fell from his hestur holding his neck in a vain attempt to keep the blood from gushing out. He didn't live long after that, as he was trampled by the others behind him.

Tam dropped his bow and drew his swords in preparation for combat. The fast approaching men were almost on him now. Another ball weapon came at him with no time to duck. He sliced at it with his sword. The impact was something he wasn't prepared for. It very nearly tore his weapon right out of his hand.

It was the first time he had gotten a good look at it. It was a simple weapon. It was three large, round stones tied together with lengths of leather rope. One of the stones caught his shoulder as it passed by. The pain was excruciating, and rendered his left arm nearly useless. How would he defend against this type of weapon? He had never seen anything like it before. He tightened his grip on his two swords, but his left arm refused to cooperate and dangled at his side.

Tam readied for the first man who attacked from his hestur at a full gallop. He dodged a vicious lance stab and simultaneously leaped toward the mounted Austican, catching him with a jab from his long sword. The dead man lolled in his saddle and wrenched the blade from his hand. He instinctively switched his short sword to his one good hand.

A short sword was, by no means, adequate to defend against men on hesturback. Tam knew he couldn't withstand another attack from the charging Austicans, so he turned and ran for Pyta. Turning his back toward a charging foe posed significant dangers, but he figured that he could run faster this way. His heart pounded with each step as if it were going to leave his chest. He could hear the low whoop of an approaching ball weapon. He would have to jump and hope it would miss. There was a thud as a weapon glanced off a nearby tree, quickly followed by a sickening crack, and an unbearable pain at the back of Tam's head. Everything went black, and he fell to the ground like a lifeless rag doll.

# Chapter 21

# WATCH FIRE

Hector preferred isolation, because people bothered him in general. He found that most of them were petty and easily offended. What was the point of being civil? If someone was making a blessed fool of themselves, why not let them know it? It was one of the reasons he had trouble with others. He had no time for foolishness. Besides, no one really liked him. From the time he was young, people had teased him for a variety of reasons, but mostly because he was shy. No, being away from everyone suited him just fine. That is why he chose the life of a watchman as opposed to a guard. Watchmen live life relatively alone. There was only one other person in his little camp, and he was asleep right now.

The camp was situated high in the eastern Wall Mountains, giving him a spectacular view of both valleys. He could see forever. He knew every tree, trail, and lake on the Ithilton side of the mountains. He used that familiarity to scan the skies for any sign of a popper, or campfire. He knew others were counting on him to see the first sign of an army, and warn the garrison.

It wasn't a large camp. It consisted of a single tent and a large unlit bonfire. If he spied a popper from one of the scouts or saw the telltale smoke from multiple campfires he would light the bonfire. Other watchmen situated in camps closer to the garrison would see his fire and light theirs. The signal would be relayed from camp to camp down the range until it reached the guards at the garrison.

This was a beautiful turn. It wasn't raining, and the sun was just warm enough. He sipped at his celis leaf tea, and enjoyed its honey like flavor.

A brief flash of orange caught his eye, and he zeroed in on it. That had come from Lost Lake far to the east. It couldn't be a scout. That was too far out of the patrol area. He could see the appearance of a small smudge of black just above the trees on the northern shore of the lake. He had to be dreaming. That wasn't a popper; it had to be a fire of some kind. He reached over and got his excluder, a short metal tube used to observe a specific area. It didn't magnify anything; it just made it easier to focus on one small area. He could see the fading black puff of smoke. There didn't seem to be any signs of a campfire or wildfire. It looked like the remnants of a popper, but it was not in the right place. It had to be his imagination.

He was looking through the excluder, and was mulling everything over when he saw a second flash near the remains of the first. There was no doubt in his mind now. That had to be a popper.

"No," Hector said aloud. "No, this can't be happening, Kyros!" He opened the tent flap as the other watchman woke with a start. He grabbed the bleary watchman and hauled him to his feet dragging him out of the tent. "Kyros, you must come quickly before it's gone."

"What is it?" Kyros had the excluder thrust into his hand by the now excited Hector. "Have you gone mad all of a sudden?"

"No, no look there on the north shore of Lost Lake. What do you see?"

"It's black smoke from a fire of some sort," Kyros said sourly.

"It's a popper. I saw it explode with my own eyes."

"But it's too far out of the patrol area. You must have seen something else."

"Have I ever seen something that wasn't there before?"

Kyros paused, and looked through the excluder again. "No, you haven't. You know what this means?"

"It means you need to get that fire lit while I ride to the garrison to let them know."

"Why you?" A ride back to the garrison meant a warm meal, and maybe a soft bed to sleep in for a whole watch.

"You didn't see it, I did. Now get that fire lit. We've wasted too much time yappin'." Hector hated arguing. He wondered how long it would take the guards at garrison to believe him.

Xacthos walked the ramparts of the garrison walls at a leisurely pace. It was perfect weather right now. It wasn't too hot or too cold. That would change in a ceanor. The fall would come, and they would have nearly constant rain intermixed with snow, but it was a beautiful turn. He loved being stationed high in the mountains, although he never got to eat the shellfish he enjoyed so much. It was a small price to pay for the peace and freedom of the alpine life. He could sit and stare out at the beautiful vistas afforded by the rocky perch all turn long and never get tired of it.

In the distance to the east, something caught his eye. One, now two columns of black smoke began to curl above the rocky mountaintop. It can't be, he thought. Watch fires? Instinctively, he started to run toward the high watchtower on the south side of the garrison. Soon he was at a full sprint, his legs pounding fiercely against the stone walkway. A guard on the watchtower called to him.

"Sir, are those watch fires?"

"Sound the alarm!" Xacthos yelled loud enough for every sentry to hear. "Sound the alarm now!"

The silence was broken by the repetitive melodic ring of the watchtower's bell as it pierced the air. The bell only tolled when there was significant danger, such as fire or the threat of invasion. Everyone had been conditioned to react the same way every time they heard it. Guards that had been idle sprang to their feet in search of a post to stand. Men asleep in their bunks sprang to their feet and, disoriented, hastily dressed.

Athon was a light sleeper that quickly roused at the first tone of the bell. He dressed in near record time, and was racing up the steps to the watchtower before many of the men had their shirts on. In moments, he emerged at the top of the long staircase to find Xacthos and several anxious looking men watching the horizon.

"What's going on, Xacthos?" Athon yelled, to be heard over the din of the bell as it pealed in a continual plea for the guards to muster.

"The watch fires are lit."

"Do you know why?" Athon wasn't expecting much in the way of an answer, but he felt compelled to ask.

"No, but I'm sure we will have a rider soon. We should assemble the men and head to the canyon."

"Agreed," Athon said. "Take everyone and head to the pass. I'll wait here for word, and join you when I know more."

Xacthos turned to one of the nervous guards. "Get all the reserve from the south and west ramparts. Have them muster with the others in the courtyard. I'll take the east and north wall, and meet you there." He quickly saluted Athon and raced down the east wall, tapping men along the way and motioning them to follow him.

Athon stood rooted on the spot, keeping his eyes open as he scanned the distance for any sign of an approaching rider. He didn't notice how quickly the entire garrison had mobilized into an orderly formation in the courtyard below. Grim–faced men had armed themselves to the teeth in preparation for inevitable conflict. Shields, pikes, and helmets, not normally part of the guard's accoutrements, were distributed to everyone not on a hestur. It took only a few moments for the full garrison complement to assemble in the courtyard.

Xacthos stood at the head of the assemblage of fighting men. As soon as he was satisfied that all the guards were there, he roared so all could hear. "Men, Preanth and his army have come to take away our lands and make slaves of our women and children. I say they have come to their doom. No force has ever breached this fortress, and none ever shall. Preanth believes we are less than worms. We will prove him wrong. We will send his army back, a mere shadow of itself. We ride, not for conquest, but for the defense of our freedom. Do not fear death for we that fight for justice shall never die! To the canyon!"

A mighty roar emanated from the throats of the entire garrison. It echoed throughout the halls in a din of fanatic resolution. The gates opened, and Xacthos charged through with a thunder of hooves and running men.

The canyon was only a half hour's ride from the fortress, and was the greatest defensive weapon the kingdom of Campsit had. It was narrow in the extreme. It was only two wagon lengths wide, and lined by sheer cliff walls on either side. It was the only way through the otherwise vertical precipice of the Wall Mountains.

Beyond the rocky trail led to the upper foothills of the mountains and then down to the valley of Ithilton. Trying to move an army though this narrow pass was suicide, a significant reason why it provided the perfect defense from invasion. Anyone moving through the pass found themselves an easy target for archers. Anyone not killed by arrows in the narrow confines could easily be stopped by a wall of fifty or so men.

Athon thought his men would be enough to repel an invasion, but that may not be necessary. A show of force, from an excellent defensive position, had always proved an effective deterrent to Preanth's army. Hopefully, they would see the futility of an attack and return home without shedding any blood. He prayed that would be the case.

He watched the bulk of his command run down the road and deploy on the barely visible canyon rim. The tactic had been devised hundreds of passes ago, but was still effective. It was now a waiting game. How long would it be before the arrows would fly in defense of the entire kingdom? It would all depend on the information provided by the watchman.

It was nearly two and a half hours before he saw the dust in the distance kicked up by the hooves of the galloping hestur. He watched the rider get closer and closer. Athon raced down the steps and arrived at the same time the rider pulled up at the gate.

"Report!" Athon ordered

"I have news," Hector said breathlessly, as he dismounted his hestur.

"Calm down, breathe deep."

Hector did as he was commanded. Still panting, he began his report. "I come from the furthest watch camp. I saw a flash far to the east of our normal patrol zone. At first, I thought I was seeing something, but it happened again when I was looking directly at it with my excluder. It was a popper, sir."

"Where did it come from?" This news was troubling to Athon. Poppers were only issued to scouts, and as far as he knew, Ithilton didn't possess them.

"It came from the north shore of Lost Lake."

"Lost Lake? I'm not familiar with that, where is it?"

"In Ithilton, near the base of the mountains in the east, I could show you on a map."

Athon turned to one of the sentries. "In the Commander's Office, there is a map of the mountains and Ithilton territories. Get it and get back here as fast as you can." The guard gave a quick salute and raced into the barracks. Turning his attention back to Hector, he began pumping him for more information. "When did you first see it?"

"Sometime between low and first–quarter sun, I think."

"You're not sure?" Athon didn't want to go on something that wasn't definitive.

"I know what I saw, sir, I just got so excited I didn't really stop to see what time it was."

"Fair enough," Athon said, noting the frustration in the watchman's voice. "How do you know it was a popper and not a fire or something else?"

"Sir, do you believe me or not?" Hector's frustration began to boil over.

"I believe you," Athon said, beginning to lose his patience with the insubordinate old man. "I just want you to tell me why you think it was a popper and not a fire or something else."

"It exploded, all right!" Hector snapped. "I saw an orange flash and then the cloud of black smoke. Then, the smoke thinned out and disappeared after a while. It was a popper. Nothing else looks like that, sir. Now stop thinking I'm insane and treat me with a little respect."

Athon's voice was low, unwavering, and measured. He spoke with conviction and authority as he rose to his full height. "Just exactly who do you think you are talking to? Did it ever cross your mind that I have the responsibility of the lives of thousands of men? Do you realize that I am making decisions based on the information I get from you? Do you think I can make a decision based on incomplete, irrational, or otherwise tainted intelligence?" Athon's words took on the tone of a low roar. "If I ask you a question, it isn't because I think you are stupid, or I don't understand what you're saying. I need to know what you have seen, and since I can't crack open your skull and get it that way, I have to settle for asking you. If that is a concept that you can't wrap your mind around, then you might wish to consider another occupation."

Hector cowered from the towering giant Athon seemed to have become. Athon could see he had made his point. He hated being hard on one of his men that obviously did his job well, but he couldn't tolerate someone not showing him the proper respect. The watchman had done what he was supposed to, and now it was time to concentrate on that instead of the heated exchange that had just taken place. He placed a reassuring hand on the watchman's shoulder. "I believe that you saw a popper. Now we have to know where that came from and why."

The guard that was sent to fetch the map returned, breathlessly clutching a large roll of parchment. "Here it is, Captain," he said, pulling up just short of the pair.

"Good," Athon said, taking the map from the guard. He unrolled the map and held it up for Hector to see. "Now, show me where this Lost Lake is and where that popper was seen."

It took a moment for Hector to get his bearings on the map, but he soon found his place and jabbed a stubby finger at the figures on the map. "There is Lost Lake, and here is where I saw the popper. See how far east it is. It has to be one of our men, but no scout I know of would be that far out of our territory."

Athon knew Hector was right, but he couldn't deny it was one of their poppers. This was perplexing news. Who would send up a signal and why? He would have to discuss this with Xacthos and get his opinion. Something gnawed at him, something important, but he couldn't think of it. It was lost in a jumble of thoughts. It would just have to eat at him for now. At the moment, there were important matters to attend to. "Thank you, for the valuable information, watchman. Go inside and get something to eat and then get back to your post." With that, he turned and headed for the almost empty stables.

The ride to the canyon seemed to be over as soon as it started. Athon's mind was lost in thought, occupied by the singular conundrum that was the mysterious popper. He found Xacthos and showed him the map and the location of the pyrotechnic bursts. They agreed that it had to be a signal from one of their scouts, but who would be in that location?

"Stenos and Cyrix both patrol areas near there, but they would never venture that far east on a whim," Xacthos said emphatically. "There has to be some reason one of them was there."

"It doesn't make sense, does it?" Athon shook his head. He was racking his brains trying to find some explanation. "What I don't understand is why Preanth would come that way. The cliffs are far too high, and there isn't a pass. The only way over the mountains is here. The forest is too dense to move large numbers of troops through, and it isn't even remotely close to the road. What is the advantage of going that way?"

"Maybe he's trying to outflank us somehow."

"No," Athon said, shaking his head. "He still has to come through this pass. He has to know we would have spotted him trying to skirt the road."

"It must be something we haven't thought of," Xacthos said. "It really makes no difference. We spotted him, and we're on high alert now. He's lost any advantage he may have tried to gain. My only worry now is Tam. If he's gone this way he could find himself in a world of hurt. Knowing him, he would do something stupid, and get himself captured or killed."

Athon closed his eyes and silently cursed. Tam, his absence was what had been bothering him. No one had seen or heard from him. He could be dead, wounded, or captured for as far as he knew. Curse that boy for his foolhardy actions! "Please, tell me someone knows where that boy is."

"I wish I could," Xacthos sighed. "I asked Brixos about it before you arrived. He hasn't seen him."

"Great," Athon said angrily. "An entire garrison full of men trained to watch out for each other, and he wanders off without anyone having the slightest idea where he is. It's amazing how Preanth hasn't marched in and killed us all in our sleep. We can't even keep track of one man!"

Xacthos didn't have a reply. Eventually, he broke the silence. "I'm sorry, Athon. I don't know what more we can do."

Athon knew he was taking out his anger on the wrong person. "Sorry, Xacthos, you didn't have anything to do with his deception. I'm worried we don't know where he is, and it's my fault."

"You couldn't have seen this coming," Xacthos said reassuringly. "He gave no indication that he would be dishonest at all. What were you supposed to do, keep him under lock and key?"

"No," Athon admitted soberly. "I should have gone looking for him when he first came up missing."

"What's stopping you now," said a voice from behind them.

"Eavesdropping is a bad habit, Brixos," Xacthos said with some irritation.

"We can't mobilize a search effort and keep this pass properly defended." Athon had already considered the consequences of going after the prince and found them to be unacceptable. "If Preanth is coming, he would take the pass by sheer numbers if we split this force up and started to look now. As much as I hate to say this, he's on his own."

"What if I go looking for him?"

"Completely out of the question," Xacthos said before Athon could respond. "You have a duty, and regardless of how you may feel, you are going to perform that duty. Now get back to the line, and we'll have no more talk of you going off on some ill–conceived rescue."

Athon watched the dejected young guard turn and slowly make his way back to the edge of the chasm. "When this is over I'm going to take every last man and hunt that boy down. When I find him, I'm going to hang him by his thumbs until his arms fall off."

# Chapter 22

# THE COLD TRAIL

I t was impossible to tell if Indura's eyes were dry because of the wind, or if she had cried until she couldn't cry anymore. It was probably a combination of both. She had no idea how long she had been running from the Austicans, or if they were even pursuing her. She was running because she didn't know what else to do.

Tam had sacrificed himself so she could evade from certain doom. She didn't know if he had escaped or if he lay dead on the shore of the lake. The only thing she could do was ride as fast as Azul could carry her toward the safety of the Campsit garrison. It had taken her some time to reach the road. Along the way she had received countless scratches and scrapes from tree limbs that clawed at her as she frantically fled through the forest, and her dress had been reduced to tatters.

Even after she had reached the safety of the road, she didn't slow down. Azul was obviously tired from the ride. His breathing was labored as they climbed the steep path toward the sanctuary of the garrison. One thing she knew for sure was that both rider and mount were exhausted from the journey. She had no idea where she was or how far she had to go. She just continued to ride, her mind lost in a near catatonic state. As she rounded a bend in the road, her hestur pulled up short and she was brought back into the present. A mass of menacing guards with pikes lowered and shields raised blocked her progress forward.

"Halt and identify yourself!" The voice seemed to come from all around her as it echoed off the canyon walls.

"I am Indura, Princess of Ithilton. I need to see Captain Athon."

"What purpose brings you here?" The voice was somehow familiar, but she was unable to place it.

She scanned the hardened faces of the phalanx that barred her way, but could not see the source of the inquisition. "I need your protection, and your help. Please, let me speak to Captain Athon." She began to sob. "Please, help me!"

The voice didn't answer her. She didn't know what to do. This reception was far from the one she had received on her first encounter. Tam wasn't here to save her. She was tired, emotionally drained, and felt alone, surrounded by her enemies. Her sobs turned into the deep anguish. She doubled over with the pain that now threatened to rip her heart out of her chest. Unable to remain seated she slid off Azul and collapsed in a heap on the ground. "Please, help me!" she cried, her piteous plea was enough to melt the heart of the most callous.

From behind the men came a sharp command. "Stand down, and make way." Athon rode through the throng, accompanied by Xacthos. He reached the sobbing heap and leapt to her side. "You're safe, Highness. No one will hurt you." He held her tear-stained face in his hands. "What happened? Why are you here?"

"Tam said you would protect me. I only came because he told me to." Sobs kept Indura from being very coherent and she fought for every word to escape her spasmodic lungs. "You have to help him! There were too many. Oh, gods! I killed my precious Tam!"

"She's delirious," Xacthos said.

"No, what she's saying makes perfect sense," Athon replied.

"It does?"

"The poppers weren't set off by a scout. Tam must have taken them with him. He was the one who set them off." Athon turned his attention to the hysterical girl in his arms. "Who did this? Who hurt Tam?"

"Austicans!" Indura said, before she lost consciousness.

Athon felt a chill run down his spine at the mention of Ithilton's most fearsome rival. He picked up the disheveled princess and handed her to Xacthos long enough to leap onto Zuri's back, and motion for her return. "Give her to me," he demanded. "She's exhausted, and we need answers."

Xacthos hoisted the slumbering beauty into the arms of his captain. "What do you think she means by I killed him?"

"I don't know, but let's hope it isn't true. One thing is for sure; she knows, and we won't get answers until she's had time to recuperate. Let's get her back to the garrison, and we'll deal with it when she's had a chance to rest."

"What about the pass?"

"Until we know more everyone stays here ready to fight, that includes you."

"What will you be doing?"

"I'm going to sit with our guest and get some answers when she wakes up."

"I'll have someone take her hestur to the garrison and tend to it," Xacthos said. "By the looks of things, it's in as bad a shape as she is."

Athon was considerably slower returning to the fortress than he was on the way there. He cradled the princess in his arms as if handling a precious fragile vase. From her appearance, she had taken quite a beating. When he arrived back at the garrison, he headed straight for the inn. Dismounting was accomplished with the aid of several guards that had to provide security for the nearly empty structure. He seconded two of them to act as runners while he watched over the princess in a room hastily provided by the innkeeper. He had several dispatches that needed to be written and sent to Campsit.

Reinforcements would be arriving soon from the valley, and the king would need to be informed of the recent developments. As far as the issue of the missing prince and the princess, he would limit the details until he knew more.

After his administrative duties were completed, he began his vigil. He sat in a chair next to Indura's bed and contemplated the events that led to her arrival. They must have conspired to rendezvous, but as to who made the plan was anyone's guess. It really didn't matter which one came up with the idea. The damage was done. All that was left was to pick up the pieces, and hope there was something left.

Sometime during Athon's watch, he allowed himself to fall asleep. The princess stirred. He opened his eyes to see her stretching. "How are you feeling?" he asked.

"I'm all right, all things considered," Indura replied sleepily. "Has Tam arrived yet?"

"No," Athon replied. "I'm assuming by that question that you were the last person to see him. What happened to you? You said the Austicans killed him. Do you know that for sure?"

"It's all my fault," she confessed, pain stabbing her conscience. "I missed him terribly, and had to see him again, so I arranged to meet him at this lake I found on a map. We had a lovely meal, and then we fell asleep. When we awoke, we saw a group of Austican soldiers coming toward us. Tam held them off while I escaped. I didn't want to leave him; he made me go."

Athon was somewhat perturbed by not having the most important question answered. "Did you see him get killed or wounded?"

"No," she admitted. "The last thing I saw, he was firing his bow at them. I didn't see anything after that."

There was a glimmer of hope that he could still be alive. He would have to act quickly if there was going to be a chance to save him, but it may already be too late. He stood and headed for the door. "You should bathe, and get ready. I'll have the innkeeper's wife, Daphne, bring you some clean clothes, and I'll be back in an hour to get you."

"Where are we going?"

"We're going to that lake to find Tam, and then I'm taking you back to your father."

Athon emerged from the inn just as a large contingent of guards rode through the main gate. Parth and Castor, the lieutenant in charge of the Deep Woods, were at the head of a column of reinforcements. Hopefully, they wouldn't be needed for long.

"Parth, Castor," Athon said genially. "It's nice of you to join the festivities."

"We came as soon as we could muster," Parth said, crossly. "We weren't sure there would be a garrison by the time we got here."

"Have a little more faith than that. How many are with you?" Athon knew there weren't many men to draw from.

"I've brought every man that could be spared, but we're just shy of five hundred. That leaves us effectively defenseless in the rest of the kingdom."

"It can't be helped. I want you to turn around and head to the canyon. I'll be there in an hour or so. You'll have your orders then."

Parth glowered. "I take it you have something else to occupy your time?"

"There are some things I need to attend to here first. When I'm done, I'll meet you there, and brief you and Xacthos on my plan. By the way, tell him to get some sleep if he hasn't already."

"I can't wait to hear the explanation for this," Castor said as they turned and left the garrison.

It didn't take long for Athon to wash the sweat and grime of the past two turns off. He changed into a clean uniform, and headed to the armory before returning to the inn. He found Indura waiting for him looking sullen, but refreshed. She was silent as they rode to the bustling camp at the canyon's rim. They found Xacthos Parth and Castor waiting for them.

"What a fine mess you've made, Athon," Parth said when the captain and princess approached.

"You're referring to what, exactly?" Athon began to bristle at the insubordinate innuendo.

"Letting Tam do whatever he pleases. That brat gets away with murder. How is it he found a way to coordinate an assignation with the princess of our mortal enemy?"

"How dare you!" Indura thundered at the insult.

Athon immediately blocked Indura's approach, and tried to dismiss the impending quarrel. "It's true he has been corresponding with the princess. I've been supervising his letter writing in the interests of easing the tensions between our kingdoms." Indura stood in shock that the captain had been privy to her correspondence.

"You did *what*?" Parth was furious.

"Have you gone mad?" Castor demanded.

"Just exactly when were you planning on including me in this information?" Xacthos said indignantly.

"I can't believe Tremmon and Aurora approved of this," Parth said dubiously. "Do they even know?"

"No," Athon said reluctantly. He dreaded the coming reaction.

"You kept it secret?" Parth said furiously, "from his parents!"

"It was entirely within my right to allow it. Unfortunately, he wasn't honest with me when it came to disclosing everything the two were discussing. I take full responsibility for that."

"The prince could be dead, or worse. Are you willing to accept the consequences of failing to perform your primary assignment of protecting him?" Parth said accusingly.

This attitude from his insubordinate lieutenant was partially justified, but entirely unacceptable. Athon drew himself up and stood nose to nose with Parth. It seemed that his replacement had gotten too used to having authority. His face was noticeably fuller, and he had started to get fat around the waist. Evidently, his lieutenant had started to like his position of authority too much. "Do you want my job?"

"I do it better than you," Parth snapped. "And, I wouldn't have let the prince act like this was his personal playground."

"I highly doubt that," growled Athon. "Look at yourself. Did you just decide to stop training the moment I left, or did you wait an entire turn before you decided to swallow an *uht*! If the reinforcements you brought followed your example, we might as well let Preanth walk in here and take over."

"None of this solves our problems," Xacthos said leaping between the two bickering commanders. "Athon, you know I would follow you to the ends of Arabella, but that was pretty stupid to let those two fraternize. Parth, like it or not, Athon is still in charge. If you continue to speak to him like that, I'll take my sword and cut that fat right out of your pompous, lazy hide! We have a number of issues right now, not the least of which is that we have Preanth's daughter." He turned and addressed Indura. "I'm guessing he has no idea where you are right now?"

She looked sheepishly at the ground. "No, no one knew about my plans. I borrowed my handmaiden's clothes, and left the castle in disguise."

"Idiot!" Castor spat.

"Fantastic," Parth said. "As far as he knows, we kidnapped her."

Xacthos turned to Athon. "He's right you know. Preanth might use this as an excuse to attack."

"My father is not the bloodthirsty man you make him out to be," Indura broke in defensively. "He's a good king, and a loving father. He's not going to attack until he knows what happened to me."

"Oh wake up, and live in reality!" Castor chided.

"Enough! We can't take the risk that he won't jump to a hasty conclusion," Athon said. "Xacthos, round up fifty men with hesturs. Make sure they have had some kind of rest recently, and have at least one scout. We're going to need someone who's an expert tracker. You and I will find Tam and take the princess back to Ithilton. Parth, you and Castor stay here and keep this canyon defended. If Preanth does attack, we want to be ready for him."

"You still have a lot of explaining to do, Athon," Castor growled.

"And, a lot to answer for," Parth chimed in.

"Fine!" Athon said angrily. "We'll deal with it if and when I get back, but right now we don't have time for petty arguments. Now, I'm still in command, so carry out my orders!"

"I'll send a rider to fetch Tremmon and Aurora," Parth said menacingly. "I have to tell them what happened to their son. It should be you, but you will answer for your crimes eventually. I hope you find him alive."

"I will," Athon snapped.

"You'd better. Don't bother coming back if you don't," Parth sneered. He turned and stormed off into the crowd of gathered men.

Within an hour, the group was assembled. The only scout Xacthos could find was Cyrix, and he had to borrow a mount from one of the guards. Once they had stocked up on provisions, they set out at a gallop. Cyrix had been shown where they wanted to go, and he assured them that he knew exactly how to get there as quickly as possible.

The journey took them on game trails in a part of the forest Athon had never seen. When they arrived at the campsite, it was deserted. Any signs of a battle had been all but erased.

"Where's Tam?" Indura asked as she dismounted and began to search the shore, as if she expected to see him any moment.

"Cyrix, see if you can tell what happened," Athon ordered.

"It's going to be hard to tell for sure," Cyrix said, scanning the ground for clues. "Lots of hesturs have been through here. I can't get an accurate count. Tam must have killed some of them. It looks like someone dragged several bodies into the woods. Maybe there's a grave site."

"Fan out and find those graves," Xacthos said.

"What do you want us to do with them," Cyrix asked.

"Dig them up," Athon said. "I want to see these Austicans for myself, and we can see if Tam is numbered among them."

The shallow graves were quickly located just off the beach, and within minutes, all six bodies had been exhumed. To everyone's great relief, Tam was not among them. The Austican soldiers were dressed from head to foot in loose white clothing that was stained with blood from their wounds. Each man had a headdress that was made out of a single strip of white cloth. The sturdy lightweight clothing was unlike anything Athon had ever felt before. He spent a long time examining the bodies, and even compared his skin color to theirs, which was significantly darker.

"What are you doing?" Xacthos asked.

"I'm looking to see if I can blend in with a crowd. I can't," he said, rising to his feet.

"Why would you need to do that?" Indura asked.

"Tam's been captured by them. I'm assuming that they intend to torture him for information. After that, I don't know. What I do know, is that we can't just allow that to happen. Someone has to go and get him, and since I promised his parents I would protect him, that duty falls to me."

"I'll come too," Xacthos said.

"No," Athon said quickly. "You're going to take command of the garrison. Ceanor knows I don't want Parth to do it, and Castor as a bad attitude right now. I don't know what happened in the last half pass, but Parth's not the same man I left in charge."

"You can't do this alone, Athon," Xacthos insisted. "We're certain to lose you, too."

"The answer is no. I have a better chance of doing this by myself, and someone needs to lead the men. You're the only one I can trust not to make a bigger mess of things. Go back there and tell them I relinquished command to you. Now, Parth may not want to relinquish that power, so if anyone tries to stop you, kill them."

"We'll be ready to leave momentarily, and escort the princess back to Ithilton," Xacthos said.

"No one is leaving now. We're all exhausted from the journey. Most of the men haven't slept in at least a turn. We'll camp here and set out once we have had some rest. Then you'll head back to the garrison, and I'll return the princess. If we show up with a bunch of guards, Preanth will most certainly suspect we had something to do with her disappearance. At that point, it doesn't matter what she says; he'll attack."

"I really think you're making another mistake," Xacthos said softly. "I should go with you. We have a better chance of success together."

Athon drew a heavy sigh. "I understand your concern, but it's my fault we're in this debacle, and I need to fix it myself. I won't risk another man's life because of my mistake."

They reburied the bodies and set up camp by the mouth of the trail to Ithilton. It was high-sun before everyone awoke, ready for the next leg of the journey. It was bittersweet sorrow as Athon gave Xacthos his armor and weapons, and bid farewell. For all he knew, it would be the last time the two friends would see each other. They simply saluted as they led their groups their separate ways.

# Chapter 23

# Eyvindir

A thon and Indura traveled for several hours before Indura broke the silence. "What will you tell my father?" She was very nervous about what the captain might say about her deception.

"The truth should suffice," Athon said, pausing for reflection, "and it's all I have. Hopefully, he doesn't kill me for it."

"Is it really necessary to imply that my father is mean and cruel?"

"The reason why I say your father is cruel is because he is."

"He is not!"

"I've seen him personally run a man through because he thought he was a spy."

"How did you see that? You've never even been in Ithilton except that once."

"If you say so," Athon harrumphed.

"When were you in Ithilton?"

"It was long before you were born."

"You were?" Indura asked inquisitively. "How did you know that the man wasn't a spy?"

"He wasn't, I was. Your father killed the wrong man. He was one of the soldiers at the palace. Your father suspected there might be a spy in his midst, so I framed him to throw suspicion off me. I had no way of knowing your father would personally execute him in front of the entire palace."

The revelation shocked the princess as if she had been hit by lightning. "You spied on my father?"

"It isn't something I generally tell people."

"Why are you telling me, then?"

"Because, you need to know what kind of man your father really is, and I probably won't live through this, so I might as well tell you. Your father got where he is by cunning and brute force. Most people who cross your father wind up paying a very high cost. He isn't known for his generosity or forgiveness; he is known for his ruthlessness."

"But how can that be? I've only ever seen him be kind to others in my presence."

"It's the way things are with him. I suppose he doesn't want to corrupt his sweet, innocent daughter. In a way, I have to admire him for that."

"If that's the case, why are you going to tell him the truth? Can't we tell him something that won't get you killed?"

"Don't you see what lying has done? The man you love has been captured. We don't even know if he was injured. He could be seriously maimed for all we know. He's most certainly going to be tortured. Can't you see that the lying and deceit need to end before more people are hurt?"

"I'm trying to do that," Indura insisted. "I don't want anything to happen to you, but if my father reacts the way you say, you will certainly die. Then who will save my beloved Tam?"

Athon knew she had a point. He wasn't much good to Tam locked in a dungeon or having his head decorate a spike. He thought for a long time, trying to formulate a plan. The thunder of hooves eventually interrupted his train of thought. Soldiers soon rounded a bend in the road and came barreling toward them, stopping only a short distance from the pair. The commander raised his hand and let out an audible heavy sigh. It was Eyvindir.

"Highness, what are you doing in the company of Captain Athon, *again*? Don't you realize the entire kingdom is in an uproar looking for you?"

"I'm sorry, Commander. I left to visit the prince. I knew my father wouldn't approve, so I slipped out."

"Your mistress and handmaiden were drugged. We presumed you had been kidnapped."

"No I left of my own accord," she insisted.

"It's true," Athon insisted. "She came to us at the garrison. None of my men absconded with her."

"Captain, we need to talk," Eyvindir said. "Unfortunately, this is not an appropriate place. Accompany me back to our fortress where we can speak in private."

Athon could see no reason to disagree with the commander, and the cadre of soldiers accompanied them on the journey to the fort. When they arrived, Eyvindir ushered them into a large office and shut the door.

"Captain Athon, I know that you are a trustworthy man, and I know you had nothing to do with the princess' disappearance. Unfortunately, things have gotten out of hand. After you vanished," nodding at Indura, "the king was certain you had been kidnapped by the prince. With your servants drugged, what else could it be? The king searched every home in the kingdom, and doubled the patrols on the roads leading to Campsit."

"Is that all?" Athon had a feeling of cold dread as his suspicions were slowly confirmed. Eyvindir looked worried, and Athon knew he wouldn't be told everything.

"For now, but it's too soon to be certain. Fortunately, with her return, his anger may subside, but for your sake, I would suggest you let me take her back to the palace. If you were to do it, it would confirm the king's suspicions, and he would kill you."

"I appreciate your candor," Athon said. "Let me be equally forthright. Indura did not come directly to the garrison to visit the prince."

"Oh," Eyvindir said, raising an eyebrow.

"Since I wasn't there, I'll let her explain," Athon said, directing his words at Indura.

Indura recounted the particulars of her rendezvous, and escape. Athon was somewhat surprised that she gave as much detail as she did. Evidently, what he had said about telling the truth must have pricked her conscience, because she didn't hold anything back. Her voice waivered and she began to cry as she told how Tam had stayed to fight so she could flee. Eyvindir sat and listened intently to her story. When she was finished, she seemed crushed by the gravity of the situation, but inwardly, she felt as if a great weight had been lifted.

"He must love you very much," Eyvindir said gently. "It is a brave man that realizes he is hopelessly outnumbered, and is willing to die to protect the woman he loves."

Indura had not looked at Tam's heroics from that perspective. He must love her as much as she loves him. He was willing to die to protect her. She felt selfish and ungrateful for her thoughtlessness. Now it was Tam who was in danger, and she wasn't lifting a finger to help him. She clenched her jaw tightly in self–loathing. She looked at Athon. Here was a man who was going to risk his life to do that which she wasn't willing to do herself. She loved Tam more than anything in the world, and now she was going to prove it. Her resolve cemented in an instant, and her duty suddenly seemed very clear. She was going to do whatever it took to ensure that Tam did not suffer a fate worse than death. Athon wouldn't be the only person trying to save him. She would see that he was brought back to safety, even if she died in the process. "Yes, I think he really must love me, and I love him."

"Your father would not approve," Eyvindir cautioned.

"My father does not own my heart," Indura spat haughtily, "or control my feelings. It is my own business who I choose to give my affection to, and no other."

"With all due respect, your Highness, your hand is a matter of state's interest," Eyvindir said. "Your father has every right to dictate who can and who cannot seek your affection, but that is not the issue here. What is the issue is what to do with you for the time being. I know you've had a long journey, and probably wish to rest. I see no reason why we can't wait until even–sun to leave for the palace. Captain, you're welcome to rest here as well before you head back to the garrison."

"Thank you for the kindness, but I won't be headed back to my kingdom. Tam is a prisoner of the Austicans. I might be able to intercept them before they get back to Austica. If I can't, I'll go into their capitol and rescue him from prison."

"You're out of your mind," Eyvindir said, shaking his head in disbelief. "You have no idea what route they are taking or where they are going."

"I'll take my chances," Athon said bluntly. "Even if it takes me the rest of my life, I will not abandon him. I don't know much about these people. Do you have any information that could prove useful to my cause?"

Eyvindir eyed him carefully. "If your prince was captured, they are most likely headed back to Austica's capitol, Dehnet. It's very far from here," he said, pointing to a map on the wall. "It's situated on the banks of this river. Between Ithilton and Dehnet is a large desert. It will take several turns to cross. If you don't take enough water for you and your mount, you'll die. If the prince is lucky, he will be sold as a slave. If they decide he has information they want, he will sit in the palace dungeon and be tortured until he dies."

"Is there any way I can get across the desert without anyone knowing?"

"Our boarder with Austica is heavily guarded, but there might be one way. Austica and Ithilton might be enemies, but that doesn't mean there isn't a demand for goods. There are caravans that take items back and forth between Ithilton and Dehnet. They leave from the village of Skaraton every few turns. If you went with them as some kind of merchant, you could get into Dehnet with little trouble. I don't know exactly how you plan on accomplishing that."

"What can you tell me about its people?"

"They're sun worshipers, and fanatical about their religion. They are led by their king, H'met. He's said to be their god in human form. They worship him, and every word out of his mouth is scripture. That's as much as I can tell you. I hope it's useful."

"It would be nice to know more, but I'll take what I can get. If I could get some provisions from you, I'll be leaving as soon as I can."

"We will give you anything you need," Indura said, before the commander could respond. "You'll need some money, too. Commander, give Athon enough gold so he looks like a merchant."

"I can't just open our coffers to him," Eyvindir said with exasperation.

"I will see that you are compensated. Do as I command. One hundred gold pieces should be plenty."

"That's an entire ceanors pay for half my garrison!"

"Do you have it or not?"

"We do, but I can't just waltz into the treasury and embezzle the payroll. If people found out, I'd have a mutiny on my hands. Even if I could, how can I explain the need for more gold to replace it?"

"This isn't a request," Indura bristled. "I'm ordering you to do it, and I *know* you won't defy me if you know what's good for you."

Eyvindir paused, gritting his teeth hard. After what seemed like an eternity, he let out a heavy sigh. "I will see that he gets it before he leaves," Eyvindir said reluctantly. "If that's all, Your Highness, I will have you escorted to our guest quarters so you can rest."

"I will need to retrieve my saddlebag before I turn in," Indura said.

Eyvindir had soldiers escort Athon to the storehouse and Indura to the stables. The commander gave specific orders that the soldier escorting her stand guard outside the princess' quarters. Indura was irritated by the directive, but didn't see any way of circumventing it. The watchful eye of the soldier was going to make her departure tricky.

She retrieved her saddlebag, and followed the lone man to a bedroom reserved for visitors. It might as well have been a prison cell for all she cared, one that she was determined to escape. She closed the door, and quickly began to make a visual inventory of the contents of the room. It was a medium sized with a few standard furnishings. There were some decorations and a cold fireplace, but nothing ornate. She just needed something heavy, but not so heavy, she couldn't lift it. She had to work quickly if her plan was going to succeed.

It took Athon only a half an hour to gather enough food and water sacks to last ten turns. It would be a lot of water weight for Zuri to carry once he filled them, but it would get lighter as both master and mount drank. He had also taken the liberty of changing into a set of civilian clothes he acquired from the garrison before he left. He was just finishing up with securing the bulky load when Eyvindir joined him.

"You work quickly, Captain," the commander said, discreetly placing a heavy pouch in his hand. "I would have thought you'd take a moment to rest."

"There's no time to sit," Athon said, slipping the pouch into his saddlebag. "Every hour puts more distance between me and Tam's abductors. I have to get going as soon as possible."

"You are wise not to wear your uniform. Did you get those here?" Eyvindir indicated the clothing.

"No, this was something I had with me." Athon extended his hand to Eyvindir. "You have my sincerest thanks for everything. I wish there was a way to repay you, but I fear that will never be possible."

"If you survive, it will be thanks enough," Eyvindir said, giving Athon's hand a firm shake. "Find your prince, and return safely to your people, but you should know that Preanth's patience has evaporated. You would be wise to keep a low profile, and return quickly."

Athon smiled and mounted Zuri. He had caught the thinly veiled warning. "If your king were more like you, we would live in a much happier world, and if we don't meet again in this life, I will see you in the next." With that, Athon spurred his hestur and headed down the road.

Eyvindir turned and headed back into the barracks. He would have to dispatch a messenger to the king, informing him of the news of the princess being found safe. He would also need to get as much rest as possible if he was going to face Preanth. He began seriously thinking of what he was going to say, and hoped the wrath of the king would be tempered by the return of the princess. He turned the corner toward his office, and nearly bowled over a raven–haired scullery maid holding a saddlebag. "Mind where you're going, you dirty oaf," he roared. She kept her head bowed in a low curtsy, and whispered a faint apology. He shrugged her off and continued to his office. What a shame, he thought, she would have pleasant features if she wasn't such a drudge.

# Chapter 24

# TORMENTOR

Pain bored into Tam's skull from the back of his head. He could feel it throbbing all the way into his eyes. His arm ached as if it had been sawed off halfway to his elbow. Waves of nausea poured over him like a drowning man in a turbulent sea. He could feel something stifling over his face blocking out the sun, but holding all the heat in. He tried to remove it, but his arms refused to obey his commands. He suddenly realized that his hands were bound to something hard. As he regained consciousness, he became aware of a rhythmic motion swaying his body to and fro, making him sicker. The steady plodding and smell of hesturs assailed his ears and nose. He was lying on his back on some kind of stretcher. He had no idea where he was. He let out a groan through his parched lips.

Suddenly, the blanket was thrown off his face. A strange looking man in a white uniform looked at him with a wry smile. "You've decided to return to the land of the living, my friend? Don't try to move, you're bound for your own good."

"Where am I?" Tam opened his eyes a crack, only to be confronted by the searing brilliance of the sun. He looked around to survey his situation. The world seemed to twist and turn as if he were moving on some gelatinous blob. Everything was out of focus and doubled, but he knew he had been completely disarmed and his armor was gone. All he was wearing now was his tunic and pants, even his boots had been removed.

He closed his eyes to stave off the inevitable sickness to no avail. With great effort, he leaned as far as he could and vomited violently. He was unsuccessful in diverting the emesis away from his body, and was now soaking in his own vile fluid.

It seemed like an eternity before the wrenching subsided and he could return to his relatively comfortable position on the stretcher. The man in white leaned over and gave him some water from a canteen. The liquid wasn't cool, but it wet his chapped lips and removed the taste of bile from his mouth.

"You should lie still, and keep your eyes shut for now," the man in white said, placing a cool piece of cloth on his forehead. "Struggling will only make you sicker, my friend. Normally, we wouldn't move someone in your condition, but your warning device changed our plans."

"Who are you?"

"My name is of little importance to you," the man in white said. His voice was gentle and kind as if Tam was his young child.

"Who would I call for if I need help: hey you?"

The man arched one eyebrow and considered this for a moment. "I am called D'jefra. Now it is time for you to return the favor. Who are you and where do you come from?"

"My name is Tam." He paused for a moment. The recollection of what had happened at the lake seemed like a dream, but it had occurred to him that maybe it wasn't, and he needed to be careful what he said. He was leery of D'jefra's kindness, and wasn't sure if he was being genuine. "I live alone in the mountains."

"What were you doing at the lake?" D'jefra said soothingly.

"I was hunting game for food."

"Who was the woman who was with you?"

"There wasn't anyone else. I was alone."

"If you were alone who did you warn with those devices?"

"I was trying to warn you to leave. It didn't work," Tam groaned with pain.

"You should rest for now, my friend, Tam," D'jefra said, rewetting the cloth on Tam's head, and moving it down over his eyes. "We will discuss your story when you have had time to recuperate. I'm sure the pain in your head has clouded your thoughts, so you are unsure of the truth. I must warn you that if you continue to lie to me, you will suffer unimaginable torment."

"Thank you for not covering my face with the blanket," Tam said. "I could barely breathe with it on."

"Sleep now," D'jefra said soothingly. "We will talk later."

It didn't take Tam long to drift into an uneasy sleep filled with unsettling dreams. He was walking through the forest on the road toward Ithilton. He traveled for what seemed like an eternity. When he finally arrived at the palace, he found it deserted. He wandered through its empty corridors searching for his lovely Indura. From the highest tower to the lowest dungeon he searched in vain. Frustrated by the fruitless search, he made his way to the Grand Hall. Seated on the top of the great dais was the princess. She sat on the throne looking regal. An ornate gold crown graced her auburn hair. He ran up the stairs excited to see her. "I've found you, at last," he cried.

"I've been here," she said placidly.

"I've been looking all over. Where have you been?"

Indura looked at him with dead eyes. "Who are you?"

"It's me, Tam," he said, stunned by her question. "Don't you remember me?"

"I've never seen you before in my life. How did you get in here?" She didn't wait for an answer. "Guards, kill him!"

He turned, and what was an empty space now was filled with hundreds of men running toward him with swords drawn. He turned again and fled. Even though he was running as fast as he could, it was as if he was trying to run through water. Although he didn't seem to be moving very quickly, he stayed one–step ahead of the soldiers who pursued him. He went through a door at the end of a passageway and found himself going down a long staircase. The soldiers followed him and kept right at his heels. He continued down the steps in a blind run, trying to evade his attackers. When he finally reached the bottom, he found another door. He quickly opened it to find Indura standing just beyond it holding a sword.

She looked at him impassively. "Liar," she said icily. She took the sword and plunged it into his chest. The blade burned like fire as it split his skin and entered his beating heart. He groaned in pain and woke with a start.

The smell of rotting vomit assailed his nostrils. He could feel the vile fluid coating his right side, permeating his clothing and hair. He felt disgusting, and was in desperate need of a bath.

They had stopped moving. The stretcher Tam was on had been moved to the ground. He opened his eyes to the darkness of a tent. The only light was the dim flicker of a small oil lamp hanging from a pole in the center of the shelter. The lamp cast deep shadows on the walls, which danced in the warm light. D'jefra sat next to him, watching him as if enthralled by his captive.

"Bad dream?" D'jefra asked calmly.

"No," Tam said slowly. "I just woke up suddenly, that's all." His mouth was so dry the words felt like a thick paste on his tongue. "Could I have some water, please?"

"Of course," D'jefra said, putting a canteen of warm water to the prince's lips, and letting him take a good, long drink. "I would offer you food, but I think we should wait on that until you've had a chance to have your stomach settle. For right now, I have some questions you need to answer."

"Where am I?" Tam asked.

"That is not important, and from now on, you will not ask any more questions. All right, my friend," D'jefra said, with a smile that seemed tinged with anger. "You will answer my questions truthfully this time, or I shall make your pain quite exquisite. Do you understand?" Tam nodded his head. "Now, who are you?"

"My name is Tam."

"Are you sure of this?"

"No, I would never lie about a thing like that."

"Do you have any idea what would happen to you if you were to lie to me?" D'jefra moved over to Tam and knelt by his side. Tam shook his head. "Do you know that when you were captured, you had a number of severe injuries? Your head was split open, and you had broken your left arm. We sutured your head and placed a splint on your arm. Have you ever had a broken arm before?" Tam again shook his head. "They can be quite painful if they haven't been properly immobilized." D'jefra untied the straight dowels that secured Tam's arm in place. "I am truly sorry for what I must do, my friend, but you must be shown what will happen if you do not tell me what I want to hear."

D'jefra cradled Tam's hand firmly in his own and grasped his shoulder with the other. With Tam's arm forming an L shape, D'jefra began slowly rotating his hand toward him. Pain shot through his arm and into his neck as the bone began to grind at the break site. Tam let out a chilling scream that pierced the air. D'jefra continued the slow progression until he was satisfied his captive knew exactly what he would do. He then slowly moved the arm back into place.

Tam was panting heavily when his arm finally stopped moving. He had never felt anything that painful before. His arm burned like fire and his fingers tingled as if they were asleep. The pain radiated up his shoulder, through his neck, and into the back of his head. He sobbed with the agony his arm had been forced to endure. Why was his tormentor doing this?

With the same sickly soothing voice, D'jefra spoke again. "I know that was painful, my friend. I don't wish to continue to hurt you, so you must be completely honest with me. If I feel that you are lying to me, I will punish you until you tell me what I want to know. As painful as this is, I can do much, much worse. I can leave you crippled for the rest of your life. If you are very good, and tell me what I want to hear, I will reward you. Instead of spending the rest of your days feeling the pain of dungeon torturers, I will see that you become a slave to a kind master. Now answer me, what is your name?"

"My name is Tam."

"Very well, Tam. Where do you live?"

"In the mountains."

"By yourself?"

"Yes."

D'jefra smiled malevolently. "I don't believe you."

He rotated Tam's arm again, this time turning it until it was nearly perpendicular to his body. The pain was excruciating. Tam's screams would be difficult for the casual observer to listen to, but D'jefra derived an immense amount of pleasure from the suffering of his enemy.

"Stop! Stop!" Tam pleaded for mercy from this stranger who seemed to derive some sadistic pleasure from this torture. "I'll tell you anything!"

"Oh," D'jefra said with a sickening grin, "I know you will, my friend."

# Chapter 25

# From Bargain to Dounie

F
rom his examination of the map in Eyvindir's office, Skaraton was more east than north of the stronghold Athon had journeyed from mere hours ago. He knew his way around most of the kingdom, and had heard of the place, but had never been there before. He had made good time, and felt the shade of a tree by a small brook would be a good place to stop to rest for a moment. While Zuri took advantage of the plentiful water, Athon rested his eyes.

The sound of approaching hoof beats jolted him awake. His vision cleared to one of the filthiest women he had ever seen riding atop a gray hestur. She came to a stop a short way from him and sat there, blinking through soot–obscured eyes. There was an odd familiarity about her, but what struck him most was the mismatched sight of a grubby maid riding down the road atop a majestic animal. She dismounted and silently led her mount to the side of the stream. As her hestur began to drink, she began washing the grime from her hands and face. Her presence reminded him that he needed to get moving, so he walked over to Zuri, who had moved from trying to drink the stream dry to feasting on the tall grass that lined the bank. He felt bad about cutting his hestur's meal short, but it would have to wait until they arrived at Skaraton. He mounted and wheeled toward the road.

"I wish you would wait long enough for me to wash some of this soot off," the drudge said with a familiar tone.

Athon leaped from Zuri's back and raced to the woman's side. There was no possible way she could be who he thought she was. He grabbed her arm and pulled her so he could get a good look at her face. "Indura, how did you get here?" The question was moot. Athon had already guessed what happened. "You shouldn't be here. You should have gone back to your father." He paused. "How did you even get out of that room?"

"A good disguise and a well–placed chair to the head."

"You need to go home right now."

"No, I'm coming with you to rescue Tam."

"No, you're not. You're getting on that hestur and you're heading back to your father. I have no time for selfish little girls."

She shook herself free from his grasp, offended at his remark. "You're right, and that's why I'm coming with you. For once, I'm not thinking of myself. I'm thinking of Tam, not me."

"No, you're not thinking at all!" Athon yelled. "This is dangerous. I could die, but at least I know what I'm doing. You can't even lift a sword."

Indura's ears burned with anger. She turned and drew the weapon she had stashed in her saddle. She wielded the sharp blade at Athon. "If I'm so helpless, then you should take this sword from my hand, and stop me before I hurt myself."

"I don't have time for this," he hissed.

With a flick of her wrist, she smacked him on the shoulder with the flat of the blade. "Fight me."

"I'm not going to do that," Athon said, turning to mount Zuri. "You're being a ridiculous child. You should go home while you have the chance."

She ran up and hit him on his backside with the sword. "Fight me, you coward, or next time I will use the edge."

He rounded on her in anger, only to be staring at the tip of the lethal weapon. "You want to fight me," he said. "Fine!" His hands moved deftly and brought a throwing knife out of a hidden pocket in his pants. He quickly knocked the sword away from his face. With his other hand, he drew a dagger concealed in his boot, and brought it even with her face. "I don't want to hurt you, Princess."

"I don't want to hurt you either, but if this is the only way you'll respect me, I will have to resort to violence."

"What do you think is going to happen here?" Athon knew that he could kill her, expending little effort in the process, but knew that wasn't an option. If they continued down this path, someone was going to be hurt.

"You have to take me with you," Indura said coldly. "I love Tam more than life. If you don't let me help, I'll just go on my own. Do you want that? Do you want me to venture alone into enemy territory?"

He knew she would make good on her threat to go it alone. He dropped the weapons to his sides, and drew a heavy sigh. What was he going to do with her? He couldn't let her come, but he couldn't just allow her to act so rashly. "Either decision is unacceptable," he said, "but it appears as if I have little choice in the matter." Athon knew if he didn't protect her, no one would. "You can come on the condition that you do exactly as I say."

She dropped her sword, threw her dirty arms around his neck, and kissed his cheek. "Thank you, Captain, you won't regret this."

"I already do," Athon said pushing her away. She looked at him and began to laugh. He looked down at what used to be a clean outfit. He was now smeared with chimney soot. "Thanks for making me as dirty as you are. You do realize you'll have to stay disguised. If anyone finds out your identity, the consequences for my kingdom and me would be horrific."

"I can stay incognito. With this disguise I'm sure no one will recognize me."

"The problem is that Eyvindir's men saw you like that. They're probably headed this way right now. Who knows how soon they will overtake us. We need to leave now and find someplace where we can get you another disguise."

"I might have an idea on where we can do that," she said, replacing her sword and mounting Azul. "You'll have to trust that I know what I'm doing."

Athon mounted Zuri, and rolled his eyes in disgust. "Fine, lead the way, but this had better be fast." The pair galloped down the road and turned southward when they came to a crossroads. They rode for nearly an hour before they came to a quaint little village surrounded by farms. At the edge of the town, they stopped at a small cottage set off the main path. The stone structure looked old, but kempt. The outside was festooned with flowers that seemed to grow from the very walls. Planters hung from the eaves, decorating the cottage in a veritable rainbow of color.

As the two riders dismounted, a beautiful middle–aged woman stepped out. Athon instantly recognized her comely face, and silky raven hair. Time, it seemed, had been very good to her. She suddenly froze as her eyes rested on the duo. As they approached, her mouth gaped and eyes widened. It was as if she had seen a ghost. A shaky hand stopped the silent scream from escaping her lips.

"Dissa?" Athon said rhetorically.

Indura turned and looked at Athon in awe. "You know this woman?"

"No," Dissa said shaking her head in disbelief, "You're dead. You have to be dead."

"As you can see, I'm very much alive. I had to leave." Athon approached her slowly, expecting her to run at any moment. "I didn't want to leave you, but I had no choice."

"You had no choice?" Dissa's voice grew terse as tears filled her eyes. "You left me all alone to rot!"

Athon caught her hand before it could find his face. "I didn't mean to hurt you."

"Get your filthy — " Dissa started, but Athon's hand had quickly covered her mouth. He picked her up and drew her inside the dimly lit cottage.

Indura followed the struggling pair inside and closed the door. "Athon, what are you doing? We need her help."

"She isn't going to help us by alerting her neighbors. It's imperative that we attract as little attention as possible. Dissa, stop fighting me, I'm not trying to hurt you." He winced as he could feel her begin to bite his fingers. "Quit biting me. Indura, talk some sense into her."

Indura took off the wig, and Dissa's struggle ceased. Her jaw relaxed and she released Athon's fingers. "Dissa," Indura said softly, "it's me, Indura. We aren't going to hurt you, but you have to stop. Please relax and just trust that I won't let any harm come to you."

Athon released his hold on Dissa's mouth and let the woman get up. "I should call the constable," Dissa hissed.

"Please, don't do that," Indura said softly. "Let us explain."

"It's Agmundir here that should do all the explaining," Dissa said sourly. "Explain why you left me to suffer at the hands of Preanth. Explain how my daughter had to grow up a fatherless servant, never knowing the man responsible for bringing her into this world. Explain it all, you coward!"

"Who is Agmundir?" Indura asked, confused by the name.

"Him!" Dissa spat. "Why, what name does he *really* use?"

"Athon — but that isn't important. I have a daughter?" Athon asked incredulously.

"You are a father, but one without honor," Dissa said cruelly.

"You're Mai's father?" Indura was dumbfounded.

"I'm not a father."

"Oh, yes, you are," Dissa said. "I didn't know I was pregnant until a ceanor after you disappeared."

"Who is Mai?" Athon asked Indura.

"She's her handmaiden, and your daughter."

"I thought you told me that Mai's father was dead." Indura said.

"He was," Dissa said, "or so I thought. I thought Preanth had discovered your treachery and had you killed. The turn you left, I was imprisoned as a traitor.

I suffered an entire ceanor in the dungeon before anyone knew I was carrying Mai in my womb."

"No one knew about our love affair, let alone our marriage."

Indura fell silent into a chair. She watched with unblinking fascination the revelatory events unfold. Although she had visited Dissa on a number of occasions, the subject of Mai's father had never really been discussed other than his death. She listened intently to the drama that was unfolding in front of her. Athon had indeed been a spy, and he had a greater impact on her life than she ever imagined. Mai was like a best friend and a sister all rolled up in one. Now, she was in the same room as the father she never knew. It was the most fascinating thing she had ever witnessed.

"One of the maids saw you leave my quarters once. From that, the king surmised that we were lovers, but no one ever guessed we were married. When Preanth discovered the truth, I was sentenced to death. Since I was Elina's servant, she pleaded for my life, and I was sentenced to spend the rest of my life locked away in the dungeon. When they found out I was pregnant, the king took pity on me, and made me an offer I couldn't refuse."

"I'm almost afraid to ask," Athon said meekly.

"In exchange for my freedom, I would give him the child when she turned ten. She would then be a servant to the queen. As far as I was concerned, he wanted me as far away from him as possible, so I was banished here. Occasionally, I get to visit with my daughter, but mostly she stays in the castle bound to Your Highness."

"If I had any idea that you were in danger, I would have taken you with me," Athon said with a sincere voice. "I wanted to take you with me, but I knew you wouldn't understand."

"It was all a lie," Dissa said bitterly. "Your whole life with me was a fabrication so you could obtain information. So, you went back to your life in Campsit. I'm sure you found someone new to share your bed. Typical man! You only do what is easy, and never what's right."

"My identity may have been a lie," Athon said, holding back the flood of emotions, "but my love for you wasn't. I loved you more than anything, and it nearly killed me to leave you. I have often dreamed of seeing you just one more time, but I knew that wasn't possible. There has never been, nor will there ever be, another woman in my life. I could never bring myself to fall in love with anyone else."

"You've been alone this whole time?" Dissa asked in disbelief.

"There has never been room in my heart for anyone but you. There isn't a turn that goes by that I don't think of you, and I'm very sorry that I abandoned you. If I had known you would be a prisoner, I would have taken you with me. Please forgive me."

"I've cursed your name ever since you left, and prayed that you were bound to purgatory," Dissa said, as tears flowed down her cheeks. "I loved you with all my heart, and you broke it. After all these passes why have you come back into my life?"

"We need your help," Indura said softly.

"Are you a Campsit spy disguised as my beloved princess?"

"No—it's a long story."

"Well, I'm not helping you until I know."

Indura sighed and told the story of her meeting Tam. How she fell in love, and corresponded with him. How she planned the secret meeting at the lake, and all the events leading up to her arrival at the cottage.

Dissa listened quietly, finally speaking when the princess had finished. "I think you're being incredibly foolish going on this expedition. Have you stopped to think about what could happen if you fail?"

"Yes," Indura said firmly, "I have."

"What do you have to say for yourself, Agmundir—Athon—whatever? Do you really think you can protect the princess and rescue the prince in an empire filled with people trying to kill you?"

"I admit, it isn't going to be easy," Athon said, "but we do have an advantage. The Austicans aren't looking for either of us. If we keep our cover we can make it in, and hopefully out without arousing suspicion."

"What exactly do you need from me?" Dissa asked the question not expecting a meaningful answer.

"A new disguise for the princess," Athon responded. "She needs something to change her appearance, so she can slip past any Ithilton soldiers that may be looking for her."

"Why should I help you? If I reported this fraud, you would be safe, and he would be taken away in irons."

"I thought you loved him," Indura said calmly. "Why would you want to see him suffer?"

"Do you have any idea how much I've suffered because of him?"

"I can't imagine, but you can't let this hate consume you," Indura cautioned. "Seeing him in prison or killed won't heal any of your pain. It will just make you feel empty, and it won't keep me from trying to rescue Tam. I'll just escape and head into Austica by myself. I love the prince more than anything, and I'll not see him suffer when I can do something about it. You said you loved Athon. You can come with us and never be apart from him again."

"No," Athon said emphatically, "I won't allow it."

"And why not?" Indura asked crossly.

"It's far too dangerous. I don't want to see her injured, too."

"I see," Dissa said coldly. "You'll put her life in jeopardy, but not mine."

"I don't want her to come at all," Athon said tersely, "but no one seems to be able to stop her. All I can do is try and keep her from killing herself."

"I can handle myself," Indura huffed. "Together we could keep you safe."

"It's all right, Highness," Dissa said, patting the princess on the shoulder. "I'd rather stay here. Agmundir would be hard-pressed to watch over both of us. Besides, I have some things to think over while you two are out trying to kill yourselves."

"When we get back, you two could be together again. Now you know he's alive, and he knows where you live. He could come and take you back to Campsit with him."

"I don't know that is possible," Dissa said quietly. "It's been so long, and there is a lot of hurt to forget. It is too much to ignore."

"Let's not worry about that right now," Athon said. "Will you help us or not?"

"Yes," Dissa said reluctantly. "I'll help you. First, we need to do something about your hair. Your natural color is too distinctive, and the soldiers will be looking for a woman with black hair. We'll have to dye it before we cut it."

"Cut my hair?" Indura exclaimed holding it like a prized possession. "Why would you want to do that?"

"Every soldier in Ithilton is looking for you, and I'm afraid that your little stunt with the guards will have them looking for a raven haired woman now. We could dye your hair another color, but I'm thinking that maybe being a woman is your biggest liability."

"What are you suggesting?" Athon questioned, sensing her train of thought.

"They won't be looking for a brown haired boy," Dissa said triumphantly, "now will they?"

"What about the clothes?" Athon was slightly more skeptical of this plan. "There's also a matter of her—well—uh—chest."

"Her breasts I can handle," Dissa said confidently, "but I'm afraid we're going to have to make the clothes. There are tailors in the village, but they might ask questions. The fewer people that know about this, the better off we'll all be. I don't suppose you have any spares?"

"I have one change of spy clothing and my uniform, but neither will fit her."

"No, but I'll wager I can use the material to make some that will fit. They will look more like boys clothing than anything I might have stashed away, but what makes these clothes different from normal ones?"

"There are pockets designed to hide weapons and other items, very useful when you can't have a belt lined with the tools for combat."

"Give them to me," I'll try to keep the pockets intact, but somehow, I don't think it will be an issue with our dear princess if they don't survive my mending."

It was low–sun before they were finished cleaning Indura off and transforming her. Dissa had used a thick, chocolate–brown tea to turn the princess' deep red locks into a wavy brunette beauty. It was now time to cut her hair, and re–dye it if necessary. Indura had cried when the beautiful strands of hair lay strewn on the floor to be replaced by a do that was shorter than Athon's. He looked at her and sincerely doubted that even Mai would recognize her.

"You'll need to decide on a new name," Athon said. "I can't very well go around calling you Indura. No one will believe you're a boy if I do that."

Indura thought for a moment. "What name are you using?"

"I've always been partial to Agmundir," Athon said quickly. "It's been a while since I've been used to hearing it, but I shouldn't have any problems answering to it."

"Am I posing as your son?"

"I would imagine that would be the most plausible."

"Then I should be Igmundir, don't you think? It will sound more like we're father and son."

"The question is will you be able to answer when I call you Igmundir?"

"I don't know," Indura said thoughtfully. "I suppose if I hear it enough I will become accustomed to it."

"You had better," Athon said, his tone weighing in on the seriousness of the matter, "if you don't, people will start to question us. The more people question our story, the more we stick out. If we're too conspicuous, that could end the whole thing. Spies depend on the ability to blend, but right now it's late, and we need some rest."

There was only one bed in the small one room cottage, so Athon slept on the floor. It was cramped on the bed, but Indura and Dissa slept soundly. Athon woke before either of the women. He had sat in the chair and stared at the sleeping love of his life. He was still processing the fact that he was a father now, and that she harbored so much animosity for him. He reflected on his decision to leave her so many passes ago. He wondered if he would make that same mistake again, knowing then what he knew now.

When Dissa finally opened her eyes, they met his. The two sat in silence, unable to look away. There was only a short distance between them, but it felt as if they were on opposite ends of the world. Athon wondered if things would ever be the same with them again. They stared at each other for quite a while before Dissa got up slowly so as not to disturb Indura's slumber.

They didn't speak as Dissa began to alter the clothes Athon had brought to complete Indura's disguise. It was high–sun before the princess finally woke up, and the trio had anything to eat. The entire turn was spent waiting for Dissa to finish the clothes. Athon felt that if they ventured outside, someone might take more interest in them than he wanted, so he saw to it that he and Indura stayed inside the cramped cottage. It was bad enough there were two hesturs outside, but a strange boy in a dress would only invite scrutiny.

Indura spent the hours talking to Dissa about Mai, and the news of Ithilton. Athon just sat and silently watched the only woman he ever loved.

An hour before late–sun, the clothes were finished with most of the special pockets intact. While Indura changed into her disguise, Athon went outside to tend to the hesturs. With the help of a tight bandage and a loose fitting shirt, the problem of Indura's buxomness was solved to Dissa's satisfaction.

With the disguise complete, Athon returned inside. He approved of the trans-formation, and for the first time felt, they might have a chance to pull off the ruse. Before they left, he had some unfinished business he needed to complete. He pulled Dissa aside and spoke quietly in her ear. "I know you might hate me, but that doesn't change the fact that I have always loved you. If I thought I could keep you safe, I would take you along, but I can't do that. If we make it through this, I want you to come home with me."

Dissa hesitated for a moment. "I need to have time to think about it," she said skeptically. "There's so much—I don't know—I guess we'll have to cross that bridge when we come to it."

"Fair enough," Athon said, conceding that he may have lost the only woman he ever loved, again. It was painful to think that instead of being forced apart by circumstance, he would lose her heart. "We need to leave now. Time is a luxury we really don't have, and we've wasted too much of it already."

Athon and Indura got on their hesturs, and readied for the long journey ahead of them. Dissa wished Indura a pleasant journey, but could only look at Athon with the internal emotional etched on her face.

He looked at her beauty one last time. She was just as lovely as she was the first turn he laid eyes on her. He felt the same love for her that he did all those passes ago. It was as if they had never parted, but he knew they had both changed. "I love you, Dissa." She returned his offering with a long, pained silence. With a discouraged smile, Athon turned and rode away with Indura.

# Chapter 26

# DUNGEON

As far as Tam was concerned, the inquisition had lasted for an eternity. He had answered every one of D'jefra's questions truthfully. Despite his honesty, his captor had mercilessly contorted his arm to force him into revealing every bit of information. Several times, he had vomited, wretched, and nearly passed out, but fate had not been kind to him, and he remained conscious for the whole ordeal. After he was finished with ruthless questioning, D'jefra re–set Tam's arm and replaced the splint. Tam's arm throbbed, and was very swollen. Even though he was in agony, he was eventually able to fall asleep again.

He was awakened before even–sun by the soldiers as they broke camp. D'jefra untied Tam long enough for him to relieve his distended bladder and clean off in a nearby stream, but it was only a temporary reprieve. The soldiers returned the prince to the stretcher that had become his filthy mobile prison, and secured his limbs tightly. The abrasive ropes had begun to chafe his skin raw.

Tam thought about trying to escape, but it was no use. He had no weapons, a broken arm, and surrounded by fourteen men who had no such handicap. He figured that for the time being, he was stuck being a captive. He had stopped trying to struggle with his bonds because of the soreness in his wrists and ankles. Soon, he settled into the routine that accompanied his situation. He was given a small amount of water every few hours, but never enough to quench his thirst. Twice per turn, he was freed to stretch his legs, but the rest of the time was spent restrained on the stretcher.

His requests for food went unanswered, and as the turns went by, he grew hungrier. His stomach became so pained by lack of food that it nearly rivaled his arm, but his pleas to D'jefra were met by an icy smile.

Each turn they traveled great distances, yet they avoided any human contact. Tam tried to pass the time by orienting himself to features he could recognize. While they were in the forest it was virtually impossible to see beyond the trees, but as they moved into the savanna of the Ithilton plains, he was able to see quite a bit. They had forded several large rivers on their generally eastward progress, but the only thing Tam could look at was the majestic Wall Mountains that were steadily retreating into the distance. Turn after turn, the monotony of the routine grew on Tam as he gradually accepted the idea that he would never again set foot on those mountains. There was no rescue from this hellish nightmare. His only consolation was that D'jefra did not continue to torture him

Tam's hope of some form of rescue faded completely when, after six turns, they began to cross a hot wasteland of sand. The heat was unbearable as the sun beat down on him constantly. His lips cracked and bled. His stomach pains had become a constant reminder of his plight, but had become almost pleasant. He was weak now, and needed help when he was allowed to be free of his bonds. He felt that soon he would die from either starvation or thirst. The only comfort left to him was sleep, but his dreams still mirrored his reality, intensifying his suffering.

It took several turns to cross the burning sands of the desert and arrive in the fertile valley that provided Austica with its substance. Unlike the plains of Ithilton, the valley of Austica was thick with cultivated vegetation. The river that cut through the green valley was larger than any Tam had ever seen. Boats, both large and small, plied through the deep water in search of fish or hauling commodities to the various cities that punctuated the landscape.

The caravan skirted the ridge overlooking the river valley for nearly two full turns before veering toward the grandest city Tam had ever seen. Everything seemed to be built of immense blocks. Large, step–like buildings dominated the landscape with tall spires made entirely of stone proclaiming the various entrances and intersections of the magnificent city. Tam calculated that hundreds of thousands of people must live here. The walls to the citadel seemed to soar higher than the ones at Campsit or Ithilton.

As they made their way through the bustling crowds of the city streets, he could tell he was attracting the attention of everyone they passed. He was a trophy of war, an oddity like an uht born with three heads and five legs. Everyone had to look at the strange man in his strange clothes.

The streets were full of the noise of people chatting, selling, buying, haggling on the price of one commodity or another, and all kinds of strange music on stranger instruments played by musicians begging for sustenance. The aroma of cooking meats wafted into his nostrils only to torment him by highlighting his starvation.

Tam noticed that almost all of the people had similar attributes. Deep brown skin and jet–black hair dominated the populous. Most of the people wore white, loose–fitting clothes of varying quality except the men building the stone edifices, who dressed in little more than a loincloth. Everyone took time from their busy lives to stare at the prisoner on parade.

They arrived at a circular building near several large buildings. Tam figured it was a palace of some sort, but as to its true purpose, he had no idea. What concerned him most was the monolith into which he was being carried. There didn't seem to be any windows, and there was only one door that was guarded by two soldiers. They passed through the small opening and into a dimly lit chamber. A frail old man approached and began examining Tam, who was too weak to protest.

"What a sorry state he's in. I take it you haven't given him much of anything to eat," the old man said, directing his indifferent words to D'jefra. "There's hardly any life in him at all."

"He wasn't worthy," D'jefra said. "I barely had enough for my men to survive the return trip. He should be grateful he got anything."

"So, you leave it to me to play nursemaid?" The old man grew cross. "He hardly has strength to move. If I have to sit and feed him until he becomes stronger, it will cost you."

"Can he be sold as a slave or not, T'lal?" D'jefra said impatiently.

"That depends on if he can recover. How do you expect me to make a profit? A slave with a lame arm makes him almost worthless. I won't quote you anything until his arm heals and he has had a chance to recover from your neglect."

"If you can't get me full price, don't even bother," D'jefra said coldly. "Holy H'met always has need of sacrifices. I'd rather take his rate than the pittance I will get if you fail. Keep me informed, and we'll settle the account later." Without a word to Tam, D'jefra turned and walked out of the door with his men.

Before the door closed, Tam took one more look at his beloved Pyta. He loved that hestur, and worried it would be the last time he would ever lay eyes on his trusted friend. If he could cry he would, but his tears had dried turns ago. The door shut with a loud bang, and he was left with the old man.

"I don't think you'll try to harm me if I take these off," T'lal said, removing the ropes from his raw and scab crusted wrists and feet.

T'lal placed a canteen on Tam's lips, and let the liquid flow into the dry and cracked mouth. The water was cool, and tasted sweet to his tongue. He eagerly drank from the flask. It was the first real drink of water Tam had since his capture. He drank with big gulps, unsure when his new captor would pull it from his parched lips. Soon the canteen was empty, and he handed it gratefully back to T'lal. The cool liquid seemed to fill his stomach, which gurgled in an unpleasant way. He felt nauseated and fought the urge to vomit up the precious water.

T'lal helped Tam into a sitting position and patted his back kindly. "It will take some time before you can drink enough to heal your lips, and restore normal function to the rest of your body. We'll just have to take things slow for now. How long has it been since you've eaten anything?"

Tam's voice cracked and sounded high pitched and foreign to his ears. "I'm not sure, but I would think it's been half a ceanor or more."

"Quite a long time for anyone to be without food," T'lal said sympathetically. "I know you want to eat a feast, but your stomach has grown used to being empty. We will have to give you small amounts of gruel to get it used to having food in it. If I give you too much, you'll just die. Slow, slow is how we need to do things."

Tam tried to stand, but T'lal pushed him back down. "You're not ready to do that yet, I'm afraid. Stay here and I'll run and get you something to eat. Be patient, your strength will return in time." The leathery old man hurried off down a corridor, and returned a short time later accompanied by another larger man and holding a small bowl filled with a thick stew that smelled of boiled fish. The steaming concoction had a kind of rancid odor to it, but Tam was so hungry he could care less if it was someone's boiled sock. The first food to touch his lips since that last meal with Indura was warm and the sweetest thing he had ever tasted. He savored each morsel as if it was a delicacy fit for a king as he ate. When Tam was finished, he gratefully handed it back. "Thank you," he creaked. "It was the best thing I've ever tasted."

"I'm sure you'll come to loathe it," T'lal said. "They all do. You'll be fed three times a turn until you're better. Once you have your strength back, we'll put you to work. If you aren't lame in that arm, we'll take you to market and see what you fetch."

"And if it's lame?" Tam asked the question not really wanting to know the answer.

"You'll be sold to Holy H'met's priests for use in the temple rituals." T'lal's dispassionate tone was that of a man stating a boring fact like the sky is blue. "You should hope that things don't happen that way. People sold to the temple rarely last a ceanor before they are sacrificed. We will take things one–step at a time right now. T'hoth here will help you to your cell after I tend to your wounds."

T'lal was quick and clinical in applying ointments and salves to Tam's many open sores, removing the stitches in Tam's head in the process. He re–splinted Tam's arm with shorter pieces of wood that allowed him to bend at his elbow. He then cradled the arm in a sling.

"D'jefra set your arm fairly well," T'lal said optimistically. "You should heal up nicely."

After T'lal was finished, T'hoth half carried the prince through the long spiral maze of corridors to a small door that led to an equally small rectangular room. It was barely big enough to lie down in, but you couldn't quite fully stretch out. The ceiling was so low that you had to crouch when you stood up, and it was only slightly larger than the door, which was just large enough to admit one man. A grimy, foul–smelling chamber bucket stood encased in cobwebs in one corner. A labyrinth of webs occupied every other corner and crevice. It was clear to Tam that this would be a windowless pit of despair. He was left inside and the door closed with a clang as the locking mechanism engaged, sealing him in the cramped, spider–infested quarters. Tam was left alone in utter darkness, helpless and hopeless.

# Chapter 27

# STYFASTR

It took a couple of turns for Athon and Indura to journey from Dissa's cottage in Dounie to Skaraton. The thriving city was alive with people eager to trade in goods imported from all parts of the kingdom, minor kingdoms to the north and south, and Austica to the northeast. In most villages and cities there was a market section, but in Skaraton the entire city seemed to be one great market. As with any border city, there was a large contingent of soldiers, but Skaraton was the largest fortress in Ithilton. More soldiers were deployed to this garrison than anywhere in the kingdom. It was the central staging point for the network of forts guarding the border with Austica. Despite the tensions between the two rivals, a flourishing trade supported a large number of merchants. It was here that the bulk of the taxes came from, making it more profitable than any gold mine.

They entered the main gate to the city with relative ease. The soldiers had looked right at them, but didn't seem to give them any thought. The streets of Skaraton were a frenetic jumble of people moving every possible way all at once. There were sellers everywhere. Merchants were hawking their wares from every conceivable corner of civilization. The din of shouting voices was tempered only by the minstrels that filled every unoccupied open space. The smell of cooking food permeated the air, making their mouths water.

"Can we get something to eat?" Indura asked, trying to be heard over the crowd.

"As soon as we can get settled somewhere," Athon answered.

It took hours to locate a suitable place that had stables for the hesturs and beds for the two travelers. Athon chose one that had security patrolling the grounds. Theft was unheard of in Campsit, but in Ithilton, it was a major concern. Athon didn't want the hesturs to be stolen while they were trying to conduct the business necessary to get them in a caravan. It was late–sun by the time they were settled, and the business in the streets had quieted down for the sleep–time. They found a tavern that was open just down the street from their inn, and at last satiated their hunger.

"So, what now," Indura asked, cramming a hot morsel of food into her mouth.

"We wait until even–sun and then we can start to look for something appropriate to sell."

"Maybe we can sell pots or something?"

Athon kept a vigilant eye out for people paying them a little too much attention, but didn't see anyone. "Maybe, I don't know. It has to be something that the Austicans want. They aren't going to make room for us if the caravan leader knows we can't sell what we've got."

"Do you have any ideas?" Indura looked at him quizzically.

"I won't know until I've asked around a little. What we get will depend greatly on what's in demand, and what we can afford."

"You should be able to afford something decent, I mean you have — "

Athon cut her short with a sharp whisper. "Shhh! We do not discuss money in the open. You don't know who is listening, or what their intentions are. You have to think, Igmundir."

"I'm sorry, father, I don't know what I was thinking," she said, not hiding her sarcasm.

He grabbed her arm and pulled her close. "I know this may be difficult for you to grasp, but it isn't like we're floating in money here, and we can't go back to the source for more of it if it gets stolen. Try and remember that we are surrounded by thieves and charlatans who will do anything to separate us from it, and if they do, our chances of rescuing Tam go to with it."

"I'm sorry, father, I will remember," Indura said meekly.

They returned to the inn, and decided to begin putting their plan into action at even–sun. The room they were given was large enough to contain two small beds, but not much else. They had chosen to obtain economical accommodations as a way to maximize their cash reserve. Athon didn't know how long it would take them to acquire the needed goods and then join a caravan, and he didn't want them running out of money before then. It was just good to have a place to stretch and rest from their travels. When they had locked the door and drawn the curtains, they both sat down on their beds and began to ready themselves for sleep–time.

"My back side is killing me," Athon groaned. "I don't think I've done this much traveling in several passes. I've forgotten how much it can take out of you."

"My chest is killing me more than my rump," Indura said, joining in the gripe session. "I've got to get out of this bandage before it kills me." She stood up and began to take off her shirt.

"What are you doing?" Athon's panicked whisper caught Indura off guard.

"I'm getting undressed," she said briskly, "so no peaking."

"You can't do that," he hissed, "and keep your voice down, these walls aren't that thick. You can't take that bandage off."

"I'm in severe pain right now," she said, lowering her voice to a whisper. "I have to get out of this before I go insane."

"How are you going to get it at back on?"

"I suppose you're going to have to do it," Indura paused a moment, "as long as you don't look."

"You want me to what?" Athon was exasperated. "No, I'm not going to do that!"

"You have no choice," she said. "I've ridden turns with this getup on, and I'm not taking it any more. It's coming off."

"I'm not staying for this," Athon huffed as he got up. He had barely gotten comfortable and wasn't happy that he had his respite interrupted. "I'll be downstairs," he said, leaving the room. "Ceanor, please save me from the folly of little children," he said under his breath as he closed the door. Why did he allow himself to be coerced into this fiasco? Here he was, far from his own lands and at the furthest reaches of the next kingdom with a confused brat who refused to listen to a word he had to say. If he managed to rescue the prince, and safeguard the princess, it would be a miracle. For that matter, if he managed to avoid insanity it would be a feat of unparalleled magnitude.

Athon headed back to the tavern. He wasn't in search of some deleterious refreshment, but more an escape from the irksome antics of the princess. A little break would be a good thing, he thought. They had to maintain the appearance of father and son migrating to the greener pastures of Skaraton, so they hadn't been apart since the stream, and hadn't bothered to obtain lodging since Dissa's.

He entered the dimly lit purveyance and located a booth in a tucked away corner of the room. It was crowded with all manner of folk seeking the refreshment offered at the bar. Most of the people were in various states of inebriation, but Athon wasn't going to be one of them. He realized this was the perfect opportunity to begin sussing out business leads, and planting his cover in a few well-placed ears.

The first step in any reconnaissance was to familiarize the territory; a fact Athon knew all too well. He knew he had to survey the people in the bar and determine which set of business rules set them apart. Men with agendas stick out like sore thumbs, even in a crowd. Some people in the tavern were there to socialize with women, others were there to commiserate with friends, a few men were there to conduct ill-reputed business, and others were there to drink themselves into an early grave. Athon had no interest in getting drunk, but knew he needed to blend in. He was alone, wasn't interested in women other than Dissa, and didn't wish to delve into the criminal element yet. That meant that in order to blend, he needed to look like he was there to get drunk. He ordered a pint of ale and began his slow deception. It looked, smelled, and tasted like his own urine. He had never understood why any sane person would down any quantity of this horrible liquid.

Alcohol was strictly prohibited in Campsit as a matter of principal. It generally caused more problems than it solved, and was banned outright at the inception of the kingdom. However, it flowed freely in Ithilton, and Athon had learned in his early spy years to mimic drunken behavior in order to blend into the crowd.

To give his breath the aroma of the foul tasting fluid, and lull his quarry into a false sense of security, he drank, but didn't swallow. After allowing it to marinate his tongue until he couldn't taste anymore, he regurgitated it back into his glass, simultaneously allowing some of the amber drink to trickle down his cheeks and onto his clothes. He did this repeatedly over the course of an hour to give the illusion he had consumed a large quantity. The only disadvantage to this particular method of deception was that it didn't take long before his clothes were saturated with ale. He always hated the part where he had to feign spilling his drink all over so he could order another one and have the barmaid clean up his mess.

It didn't take the whole hour for Athon to spot his target. A middle-aged man was making himself popular with the local wenches by throwing money around. He was loud, dressed richly, and was sandwiched between two ladies of the evening. In this city, that meant that you had money to spend and you wanted to show it off.

Athon knew that all systems based on money had an imbalance. Money made by trading goods wasn't always fair on all ends. The richest and most influential were the middlemen who brought buyer and seller together. He needed to acquaint himself with one in order to secure a spot in a caravan.

"Another round for my lovely companions," the rosy-cheeked man said with a bilious roar. His companions had been giggling non-stop as he told pathetic story after story. The man was about the same age as Athon with a balding head and a protruding belly. He wore a large, flowing robe–like garment that was tied about the middle with a yellow sash. The chest of the vestment gaped open like some obscene mouth for all to see his abundant chest hair. Around his neck, several thick gold necklaces hung, attesting to his wealth and status. He was loud, lecherous, and drunk on more than ale.

It was time to make his move. Athon stood, mug in hand, and stumbled toward the man's table. It had been a while since he had called upon his acting skills, but he found it came as naturally to him as riding Zuri. He arrived at the table and almost tumbled into the vacant chair directly across from the garishly dressed man, splashing ale liberally on the floor and table.

In his most convincing drunken voice, he slurred his salutation to the three revelers "Ssssay friend, why don't you share one of these fillies with me?"

The girls giggled at Athon's antics, but the gentleman was visibly annoyed by this unsolicited interruption. "Look what we have here, girls, it's the village idiot." Everyone within earshot laughed at the hilarity of the gaffe.

Athon pretended not to understand the cynical comment directed at him, and turned his head in an effort to locate the aforementioned idiot. "Where?" There was a long pause as he acted as if he was too inebriated to think straight. "Wait," he said as if realizing he was the butt of joke, "you're talking 'bout me? Thhash no way to talk to a friend."

"You're quite right, my good chum," the man said, "where are my manners? I would order you another drink, but I fear that you've had enough already."

"Thhersh no need to worry about me," Athon said, "I've still got some left."

"What's the occasion?"

"Huh," Athon said, slowly blinking at the question.

"You're quite drunk. You don't seem like the type of man who's down on his luck, so you must be celebrating something."

"You're very ass—astute. I am celebrating my good fortune to come."

"Wonderful," the man said clapping his hands loudly, "you've got something on the horizon. Good for you."

"You know wanna' know what it is?"

"I'm all ears."

"I just got inta town, and I'm gonna make a fortune."

The man suddenly took a keen interest in what Athon had to say. Men who make a great deal of money are always interested in making more, especially if they can easily take it from a fool. "How do you plan on doing it?"

"There are these caravans that go to Awest — *hic*," Athon feigned a hiccup to reinforce his appearance as a drunk. He belched loudly and continued. "'Scuse me. As I was saying, there're these caravans that go to Awe — sticka. I hear a man can buy somethin' here and then sell it for ten times that if'n he can cross that desert. Then you buy somethin' there and then sell it here for a tidy profit."

"Indeed, there is a lot of money to be made doing that, but it is hardly ten times the profit."

"How would you know? You don't seem like the kinda guy who'da cross the desert."

"You are observant. If you're good at haggling, you can make out quite well. If not, you can lose your shirt. Can you negotiate?"

"I can sell water to a drowning man, on account I'm so handsome," Athon said, smiling with a big, toothy grin. "See you are sold on me already, and I don't even know what to call 'ya."

"I'm known as Styfastr, and I have the reputation of being the best trader in all Ithilton."

"So, you're the guy I should be talkin' to," Athon said, reaching over and shaking Styfastr's hand.

"Yes indeed, but I never discuss business in front of the ladies," Styfastr squeezed the women tightly to him and kissed each on the cheek. "Now is the time for pleasure, not business. We can talk after high–sun."

"Is even–sun too early? I want to get shtarted as soon as possible."

"I doubt you will be moving that early, and I know I won't be out of bed before the second–quarter rolls around. No, high–sun will be the earliest we can discuss business."

"Bud, I don't wanna' mish the caravan."

"You will," Styfastr said. "They leave at even–sun. I can't get you on that one, so you'll have to wait five turns for the next one. I think once we have the chance to talk, I will be able to point you in the right direction."

Athon silently cursed his bad luck, but knew there wasn't anything that could be done about it. He would have to wait for the next caravan. They couldn't risk trying to go on their own, and trying to get on without some kind of cargo would raise everyone's suspicion. "You're a really great guy. But, how will I find you?"

"I will meet you here and then take you to my shop. I would tell you where it was, but I'm afraid you're probably too drunk, and too new in town. You would get lost for sure."

"What a great guy you are," Athon said, slapping Styfastr hard on the shoulder. "You'll make a great partner."

"You know who I am now. Since we're going to be partners I need to know your name."

"Agmundir of Nidaros," Athon said, proudly raising his glass to toast his adopted hometown.

"Well, Agmundir of Nidaros, I think this will be the beginning of a wonderful relationship, a toast to your coming prosperity." With a clink of glass goblets, they sealed their partnership with a long drink of ale. A close observer would notice that the amount of liquid in Athon's glass hadn't changed. "You should rest, my friend. You will need to be at your sharpest if you're going to negotiate with me."

Athon nodded his head in agreement, and stumbled as he stood up. He called the barmaid over to the table, and slapped down a gold piece. "Buy my new partner anything he wants." With that, he clumsily shambled through the street and back up to the dark room.

Once the door was locked, and he was certain he hadn't been followed; he lit a small lamp and looked over at the princess. She was fast asleep on the bed. His rather noisy entrance hadn't woken her. He changed into his dry uniform and began washing the ale soaked clothes. He only had the one outfit thanks to the princess, and he couldn't very well go around dressed like a Campsit guard or smelling like a brewery. It took a full three washes before he was satisfied the foul odor had gone.

He would have thought that all of the noise would have caused Indura to at least stir, but she remained blissfully unaware that he was even there. When everything was set and drying, he retired to his bed and quickly drifted off to sleep.

# Chapter 28

# LAW OF H'MET

The sound of his bare feet on stone was comforting. He detested sandals and only wore them when he was outside on unholy ground. The stones of the palace had been sanctified, and worthy of the presence of his unshod foot. He was the holy son of the only true god Sakphata. His presence was divinely required to save the population of the chosen people from the heresy of unbelief. He was Holy H'met, and his people worshiped him and the generations of progenitors going back to the creation of the world. All of them had risen in the sky to become one with Sakphata.

It was the presence of deity that saved his people from the wrath of Sakphata, god of light and creation. H'met was, in all respects, divine. He was a handsome man with strong, chiseled features. His perfectly round head was devoid of hair, making him smooth like the face of his father–god. His brown skin was golden color and almost radiated with the luminance of his countenance. His blue eyes were highlighted by the eye makeup that was customary for the god kings of Austica.

All fell to their knees as he entered the believer's throne room, gracing them with his divine presence. No one would raise their heads until he had left. They were unworthy to gaze at his glory. The men bowing low at his feet were the reason he was here. The thirteen soldiers knelt behind their leader. This leader needed to account for their apparent failure and atone for their sins. "D'jefra, you have returned earlier than expected. Were you unable to do as you were told?"

"Holy H'met, who is infinite in wisdom, I have returned with the answer you sought."

"You were sent to discover the route behind the Ithilton defenses. You found such a route so quickly?"

"No, your magnificence, we discovered that no such route exists. We were able to penetrate deep behind the defensive forts to the mountains that run along the far southern border of the land, but found that there is a large area that is impenetrably guarded by a rival kingdom. We were discovered, and our presence was relayed instantly to other guardians by a fire I have never seen before. We fled back the way we came, before the forces of the kingdom could be mustered against us."

"You fled?" H'met's voice was even and cold. "How do you know they would have found you if you had pressed forward."

D'jefra was sweating. "We encountered and captured one man who says he is their prince. He told us there were many such guards who would alert the others to our exact position before they would track and kill us."

"How do you know that the others saw this fire?"

"Shortly after our confrontation, we saw the smoke from several fires in the mountains that were too evenly spaced to be coincidence. I know it couldn't be long before we would face a force that would overwhelm my small reconnaissance force." He then proceeded to relay all of the intelligence he obtained from interrogating Tam.

H'met seemed to be very interested by the fact that Indura had nearly been captured. What a pity his men were inept, and not chased her down. They hadn't had the wits to know her importance at the time. He scowled at the man who had been, up until this point, one of his most trusted generals. He had counted on this man finding a way to the rear of the Ithilton forces, or die trying. The fact that D'jefra was kneeling at his feet, very much alive, showed that he was cowardly, and valued his own life more than the success of his mission. Still, they had managed to make it deep into enemy territory before being discovered, and it wasn't clear if Ithilton was aware of the breach in its security. This was a difficult decision. Good generals were so difficult to come by, and D'jefra had demonstrated in the past that he was the best. "Do you think Ithilton was made aware of your incursion?"

"Holiest H'met, it was the princess who identified our party. It would be foolish to assume that she did not alert her father when she returned to the palace. It is likely that they will be watching that route should we attempt to go that way again."

The anger that had been simmering boiled over. H'met knew he couldn't be seen to tolerate failure, especially from his elite, beloved general. In his life, he had never had to raise his voice for his word to be obeyed. His word was followed with fanatical precision, and was never questioned. He stood to his full height and stretched his hand out to the men who had remained prostrate before him during this accounting. "You were the best men, handpicked from the ranks of my loyal army. I trusted you above all else to seek out the weakness in my enemies defenses. You were to return triumphant, or not at all. This, you have not done. I will not tolerate cowardice in my army, and you are all cowards. Because of your failure, Ithilton now knows of their weakness. They will close the gap in their defenses and our opportunity to circumvent their main forces has been thwarted. None of you shall live. Guards, take them into the barren waste and behead them. Do not sacrifice them at the altar, but let their blood be spilled on the sand, to nourish nothing. Erase their names from all documents and letters, and let the name of D'jefra become a curse. Go to their houses, defile the women and then sacrifice all who live there. Let their blood atone for the sins of these men. As for the men who died in the wilderness of Ithilton, let their names be remembered and their families be unharmed. The Prince of Campsit shall rot in the dungeons of the slave master, as we may have use for him later. My word is law."

H'met walked calmly out of the room. He could hear the condemned men openly crying, but none begged for his life. They wept because they knew it was a grievous sin they had committed, and the punishment was difficult to bear. They would not redeem themselves in this life by being sanctified by sacrifice. Their souls were destined to wander forever without rest because their bodies would not be prepared for the journey to the afterlife. It was a righteous punishment.

# Chapter 29

# DEAL WITH THE DEVIL

Indura was having one of those dreams again. Tam was holding her in his muscular arms in a tender, but firm embrace. It was exquisite to feel his lips softly caressing her cheek, finding their way to her mouth. His touch was warm and gentle, and made her pulse quicken as he stroked her back lightly. Being with him always gave her goose pimples and made her spine tingle all the way to her toes.

Out of nowhere, soldiers appeared in the distance, racing toward them on hesturs that moved like lightning. Terror gripped her, and she knew they would kill them both. She pulled and tugged at him in an effort to get him to try to flee. He wouldn't budge. Instead, he turned and drew his sword. She turned to go, but stopped herself. She wouldn't run this time. She would stand and fight with her love. She looked around but there was no sword to be found. She asked him for one, but he didn't have another. She was defenseless, but stood her ground, shaking so hard her knees knocked together.

Indura tried to whisper, "I love you" to Tam, but he was suddenly gone. The soldiers had vanished too, and she was standing in a dark corridor. It was just light enough to make out the walls on either side, but she couldn't see far in front of her. The fear she had felt at the approaching soldiers had increased to the horror of being alone in a strange, dark hall. From the inky blackness, she heard Tam's faint cry for help.

She charged down the passageway, not knowing where she was going, but listening intently to the pleas, as they got louder and louder. After moving for hours through a seemingly endless maze, she found the door that stood between her and the only man she'd ever loved. It was a tiny little door, barely large enough for a man to squeeze through. In the center of the door, there was a miniature barred window just large enough for his hand to stick out. On one side was a large metal handle that was disproportionate to the rest of the door.

She grabbed the handle and pulled with all her might. The door opened with a sudden jolt that threw her on her back. Something fell out of the small room and landed on top of her. When she came to her senses, she found it was an emaciated corpse, but she couldn't see the face. In horror, she turned it to discover the identity of the near skeletal remains. Before she could learn the identity of the body there was a blinding flash of light, and then a palpable darkness.

Indura bolted to a sitting position in her bed. Her heart was pounding hard and she was sweating profusely. It was dark in the room, with only a faint bit of light spilling in through the cracks in the curtain. Out of the darkness next to her came the familiar voice of Athon.

"Bad dream?"

"Yes, very bad."

"You mind me asking about it?"

She normally didn't share her dreams with anyone but Mai; however, Mai wasn't there. Athon was her father though, so maybe it was the same thing. "It was Tam. He was in some kind of dark prison. He had wasted away as if he had been starved to death, but something happened as soon as I freed him. It was like nothing I've ever experienced in a dream. I fear something terrible is happening to him, and if we don't do something soon, he'll die."

"It was only a dream, Indura. You shouldn't let it worry you."

"You don't understand. My dreams come true."

Athon's voice betrayed his cynicism. "You can't be serious. Dreams are dreams and nothing more."

"I'm going to tell you something that I've only ever told Mai. Before I met Tam, I had a dream about him. I knew his face long before I ever set eyes on him. When I saw him, in that dream I knew that I loved him. I've loved him since that moment, and I know that I will never love anyone else."

"Let me get this straight. You had a dream about Tam before you met him? How do you know it was him? Couldn't it have been someone else? It could have been someone that you've met before, but had forgotten about."

"I know what I dreamt," she growled. "It was Tam, and no one else. I know it. You can scoff all you want, but I won't change my mind. If you can't accept that fact, then you're a fool."

"Is that why you've risked everything to come on this suicide mission? Because you think you had some kind of vision?"

"That isn't why, and you know it," Indura said defiantly. "I don't expect you to understand. I love him. How it happened is irrelevant."

"I guess I'm just trying to understand why you would risk your life for a man you barely know."

"I do it because he risked his life to protect me. I think I owe it to him to return the favor. Why are you doing it?"

Athon sighed heavily. "It's my responsibility to protect him. I made an oath that I would do that, and I have failed. My command, my life, and my honor depends on me bringing him back safely to his parents. Thanks to your stubbornness, I have no choice but to rescue him, and keep you safe in the process. If I manage to pull it all off, I might get to live, but if I don't, then Campsit will fall into a war I caused. The destruction of all that I know and love will be entirely on me."

Indura sat, staring into the dark void at the man she entrusted her life to, but hardly knew. It had never occurred to her that Tam's sacrifice had such far-reaching consequences. "We can't fail. Just so you know, it isn't your fault; it's mine. I caused all this, and I have to make it right." Tears began streaming down her face, and her voice choked with emotion. "So many people have died because of me. I can't let Tam be one of them. I would rather die trying to save him than live another moment with the guilt of knowing that I did nothing after he sacrificed so much for me. I don't want to live, knowing that I killed the only man I've ever loved."

"You said we."

"Yes, I did. You're not in this alone. Like it or not, I'm coming with you, and together we will save Tam."

"I just hope that when we find him he'll be alive."

"I know he's alive. I can feel it in my blood. It courses through my veins with every beat of my heart. I know it like I know the sun will always shine."

The emphatic tone of Indura's voice moved Athon. He took courage from her optimism, but it was tempered by the enormity of the task that confronted them. He knew that they faced insurmountable odds, but whatever the obstacle, he would do his best to overcome it. He got out of bed and felt his way to the window. He cracked the curtains and gazed out into the blinding light of the first-quarter. His exhaustion needed more sleep before it abated. "Even-sun is still hours away. Do you think you can get back to sleep?"

"I don't know."

"Try, we could have a very long turn ahead of us." Athon said as he made his way back to his bed.

Sleep came quickly to the captain, but Indura sat for a long time trying to divine the meaning of her vision. The vivid imagery troubled her. What was going to happen to her precious Tam? Was he trapped in that dark horrible place? Would he die if she didn't get to him in time? What would her father do to the people of Campsit if she died? She didn't have answers to any of these questions. Her mind wrestled with the problems while she lay there, listening to Athon's rhythmic breathing. It made her sick to her stomach just thinking about the number of people whose fate rested solely on her choices.

She didn't know when she fell asleep, but it was well past even–sun when Athon opened the drapes, filling the room with light. He left the room while she bathed and got ready, but she found it nearly impossible to wrap the bandage tight enough to minimize her chest sufficiently to pass as a boy. She was going to need his help to put it on, but she had serious reservations about letting any man in a position where he could ogle her. She considered carefully everything she knew about him, and decided he was not the kind of man who would take advantage of the situation. He returned to find her waiting.

"I brought some food. I thought we would eat here and then make our way into the market to get a feel for our surroundings. We have to be back here at high–sun to meet with a man about getting on the next caravan. I'm afraid the last one left about three hours ago."

"While we were asleep?" Indura asked with alarm. "Hurry and help me with this bandage. We might be able to catch up to them."

"We aren't going," Athon said bluntly. "We didn't make arrangements to go. The caravan allows merchants to cross the border without fear of attack from soldiers or bandits. The men guarding it would most certainly think we were robbers, and kill us for our trouble. I don't like it any more than you do, but we have to bide our time, or this won't work."

"Fine," Indura finally said, accepting that he knew what needed to be done to be successful in this instance. "You still need to help me with this bandage so that I don't look like a woman." She read the exasperated look on his face, and knew she needed to give him a real reason. "I tried to do it myself, but I can't get it tight or smooth like it needs to be."

"Being alone with you on this outing is compromising enough without having you — ugh — expose yourself to me."

"I won't be exposed," she said, trying to pacify him. "I'll do the front part; you stay behind me and just pull it tight. All you will ever see is my back."

"I'm a lot taller than you," he protested trying to see a way out of this.

"Then sit on the bed and do it, but it has to be done. I can't go out pretending to be your son with the figure of a woman."

"All right," he said, "but, just this once."

"We will have to do this every turn until we're traveling with the caravan."

"Are you kidding me?"

"I'm not going to feel like there is a fat man sitting on my chest all turn unless I absolutely have to."

"You're going to send me to an early grave, and then I'll spend the afterlife in purgatory." He plopped down on her bed, and shut his eyes, hoping that this would end quickly.

It took several attempts before Indura was satisfied with the outcome. While they ate, Athon explained had happened while she slept, and their appointment with Styfastr at high–sun. In the interim time, they would peruse the wares at the marketplace and try to assess what commodity would sell, and which one would best fit their budget and disguise.

The market was a hubbub of activity with shopkeepers constantly yelling to attract the attention of passing buyers, or haggling to negotiate the best deal. There was everything imaginable from both kingdoms. Some of the items Athon had never seen before. The scent of exotic spices filled the air. All kinds of art were shipped in from the far away kingdom from necklaces to statues. Athon had to remind Indura that it was unnatural for a boy to be browsing jewelry, to which she replied that she was simply doing "research". Athon wasn't as interested in what was from Austica, as he was trying to find out what products from Ithilton were in demand at their destination. After a couple of hours, he reasoned it was time to return to the tavern and await Styfastr.

When they arrived at the inn, they found a secluded table. Athon noticed that the barmaid had taken a peculiar interest in them. They didn't have to wait long before Styfastr, dressed in a fine, long, red silk robe, entered and spotted them. He looked like a walking bloated flower.

As Styfastr approached the table, Athon whispered in Indura's ear. "Just let me do all the talking." He stood and motioned for the portly gentleman to sit opposite Indura.

"I see you remembered our appointment," Styfastr said, shaking Athon's outstretched hand vigorously, and then plopping down, causing the bench to groan under his weight. "You were so drunk last night, I didn't think you would remember your own name, let alone that you and I had talked." Indura shot Athon a wicked glare, which he stealthily waved off. "Speaking of names, yours has completely escaped me."

"It's no problem. I'm Agmundir, and this is my oldest son, Igmundir." With a slap on her shoulder to emphasize her identity as a boy, and reminded her that she needed to be in character.

"Handsome young lad," Styfastr said. "I'm sure he takes after his mother."

"He reminds me of her constantly," Athon said, giving Indura a sly wink. "Are you ready to do some business?"

"Absolutely, my friend, but I never discuss business on an empty stomach. If you want my help getting on the caravan, you need to stop me from starving." He hailed the barmaid and proceeded to order enough food to feed five men. Indura looked at him in stunned disbelief. "You disapprove, young man?"

"I don't see why a person who obviously enjoys the finer things in life tries to gorge himself to death."

"My dear boy," Styfastr said, grabbing a goblet of wine the barmaid was conveniently holding. "I enjoy the finer things in life. Some might call me a glutton and a slob, but I believe life is short, and you should enjoy as much of it as possible while you can. In any case, food always tastes better when someone else is buying."

The food arrived, bringing with it a tantalizing aroma. It had been hours since the last time she ate, and the thought of all that food made Indura salivate. She wondered if the fat man would miss a small helping of his feast. She gripped Athon's hand under the table. He looked at her and caught her hungered expression. He grabbed the barmaid before she left and ordered them both a meager meal.

About half way through the feast, Athon broke the silence. "So, what do we need to do to get on the next caravan?"

"Do you have animals to transport yourselves and the goods to Dehnet?" Athon nodded his head. "Good. Do you have something to sell when you get there?"

"That's what we're looking to acquire. What's in demand?"

"There are many things we have that the Austicans want, but what's turning the highest profit right now is salt crystals."

"Salt?" Indura said with disbelief.

"Scoff if you want," Styfastr said, shoving a large section of steak into his mouth, "but they don't have any salt mines there. Oh, sure, there are places that harvest the crystals from the sea, but what they really crave are the big ones from the Ladton mines."

"What's so special about it?" Athon was intrigued by the idea of having something truly valuable.

"It tastes better, and it's all in one piece, so you have to grind it to use it. It's a status thing with them. It's bulky and heavy, so you can't take large quantities by hestur or awr. You can't take a wagon or cart across the desert, although many a fool has tried. With all the water you have to take for yourself and the beasts, there isn't much room for cargo, even less if you only have a hestur and not an awr."

"What's an awr?" Indura asked.

Styfastr rolled his eyes. "You sheltered boy. An awr is a desert pack animal that can go long periods without water. They look like a hestur has crossbred with an uht."

"Back to the subject at hand," Athon said, not wishing to linger on their ignorance of desert animals. "How profitable is it?" Making a profit was not his goal, but he needed to seem like it was.

"Let me put it this way," Styfastr said, clearing his throat. "If you're a good haggler, in ten trips you and your son will never have to work again, although there is no such thing as too much money."

"I take it this isn't the easiest way to earn a living or everyone would be doing it."

"Not even remotely. If the desert doesn't kill you, then thieves and robbers will. The caravan has its own soldiers that guard against highwaymen, but if you straggle, they won't help you. If you're lucky, robbers will kill you before they take everything you have."

"If we aren't lucky," Indura asked.

"Then they will take all your possessions and leave you in the desert to die of thirst. Those aren't the only people who will try to kill you, of course. Sometimes, the Austican soldiers will be the aggressors. They come and make you pay an additional toll to cross their territory."

"Doesn't the caravan take care of that?" Athon was beginning to see how this could be an expensive venture.

Styfastr chuckled. "They do, but there is a lot of money at stake. Soldiers don't get enough to make them honest men. If you can't pay the toll, you will be slaughtered on the spot. Anything you have will become theirs," he could see the despair on Indura's face, "but wait, there's more. Once you've arrived, there will be all manner of people trying to separate you from your cargo. Some try to lure you away from the rest of the caravan, and then rob you. Others wait until you're asleep in the inn, then sneak into your room and take your gold. You could walk away penniless, or they might slit your throat as you sleep just to make a point. Despite the danger, the rewards are substantial for men who can survive long enough to make it back to Skaraton. Do you think that you're up to the challenge?"

"I'll stake my life on it," Athon said firmly. "Are you the sort of man who would try to swindle us, or are you actually interested in us making a profit?"

A serious look replaced the perpetual jovial expression on Styfastr's face. His honor had just been called into question, and it was apparent that he was not used to having that happen. "I make all my money legitimately, which is more than I can say about a lot of my competitors. I make lots of money on my courier's backs, and I depend on them making many trips back and forth. The best ones take what I tell them, and with a portion of the profits buy exotic items and bring them back where I buy them for a small profit. I sell the imported goods, and we both make money coming and going. It's a beautiful relationship."

"Fair enough," Athon said, trying to assuage the offended merchant. "I didn't mean to insult your honor, but I have to know who I'm dealing with."

"I like your father," Styfastr said to Indura. "He's very smart. I thought he was a bit of an oaf when I first met him, but now I see that he's a sensible man. I think we can certainly do business together." He punctuated his statement by saluting his host with his full goblet and taking a large gulp.

"I know we have a few turns before the caravan leaves, but I don't want to waste any time." Athon knew he had to be patient, but every hour that passed without knowing what happened to Tam made the likelihood of them finding him unharmed more remote. "When can we go to your shop and discuss the terms of our deal?"

"After I finish with this absolutely gorgeous meal," Styfastr said. "I hope you're not too rushed. It takes me hours to eat a feast like this."

Indura was visibly disgusted by the gluttonous boast, but he wasn't exaggerating. They sat and waited for an hour before Styfastr announced that he was finally finished, and they exited the inn to head to his shop. The emporium was guarded by two well-armed soldiers who were part of a small army of private soldiers that guarded trading establishments in Skaraton. Once inside, Athon and Indura got their first look at the import/export business that made their host so wealthy. There were shelves of large pink and white salt crystals of various shapes, size, and shades to one side. Jars of colorful, exotic–smelling spices were on the other. Intricately woven carpets and tapestries hung from every conceivable space; with the floor occupied by a large red rug. Large, soft, brightly colored pillows occupied the center of the room, and Styfastr gestured for them to sit as he plopped himself down on the largest one.

Styfastr explained how the transaction would actually occur. He would need twenty gold pieces up front to pay the fee to get on the caravan. He highly suggested that they keep five gold pieces on hand for bribes and another five for food and secure lodging. Last, but not least, they would have to buy the salt from him before he would agree to even start the process.

It took a few moments for Athon to figure out how much they could carry all together, and then it was a matter of negotiating the price for the salt. It had been a while since he was placed in a position where he had to negotiate a price, but it was something that came naturally. Even though Campsit had no monetary system, bartering wasn't uncommon.

It was an intense haggle, but Athon was able to secure what he needed for forty gold pieces. He was slightly hesitant to hand over that much money on the promise that it would be made available just before they left, but Styfastr assured them that it would be safer if he held onto it in the interim time.

Athon and Indura left the shop and made their way through the teeming city streets back toward the safety of the inn. "Why did you do that," she asked.

"Do what?"

"Give all our money to some stranger. How do we know we can trust him?"

"Look at it this way," Athon said. "If he tries to renege, I'll kill him. He may not know that at this point, but I'll make myself clear when I kill whoever he has guarding him. I don't think he is likely to. Did you see how upset he became when I challenged his word? That was genuine. A man like that may have a few vices, but he keeps his word or he doesn't stay in business."

"What if he doesn't and we can't get on the caravan?"

"That isn't going to happen."

"But what if it does? How will we help Tam if we're out of money?"

"My plan does not depend on us having money. Money is one of the tools I'm using to help us complete our mission, but our success doesn't hinge on it. One way or another, we'll find a way to get into Austica. This is just the best way. All the others are more complicated and risky."

"How will we get back?"

"I'm not sure of that just yet. I need to get there and retrieve Tam before I'll know that answer."

"Let me get this straight," Indura said, coming to an abrupt halt. "You planned how to get in, but you haven't even thought of how to get out?"

Athon grabbed her by the arm and began forcibly guiding her back to the inn. "It's impossible to know how to get him out when we don't even know where he is or what's happened to him. You can't plan something if you have no knowledge of what obstacles there may be. We have to hope that we can locate him quickly, and he won't be heavily guarded."

"Can't you just kill whoever is in our way?"

He looked at her as if she just said the stupidest thing in the world. "I'm not invincible, I have no armor, and I only have a few close quarter weapons. I also have the great disadvantage of not knowing the terrain or the military customs. I can't take on the entire Austican army by myself, so we don't have the luxury of using brute force. We need to use our heads. Now start using yours, and stop thinking that you're the only one who cares about Tam."

"At least tell me we have a chance," Indura said, pouting at the chastisement.

"We stand a better chance doing it my way," Athon said gently. "You need to trust me. This isn't the first time I've had to do something difficult with limited information."

She looked at him quizzically. "You've done this before?"

"Not quite."

"Were you successful?"

"I suppose that depends on who you ask."

"I'm asking you."

"Not always," Athon's answer was sarcastic and blunt.

"What do you think our chances are?"

"Not that good."

She glared at him. "Is that supposed to make me feel better about this?"

"Would it help you if I said they were good?"

"No, I'd think you were lying."

"Then we're on the same page." Athon noticed a group of soldiers working their way through the crowd. They seemed to be stopping every woman they came across. "We need to keep our heads down until we leave. No going out into the streets, especially you."

They disappeared quickly into the inn, blissfully unaware that there was a

man who had been following them close enough to overhear their entire conversation. He turned and headed back down the street. It wasn't necessary to
follow them into the inn, she could handle the surveillance inside, he thought.
His master would be interested to learn what he knew, and he needed to get
back as quickly as possible.

The next three turns passed interminably for both Athon and Indura, but
particularly for the princess. He could leave the room anytime he wanted to,
but she had to remain inside unless they were eating at the tavern. It was long,
boring, and hot. The room seemed to suffocate her. There was very little air-
flow, and the desert heat had baked her skin dry. She itched, and longed to rub
soothing oils on her arms and chapped lips. How could anyone live like this?
She was a princess, not a prisoner. The only relief seemed to come after high–sun
when the clouds would boil up into dry thunderstorms. It was as if the sky was
teasing the desert grasslands with the promise of rain, but refused to quench
its brown, sunbaked crust. The only benefit was the shade the clouds provided
from the ever–present sun, and the winds that moved the otherwise stagnant air.

Athon spent most of the time walking in the market, talking to the purvey-
ors who he recognized as being Austican merchants. He tried to get as much
information about their homeland as possible on the guise of looking for a place
to sell his wares once he reached Dehnet. He tried to spend as little time with
the princess as possible. It wasn't that she annoyed him so much, but she was a
constant reminder of the perilous situation.

The only time they enjoyed together was when they ate in the tavern. They
tried to avoid hours when it was busy, to avoid attracting undue attention. It
was third–quarter sun on the eve of the fourth turn when they sat down for
their last meal before they left. In a few hours, they would load everything and
move to the staging area to await the departure of the caravan.

They were waiting for their food when Styfastr entered the room and wad-
dled up to their table. Indura transferred herself to Athon's bench to allow the
lumbering gentleman space to sit.

"Thank you ever so much," Styfastr said, as the bench once again noisily
protested his weight. He was wearing a brilliant green robe, with bright yellow
edging, and accentuated by numerous gold necklaces. "I won't be eating with
you this time, as I have other business. I thought I would just quickly check on
you to make sure you were still going to honor our agreement. I trust you are
all ready for your journey?"

"Everything but our cargo," Athon said.

"I'll be in my shop two hours before even–sun. We can load you up with plenty of time to join the caravan."

"We'll be there on time or my name isn't Agmundir."

Styfastr smirked and an evil grin began to grow on his face that made the hair on the back of Athon's neck stand on end. "Interesting you should say that."

"Why is that?" Athon said, dryly ignoring the knot growing in his stomach.

"Because I don't think you are who you purport to be," Styfastr said menacingly. Indura froze, and gripped Athon's leg.

"Oh," Athon said calmly, as his hand fondled the hidden handle of one of his throwing knives. "Who exactly do you think we are?"

"You know my business isn't just simply importing and exporting goods," Styfastr said, his face contorting with his maniacal smile. "I hear all kinds of rumors from inside and outside the kingdom. People talk and my ears hear everything. I hear all manner of news from all corners of the known world. I have even heard about the princess who knocked a guard unconscious with a chair, and then absconded with half the payroll of one of the kings own garrisons. How she managed to disguise herself as a drudge and escape with the Captain of the Guard of Campsit, of all places." He leered at Indura who was frozen with wide–eyed horror. "The last time anyone saw the lovers, they were headed here. It's rumored they are trying to elope to Austica. Isn't that absolutely rich? Here's the thing. No one can find them here. There isn't a couple that hasn't been under suspicion and questioned repeatedly."

Indura clenched her teeth. Her grip on Athon's leg tightened, as Styfastr continued his tale at a low whisper. "You see, I think the soldiers are looking for the wrong people. I think the princess and the captain are smarter than the military gives them credit. I think they changed their identities so radically that they decided not to pose as man and wife, but two men entering the city to avoid detection. There's only one problem with that theory, and that is: the princess is much too young and beautiful to pose as a man, but she might pull it off if she were to look like a boy. If they posed as father and son they might fool everyone, but they couldn't fool me. Now, could they?"

Unlike Indura, Athon stayed calm. There weren't many people in the tavern, and a rapid strike under the fourth rib on the left side would silence the overgrown sea mammal quickly. No one would even notice in a place like this until he started to stink, and by then, they would be long gone. "If you're as smart as you say, why didn't you go to the soldiers with this wild theory of yours?"

"You see, it isn't a theory," Styfastr gloated. "I've had people watching you since you got here, and from what I've heard there can be no other explanation as to why you behave and talk the way you do. Who's this Tam by the way, and why is it he needs to be rescued?"

Athon silently cursed himself for not guarding their conversations better. He thought the din of the market would mask their voices, but apparently, he was wrong. "That didn't answer my question," he growled.

"You're quite right," Styfastr said. "I've always thought you were brilliant, but you're getting sloppy. I haven't said anything because I'm waiting for a reward to be published. I have to make it worth my while."

"So, it's money you want?" Indura hissed.

"You can *never* have enough, and your measly forty gold isn't enough to keep your dirty little secret." Styfastr turned to Athon. "I don't blame you. Even disguised as a boy, she's beautiful."

"We aren't lovers!" Indura said, through her teeth trying to keep her voice low.

"I don't know what you think is going on, fat man," Athon sneered, "but your little tale is not entirely accurate. You may have penetrated our disguise, but our reason still escapes you. You can only guess as to what we're doing, and that bothers you. A puzzle you can't solve by guessing. You have a *need* to know why, or you'll go mad."

"My, you are perceptive, Captain," Styfastr said, turning his attention to the taller man. "She's too feisty for you, I can see. It must be this Tam fellow who really has her heart."

"Do not speak his name, or I'll cut your heart out and stuff it down that vile, loathsome throat of yours." Indura growled loud enough to attract the attention of everyone in the tavern.

"Keep calm," Athon said, in a stern but quiet voice. "No one else knows about this, or the soldiers would already be flooding the room. I can't help but think there's something you believe will be better than a reward."

"How Preanth ever mistook you for a simpleton, I'll never know. There is still a matter of the salt. You see, I still can't get enough of it into the hands of the people who want to give me all their gold."

"The money you would receive from the shipment's going to be that much, is it?"

"If you give me your share, I'd be a fool not to let you go on your suicidal romp."

"We'll still have expenses once we reach there," Athon said.

"Like what?"

"We need to procure a hestur for Tam, and stealing it would attract too much attention."

"Is that all, or do you have more?"

"I don't see how you will profit if we can't get your money back to you," Indura growled.

"That's the beauty of my plan. You aren't my only agents on this venture. Once you've sold your shipment, you will give the money to one of my men, and they will bring it back to me instead of their usual cargo, minus a very small percentage, of course."

"After we pay for the hestur, we'll give your man everything else minus fifty. If we make it out alive, I'll give you whatever we don't spend."

"And if you don't make it out?"

"Then, you still get your precious money," Indura spat, "and no one will ever know our little secret. I'm sure that if anyone knew you discovered who we really are, there wouldn't be enough money to buy you out of the prison. My father would lock you away for keeping that secret."

"With a threat like that, I might have to reconsider my generous offer."

"Oh, I know you'll hold your tongue," she said venomously. "You see, my father listens to me. When he learns of how you wanted to kill my protector and turn me into your own personal plaything, his wrath will be incalculable."

"He won't believe you," Styfastr said. Fear replaced the power–driven menace that occupied his face just a moment before.

"Who do you think he's likely to believe?" Indura began, driving her point home. "Does he believe me, his beloved daughter, or a man who would sell his own mother into slavery if it meant he would get paid?"

"She has a point," Athon whispered as he began to caress Styfastr's leg with the edge of his knife. "You know, Preanth is a cruel tyrant, but adores his daughter above anything. If he thinks for a moment that she could be telling the truth, it doesn't matter what you try to say. You'll be dead before you can finish your first word. A word of caution: if I sense that you're going to back out of our arrangement, there won't be a force that can stop me from killing you, and that's a fact."

"It's true," Indura added with a smirk. "There isn't a single man in my father's army who could stand in combat with him."

"If you keep quiet, you stand to make a lot of money," Athon said, keeping his voice low. "If you open your mouth, there isn't anyone who can save you from what the two of us will do to you."

Styfastr was sweating. "You have my word."

# Chapter 30

# DEHNET

E ven–sun couldn't come fast enough for Indura. She found it difficult to sleep thinking that soldiers could burst through the door of their room at any moment. Eventually, she succumbed to her exhaustion and dozed off. Athon, however, stayed awake the entire sleep–time. At first–quarter sun, he woke the dazed princess, and they began loading their hesturs for the long journey across the desert. Two hours before even–sun, they made their way to Styfastr's shop. The soldiers standing guard outside unnerved Indura despite Athon's urging her to stay calm. Her tired mind conjured up images of them rushing to arrest them, but it didn't happen.

Styfastr arrived with several men and hesturs. He led them all into the shop and loaded them with the salt crystals that lined his wall. After all the cargo had been stowed, he pulled Athon and one of the couriers aside. "This is Botulfr. He's my oldest and most trusted courier. He will be your guide to Dehnet. Stick close to him the entire time. He will ensure you get there safely, and find a good buyer for you. When you're done obtaining the hestur, he will take the money and bring it to me. I trust this man with my life, and you should too."

"No harm will come to you as long as you do what I say when I say," Botulfr said curtly. "I've been doing this longer than anyone else, and I know the dangers all too well." He pointed to a large scar running down the right side of his face and neck. "This is one of many attempts by thieves to rob me, but I don't die so easily. You have other business in Dehnet than selling salt?"

Athon nodded. "We will stay longer, but should return with the next caravan if all goes well."

"I wouldn't stay there any longer than I needed to if I were you. Austicans are highly suspicious of foreigners, and there are many evil men. Visitors have a way of becoming permanent residents if they aren't careful."

"I believe he can take care of himself," Styfastr interrupted.

The staging area for the caravan was at the city's eastern gate. The small caravan of Styfastr's salt couriers arrived about the same time as the main group. Most of them knew each other, but there were a few newcomers. A large contingent of soldiers made their way through the assembling merchants, stopping at each briefly.

Athon whispered in Indura's ear. "Just relax and let me do all the talking. Don't say a word, even if they speak to you directly, and whatever you do, don't look frightened."

When the soldiers arrived at the group of couriers, they immediately approached Athon. "You're new here," the leader said. "Who are you and where do you come from?"

"I am Agmundir of Nidaros and this is my eldest son, Igmundir."

"Are they with you, Botulfr?"

"They are."

"Do you vouch for them?"

"Have you ever known Styfastr to take on anyone he thought was questionable?"

"I'll take that as a yes," the leader said, annoyed that the courier had not answered his question directly. "What about this boy? Why is someone so young taking this journey?"

"He is lighter than me, and can carry more salt," Athon said. "I am teaching him a trade so that he can take my place when he gets old enough to do it on his own."

"I want to hear it from him. Speak up, boy, why are you here," the leader demanded. There was a long pause as Indura looked at Athon nervously.

"He's mute," Athon said, "and cannot answer you. Why are you inquiring of us so vigorously? We've done nothing wrong."

"We're interviewing all newcomers," the leader said. "We're looking for a pair of criminals, a man and a woman who are traveling together. We heard they may try to join a caravan."

"Do I look like a woman to you?" Athon asked indignantly.

"I'm only doing my job," the leader said defensively. "I must question everyone I don't recognize. You're free to go." He then spurred his hestur, and the soldiers continued to make their way through the gathering crowd of merchants.

Athon breathed a sigh of relief, and looked at Indura. She felt as though she was about to faint with the stress of a narrow escape. Just before even–sun, the caravan leader called everyone into formation, and they were soon traveling down the road headed toward the desert. There were brief, regular stops along the way so the caravan members could water their hesturs or rest themselves, but they never lasted for very long.

For three turns, they traveled stopping only long enough to water the hesturs. For the most part, the journey was uneventful. They had seen several Austican patrols and one or two potential raiding parties, but none ever came close enough to worry Botulfr. When the Dehnet river valley came into view, it was a most welcome sight for everyone. It meant that sleep would soon come for the weary band of merchants.

The journey was especially taxing on Indura. She traveled in complete silence, pretending not to be able to speak, which at times drove her nearly to tears. It was hot, and the bandage around her chest didn't help anything. She succumbed to exhaustion several times, and Athon had to hold her up to keep her on Azul.

Shortly before high–sun on the third turn, they crossed paths with the departing caravan. Two hours later, the city of Dehnet came into view. When the long train of hesturs finally entered the gates to the city it was late–sun.

Once in Dehnet, Botulfr insisted on his choice of inn where they would stay. He said it was the only place that was safe. The rooms were large, and each contained its own private bathing area.

Indura used the bath first while Athon slept. Afterwards, Athon bathed and cleaned his clothes. He put on his uniform while they dried. Sleepily, he sat then leaned over and fell to dreaming at the edge of the bed. Indura was still fast asleep. A knock at the door startled them both. Athon, still in uniform, only opened the door a crack. Blearily he blinked into the passageway.

"I see you're still recovering from the journey," Botulfr said with a laugh. "It will be high–sun in an hour. I'll give you that long to wake up and then I'll return to take you to the market."

Indura went back to sleep, and Athon took advantage of the opportunity to change back into his spy clothes. They were still damp, but they'd dry soon enough. He spent the better part of an hour helping her wake up, and helping her put the bandage back on. Her clothes were filthy, and they smelled bad, but they would have to deal with that later. When Botulfr knocked on the door again, Athon slung the saddlebags holding the salt over his shoulder and they left for the market.

The inn was situated to one side of the city's central shopping district. Its entrance had a commanding view of the great court that was the marketplace.

Athon and Indura had both been too exhausted to appreciate the scope of its size. Compared to Skaraton, this market was enormous. It housed thousands of small kiosks and carts selling everything imaginable. On each side, there were various shops, restaurants, and inns in great buildings made of mud bricks. Tens of thousands of people and animals created a chaotic cacophony. The scent of cooking food and animal dung was both nauseating and tantalizing at the same time. The other couriers joined them as they admired the spectacle. Four strange, armed men were ascending the brick steps toward them.

Botulfr hailed them, and turned to Athon. "This is our escort to the emporium at the other side of the market."

"Why didn't we get a room at an inn closer to our objective," Athon inquired.

"It's *safer*," Botulfr replied. "These men will escort you through the market, so you must not stray from the group, or you'll wind up dead, or worse."

It took over an hour to negotiate the crowds and reach the well–apportioned shop. They were eagerly greeted by the owner, who welcomed Athon's additional cargo. The negotiated price was an equal measure of gold for each intact salt crystal. The salt dust was also weighed and measured, but was paid at a considerably reduced rate of a half measure of silver.

Athon had never had so much money in his possession in his life. No wonder Styfastr was so eager to get his hands on the gold he and Indura were getting for this shipment. The entire process took nearly two hours to complete the weighing for all of the couriers. It was late when the group returned to the inn, and all but Botulfr left them.

"We should go to your room to complete the transfer of gold," the courier said.

"There's still the matter of acquiring a hestur," Athon said sternly.

"Very well," Botulfr said with a sigh. "I will meet you at your room after I've secured my bags. There is a hidden compartment at the foot of your bed. I suggest you hide your saddlebags there. Take only what you need to get your hestur. I will arrange for an escort to take you into the market."

They returned to their room, and located the drawer in one of the corners of the bed. Athon figured that it would cost two hundred gold pieces for the hestur and the riding tack. He put the coins into his purse just as Botulfr arrived with their escort. Botulfr introduced their heavily armed, burly guide as K'tifu, and then left.

Indura looked at one of the food vendors, and tugged at Athon's arm. "I'm starving. We haven't eaten in almost a full turn."

"As soon as we get the hestur back to the stable we can head to the tavern."

"I don't know if I can wait that long," she moaned.

"I'm hungry, too; but we need to get this done before everyone packs up and heads home." Athon turned to K'tifu. "I assume that we only have an hour or so before the market closes?"

K'tifu's voice was deep and booming, a perfect match for his barrel chest. "You are correct. Most of these carts will be gone in an hour. I will take you to a man who sells hesturs just off the south end of the square. His name is N'jafe. He has good animals, and is an honest man, but we must hurry or he will be gone as well."

N'jafe's cramped stables were in an alleyway just off the main square. N'jafe was a skinny man who was missing most of his teeth. Athon hoped his hesturs were better kempt than he was. In all, there were about ten animals in a corral that was barely big enough for one to roam freely. K'tifu introduced his charges to the eager owner, and the demonstration began.

As the peddler began extolling the virtues of each hestur, a black stallion caught Athon's attention. He tried to shake off the feeling that he'd seen that very hestur before. "When did you get that big black one?"

"You have a good eye," N'jafe said approvingly. "I acquired that one not long ago. He's a little tired from a long journey, but I assure you, he's in perfect health."

"Do you know who he belonged to before you bought him?"

"I'm told that he was won in battle, and I assume the former owner is either dead or a slave."

Athon couldn't believe his luck. How fortunate he was to be led to this stable. He almost couldn't contain his excitement, but he had to be sure. "I'd like a closer look to check it for disease. I don't want a hestur that's going lame."

"Of course," N'jafe said. He grabbed a bridle, fetched the large black hestur, and brought it back to the eager buyer. The blemish free coat was covered in a heavy layer of sand and dust, but it was free of any sign of injury.

"I'll take it," Athon said quickly. "You said that this animal was won in battle. Did you acquire the tack that was on it?"

"Of course," N'jafe said. "What good is a hestur without it? It's plain, but it's in good condition. I'll just go get it for you." He handed Athon the reigns and disappeared into a small wood shed next to the corral. When he emerged, Athon knew immediately where the saddle had come from. It was Campsit tack. This was none other than Tam's hestur, Pyta.

"What would have happened to the owner if he wasn't killed?"

"Sold to a slave trader, no doubt," N'jafe said somberly.

"You wouldn't know which one, would you?"

"I heard a rumor that a strange man was brought into the city by a group of soldiers. He was taken to the slave prison in the central square, but I don't know if that's true. It is rumor after all. I don't know why you would care about that. They don't sell slaves to outsiders."

"Just curious," Athon said trying to cover his inquiry. The negotiations were intense. The original offer was for two hundred and fifty gold pieces, but Athon was able to negotiate it down to two hundred. It was worth it. They had proof Tam was alive, and they had a good idea where he was being held. They saddled Pyta, but didn't mount him.

They made K'tifu take them to see the building N'jafe had indicated where Tam was being held. The guard reluctantly agreed, but he wasn't happy about it.

Athon made sure to note the route they took to reach the round, windowless building. It was located adjacent to one of the larger ziggurats. A cursory glance told him just how dire the situation was. There were only two guards, and one door from the look of things, but the square had many soldiers patrolling it. He could take out the two guards, but the others would certainly notice.

A man approached the building's entrance, waved at the soldiers, and simply walked in. Athon was a little stunned that ingress seemed so rudimentary. He couldn't see inside, so there was no telling how many soldiers were waiting just beyond the door, but the man didn't acknowledge anyone before it shut.

It was quickly apparent that getting in without alerting the entire city would be impossible. They might make it inside, only to find more soldiers, with reinforcements cutting off their sole means of escape.

Athon needed to think this through. First, he needed to make sure he knew where he was. If they could get to the prince, they would have to leave the city quickly, and he had to know the fastest way to the gate. An enormous building occupying the far side of the square was a good landmark. "What is that?"

"That is the Believer's Temple," K'tifu said. "You do not want to go there. They would kill you because you are not Austican. You are infidels. That is a holy place where they sacrifice people to ensure our salvation."

"Are there many of these buildings in Dehnet?"

"There are five temples. Four represent a point on the compass. This is the most sacred, because it is next to the palace of the Holy H'met. He is the physical manifestation of the divine God, so only holy people can enter there."

"I don't suppose you've ever been there?"

"I am not holy enough, but I would not go in there, even if I was. I do not relish seeing the infidels blood spilled like my countrymen."

"You say people are murdered in some kind of ritual?"

"It is not murder," K'tifu said defensively. "The people who are sacrificed are infidels, and can never believe. Their blood atones for their sin, and washes our people clean. You do not understand, because you are an unbeliever."

Athon shrugged. "I suppose so." Indura looked at him and pleaded with her eyes. He could tell she wanted him to storm the building right then, but he knew that if he did, it would only end in disaster. He shook his head slightly, and turned to head back to the inn. She hung her head and began to cry softly.

"The man who was captured is your friend, isn't he," K'tifu said. Athon didn't know how to answer so he stayed silent. "I sympathize with you, but do not get any ideas about trying to rescue him. You would not get far before they caught you."

"So, you know we're here to do more than just trade salt." Athon was not relishing the idea of taking on the muscular guard. He was easily the same height as Athon and obviously stronger and better armed. "What do you plan on doing about that?"

"Nothing," K'tifu said calmly. "Even though you are infidels, I sympathize with you. I would hope if I were being held as a slave, my family would come for me, too. I think it's noble that you would come all this way, but it's for nothing."

"We had to try," Athon said. "We didn't even know if he was alive. What do you think will happen to him?"

"If he is lucky they will sell him as a slave. If he is not, they will sell him to the temple priests to become a sacrifice."

The walk back to the inn felt like a forced march back to Skaraton for Indura. With each step, her hope faded. The pain in her heart overwhelmed the pain in her stomach. They had come so far only to fail.

"How do you wind up in there?" Athon asked.

"Be in the wrong place at the wrong time," K'tifu said bluntly. "Our army is strong. They conquer the unbelievers and enslave them. If they see an unbeliever, they will take them to a slave house, like that one. Soldiers on the street sometimes take infidels they find without an escort who is a believer, but I would not recommend getting in that way. The only way out of that building is as a slave, or a sacrifice."

"Has anyone ever escaped?" Indura asked.

"No, there is no hope in a place like that."

"I'm surprised you haven't tried to take us in if you know why we're really here."

"It is my job to protect you, not enslave you. Besides, I do not believe it is right, but most people disagree. Men should be free. They are not meant to be in chains."

When they arrived, they bid K'tifu farewell, and put Pyta in the stable with Azul and Zuri. Neither one of them had much of an appetite, but Athon insisted they have something to eat. After the meal, they returned to their room, still tired from the journey. When the bolt finally clicked shut, Indura fell onto the bed face first and began weeping loudly.

"Crying isn't going to help the situation, Indura," Athon said as he sat down next to her and placed a loving hand on her shoulder.

"All this way for nothing," she sobbed.

"What makes you say that?"

"You heard him. He said that it was useless to try to get him out of that prison."

"Things may seem hopeless now, but I just need time to work out a plan." Athon said, softly stroking her short hair. "One thing's for sure; we need to get some rest. Our hesturs need to be fresh enough to make the journey back to Skaraton. I'm going to go find Botulfr and give him Styfastr's money. You need to stay here until I get back." She nodded, still crying inconsolably. The hope their quest would not be in vain had been crushed. How could they rescue her beloved Tam?

# Chapter 31

# NIGHT FALLS

Three turns had passed, and Athon could not solve the problem that plagued him. He had gone with K'tifu to the prison, and then to the main gate at different times, to determine the best options for rescue. During that time, Athon had learned why K'tifu was willing to help them.

K'tifu was the son of a slave who was taken when the Austicans had conquered his mother's homeland. His mother was beautiful, and her master took her as one of his concubines. She and her family were doomed to remain slaves until they died, and he could never forgive his father for that injustice.

Athon couldn't fathom how anyone could justify owning another person. He could only take pity on K'tifu's situation, and appreciate his help.

Athon committed the routes to the prison to memory. He carefully noted the position of every sentry and guard, and burned the images in his mind. He borrowed writing tools and parchment from the innkeeper and had drawn as detailed a map as he could remember. He worked the problem repeatedly in his mind, but always came up with the same outcome. The guards at the gate would stop them before they could ride out of bow range, and even then, they could mount a pursuit that would quickly overtake the three fugitives.

The big problem would be eliminating the guards at the front door without anyone taking notice. Even at odd hours, there were too many people to take them on without someone seeing the carnage. Stealth and the element of surprise was everything. The soldiers had an unobstructed view of the entire square, a giant wall at their backs, and plenty reserves. The building's curve offered no advantage. The backside of the structure abutted the temple grounds, and there were plenty of people there to prevent someone from sneaking up from the blind side.

There had to be something to distract every soldier in the city, and he wasn't sure how that was going to happen. If there was a grain mill close, he could try to find a way to cause an explosion, but he hadn't seen anything like that on his outings. He needed more time and, it was in short supply.

He figured they had enough money to last ten turns, and after that, they would be broke. Without a suitable base of operations, no plan would ever come to fruition. He bent all his will to discovering the solution, but it eluded him. For all of his knowledge of tactics, he could think of nothing that would help him.

Indura, on the other hand, had taken to moping about the room. She barely ate, and had fits of crying and rage. She loved Tam, and the thought that he was languishing in some rodent infested hole was more than she could bear. The waiting was unacceptable and interminable. Unlike Athon, she never left the room. She stayed inside, locked in her own self–imposed prison. Sleep offered no respite from the emotional toll the delay had taken on her. Her dreams were vividly horrific. They centered on finding Tam in a dark cell, but by the time they got to him, it was always too late. Her patience was wearing thin, but all she could do was sit at the window and worry.

"Haven't you thought of something yet?" The statement had become Indura's frequent cry in an attempt to perturb Athon into action.

Athon dropped the pencil in frustration and disgust. "For the last time, no. I can get us in, but escaping is impossible."

"Why is it so hard? Can't you think of something?" She was beginning to nag. Her voice was as irritating to him as nails on a chalkboard.

"Listen, you spoiled little brat, I'm thinking as hard as I can, and the problem hasn't changed. I still can't get how to find Tam without alerting every soldier in the city. What we need is a big distraction. Something that will make the guards not notice what's happening."

"Sorry Athon," she said dejectedly. "I didn't mean to—" her voice trailed off as she was distracted by screaming from the streets below. People began panic.

"Didn't mean to what," Athon asked as he too came to the window. "What in Ceanor's name is happening out there?"

"I don't know," Indura said slowly. They looked out on the plaza beneath the window and saw people gesticulating wildly toward the sky. "I think I know what they're all screaming about. Look at the sun!"

It was nearing high–sun, and a dark shape appeared to be taking a bite out of the brilliant orb. Athon first thought it was a cloud, but the sky was completely clear. He turned his attention from the blinding light to the people below. The panic swept through them like a wildfire through dry tinder. People began fleeing the market in a mad dash to escape the doom they so evidently felt.

A thought hit Athon like a bolt of lightning. "We need to get to the hesturs right now!" he said.

"Why?"

He frantically started packing whatever wasn't already in their saddlebags. "Hurry and pack! We need to go now if we're going to have a chance."

"A chance at what," Indura said not moving from her perch.

"These people worship the sun, right?"

"So?"

"If they're so devoted that they have five temples dedicated to one god don't you think that they would be more concerned by an event that took that god away, even for a moment? All we needed was a big distraction. Get moving this is it! There's no telling how long this is going to last!"

The doors of the holy royal palace burst open, and the old priest, R'mal, ran as fast as his atrophying muscles would allow. As Chief High Priest and, it was his duty to inform Holy H'met. He had already given his subordinates the order to call the people to prayer, and bring infidels for sacrifice. H'met needed to be told that his father was locked in an epic battle.

They had seen the evil wanderer Dortic vanish from the heavens. The moon had always been erratic as it wandered aimlessly through the sky, but it had never crossed paths with Sakphata—until now.

R'mal finally reached H'met's holy bedchamber. He stopped for a moment to bless himself before entering, and then calmly opened the door. He was one of the few people who were holy enough to speak to the God King, but he could not just burst in.

The room was filled with the king's wives and concubines. These women were blessed above all others, and were the only ones, besides the high priests, who could be in the presence of his glory. They bore and cared for his majesty's many children but were never let out of this part of the palace. They turned and looked at the old man, but he paid them no mind.

R'mal found H'met sleeping naked on his enormous bed. "Oh wise Holy H'met," he began. "A calamity most grave has occurred."

H'met stirred and he turned to the priest in a blissful haze. "Calamity, you say," H'met said yawning. "What could necessitate disturbing my slumber?"

"Oh, Holiest H'met it is my solemn duty to inform you that your father is locked in battle with Dortic."

"Locked in battle—with Dortic?"

"It can be no other," R'mal said, sensing that he may have offended the God King. "He hid his face so that he could catch your father unaware. He has always been jealous, and has now come to cover all the land in darkness. Come and you shall see how he has taken some of your father's divine form for himself."

H'met got off the bed and moved through the crowd of frightened women to the open courtyard that adjoined his royal bedchamber. It formed the center of his personal living quarters, and was his private sanctuary away from people who would soil his purity with their gaze. When he looked up, he was stunned. The women saw the calamity and began to wail and scream in terror.

H'met turned to his chief high priest with fear in his eyes. "My father must not lose this battle. I must give him sacrifices, so that he might have the strength to defeat the devious wanderer. Go to the temple and ready it for my presence. I will give the offerings myself."

R'mal bowed low and quickly walked to the exit, only to run once he had gone beyond the walls of the holy apartments. It would take many sacrifices and prayers to insure that Sakphata would be victorious in this fight.

# Chapter 32

# RESCUE

I t was fortunate Athon had purchased all the supplies before this turn of events. There was no way that they would be able to accomplish it as people ran through the streets in a crazed panic. Many were running to the temples, and others were running to hide from the sight of the growing darkness. All of it made for a chaotic scene that slowed their progress toward the prison. The hesturs sensed the panic, and even though they had been trained for combat, they were skittish. They had left so quickly they hadn't bothered to put Indura into her bandage. Athon didn't think that would be much of an issue because people had other more pressing matters. They finally reached the square that had amassed a large crowd near the temple, but all eyes were focused on the sun. No one was paying any attention to the three hesturs that rode up to the prison's only door.

The two guards stood with their backs turned until the hesturs were right next to them. They too, were watching the sky with anxiety. At last, when the steady clopping had stopped close behind them they turned, but it was too late. Athon struck both of them simultaneously in the neck. The knife dug deep, slicing each of their vital arteries and resting in their windpipe. They couldn't make a sound as the lifeblood flowed out of their bodies and onto the warm stone streets.

Athon grabbed them both by the neck and dragged them into the building as Indura tied the hesturs to a nearby post. The welcome room of the prison was dim, but their eyes quickly adjusted. From the adjoining room they heard a shuffling noise, and a thin voice call out. Evidently, whomever it was thought the guards had brought someone.

A frail man entered the room just as Athon closed the door, and cried out as soon as he saw the two lifeless guards on the floor. "T'hoth, help!"

Athon leaped at T'lal as he tried to run out of the room. Athon's blood–soaked hands were slippery, but he managed to grab him by the collar before he could escape. With one smooth motion, he halted T'lal's forward progress, whipped him around, and slammed him against the wall. The force of the impact knocked the wind right out of the jailer, and he collapsed, gasping for breath.

"I didn't know you could kill him just by throwing him against a wall," Indura said mockingly.

"I didn't kill him," Athon said, wiping his hands on the old man's shirt.

"What are you waiting for?"

"He may know which cell Tam's in," Athon said scanning the next room for anyone else. "We will need him alive for that."

"Right," Indura said, raising her short sword even with the gasping man's face. "Tell us where Tam is, and we might let you live."

T'lal continued to struggle for breath, but acted as if he hadn't heard them. Athon didn't know whom the man had summoned, but he was certain that he didn't want to find out. He continued to split his attention between the next room, and the writhing mound of flesh at his feet. "Where's the prince?"

"W—we have only slaves here," T'lal gasped. "There is no prince."

Indura grabbed the bald man by his ear and hoisted him to a standing position. She held the blade to the side of his throat so the flat pressed against his exposed carotid artery as it pulsed beneath it. In a steady, calculated tone, she growled at the man in her grasp. "You will tell me where he is or I'll cut your head off." Athon looked at the princess in stunned awe. It was vile hearing those venomous words come out of her mouth.

"I tell you, I don't know who you're talking about," T'lal said, getting his breath back.

"You lie," Indura said, viciously turning the edge in preparation for the killing stroke.

"Soldiers would have brought him in several turns ago. He may even be severely injured. He would have been dressed in green and brown with a cloak."

"I know the man who you speak of, but you will never find him if I tell you where he is," T'lal said. "I must take you to him."

"Is he locked in a cell?" Athon asked.

"Yes."

"Where's the key?" Indura hissed.

T'lal took out a single key attached to a cord around his neck. "There are only two, and I have one. I will take you to your prince now, but it will do you no good."

"Why is that," Athon asked.

"He is dead," T'lal said without even blinking.

"No!" Indura screamed, as she raised her sword. "That's a lie! Take it back! He's not dead!"

"Take us there," Athon said calmly, stepping between Indura and the jailer. "If he's dead, then we'll take him back to receive the proper burial. You understand? No one else has to die."

The old man nodded. "I understand." T'lal turned and grabbed a lamp on his way out the door leading to a confusing maze of winding corridors. He led them through the structure, turning around every now and then. By the time T'lal stopped in front of a skinny, windowless door, Athon and Indura were lost. He turned the key and opened it. The hinges squeaked loudly as they swung back to reveal a motionless form in one corner.

"Stay with him," Athon ordered. "If he tries anything, kill him."

"With pleasure," Indura said coldly.

Athon stooped to enter the dimly lit room. The flickering lamp wasn't bright enough to see clearly. "Give me that," he ordered. T'lal complied with a sly grin on his face. Athon took the lamp and with the other hand rolled the lifeless figure over. The light flickered wildly as the door closed on him, but it didn't go out.

The cold steel clicked into place, blocking the light from Athon's lamp, and Indura was left in the dark. She let out a shriek and plunged forward to stab T'lal, but found only air.

A cold maniacal laugh emanated from the darkness. "I know my way around this prison with my eyes shut, but you do not. You have no light, no key, and no h—" He was not able to finish the sentence as Indura's wild swing connected with his chest.

She could feel the flesh give under her blade and she grunted as she plunged it in to the hilt. "That is for killing Tam!" The sword was yanked from her hands as he fell over dead. "Athon help!"

He tried the door, but it was no use. It was heavy and locked. The body was definitely not Tam. He could hear Indura, but he couldn't get to her. "You need to get the key. I can't open this door, it's locked."

"I don't know where the key is," She cried, her hands trembling uncontrollably. "I can't see a thing."

"What happened to the old man?"

"I killed him," she said, a nauseating feeling gripped her stomach when she realized she had taken a life.

"Feel around for his body. He must have it on him somewhere."

She quickly located his fallen remains, and freed her sword. She felt around, and eventually found the key. There was a small flicker of light leaking under the door, but it took a few moments before she found the keyhole and was able to free Athon. With the light now restored, she felt safer. "Is he dead?"

"Yes, but it isn't Tam," Athon said.

Indura breathed a sigh of relief. "What do we do now?"

"This would have been easier if he were alive," Athon said, looking at the fallen jailer.

"If he lied about where he was taking us maybe he lied about Tam being dead," Indura reasoned. She began calling at the top of her voice. "Tam! Tam where are you!"

"Quiet down," Athon said sharply. "We don't even know if we're in the right place, and there's at least one more jailer out there."

"How do you suggest we find him," Indura asked indignantly. Suddenly there was a low thump from the opposite side of the hall. It repeated itself again, but this time there was a faint voice accompanying it.

They traced the noise to a door just opposite T'lal's body. It was difficult to make out exactly what the voice was saying, or if it was even a man or woman. Indura placed the key anxiously in the door and unlocked it. The room beyond was the same size as the other cell, and was infested with spiders that quickly hid themselves as the light hit their webs.

Indura fell to her knees, weeping with joy as she recognized the sole occupant. "Oh, my darling Tam, you're alive!"

They pulled him out of the horrible cell. He was filthy, and smelled like a cesspool, but he was very much alive. Overcome with joy, Indura cradled him in her arms as if he was made of fine porcelain. She looked into his deep blue eyes, and suddenly all of the hardships they had endured melted away. She was with him again, and no one was going to separate them. She loved him so much. Without thinking, she bent down and kissed him full on his cracked, chapped lips.

"Are you real?" Tam reached up and touched Indura's face in disbelief.

"Yes, it's really us. We've come to save you from this terrible place." Athon brushed off several spiders from his beloved prince's uniform, and nearly cried himself. Anger, sadness, joy, and the need for revenge flooded his soul as he examined his ward for injuries. Other than a healing cut and a broken arm, he was all right. "We need to get moving if we are to get out."

"I thought I was dreaming. I didn't think you'd come." Tam began to cry. "I thought you would forget me."

Indura's heart wrenched with pain thinking that Tam would believe that she would forsake him. "No, my love, I could never forget you."

"We love you too much for that, Tam," Athon said, choking back the emotion. "Time is not our friend. We can discuss this all later. We need to be on the move."

"We're lost, Athon," Indura said helping Tam to his feet. He was too weak to walk by himself so Indura wrapped his good arm around her and supported his weight on her shoulders.

"I'm not completely sure of this, but I think I might know how to get us out of here," Athon said confidently. "The jailer might have thought he confused us by his route, but I have a very good sense of direction."

Tam looked at the crumpled heap that was T'lal. "Where's the big one?"

"We haven't run into him yet," Athon said pulling them down the corridor, "and I'd like to keep it that way."

Athon led the others into the dark maze of twists and turns. After a while, they saw a light ahead of them and heard the unmistakable sound of men's voices coming from an open door leading to the a room beyond.

"I don't care what you say, those guards are dead, and the slave master is nowhere to be found," said one voice.

"The master said to find him and get all the slaves for sacrifice," said another.

"I'm not going in there; it's dark," said the first voice.

"Hello," cried a third closer to the door. "Hello?" The face that poked out of the threshold was not prepared for what it was facing. The poor man never even saw the throwing knife coming before it split through his eye. The wounded man howled in pain, and reeled backward cradling his face in his hands.

There was a startled cry from the room beyond and the two men who were bickering burst through the opening with swords drawn. The lamp Athon had been holding shattered the instant it hit the mud brick wall, spraying oil everywhere, including one of the soldiers. They panicked as the threshold burst into flames. As one man beat furiously at his clothes, which were now on fire, Athon leapt to engage the other with two daggers drawn.

Athon knew his small weapons were no match for a sword, but in these close quarters, his daggers made the perfect tool for attack. The soldier was very much off balance, and had never faced an adversary who fought so aggressively.

With one hand, Athon engaged his opponent's only means of defense while the other sunk its deadly point deep into his chest. The second soldier was still franticly trying to extinguish himself when Athon turned to engage him. The unfortunate man never stood a chance, and fell before he realized he was in mortal danger.

A thunderous roar from the darkness behind them sent Indura spinning to locate its source. It was none too soon, as a large, burly man came into the flickering light of the still burning oil. Without thinking, she propped Tam on the wall next to them and turned to face her attacker. He had drawn a large knife and continued his charge.

"I'll cut you into ribbons!" T'hoth shouted.

Indura said nothing, but tried to quell the fear that was rising from the pit of her stomach. She was still trembling from killing T'lal, but she tried to remain calm, like Glafindr taught her. Things moved so quickly she barely had time to parry his first swipe. It was so forceful, she nearly lost her grip on the hilt of her sword, but she stood firm. He continued to press her, but she stood her ground between the giant and the man she loved. She protected Tam like a she–trague protecting its young. She dodged several wicked slashes and countered with a vicious thrust of her own, nearly overreaching in the process. The duel raged for what seemed like an eternity to her, but it only lasted a few moments. The end came when she ducked to avoid his knife and spun quickly, bringing her blade high above her head, only to bring it slashing down on his exposed neck. T'hoth's nearly decapitated body landed with a thud at her feet. She turned and caught Tam's shocked expression.

"Where did you learn to fight like that?" He asked.

Indura was shaking, and she was so frightened that his words seemed comical. She began to laugh, despite her feelings of fear and horror. "We have so much to catch up on."

"We don't have time for this," Athon said, returning to the hallway after finishing off the last of the three men. "More could be coming any moment. We need to leave, now!" He had retrieved his throwing knife, and armed himself with a sword from one of the dead soldiers. He offered one to Tam. "Do you think you can wield one of these?"

"I'm not sure, but I'll try. What about the other prisoners?"

"We don't have time," Athon said, helping Tam through the building flames.

"We can't just leave them to burn to death!" Indura was shocked by Athon's callousness.

"This is the only exit and it's on fire! We're leaving!" It was a difficult decision for Athon, but he would have to live with it.

Athon halted their progress in the antechamber, and handed Tam over to Indura. He warily checked the reception area, but only found the bodies of the two guards. He readied the unfamiliar sword and exited the structure. There were five confused soldiers milling around the entrance. Apparently, they hadn't heard the commotion inside.

Athon didn't wait for them to react. The closest soldier fell as the sword came down on his exposed torso. Athon spun to regain his momentum and sliced at neck level, catching two men with the deadly blow. The remaining soldiers retreated out of sword range, but that didn't stop Athon's assault. He could see another man approaching, and knew he would soon be outmatched.

With the deft skill of a trained warrior, Athon grabbed a throwing knife and let the missile fly at the furthest assailant. It caught the man in his right shoulder, disabling his sword arm. Without missing a beat, Athon engaged the nearest soldier who parried his first swipe. He knew he was in trouble. Without the element of surprise, he would be no match for a person who was familiar with the curved blade.

Campsit swords were designed to maximize the lethality of the dual sword technique. They were short, straight, and light so the guards could use them to stab accurately with one hand. This long, heavy, curved blade was made for brute force slashing. It was a clumsy weapon meant for conscripted troops, not highly practiced warriors. However, Athon knew the more you used a weapon the more proficient you were. This soldier obviously knew the fighting style best suited for this sword.

The wounded soldier had withdrawn the throwing knife, and moved his weapon to his clumsy left hand. Athon was now fighting two opponents, even though one was only a minor threat. The third soldier was almost on them, and had raised his sword to strike the killing blow. Athon could see him in his peripheral vision, and knew the battle was almost over.

With a mighty slash, the approaching soldier struck Athon's antagonist. He screamed in pain. Athon's attention was drawn to his new benefactor. It was K'tifu. Athon didn't wait for an explanation. He ran his sword through one soldier while K'tifu finished off the other.

Athon was stunned. "How did you know?"

"You are a smart man, and would be foolish not to take advantage of this opportunity. When I saw the sign I knew merciful God did not want your friend to die."

Athon saw Indura in the entrance with Tam. He waved them out, and put a hand on K'tifu's shoulder. "Thank you for helping us."

Smoke began flowing out of the prison door. K'tifu looked around, and started dragging two of the bodies toward the building. "No one has noticed yet. Get rid of these bodies. The smoke will bring many soldiers. If they don't see them right away, it might give you some time."

Athon followed suit, and had the dead piled in the reception room by the time the smoke became a thick choking column that poured from the entrance. They shut the door to hold back the smoke, but it was only a matter of time.

The sun had nearly disappeared behind the veil of the large moon. All that was left was a large crescent that was rapidly retreating. There was still enough light for Tam to recognize his hestur, Pyta. As Athon pushed him up onto the saddle, he asked an obvious, but irrelevant question. "Where did you find him? I thought he was gone forever."

"We'll explain later," Athon said urgently. "Right now, we need to get out of here before someone finds us."

"You did not get the other slaves?" K'tifu asked.

"There wasn't time," Athon lamented. "The fire almost blocked our own escape."

"It is better this way," K'tifu said solemnly. "They will not have to live a thousand deaths in bondage."

"We have to leave K'tifu," Athon said. "It's best if none of us are around when they figure out what happened. I am grateful for all you've done for us, and I will never forget this."

Indura gave the muscular giant a hug. "I cannot repay you right now, but if you ever find yourself in Ithilton I will find a way."

K'tifu smiled. "There is no debt here. I am doing God's will, and he shall pay more than any man can. If you hurry, he will protect your exit." He raised his hand in salute, and ran away. Just before he rounded a corner, he yelled over his shoulder. "May your journey be swift and peaceful."

The three renegades spurred their hesturs into a fast trot and headed for the main gate. The timing was perfect. They were able to exit the panicked city before the last light had faded and the world was plunged into darkness.

H'met was covered with a thick coat of blood. He stood atop the ziggurat with his arms outstretched in supplication. His right hand held the ceremonial dagger that was dripping with the crimson liquid. The heart from his latest sacrifice pulsed in his left hand. The lifeless corpse of the infidel slave rested on the alter as it exsanguinated into the waiting pitcher at the base.

He addressed the crowd of believers at the bottom of the temple steps. "Sakphata has accepted the offering. It is my hand. It is my father's hand. They are the same." He threw the heart on the roaring fire to his right. "My father shall eat of the flesh." He raised a pitcher high above his head. "I shall drink of the blood. My father and I are the same. We are one god."

H'met looked out at the mass, and something caught his eye. An orange glow came from across the square. He could see a dark plume rising above the unmistakable flames that now glowed and intermingled with the smoke. It was coming from T'lal's prison.

Fire was only way H'met's father could consume the flesh and blood of an atonement. It was obvious that his father had understood his desire for the sacrifice of many. Truly, his father was in dire need to circumvent the ritual at the altar.

H'met pointed at the prison. "I am my father, and my father is me! See that we consume the sacrifice by holy fire! Their strength shall add to ours and defeat the evil one! We shall prevail!" The crowd roared.

The sun was only gone for a short while before it began to emerge from its black curtain. As the light returned, they pressed their hesturs to a gallop. They needed to get as far away from Dehnet as they could. It wasn't until the sun had completely emerged from the shadow of Dortic that they slowed to a quick, but steady gait.

Athon looked back to see if they were being pursued when he saw the black column of smoke coming from near the central ziggurat. One more distraction he thought, and if they were very lucky, no one would know they were even gone. He didn't delude himself into thinking they were remotely safe. There were still bandits and patrolling soldiers. He hoped that they were as superstitious as the people who lived in Dehnet, and they would have better things to do than wait to ambush travelers on the trade route between the two kingdoms.

# Chapter 33

# UNWELCOMED HOME

The journey through the desert took several turns, and Tam and Indura were inseparable. Tam didn't want to talk about his imprisonment, but was very interested in how Athon and Indura had managed to find him. He listened intently as Indura recounted the tale of her adventures with Athon. Tam was particularly interested in the revelation that Athon was not only married, but that he was Mai's father.

Indura's curiosity finally got the best of her, and she cajoled Tam into telling them what happened to him. Methodically he relayed the story of his capture, torture, and imprisonment. The narrative was so painful they were all left in shock when he finished. Many questions remained unanswered, but neither Athon nor Indura wanted to force him to relive the horror. They journeyed in silence, each trying to process their emotions.

To everyone's surprise, they managed to cross the desert without seeing a single person. When they reached the savanna, they found they were off course. They spotted the walled city of Skaraton far to the northwest. Athon didn't want to stop there, but he knew Tam needed a place to rest for a few turns. There was also the matter of the few gold pieces he had left in his purse that he had promised Styfastr. They would deal with that once they had rested and had sufficient provisions.

Before they got close to the city, Athon helped Indura put her bandage back on. Athon wasn't sure who would recognize them from before, but he didn't want to take any chances. Only one person knew her real identity, and he wasn't going to tell anyone. They entered through the west gate to minimize the potential for someone to place them in the last caravan.

They located a different inn with a room that would fit them all. It was small, but it had four beds and a large tub for washing and bathing. It was third–quarter sun when they settled in. While Tam was washing up, Indura and Athon left to procure the necessary provisions and clothes. Surprisingly, no one felt the expected exhaustion after a three–turn journey across the sand without rest.

When Athon and Indura returned to the inn after two hours, they found Tam still scrubbing the stench and grime from his body. "We have clean clothes, if that's what you're waiting for," Athon said.

"Thanks, but what I really need help with is scrubbing my back. I can't get everywhere with only one arm."

"I'll take care of you." Athon took the brush and soap from the prince and began to vigorously remove the remaining black grime from the prince's back. He counted numerous spider bites all over Tam's body. They were swollen and red, but nothing more. It angered Athon to think that any person could be subject to such horrendous treatment.

When he was satisfactorily clean, Tam changed into the civilian clothes Athon had purchased in the market. They were a little big on him, as he had lost a great deal of weight in captivity, but he figured that would change as things returned to normal.

The trio had a nice meal at the inn's tavern and then retired to the room to sleep. They all needed plenty of rest, but that was not the case for Tam. He woke up in a sweat, not knowing where he was.

"Bad dreams?" Athon had awoken at the sound of the prince sitting up. He whispered softly to avoid waking up Indura.

"Very bad," Tam said, panting heavily.

"You're dreaming about the prison?"

Emotions, that he struggled to contain just beneath the surface, finally boiled over and came gushing out. He began to cry as he realized, although he was no longer captive, the experience would always be with him. "I'm in the dark, and I can't find a lamp to light. Little creatures are nibbling at me. I try to get away, but I'm tied to the floor. Someone comes in and starts bending my arm, then I hear them laugh, and then I woke up. I can't get that laugh out of my head."

"I'm sorry, Tam. I'm sorry that I've failed you. I should have never put you in this position."

"Don't blame yourself, Athon," Tam said softly. "The whole thing's my fault. I didn't tell you I was meeting Indura. I should have, and I'm sorry I didn't. I just wanted to see her so badly."

"I know." Athon got up and sat on the edge of Tam's bed. "She loves you very much. I didn't realize how powerful that love was until she insisted on coming with me. As far as blame is concerned, I think all three of us had a hand in it. In the end it doesn't matter who's at fault. It matters that you're safe now, and we're out of that horrible kingdom. Don't dwell on the details of the past. Draw on the love that she has for you. I don't think I've ever met a woman that was so devoted in my life."

"I haven't either." Tam lifted himself up on his good arm and looked over at the princess as she slept. He watched the rhythmic rise and fall of her body as she breathed. "I hope I'm worthy."

"I think you are." Athon placed a reassuring hand on Tam's leg. "Remember, you stood and faced those soldiers to save her. You could have run, but you didn't. You stood your ground and covered her escape. You were brave in the face of certain death. If you hadn't done that, things would be very different. You probably would have both been hunted down and killed. No one would know what happened to you, and we wouldn't even begin to know where to look. I would say that you are more than worthy of her, and she is worthy of you. I have a great respect for both of you, and for the love you share. Most people will never know that kind of love. You're both very lucky."

"What about you and Dissa?"

"I love her very much, but I'm afraid she doesn't feel the same. I made a mistake, leaving her the way I did. If I could change things, I would have taken her with me, but I was a coward. I left her to suffer at the hands of Preanth, and she is very resentful. On our way back to Campsit, we'll stop and see if she will come with us. If she does, then there is some hope that I can undo the damage, but it has been so long, and she has so much anger."

"She will change her mind. You're a great man, Athon, and I'm proud to know you." Tam tried to verbally relay his sincerity. "Thank you. Thank you for coming and getting me. I don't know how I'll ever be able to repay you, but I wanted you to know that I'm so grateful. Thank you."

"You're welcome," Athon said, wiping away the tears streaming down Tam's face. "Just don't make a habit of getting captured. Now get some sleep. We still have a long journey ahead of us."

It was high–sun before they woke up. They spent the next few turns at the inn giving their hesturs a chance to recuperate. At even–sun of the third turn, Athon left early for the market, and told Indura and Tam to be ready to leave when he got back. After he purchased enough provisions for the next leg of the trip, he ventured to Styfastr's shop. The look on the merchant's face said it all.

"If I didn't know better I'd swear I was dreaming!" Styfastr didn't bother to extricate himself from the plush cushion. "Botulfr said you had disappeared during the event with the sun, and he hadn't expected you to live. I knew better. I knew you wouldn't let a little thing like an entire army stop you. I take it you rescued the prince, and are here to give me my money?"

"I don't know why I'm shocked by your greed." Athon took his purse and tossed it at the fat man's feet. "This is what's left after our expenses, and as per our arrangement, I'm giving it to you. I assume that you will keep your end of the bargain and not breathe a word to anyone else."

"I am many things, but dishonest is not one of them." Styfastr picked up the leather pouch and began counting its contents. "I'm only sorry that you're going back to your old life. Knowing you has been quite profitable."

"I'm sure it has, but all good things must come to an end. I thank you for your discretion." Athon turned and walked out. When he arrived back at the inn, he found the royal couple waiting on their hesturs.

In less than an hour, the trio had put a fair distance between them and Skaraton. The journey to Dissa's was less stressful. It didn't seem as though time was an enemy, and the threat of being discovered by soldiers was not as great. No one was looking for three men traveling together. Since they didn't have any money, they slept alongside the road when they got tired.

Finally, they arrived at Dissa's small cottage at the edge of the village of Dounie. She was tending to her vegetable garden. When she saw them, she hurriedly ushered them inside. "Quickly, before anyone sees you!"

Indura leaped off Azul and ran up to hug their hostess, but was quickly waived inside. "What's wrong?"

"There are soldiers in the village looking for you. If they find you here, we're doomed."

"When did they arrive?" Athon pulled Tam off Pyta and rushed into the cottage.

"They came by shortly after you left, and have been staying in the village ever since." Dissa was anxious and closed the door as soon as everyone was inside.

"Do they know you helped us?" Indura suddenly became very anxious for her dear friend.

"I'm not sure, but I can't think of any reason why they won't leave. Perhaps one of my neighbors saw your hesturs and told them about it. You should go now before they catch you."

"Do you have a hestur?" Athon began searching the house for a bag.

"Yes," Dissa said. "Why do you ask?"

"Because you're coming with us."

"No, I'm not."

"Dissa, it isn't safe for you here," Indura said somberly. "If the soldiers find out you helped us, they will most certainly throw you in prison. I can't let that happen again. You need to come with us."

"Indura's right." Athon found an old saddlebag under the bed, and began packing what belongings he could. "Take only what's necessary. Indura, you and Dissa get that hestur saddled and ready to go. I'll pack what I can here and meet you outside."

"I can't just drop the life I have here. What about my daughter?"

Indura grabbed Dissa by the arm and began pulling her toward the door. "You can see her every time I come to visit. Athon knows what he's doing, Dissa. You need to trust him."

"Trust him?" Dissa pulled away and retreated against the wall.

"Please trust him," Indura said softly. "It isn't safe for you here anymore. I won't be able to protect you from my father, but Athon can, if you come with us."

"We need to hurry," Tam chimed in.

"I made the mistake of leaving you last time. I'll not repeat it again." Athon looked at Dissa in a desperate plea for rationality.

"If I go, it doesn't mean that things have changed between us," Dissa said sternly. She turned and headed for the door.

"Fair enough," Athon said. It hurt his heart to know she harbored such feelings for him, but he was glad she was coming.

It didn't take long for Dissa to be ready to leave, and they were soon galloping down the road. Athon wanted to put as much distance between them and Dounie as he could. After an hour, they returned to a steady trot, as Tam's arm could no longer take the abuse of a full gallop.

The next several turns passed by with everyone experiencing a great deal of anxiety. The threat of being pursued by soldiers had been renewed by the revelation that they had been watching Dissa's village. Athon hoped they could make it to the forest without being caught by any patrols. He didn't know how they were going to return the princess, but after what she had been through with Tam, he wasn't sure she would want to leave his side. The two royals didn't stop talking while they traveled, while Dissa and Athon remained silent.

When they had traveled for nearly half a turn in the forest without seeing anyone, Athon felt they were in the clear. They were nearing the site where

Indura's company had been ambushed by the tragues when his blood began to run cold. He could hear the sound of a wagon and hesturs on the road up ahead. As they turned a corner, they were confronted with a chilling site. A group of Ithilton soldiers was escorting a convoy of wagons toward Campsit.

There was nowhere to run to, and not much point in hiding. Athon did the only thing he could think of. "Hail, sons of Ithilton!"

The soldiers wheeled at the salutation and quickly surrounded the small group with weapons drawn. "Who dares travel this road?"

"I am Athon, Captain of the Campsit Guard." He pointed to the rest of the group. "This is Indura, Princess of Ithilton, Tam, Prince of Campsit, and Dissa, maid of Ithilton. We seek an audience with your commander."

"This one cannot be the princess," the lead soldier said. "He looks like a boy."

"I am the princess."

"You have short brown hair. The princess' hair is long and red."

"I cut it, and dyed it so that I might disguise myself, but if you look closely, you'll find it is very much red." Indura pulled her hair up so that the soldier might have a closer look at the roots. He moved in and examined her closely.

The tension was high for a moment, and then he addressed the foursome. "I don't see it, but you shall have your request. We will take you to our king, and then he will decide what to do with you. Surely, he will know his own daughter. If you are not who you say you are, then he will most surely put a swift end to your days of lying."

Even Indura's blood went cold with the thought that Preanth was camped with his army, laying siege to the garrison. The soldiers surrounded them and escorted them around the caravan and up the road to the Great Meadow.

The meadow and the surrounding forest were filled with the tents of tens of thousands of soldiers waiting to do battle. They rode through the midst of them to a large tent in the center by a pond. When they arrived, the leader of their escort commanded them to dismount and to remain outside; he then walked into the temporary royal palace. A short time later, a small cadre of men emerged. Athon recognized Eyvindir as well as the king.

"I'm told one of you is my daughter in disguise. Step forward so that I might look at you closer."

Indura ran forward and threw her arms around her father. "I've missed you so very much."

The maneuver caught everyone off guard, and the king stood stunned. He waived off his guards and pushed her away so that he could get a better view.

He examined her closely, looking at her hair and eyes. Eventually, the glimmer in his eyes bespoke his recognition. "What have you done?"

"I'm sorry father. It will grow out, and the dye will fade eventually."

"Do you have any idea how much anguish you've caused me? Your mother and I have been worried sick. We searched the entire kingdom looking for you. When we discovered the letters you kept from that boy, we thought he must have spirited you off. I nearly went out of my mind wondering what happened to my daughter. How she must have gone mad with lust over some rapscallion."

"I'm sorry, father, I should have told you. As you can see, I'm perfectly fine, but why are you here?"

"We are here to see that you return home. I deduced that these men must have been holding you captive. Even though they denied that you were with them, I couldn't believe it. You would never run off into danger."

"I did, and I would do it again."

"Why would you say such a thing?" Preanth frowned. "They must have placed a spell on you. My daughter would never behave so foolishly without some nefarious influence." He turned to Athon and Tam accusingly. "You've done this to her. Release your magic at once!"

"I'm under no spell, father."

"She is under the influence of a great magic, but it is one that is beyond our capacity to undo," Athon said, and everyone turned their attention to him.

"What magic is she under that you cannot release her?" Preanth demanded. "Surely if you're powerful enough to place her in a trance, you can undo it."

"She is under the most powerful magic in the world. She is in love, and neither you nor I can undo that spell."

Preanth looked at Athon in stunned disbelief. "My daughter is in love with this worthless boy?"

"He is not worthless, father," Indura protested. "He defended me when the Austicans came and attacked us. He did not cower when the odds were stacked against him. He is a man worthy of being called your son."

"I've had enough of this madness." Preanth pushed Indura to the side and stepped toward his three prisoners. "Go inside, Indura, I will deal with you later. You and your countrymen will pay dearly for this intrusion, Prince. I'll lock you up until your hold over my daughter has been removed, lay waste to your cities, and enslave your people."

"On behalf of my people, I make you an offer, oh mighty king." Tam bowed low before Preanth. "Spare my people and you may take my life. Your daughter cannot love a dead man."

Indura screamed and threw herself between her father and Tam. "No!"

"You would give your life for the sake of your people?"

"Yes, but you must promise me that you'll leave Campsit in peace. If you refuse, my people will fight to the last man to keep you from your prize, and I swear to you that your army will meet its doom on this mountain."

"Done!" Preanth motioned for his soldiers to move on Tam. "Take him and kill him. Let his head adorn a spike."

Indura gave a blood–curdling scream. She drew her father's sword and menaced the approaching men. "If he dies, then so do I! You will have to kill me first!"

Preanth stared at his daughter as if he was looking at a stranger. "What do you think you are doing? Put that thing away before you hurt someone."

Athon stepped forward and placed a loving hand on Indura's shoulder. She was startled and wheeled, but lowered the sword when she saw who it was. "You've killed enough, Highness. Give the sword back to your father."

Indura began to cry. "But, I can't let them hurt Tam."

"No one will die today. Please, trust me, and do as I ask." Athon's voice was calm and reassuring. Reluctantly, she turned and dropped the sword in the mud at her father's feet. "Your Majesty, killing will not settle this matter. You might think that depriving the prince of life will end your daughter's infatuation, but it will only make matters worse. It is no secret that you love your daughter. If you kill Tam, or harm his people, you will only turn her against you. I don't think that's what you want. You may not understand what is going on, but I have witnessed your daughter's resolve firsthand. Whether you like it or not, your daughter is madly in love with him, and not even the threat of death will change her mind. I have seen her take on men many times her size in mortal combat, and they stood no chance against her fierce will. The only person who rivals her passion is Tam. He took on twenty of Austica's elite soldiers and slew six of them before they overpowered him. He did it all to keep them from capturing your daughter. I think the only way you will keep her, is to let her love the man she wants."

Preanth considered Athon's words carefully, and looked into his daughter's pleading, tearful eyes. "I cannot stop you any more than I can stop the ocean with a broom." He turned to the dumbfounded prince. "If I allow you to continue to see my daughter, you must promise me that you will be worthy of so great an honor."

"Does that mean you will let him live, and court me, father?"

"As much as it pains me to say it, yes, I will grant him my blessing to seek your hand."

"What about my people?" Tam stepped forward and looked the king in the eye.

"I will take my army and go back to Ithilton."

Athon eyed the two royal lovebirds with some suspicion. "What do we do about these two? We can't keep having them run off. They need supervision."

"And, chaperones," Dissa chimed in.

"I should discuss it with your king." Preanth said, directing his words to Athon.

Indura raced to her father and gave him a tight hug and a kiss on the cheek. "Thank you, daddy!" She turned and approached her beloved Tam, caressing his handsome face with one delicate hand. "I love you, my darling." He wrapped his one good arm around her waist, pulled her close, and kissed her for everyone to see.

## The End

# APPENDIX

List of terms used in the book:

Pass — One pass is similar to a year.

Turn — Is equivalent to one day. It is measured from low–sun to low–sun.

Ceanor — The larger of the two predictable moons, named after the Arabellan god of creation. Ceanor is used to calculate a month. Depending on context, Ceanor can refer to a unit of time, the name of a specific celestial object, or a deity. It is sometimes used as an exclamation or oath.

Dortic — Middle moon, named after the Arabellan god of mischief and evil. Has an irregular orbit that causes it to wander in the sky. Known also as "The Wanderer".

Sakphata — The name given to the sun, and the Arabellan god of creation, light, and war.

Thebon — Smallest visible moon. It has a regular orbit, and is the closest of the three major moons of Arabella.

Awr — A genetically engineered beast of burden. Introduced to the Austicans twenty-five passes prior to the events in DARK ESCAPE. It is similar to a camel in most aspects, and was bred from the domesticated animals of Arabella. It is ideal for traversing desert terrain due to its ability to go without water for extended periods.

Eryr — A large raptorial bird with wingspans up to ten feet. They make their nests on cliff ledges. Symbol of the house of Themis.

Hestur — A domesticated beast of burden similar to a horse.

Kanni — A large rodent similar to a hare.

Kyhdue — A bird that can vary in size from small to medium. Some varieties have a unique ability to return to a designated nesting point. Used by military and spies for communication.

Marmmot—A big game animal similar to deer. Used for meat and leather.

Sculphound—A large canine with feral and domesticated breeds.

Trague—Very large feline predator with jet black fur. The typical male trague can weigh up to 1500 pounds, and can be up to eight feet long, not including the tail. They are very powerful, and are heavily muscled. The most powerful muscles are found in their jaws and forepaws. They have sharp retractable claws, which can easily tear through the thick hides of their prey. Despite their massive size, they are highly agile, making them effective hunters. They have superior vision, hearing, and sense of smell. Other than humans, they are the undisputed apex predator on land in Arabella. The only comparable earth animal is the Bengal Tiger, however the trague would be larger, and more aggressive.

Uht—A long necked, wool–bearing mammal roughly ten to twelve feet tall. Their bodies are slightly smaller than a hestur, but look larger with a full coat of wool. They are herd animals, and used for wool, milk, meat, and leather.

Atole—A dark brown drink brewed from the nuts of the Kawa tree. It has a chocolate cinnamon flavor.

Celis—An amber colored drink made from the fruit of the Celis tree, and usually reserved for special occasions due to its rarity. It is sometimes fermented into celis wine.

Domn—The name for a formal Ithilton training facility for martial arts and combat.

Tvinga—A brutal game with almost no rules. It is similar in play style to rugby. Two teams, in full battle armor, attempt to score against each other by moving a round leather ball from one side of a large field to the other without the ball touching the ground. The winner is the first team to score four goals. No forward passing is allowed, but the ball may be tossed laterally, and behind the ball carrier. Players can, and usually do, punch opponents to force a turnover. The only rules on physical contact are limited to avoiding blows to the head, neck, groin, kidneys, or joints. The penalty for hitting these "soft points" is receiving unblocked facial blows from the entire opposing team. Due to the violent nature of the game, no weapons are allowed, and the royal family may not play. Tvinga is a popular game with the guards of Campsit.

Aaron is an Emmy® award winning television journalist, now an author of science fiction and fantasy. During his college years, he taught science at the Hansen Planetarium in Salt Lake City while he studied Biology, Political Science, Physics, Communications, and Sales. He worked as a full-time Emergency Medical Technician at a local hospital to earn money while he attended school.

His first job in television was working as a photojournalist/master control engineer at a small station in Idaho. He returned to Utah as a photojournalist and continued to dabble in technology and engineering. He learned satellite operations, and developed techniques to broadcast live from remote locations with unorthodox technologies.

He advanced to the position of Managing Editor at a Midwest television station, but returned to Utah to be closer to his family. He still works in television, and writes during his spare time.

DARK ESCAPE is the first book in the TALES OF ARABELLA series. The inspiration for the books came from his wife Sandy. She wanted a story set on a world where the sun never sets. The result is Arabella.